G.M. TRUST

GARDEN OF LIES

ISBN 13: 978-1-7321458-0-1
ISBN 10: 1-7321458-0-6

Scripture taken from THE HOLY BIBLE, King James Version, Henry S. Goodspeed & Co., New York, NY. 1877 edition. All rights reserved.

For Eve,
the mother of all living

"There are things known
and things unknown,
and in between are the doors."

Jim Morrison

"Alice opened the door
and found that it led
into a small passage..."

Alice's Adventures in Wonderland
Lewis Carroll

TABLE OF CONTENTS

GARDEN OF LIES

CHAPTER 1

DANCE WITH FATE

July 1971

Veiled by the summer evening haze, the sun's glow was deceptively mellow. It hovered in the west, beyond the Hawkins Middle School softball diamond, like an enormous tangerine sphere magically suspended in the sky. Past the school property, the countryside was a patchwork of cultivated fields, pastures and woodlands. Sturdy barns and outbuildings clustered around tidy farmhouses, and whitewashed fences bordered green meadows where black and white dairy cows grazed.

The honeyed scent of corn lush with tassels lingered in the air, as the players exchanged places on the ball field. It was the bottom of the ninth inning and the last chance for the Belleville Ladies Softball Team to score against Hawkins.

Coach Kevin McKenna wiped his brow and adjusted the ball cap on his dark hair. "Oh shit!" he hissed, when Peggy Boyle picked up a bat.

Jessie Daniels flashed Kevin a dirty look. The eldest son of a prosperous farmer, Kevin was twenty-five and attractive, but she didn't mind letting him see her displeasure.

Jessie hoped Peggy hadn't heard anything. A buxom redhead with naturally curly hair, Peggy weighed at least two-hundred pounds and was scarcely five feet tall. The odds of her making it to first base against Hawkins were slim to none, but the last thing she needed to hear was Kevin's derogatory expletive.

The hotshot pitcher smirked as the plump housewife stepped up to the plate.

Jessie crossed her fingers, hoping Peggy wouldn't strike out again in front of these gum-chewing, wise-ass tomboys.

Sweat beaded on Peggy's forehead as she shifted nervously from foot to foot, clutching the bat.

Grinning, Vicki Stambaugh gave a thumbs-up to her team and burned one toward home plate.

Peggy flailed at the ball and missed.

"Strike," the umpire called, and the Belleville team let out a collective moan.

Kevin masked his irritation. "Relax, Peg. Wait for the ball to come to you."

Peggy waited, and the ball blew right by her.

"Strike two," the ump said, and the Hawkins team whistled and cheered.

Vicki took a bow, then began her third wind-up.

Jessie said a quick prayer. If Peggy didn't get on base she'd be humiliated, and the smug pitcher would gloat.

The speed of Vicki's final pitch was awesome. The ball ripped through the air and smacked Peggy's arm with a sickening thud.

"Ow!" she cried, dropping the bat. Tears spilled down her cheeks, as she moaned and clasped her hand over the bright red welt blossoming on her arm.

Kevin ran to her side and put his arm around her shoulders.

"Hang in there, Peg. I know it hurts." Passing her his handkerchief, he massaged the injured arm until she regained composure.

"Ready?" the ump inquired. Peggy nodded. "Then take your base."

Peggy lifted her chin and started down the line to first base.

"Time out!" Vicki hollered, and strode off the mound toward the home plate ump. "The batter deliberately stepped into the pitch. You can't give her the base!"

The umpire narrowed his eyes. "It was a bad pitch."

"Like hell! That fat cow couldn't get to first base any other way."

"Watch your language, Miss," the ump warned, and summoned the first base umpire to home plate for backup.

Over on the Belleville bench, mutters of disgust arose. Ann Miller shook her platinum-blonde head in annoyance. "That Vicki, what a *prima donna*! She just can't handle the ump ruling she threw a bad pitch, especially after she won the state championship for North Central last year."

"Yeah, she thinks she's hot stuff," Jessie said, twisting the end of her long black ponytail. The Hawkins team consisted almost entirely of graduates of North Central High's 1970 championship team. Athletic scholarships for females were few and far between. They seemed to be reliving last year's glory by playing in the summer recreation league. Hawkins knew every trick in the book, and the umpire had already changed one call in their favor. This time Jessie hoped the call would stick.

Except for Audrey Reddon, Ann Miller and herself, the Belleville team was a group of housewives out for some fun. She and Ann had graduated from Archbishop Moore High School, which never had a softball team, and each had learned the basics from a brother. Audrey had played for Mansfield High's formidable team before Jessie met her at Concord Community College last fall.

The bickering between Vicki and the umpires continued on the infield. Jessie left the bench and picked up a bat to take some practice swings, while keeping an eye on the altercation.

The Hawkins coach tried in vain to quiet his pitcher. Red-faced with fury, Vicki continued to flay the umpires with invective.

The home plate ump put his hands on his hips and got into Vicki's face. "One more word out of you, Miss, and you'll forfeit the game."

"What?" Vicki sputtered. "You can't—"

"Shut up, Vicki," the coach said, placing a warning hand on her arm. Both umps glared ominously at Vicki. Shaking off her coach's hand, she stomped back to the pitcher's mound.

Jessie stepped into the batter's box and took a deep breath. A ripple of tension coiled her stomach.

Behind her, teammates made sounds of encouragement and approval. This was Belleville's last chance to get on the scoreboard, and she knew they were depending on her. But the odds of getting Peggy to second base were about as good as pulling a rabbit out of her hat. The Hawkins pitcher was deadly, Peggy was slow, and the breaks hadn't been going Belleville's way.

Jessie took a deep breath and willed herself to relax.

Vicki swung her arm around to loosen up, then poised for the throw. The pitch seared the air, but as soon as Jessie got a fix on the ball, everything clicked. Her bat connected with a sharp crack.

Startled, Vicki watched the ball soar past. Her outfield scrambled into motion, but the center fielder misjudged the ball, giving Peggy the extra time she needed to make it to second base.

The Belleville team burst into cheers.

Kevin clapped and let out a whoop.

Audrey Reddon strutted into the batter's box. Tawny and tanned, she sported the short-cropped hair and well-honed body of a dedicated female jock. She never lost her cool under pressure and knew exactly how to shake up a pitcher. Grinning wickedly, she took her batting position.

Just as Vicki began her wind-up, Audrey walked away from the plate and waved her bat around. She paused and examined the tip, tapped it on the ground for good measure, then strolled back into the batter's box. She made an ugly face at the pitcher. "Sock it to me, baby!"

Vicki scowled and fired off her first pitch.

"Ball," the ump called out.

Audrey stepped away from the plate again and eyed the pitcher. Vicki looked steamed. Good. That meant Audrey was getting to her. Audrey smiled and moved back into position.

Frowning, Vicki concentrated on her next throw.

"Ball two," the umpire said.

Bafflement flashed across Vicki's face, then anger. She wiggled her shoulders and hands to loosen up, then poised herself once more. In a blur of motion, she smoked the ball toward home plate.

Audrey swung, cracking a line drive into left field.

The Belleville team leapt to their feet, screaming with excitement, and urged the runners on.

Jessie caught up to Peggy and tried not to step on her heels as she lumbered toward third. Audrey rounded first and headed for second.

The left fielder snagged the ball at the edge of the cornfield and hurled it toward third. Gasping for air, Peggy struggled to round the base. Jessie was forced to hold back until the bag was clear and tagged it split-seconds before the ball smacked into the baseman's glove.

The third baseman whirled and threw the ball to second.

Audrey dove into a slide and hit the bag just before the ball got there. The second basemen spun and whipped the ball toward the catcher.

Huffing and puffing, Peggy propelled her jiggling bulk along the last few yards to home plate. The ball smacked into the catcher's mitt with time to spare, but Peggy's chance to score at last was not to be denied. She plowed into the catcher like a rolling boulder. The ball flew out of the catcher's mitt, and Peggy flattened her to the earth in a cloud of dust.

Belleville erupted into wild cheering.

"She's out!" the umpire roared.

Jubilant shrieks subsided into catcalls and booing.

Peggy struggled to her feet and began to brush herself off, but the catcher flopped around on the ground like a dying fish.

Vicki left the mound and ran to the catcher's side, reaching her at the same time as the coach.

"She's had the wind knocked out of her," the ump said to the Hawkins coach. "Do you want to substitute?"

"No. She'll be all right in a minute."

Kevin protested the call, but the ump refused to listen.

Hawkins resumed the field. Vicki struck out the next two batters, and the game ended 36-0. The Hawkins team raised their arms and crowed.

"What a bunch of assholes," Ann said.

"You got that right," Jessie replied.

The home plate umpire walked around the backstop heading toward Ann. She'd been flirting with him all evening, but now she gave him a look that would have fried steel then turned her back with a haughty toss of her platinum-blonde head. He tried to say something, but she ignored him until he gave up and walked away.

"You sure gave him the cold shoulder," Jessie said, unfastening the rubber band securing her long black hair.

Ann's hazel eyes flashed with fire. "I don't care if he's cute. He could have let us score one run, at least. Peggy had as much right to try to score as the catcher had to make the play. By the rules, Peggy was safe when the ball popped out of the catcher's mitt."

"I know," Jessie said, and glanced in Kevin's direction just in time to see him leaving with Bob Parker, the team's portly, ginger-haired manager. That was strange, because Kevin had carpooled to the game with her and Ann. He looked so angry, Jessie wondered if he was going to show up at their favorite post-game haunt.

❦

Ann circled the parking lot of Logan's bar, as Jessie scanned the tightly packed mix of vehicles searching for an empty space. "I don't see Bob's car anywhere."

"That sucks," Ann said. "It's always more fun when Kevin's with us. He's so sexy and funny, and I love his dark hair and brown eyes. I don't know what his problem is, stalking off to Bob's car without speaking to anyone."

"Me neither." Jessie hid her disappointment. Kevin's behavior after the game seemed totally out of character. He flirted with her occasionally, and she hoped one day he'd ask her for a date. However, Ann had a way of monopolizing his attention. Even though Ann was secretly engaged to her boyfriend, she still loved attracting every guy within her radius.

They snared a parking spot and headed for the door of the cedar-shingled building. Its solitary window teemed with neon beer advertisements. Inside, the jukebox glowed with multicolored lights and blared out a rock 'n' roll hit. A blue haze of cigarette smoke hovered over the crowd at the bar, like a testosterone-fueled cloud.

Jessie cringed when each man cocked his head toward them as they walked past, admiring the way their figures filled out the gold T-shirts and green shorts of their uniforms. Running the gauntlet always made her feel uncomfortable but Ann reveled in it, smiling and swaying her hips provocatively.

The rest of the team had arrived early enough to push some tables together in the back corner. Wisecracks about the game were already zinging among the women.

"Hey Peggy, you sure got what it takes, baby!"

"That umpire must've had his head up his ass not to see the catcher drop the ball!"

Jessie and Ann ordered beers from the waitress, lit cigarettes, and joined in the repartee.

◦⊶◦

Kevin was so angry he didn't want to go to Logan's, even though hanging out with the girls was the highlight of Bob's week. He knew Bob was taking it slow driving him home, hoping he'd change his mind. If Kevin hadn't bet fifty bucks that the team would score a run against Hawkins, he wouldn't have been so pissed off.

"Goddammit, Bob, all they had to do was score one run. *One stinking run.* You'd think those dumb broads could manage that. The other coaches will never stop rubbing it in."

"Look, our gals didn't know you had a bet riding on the game. We got blindsided tonight. It wouldn't surprise me if the home plate ump was in on it. Come on, let's go to Logan's so the girls don't get too bummed out. It won't be good for team morale if we don't show."

Kevin took a deep breath. "You're right. I guess we'd better go."

After they arrived at Logan's and ordered beers, the routine rehash of the game irritated him all over again. "You girls had the crappiest batting and fielding I've ever seen."

The women rolled their eyes and ceased joshing. Silence reigned around the table.

Braving the static, Jessie spoke up. "What did you expect, against the Hawkins team? Most of them were All-Stars in high school."

"And what did you think you were doing, screwing around out there tonight?" he shot back.

"I don't know what you mean."

"You should!"

"I got a hit every time, and I *nailed* that runner. It wasn't my fault Hawkins got the ump to change his call."

"You can't prove that to a jury!"

Bob intervened. "Come on, Kevin, back off. Everyone screwed up tonight *except* Jessie, and she's one of our best players."

Kevin scowled. "I don't believe it."

"I can prove it." Bob pulled out the logbook and checked the stats. "Yeah, I was right. She has the highest batting average on the team."

Jessie flashed Bob a dazzling smile, then slid her fingers through her hair and flicked a length over her shoulder. She gave Kevin a saucy look. "See? Where would you be without me?"

She didn't like the dirty look he gave her, and she wasn't going to sit there and listen to him grump. She got up to get another beer.

The crowd around the bar was full of rowdy studs. Jessie hoped she wouldn't have to wait too long to get the bartender's attention. A hand squeezed her ass. Jessie turned and saw a good-looking guy with a teasing grin and hair like a lion's mane. She pushed his hand away. "You don't know me well enough to do that."

"I'd sure like to," he said and grabbed her butt again.

She slapped his hand off. "I wouldn't do that again, if I were you."

He grinned and reached for her once more.

"Stop it, Dennis. That's enough," a masculine voice ordered. Jessie turned and recognized Kevin's younger brother Mike.

Dennis glared at Mike, then shrugged and picked up his beer.

Mike gave Jessie a reassuring smile. "Can I buy you a drink to make up for the bad manners of my friend here?"

"Yes, I'd like that."

"What are you drinking?"

"Rolling Rock."

Mike called the bartender over to place the order.

Jessie had never had a real conversation with Mike before. He was strikingly handsome and stood about six-two, with medium-length dark hair and brown eyes. She'd met him for the first time only a few weeks ago.

She'd been out riding her horse, Rio, who was acting up in the road, pretending he'd seen the reincarnation of a snake that had been struck and mortally wounded long ago. Mike had driven round the bend, slammed on the brakes and left a lot of rubber on the road to avoid hitting them. That conversation had been short and heated.

Jessie recognized the car as one she'd seen parked at the McKenna farm. When she'd first moved to Concord County in sixth grade, she'd attended St. Mary Magdalene's parish school with Kevin's youngest brother, Johnny—before he was expelled. Although Kevin and Mike had both long gone on to Mansfield High back then, identifying the fuming driver as Mike wasn't difficult.

"How did the game go?" Mike asked. "Win or lose?"

"Lost, as usual. We were playing the *Amazons* from Hawkins."

The bartender handed Mike two beers. He passed the Rolling Rock to Jessie.

"Thanks." She took a sip. "It was a shutout—Hawkins won 36 to nothing. The highlight of the game was Peggy Boyle creaming their catcher at home plate."

"I'll bet that was something to see."

"Peggy bowled the catcher right off her feet, and the ball popped out of the mitt. But the ump ruled in Hawkins' favor. He seemed to think Peggy could stop on a dime."

Mike chuckled. "That'll be the day. Sounds like a rotten call to me."

"Yeah, but now Kevin's getting on our case. He says we were lousy. What did he expect against Hawkins?"

Mike glanced in Kevin's direction. Jessie looked over and saw him glowering at them. Mike grinned, then turned his attention back to her. "The Hawkins coach bet him fifty bucks that you girls couldn't score one run against his team."

"Oh," she said. "So that explains it."

A slow song started playing on the jukebox. "Would you like to dance?" Mike asked.

Slow-dancing wasn't Jessie's thing. The couples out on the floor were hanging all over each other, and there was no grace or elegance to it. She knew Mike's reputation well enough to realize his invitation was simply a ruse to feel her body pressed against his. Still, it felt good to be asked.

"Okay," she said.

Mike led her onto the floor and held her in an embrace no one would mistake for ballroom dancing. As soon as the song ended and a rollicking number came up on the jukebox, he took her back to the bar to finish their beers.

She was pleasantly surprised when he started talking about horses, but the loud music made conversation difficult, and the dialogue lurched to a halt.

Mike tossed a tip on the bar. "Can I drive you home?"

Jessie hesitated. She'd like to spend more time getting to know him—he was the first guy she'd met who liked horses—but he had a reputation for being an octopus. "No thanks."

"Oh, come on. Let me drive you home. It'll be quieter in the car, and we can talk more about horses."

The girl who'd told her Mike had eight hands escaped with her virginity intact, so Jessie didn't think she'd have to worry about that. But she wanted Mike to understand she wasn't jumping into his car all hot for a make-out session. Jessie had no intention of losing her virginity before marriage, just so she could be another conquest on some guy's scorecard. She was holding out for true love and didn't want to be used like the other girls he'd seduced and tossed aside. "If you take me home we can talk but nothing else."

"Don't worry. I won't give you a hard time."

Jessie needed to let Ann know she was riding home with Mike. But she was so ticked off at Kevin for taking his anger out on the team because he'd lost a stupid bet, she didn't even want to go near him. Reaching the table, Jessie was glad Kevin acted like she was invisible.

When Kevin realized Jessie was leaving with his brother, he was ticked. She was a good-looking girl, but too quiet to have made much of an impression on him. Ann was more his type—flirty and overtly sexy—but she had a steady boyfriend.

Although Kevin preferred girls with bigger breasts, Jessie had great legs and the most beautiful hair he'd ever seen. It tumbled down her back in long black waves that shimmered like a starry night.

The idea of Mike picking up a girl from his team galled Kevin. It wasn't the first time Mike had tried poaching on his territory, but they'd come to a truce. Although Jessie wasn't technically his girlfriend, she was still one of the girls on his team. Kevin felt sure Mike wouldn't get past first base tonight, but it was time to make his move if he wanted to cut his brother out of the action.

CHAPTER 2

CHASING RABBITS

Ann stirred and cautiously opened one eyelid to gauge the level of brightness coming through her bedroom curtains. Morning—late morning. Her ears picked up muffled sounds downstairs. She stretched lazily, like a cat, savoring the fluffy comfort of her bed.

Once her eyes adjusted to the light, she looked across the room toward the framed photo of her fiancé, Mark Wilson, enthroned amid the bevy of cologne bottles on her dresser. Ann smiled, remembering what they'd done in this very room the last time they'd been together. It was wonderful making love in a real bed, but it was usually impossible to spend any time alone in the house. Her parents were too vigilant and her little brother too big a snoop.

Ann looked toward the locked bedroom door with satisfaction. Thumb-tacked to the back, where it would least offend her mother, was a poster of the brooding sensual face of Jim Morrison, the lead singer of The Doors. Having Jim Morrison's poster on the door that shut out her parents' world was more fitting than they would ever know. Along with many others in her generation, Ann had heard the siren song and crossed into a world her parents couldn't begin to understand.

Today, she would open the door to that world to one more.

⌘

"Good morning," Lorna Miller said, looking at the clock when Ann entered the kitchen. "Did you sleep well?"

"Like a baby," Ann replied sweetly, knowing her mother was none too pleased that she slept late most summer mornings—but her mother had lost that argument long ago.

"I have an appointment at the beauty shop at noon. Your brother is over at Nick Wheeler's. There's a sandwich in the fridge for him if he comes home for lunch."

Ann waited with barely concealed impatience for her mother to leave. The phone call she intended to make wasn't one she could afford to have anyone overhear. The minute the car engine started she began dialing.

When Jessie answered, Ann exhaled. "Jess, it's me."

"Hey, what's up?"

"Come on, you know. What happened when Mike took you home last night?"

"Nothing really."

"I know his reputation better than that."

"I didn't say he didn't *try*."

"So he was all over you—I thought so," Ann said, excitement rising. "What did you do to stop him?"

"I told him I'd bite him."

Ann chuckled. She had to hand it to Jessie, even if she couldn't figure her out half the time. "So what did he do then?"

"He said he was just testing—and if I didn't like it, he wouldn't do it again."

"And you *believed* him?"

"He said he just wants to be friends. He asked me to give him riding lessons."

"How can you be so smart yet be so stupid about people? He doesn't want to ride your *horse*."

"He said he'd meet me at Logan's after Thursday's game to work out a schedule."

"Well, don't say I didn't warn you," Ann said. "By the way, I've got a favor to ask you."

"What?"

Ann took a breath. This part was going to be tricky. "Look, if Kevin gets out a joint sometime, I don't want you to say anything. I know you don't smoke pot, but don't embarrass me—okay?

"It really isn't any of my business if you want to smoke grass."

"Listen—if he passes the joint to you—take a quick drag and pass it on. Don't go into a stand. Act cool."

"Ann! How can you ask me to do a thing like that? If you want to smoke pot, I won't make a scene, but don't ask me to."

"That's not good enough! Think of what would happen to my reputation if it got out you don't smoke dope. Kevin would laugh himself silly. I'd be ruined. I told him you were cool."

"I can't, I just can't!"

Ann loved getting high and usually did so behind Jessie's back, but she and Kevin had come up with a plan to protect Jessie from Mike so she needed to persuade Jessie to go along.

"Heck, you smoke cigarettes, don't you? It isn't going to hurt you to take a puff from a joint."

"My parents gave me permission to smoke and drink," Jessie said. "They don't want me to take drugs."

"Hey, you owe me a favor! If it wasn't for me, you never would have been invited to the good parties in high school."

There was only silence in response. Ann knew that her rebuke had stung. She softened her voice. "When I first met you, you acted like you'd been raised in a convent. You would have been a social failure without me, and you know it. You're pretty enough, but you're too shy and unsophisticated to make it on your own. I helped you out, because you're nice and I like you. So, please, just do me this *one* favor."

Jessie knew perfectly well that her high school years would have been miserable without Ann's help. But she had always been Ann's backup when Ann forgot her homework or lied to her mother by claiming they were hanging out, when Ann was really out with Mark. However, Ann had gotten her a date for the prom, otherwise she wouldn't have been able to go, so she did still owe Ann one. But this?

This was a real dilemma. Jessie had always obeyed her parents, been a good student, and done her chores without being told. She hadn't gone behind their backs when she started smoking, like Ann did to her parents. Nope, she'd come right out and asked permission first. But that was before they'd betrayed her. Before the awful day her father had said the crushing things he said to her, upending her life and goals.

She wasn't sure how much loyalty she owed her parents anymore, but she still owed Ann one. Besides, her father once told her he'd tried marijuana back in the day, when it was legal, just to see what it was like. "Okay," Jessie said, "I'll do it."

"Thanks!" Ann exclaimed. "I'm sorry, but I've gotta run. See you Thursday."

Kevin heard the phone ringing just after everyone sat down to the midday meal. "I'll get it, Mom."

"Thank you," Maria McKenna said, and passed the mashed potatoes to her husband, Joe.

Kevin picked up the receiver. It was Ann. "I found out what you wanted to know." She then proceeded to fill him in. "Everything's a go on this end."

"Great. Thanks for calling. I'll see you Thursday." Kevin hung up and seated himself back at the table.

"Who was that?" Johnny asked, spearing some ham before passing the platter to Mike.

"Oh, Bob just called to say he's going to make it to the game after all," Kevin said. "I won't have to log the stats for the team." He took the platter of ham from Mike and grinned.

Jessie sat on the front porch with her family's Labrador Retrievers, Blackjack and Tar Baby, sprawled at her feet. A bumble bee hummed among the jewel-toned blossoms of the flowerbed edging the base of the house. Her gaze followed it as it buzzed off across the lawn in the direction of the barn, then she turned her attention back to the bottom of the lane. A flash of sunlight glinted off chrome, just before the sound of tires crunching on gravel alerted Blackjack and Tar Baby.

The dogs started barking, but quieted at her command and began wagging their tails in greeting as Kevin's powerful black Chevy Caprice pulled to a smooth stop in front of the house. Jessie was disappointed to see the convertible's top up; it was more fun to ride with it down.

"Goodbye, Mom. Goodbye, Dad," she called through the screen door to her parents, who were reading the evening paper in the living room. She grabbed her softball glove and walked to the car. Ann was sitting in the front, so she climbed into the back.

Along Route 32, Kevin slowed and turned off into a lay-by sometimes used by fruit and vegetable vendors catching the rush hour traffic. It was deserted at this time of day.

"Is something wrong with the car?" Jessie asked.

Kevin shook his head, then reached under the seat and pulled out a bag of marijuana. He took a pack of cigarette papers from his pocket, selected one, and began rolling a joint.

A twinge of fear shot through her. She glanced toward the roadway, wondering if anyone in the passing vehicles could see what was going on. She shook off a shiver of apprehension. It would be almost impossible for motorists traveling at highway speed to see into a dark car parked in the shade by the produce stand.

"Ann, light this for me," Kevin said, passing her the reefer. He stuffed his stash back under the seat, put the car in gear, and pulled onto the roadway.

Ann lit the joint. Pungent fumes drifted from the glowing tip as she took a drag and passed it to Kevin. He took a hit and held it out toward the back seat.

Jessie hesitated, then reached for it. She put the marijuana cigarette between her lips, repressing a pang of guilt. The end was damp with saliva, which was somewhat repellent, but she took a deep drag, like Ann had just done. The smoke was so harsh she almost choked, but she held it in as long as she could and hoped her performance was respectable. She didn't dare look to see if Kevin was checking her out. With a steady hand, she passed the reefer over to Ann.

When it came around again, Jessie was taken aback. She hadn't counted on this. Obviously she'd been naïve to think people took one puff and put the thing out. If this was how it was done, she could hardly fake smoking it until they were finished. She'd promised Ann, and now she had to deliver.

Bracing herself, she took another drag.

A languorous sensation stole over her body and she felt quite pleasant. It was amusing—in fact, everything was amusing. By the time they reached the ball field, she was laughing herself silly at anything that was said.

"Hey, straighten up, okay?" Ann admonished as they got out of the Caprice. "Put your sunglasses on, and keep them on, so people can't see your eyes."

Ann knew Jessie had only inhaled deeply to act cool, just as promised, but she hadn't anticipated the stuff hitting her so hard the first time. Jessie's fielding wasn't off that much, but her batting sucked. Although the teams were evenly matched, things deteriorated fast.

Kevin tried to downplay the situation and pretend things weren't as bad as they seemed, but Bob paced back and forth in frustration, and moaned over every error.

The game ended in such ignominious defeat that Bob sat on the bench and covered his face with his hands. When Kevin asked if he was going to Logan's, Bob shook his head and walked to his car without speaking.

Jessie was still feeling effects from the pot. On the way to the car, Ann had to remind her to take off her sunglasses because it was getting dark. Riding along, Jessie found it so enjoyable spacing out that Kevin passed the turn-off for the bar before she noticed. "Hey, aren't we going to Logan's?"

"Ann has to get home first," Kevin said. "Her parents want her in early tonight."

When they drew up to the curb in front of the Millers' brick colonial, Ann checked her watch. "I don't have to be in yet. Can you stay and talk awhile? My parents drive me crazy. They're on my case all the time. Do this, do that. 'You've already seen Mark twice this week.' Blah, blah, blah."

Kevin nodded, then rolled a joint and handed it to Ann. "This will mellow you out so you can handle the old folks."

Ann offered Jessie the reefer, but she passed. She'd done enough for her friend, and she didn't want to be high when she met Mike at Logan's. She didn't want to hurry Ann, but she became annoyed as the conversation dragged on.

When Ann at last took her leave, Jessie climbed into the front seat. Kevin continued speaking as if he was in no hurry to be anywhere. Although she hated to be rude, she was forced to interrupt him. "Don't you think we should get going?"

"Oh, sorry." Kevin glanced at the luminous dial of his watch. "It's getting late. I'll take you home."

"Aren't we going to Logan's?"

"Nah, I'm tired, and it's too late now. Everyone will be gone."

Jessie wasn't about to mention she'd planned on meeting his brother at the bar. If Mike didn't see her with the rest of the team when they walked in, he was probably gone by now, too.

⸙

By Saturday, Jessie was tempted to call Mike and explain about the foul-up, but she dithered and procrastinated all day. She hadn't realized how strong he was until he pounced on her when he'd taken her home from Logan's after the game. The attraction she felt toward him was chilled by the fear that he would take by force what she wasn't ready to give. However, he'd laughed when she threatened to bite him and released her.

Jessie wanted to establish a relationship with Mike that revolved around a common interest. He'd asked intelligent questions about horses, and she didn't think all of his interest was feigned. Riding lessons would provide the opportunity to develop a relationship and allow her to set her own parameters, but calling Mike first would give him the psychological edge.

She considered riding Rio along the road past the McKenna farm on the off chance she might see him. She often went that way to get to her favorite riding trail. However, the roadway was busy with careless weekend drivers, and in some spots it was so narrow it could be dangerous whenever there was traffic.

In the cool of the evening, Jessie headed for the barn to turn the horses out. Blue poked his head over the stall door and nickered. A dapple gray of unknown ancestry, he'd been her very first horse. She unlatched the door and patted him on the neck before setting him free.

She had joined the local Pony Club when she first moved to Concord County and was interested in combined training. After she had progressed as far as she could with Blue, her parents had purchased a more challenging animal for her. Rio del Oro was a fiery Anglo-Arab of a rich golden chestnut color. A real handful to ride, Rio was quite capable in the dressage arena and could jump like he was born to fly.

Rio pawed the straw impatiently until she opened the door of his stall. With a flick of his tail, he dashed after Blue. Blue pricked up his ears and the two geldings raced away.

Jessie leaned on the gate to watch the horses and caught herself daydreaming about Mike. All was not lost. This coming Monday, after the game, the team would surely go to Logan's. And there was a good chance Mike would show if he truly wanted riding lessons.

Monday evening, the Belleville team met at the Rendale Middle School ball field. Energy seemed to flow through the group as if Thursday's defeat had revitalized them. They quickly took the lead in the game over Rendale's mediocre team and managed to hold on to their two-run advantage until the end.

The team was jubilant as they crowded into Logan's.

"The first round is on me, Judy," Kevin said to the waitress.

Bob reviewed the stats while they waited.

Judy returned with a tray full of drinks and distributed them around the table. After handing Kevin his beer, she tucked the tray under her arm. "Thanks for lending me those books by Dostoyevsky for my course last semester. I've got them out in the car. I apologize for taking so long to return them."

"That's okay. I know how expensive college can be. I'm glad I could help out. So how did you like Dostoyevsky?"

"He's deep."

Kevin nodded and took a sip of his beer. "In *The Brothers Karamazov*, he said that all things are permissible if there is no God. So what do you think? Was he arguing for or against the existence of God?"

Judy smiled. "I think I have to get back to work, but maybe we can talk later."

Jessie never dreamed Kevin's reading extended beyond *Hoard's Dairyman*. "You've read Dostoyevsky? Didn't you major in agriculture?"

"Actually, I was a Liberal Arts major before I switched to political science."

"But you're a farmer. Didn't your parents want you to study agriculture?"

"Yes, but I told them I wanted to go to college to get an education. My father's perfectly qualified to teach me everything I need to know about running our family farm."

"So why did you switch to political science?"

Kevin took a swig of beer and set the bottle down. "I love great literature, but one of my professors convinced me that the political arena has the most impact on people's lives. He persuaded me to change my major, and it was the best decision I've ever made. I find politics fascinating."

Peggy chuckled. "The only thing I find fascinating about politics is the Kennedys and their affairs."

"You can say that again!" Ann declared.

"Oh, by the way," Peggy said. "I'd like to throw a barbecue next Saturday to round out the end of the softball season."

Jessie inwardly sighed. She always felt ill at ease in large social gatherings, but Peggy would be offended if she didn't put in an appearance. Everybody would show up with a husband or steady boyfriend—with the possible exception of Audrey—which meant having to socialize with a lot of people she didn't know and doing it all alone.

She couldn't exactly ask Mike without blowing her strategy. In fact, he hadn't shown up at the bar tonight, much to her disappointment, and she wondered if he was mad at her.

Oh well, the barbecue might not be too bad—at least she could talk to Kevin about books.

❦

Mike didn't show up at Logan's after the next game either, and Jessie suspected she'd spoiled her chance by not getting in touch with him right after the missed rendezvous. If he had really liked her for herself, surely he would have called, but if he only wanted to get laid, he already knew she wasn't giving it away.

The week following Peggy's barbecue, Kevin phoned and asked for a date. By now, Jessie figured Mike wasn't interested in a real relationship and saw no reason not to accept. She wasn't going steady with anyone. Although she was dating one other guy on a casual basis, he hadn't asked her out for some time.

Kevin picked her up early Friday evening, explaining that he needed to check on a crop of soybeans on the way to the movie theater in Mansfield. The Caprice's top was down, and Jessie's hair billowed like a flag in the wind as they wound their way along the twisting country roads.

The soybeans were growing on a leased track of bottom land in a crescent-shaped valley carved by the river. The hills surrounding the valley were thickly wooded and there were no houses in sight.

Kevin turned off the road onto a dirt track that bordered the edge of the field. He followed it until the curve of a hill obscured the car from the road, then stopped and got out. She walked beside him as he inspected the crop. When the task was completed, they sat in the car and smoked a joint, then began to talk about anything and everything that popped into their heads.

The blazing sun descended below the wooded hillside, casting dark shadows that soon merged with dusk. Tendrils of mist rose from the river like spirits gathering at a séance. Lightning bugs stirred in the gloaming, spangling the field with dainty lights that floated to and fro in a magical ballet.

"Look, it's lovely!" Jessie exclaimed.

Kevin glanced through the windshield. "If the lightning bugs are out already, we'd better get going, or we'll be late for the movie."

"Wait a minute. I want to ask you something."

She leaned over and touched his hand to stop him from turning the key in the ignition.

Kevin could feel Jessie's body heat. His gaze fixed on the gap in the vee of her blouse. The cleft between her breasts was visible, stirring his loins. He drew in his breath, heady with anticipation.

"Did you believe in fairies when you were little?" she asked, breaking the spell.

"Are you serious?"

"Of course," Jessie said. "I thought fairies flew around disguised as lightning bugs. Even though I don't believe in them anymore, watching the lightning bugs reminds me not to take too much for granted. There's probably a lot more to everything than meets the eye."

"You mean you think there's a supernatural?"

"Yes, don't you?"

"Well, I sure don't believe in witches and haints." Kevin started the car, half-annoyed but half-amused. The headlights cut a swath through the darkness that gyrated as the convertible bumped along the uneven track.

Jessie felt a little foolish but continued, "Einstein said that matter and energy are really the same. Matter is just a different expression of energy that we perceive as having material being. Our brains interpret what we see, but what our eyes see and what the cosmos really is aren't necessarily the same thing. There could be all sorts of dimensions, and we could be designed to live and perceive things in only one arrangement of them. There could be another kind of life in a dimensional format that supersedes ours but is capable of interacting with our world."

"You know, Jessie, only yesterday I'd have bet a million dollars against meeting a girl who talked about fairies and Einstein in practically the same breath."

"Gee, I guess I shouldn't have said anything. Now you probably think I'm weird."

"No," he said. "I think you are bewitching."

A sweet thrill tingled through her. Kevin sounded genuinely attracted to her. Although it was a little disappointing that he wasn't into horses, she loved talking to him. As much as Mike appealed to her physically, she preferred to be wooed—not pawed. Perhaps it was just as well that things hadn't worked out with Kevin's brother.

On the first day of the fall semester, Jessie pulled into the Concord County Community College parking lot and was vividly reminded of her bitter disappointment the year before, when her parents decided against sending her to the state university. If financial hardship had been the reason, she wouldn't have minded, but it wasn't, and the worst part was that the blow had been so unexpected.

Sex discrimination was pervasive, but her parents had encouraged her to excel in school with the aim of becoming a career woman. Homemaking and motherhood had never been high on her list of goals. It was difficult to have a career and raise a family. She knew that first-hand; her mother was an operating room nurse at the local hospital.

Although her father always regarded her mother with respect, many husbands treated their wives like servants. Ann's mother danced to her husband's tune and acted as if he was some sort of demigod. Jessie's dad didn't do housework, but he liked to cook, and he didn't expect her mom to wait on him hand and foot.

Militant feminists had taken to the streets to protest inequities in education and employment opportunities, and Jessie agreed with most of what they stood for. Her parents hadn't raised her to become a housewife. However, her younger brother, Rick, had always been favored over her for one reason, and one reason only—he was their son. He was now a high school senior, and could go to the college of his choice, while she was only permitted to attend community college despite having achieved high marks in a demanding college preparatory regimen at Archbishop Moore.

She'd never forget the day she confronted her father with the fact that her grades had earned her as much right to go to a decent college as Rick.

"I'm sorry," her father said. "The tuition where Rick wants to go is awfully high. Your mother and I have too much income to qualify for student aid, and we don't want to risk taking out a second mortgage."

"But you can afford to send us both to the state university. Why are you doing this to me?"

"Rick needs a good education so he can support a family. Don't you understand?"

"I understand perfectly, Dad. But if I can't go to college to earn a bachelor's degree, then I'm going to join the Air Force. The recruiters came to school, and I passed all the tests. In the military I can further my education on my own."

"There's a war going on, for godsake!" he exclaimed, concern filling his voice. "You've led a sheltered life. You have no idea what the world out there is like."

"I have to find out sometime," she replied flippantly.

"In Heaven's name, girl, I'm begging you not to do this."

She looked him in the eye. "If you don't love me enough to treat me as well as my brother, why should I care?"

"I'm sorry, I know it's seems unfair, but I gave my word to Rick. I cannot break my word."

"That's a cop-out. I'm joining the Air Force."

"No, you will not!" her father exclaimed. "You will attend Concord. If you disobey me, you'll leave this house never to return—and as far as I'm concerned, you'll be dead!"

His words pierced her heart like a dagger. Did he value her love so cheaply, he'd slaughter it for his pride?

"You have no right to do this to me," she replied in a brittle measured voice. "Rick doesn't deserve it, and you know it. I'll obey you because you are my father, but I'll never trust you again."

A few days later her science teacher, Mr. Hartman, took her aside and asked about her college plans in hope of convincing her to pursue a science degree. She'd first come to his attention when the "correct" answer on a multiple-choice test implied there were only four dimensions. Einstein had identified the fourth dimension as time, but that didn't mean there weren't more. She left the answer blank, sacrificing her grade rather than concede. She also refused to accept the tenet that the speed of light was the fastest thing in the

universe, arguing that no one knew enough about the physics
of the cosmos to postulate such an all-encompassing axiom.

"I'm going to Concord Community," she said.

Hartman's eyes widened. "You've got to be kidding."

"No, that's where my parents want me to go."

"Sending you to community college is a waste! You're one
of my best students—I love the way your mind works. Don't
worry, I'll talk to them."

"Please don't bother," she said. "My father has made up
his mind—and nothing can change it."

She'd walked away from her astonished teacher without
looking back. She didn't want him to see her tears. Given the
arguments they'd had in class, she never dreamed he thought
of her as one of his favorite students. Although she was good
at science, she wasn't interested in a scientific career; she'd
always dreamed of going to art school. Her parents had once
promised she could, but then told her becoming an artist
wasn't likely to afford her any kind of living and insisted she
become a school teacher instead. She'd been willing to settle
for the state university, reasoning she could take all the art
electives available, become an elementary school teacher, and
then save her money to attend the Art Institute. At least that
had been her goal until her parents had nixed that, too.

The Bible said to honor thy father and thy mother. She
was not yet of legal age and felt it was a sin not to obey. She'd
continued down the hall to the school office to inquire about
an application to Concord.

The parking lot was only just beginning to fill up, and
Jessie was able to get a spot close to the cafeteria. It had a low
profile and neutral hues like the rest of the campus buildings,
which were connected by meandering concrete walkways. The
campus was still too new to look comfortably at home in the
landscape. Even at this early hour, the late summer heat was
making itself felt. She hurried inside to escape the humidity.

The air-conditioning hummed a soothing chill into the
virtually deserted cafeteria. Jessie ignored the savory aroma of

bacon and sausage, and grabbed a cup of coffee. She exchanged good-mornings with the woman at the cash register, feigning more good cheer than she felt.

It was her sophomore year, so she had her pick of classes, but she had a lot of time to kill, because she dropped Rick off every morning in time for Archbishop Moore's eight-fifteen homeroom start. Everything revolved around Rick's schedule, which meant she also wound up waiting around for him to finish football practice in the afternoon. He was on both the football and baseball teams—thank God he didn't play basketball, too.

She sat down at a table and pulled out Tolkien's *The Return of the King*. The story was so absorbing she was annoyed when a voice interrupted her reading.

"Hello, Jessie. Do you mind if I sit down?"

Looking up, she was startled to see Patty Jensen.

Patty had been a year behind her at Archbishop Moore. She still wore her hair in a no-nonsense bob and was dressed in a tailored white blouse and A-line skirt. She might as well have been wearing their high school uniform—all she lacked was the blazer—but that was Patty for you. Until Jessie had gotten her driver's license, she'd ridden the school bus to Archbishop Moore with Patty, and they'd occasionally hung out together, although they weren't close friends.

"Please do sit down." Jessie shut the book. "I never expected to see you here. You always got such good grades. I thought you wanted to go to the state university?"

"Yes, and I will. But remember, I have two younger brothers, so Mom and Dad said we'd all need to start out at Concord."

At least some parents are fair, Jessie thought.

Patty pulled out a chair and seated herself. "I've been wanting to talk to you. I heard you're dating Kevin McKenna."

"Yes," she said, surprised that Patty knew. "How did you find out so fast? We haven't been dating long."

"You wouldn't date him at all if you know what's good for you."

"What?"

"You're still a virgin, aren't you?"

"Of course."

"Well, you won't be much longer if you keep going out with Kevin McKenna."

"What's that supposed to mean?" Jessie snapped, offended that Patty might think she took chastity too lightly.

"It means he's dangerous, and you can't handle him!"

"What are you saying?"

"Look, the McKennas are bad news. You aren't dealing with nice guys anymore—or even guys who would stop short of raping you, if you won't give them what they want."

"Come on. How can you say something like that about Kevin? Mike maybe, but not Kevin. He just kissed me for the first time on our last date."

"All of the McKenna brothers are the same."

"How do you know?"

Patty's eyes darkened. "It doesn't matter how I know."

"Can't you give me a hint?"

"No. I'd never reveal anything told to me in confidence. Promise me you'll never go out with him again."

Jessie saw the concern in Patty's eyes, but she didn't think it was fair to judge somebody without hearing any facts. And she'd already accepted a date with Kevin for the weekend. He was throwing a big party and was counting on her being there. It would be extremely rude to back out at the last minute. "I can't make a promise like that without more information."

"Well, don't say I didn't warn you." Patty stood and strode off.

"Wait!" she called, but Patty kept on walking.

Jessie shrugged and opened her book. Mike and Johnny were pretty wild. Until now, the worst she'd ever heard was that they drank too much, raced cars illegally, and were fast with women.

Kevin had graduated from college and was working hard to modernize the family farm. He was active in state and local politics, and had been the campaign manager for a popular Democrat in his successful bid for the state House.

Moreover, Kevin shared her interest in books and said he found her intriguing. She knew he was sexually experienced, but so far he'd acted like a gentleman, taking things slow, which made her think he liked her for herself and was looking for a serious relationship.

Just to be on the safe side, however, she told Ann what Patty said. But Ann said not to worry because Patty probably had rumors about the brothers confused.

CHAPTER 3

THE DOORS OF PERCEPTION

"There," Ann said, studying her eyelashes in the bathroom mirror, "Perfect!" She screwed the mascara wand back into its container, then peered closely at the center part in her hair. Good. The roots of her natural color still weren't showing.

She zipped the makeup bag shut and returned to her bedroom. Closing the door, she tossed the bag on the bed and walked to the full-length mirror.

Ann examined her reflection, giving her outfit a final once over. The pink gauze top revealed the globes of her breasts and the peaks of her nipples in a provocative manner. She turned and regarded herself in profile. The top looked fabulous without a bra, and she was pleased with the effect. Her bell-bottom jeans were skin-tight, with just the right degree of fading to be chic.

She would look so hip at Kevin's party tonight, and going braless showed real sophistication. It would do a number on the guys, and all of the females would envy her sex appeal— except Jessie, who occasionally went braless, but only as a feminist statement. Ann reveled in the freedom the sexual revolution had inspired and used it to her advantage, but she wasn't wrapped up in the feminism thing.

She did a pirouette and blew Jim Morrison a kiss. Too bad he'd died in July, but life must go on.

The sound of Mark's Mustang coming down the street rumbled through the open window. Ann ran downstairs, breasts bouncing. Her father was taking his regular evening constitutional—beer—and relaxing on the recliner in the family room watching TV. If she got to the door before he did, then she and Mark might get away with a quick hello and goodbye from the foyer. She didn't want her father to notice she wasn't wearing a bra.

He was so engrossed in the program the ruse worked. Ann breathed a sigh of relief as she and Mark escaped without incident. They managed to arrive at the McKenna farm on time.

Kevin was just coming out of the barn and walked over. "Hey, could you do me a favor? I'm running late. Would you mind picking Jessie up? She's probably wondering where I am."

~~~

Jessie sat in the rocker on the porch with Blackjack and Tar Baby to keep her company. She had a bikini and a towel packed in the tote bag beside her. It was the weekend after Labor Day, and she was glad the weather had held for the party. This time of year it could change overnight. The McKennas had a pool, and she wanted Kevin to see her wearing her new bikini.

Tires crunched on the gravel drive, and she recognized Mark's green Mustang through a gap in the trees that obscured the entrance of the lane. Mark brought the car to a stop near the porch and climbed out.

Tall and gaunt, with shoulder-length brown hair, he wore a plum-colored embroidered shirt open to the waist. His signature peace-symbol pendant swung on a thong around his neck.

"Hey, babe, looking for a ride? Kevin sent us. He's running late."

"Thanks." Jessie climbed into the back seat. Arriving at the McKenna farm, she was surprised to see so few cars. She thought Kevin had invited the whole softball team.

The farmhouse was a huge Victorian-era two-story with a wraparound porch. The clapboards were painted a trim white, and coal-black shutters flanked the windows. Several red-brick chimneys punctuated the gray slate roof.

Ann and Mark led the way to the front door. Mark rang the bell. After a minute or two, Johnny opened the door. He bowed and waved them inside. "Come one, come all! Welcome to the hall. The night is young, and the partying has begun."

Stepping into the front hall, Jessie noticed a big room on her right with a comfortable looking leather sofa and easy chairs arranged around a television set. To her left was an elegantly furnished living room with a fireplace.

"Kevin's still in the shower," Johnny said. "Follow me."

He led them down the hallway alongside the staircase and into a large dining room filled with mahogany pieces. An open door on the right revealed an office and the one directly across from the hallway led into a sizable kitchen, but both rooms were as deserted as the rest they'd passed.

Jessie had yet to see Mr. and Mrs. McKenna.

Ann looked around. "Are your parents home?"

"Nah. They're babysitting my oldest sister's kids overnight. Time to party."

Johnny veered to the left and led them across the dining room, then through a set of French doors into the rec-room addition that flanked the western side of the house.

Sliding glass doors overlooked the pool, affording a panoramic view of the Shadow River bordering the cow pasture beyond. At the far end of the room a cluster of casual chairs and two studio couches provided seating, leaving the center clear for dancing. A stereo cabinet stood against the wall, with a slew of 45s stacked and ready to play, along with several albums.

Mike, Dennis and one of the summer league umpires manned the bar, garbed alike in worn jeans and dark T-shirts. Jessie avoided making eye contact and followed Mark and Ann to the seating area. Mark took drink orders and headed for the bar. This was fine with Jessie; she wanted to stay as far from Dennis as possible, and she didn't know what to say to Mike.

Mark returned with the drinks, and a few more people entered the room. Jessie didn't recognize any of them. Johnny went to the stereo and started the music. Mark and Ann got up to dance, and Jessie sipped her drink feeling more awkward by the moment. Mark asked her to dance after Ann decided she'd had enough, but he was only good for one dance, otherwise Ann would be perturbed.

Bob Parker arrived, dandied-up, his ginger head finally minus the team's green-and-gold ball cap. He wore a bright blue Western shirt with black piping and a bolo-tie secured by a silver concha. He said hello to the guys at the bar, grabbed a beer, and headed over. "Good evening, ladies—Mark," he said. "You two gals sure are looking beautiful."

"Thanks," Jessie said.

Ann smiled and fluttered her eyelashes. "You look mighty fine tonight yourself, Bob, almost good enough to eat."

Mark gave her a sharp look.

Bob grinned. Ann sure knew how to stroke a guy's ego.

"Would you like to dance, Jessie?" he asked.

"Sure," she said, wanting to be gracious.

When the song was over, Bob excused himself and went back to the bar to chug a few with the guys. Drinking was his forte, not dancing, so Jessie returned to the couch.

Ann and Mark were arguing in low tones.

"You just ignore how it makes me feel, Ann, no matter how many times I tell you," Mark grumbled.

"But it isn't like that. It's just fun. Besides, I'm not a married woman—yet—and whose fault is that?"

The bickering made Jessie uncomfortable. Wondering where Kevin was, she decided to get up and dance by herself awhile.

At last, Kevin walked into the rec room, his dark hair damp from the shower, wearing a simple sport shirt and jeans. He paused by the bar to talk to the guys, and Jessie saw him wave her over.

Kevin acknowledged her briefly, but resumed conversing with Bob, leaving her in limbo. It was humiliating to be ignored while Kevin chatted with Bob. Mike was too close for comfort, but at least Dennis had left the room.

Mike gave her a sidelong look, then made a crude remark to the umpire about women who were so hard up they had to dance by themselves. The umpire sniggered.

Jessie felt a flush of embarrassment. She realized Mike must be mad at her for missing the rendezvous, then turning around and dating his brother, or he wouldn't have said something so rude. But it was too late to apologize. And it was too late to explain that when he didn't get in touch to arrange riding lessons, she didn't think he was really interested.

Kevin was oblivious to what was going on, and she felt too abashed to hang around. She decided to return to her seat until he had more time for her.

Ann was now arguing heatedly with Mark. "If we get married out of state, no one will find out."

Mark shook his head. "I can't take that chance, and you know it. I still have three years of college to go. If my parents find out, it's kiss college goodbye."

Jessie tried to pretend she hadn't heard anything. She picked up her glass and began to walk away, but Mark waved her back. "Would you like another drink? I'll get it for you," he said, eyes pleading.

"That's a good idea." She handed him her glass. He grabbed his own as well and started off.

"*Excuse me!*" Ann held up her empty drink, clinking the ice cubes for effect.

Mark turned around and took Ann's glass. He gave Jessie a weary look and made for the bar.

Ann pulled out her cigarettes and viciously struck a match into flame. She inhaled deeply, then let the smoke out slowly.

Another record dropped into place on the turntable. "Light My Fire" began to play.

"Dance to that, Jessie, would you? I haven't seen you do that one since Brenda's party."

Brenda's party had been the highlight of their senior year. Brenda's father put on a big bash at the American Legion for her eighteenth birthday and hired a local band that was so talented they soon moved on to Vegas gigs. Jessie had never been invited to a high school dance and was determined to dance at Brenda's party, whether any guys asked her or not. So she danced alone, doing routines she'd made up and practiced at home. Murmured comments soon turned into vocal approval.

Mike's dig had offended her pride, and she refused to be cowed by his derogatory remarks. No doubt he'd be watching her every move. She stood and walked to the middle of the empty floor. Poising herself, she cleared her mind to allow the spirit of the music to flow through her, then began her interpretation of the song.

Ann saw Mark struggling to corral three full glasses and pointed to Jessie dancing. He left her drink on the bar and carried their highballs back to the couch. Mark handed over Ann's glass and seated himself. For a moment they sipped their highballs in silence, then Ann picked up where she'd left off.

"Marry me. You promised you would."

"I will. I just can't do it right now."

Ann narrowed her eyes. "Maybe you'd rather break up? Then go ahead. I can have any man I want, and you know it."

"All right," Mark snapped. "Let's go. I'm not going to continue this in front of all these people."

He called over to Jessie, "We're leaving for awhile, okay? I left your drink on the bar."

When the song ended, Jessie realized that Kevin was no longer in the room. The top of the bar was cluttered with matching glasses, some nearly full and some empty. She couldn't tell which was hers.

"Does anyone know which drink is mine? Mark said he left it here."

Mike spoke up. "What were you drinking?"

"Bourbon and Coke."

He pointed to a glass. "That one's yours."

She picked it up and went in search of Kevin. Hearing voices coming from the kitchen, she headed there.

Johnny was holding court around a huge oak table in the center of the room. He looked up when she entered and waved her over. "Hey, Jess, come here and let me introduce you to my friends."

Johnny's friends were all students from Mansfield High, where he was a big man on campus. Although he was the same age as she, he still hadn't graduated from high school. She'd seen him from time to time since his expulsion from parochial school in seventh grade. He was a star on Mansfield High's football team and she'd watched him play many times, while rooting for Archbishop Moore and cheering Rick.

Johnny introduced her as "Kevin's girl," and there were several "oohs" and "aahs." The girls seemed awed by her status, although she was surprised that Johnny characterized her relationship with his brother in such terms. Kevin hadn't asked her to go steady yet. Maybe he was getting ready to.

"So, Jess," Johnny asked, "how do you think Archbishop Moore's going to do against Mansfield at the homecoming game?"

She sipped her drink thoughtfully. "Well, you guys are sure tough to beat, but you're still going down."

"No way!" he exclaimed.

They commenced arguing good-naturedly.

Jessie began to feel light-headed. The room seemed to be growing warmer, and it was difficult to hear Johnny over the magpie chatter of the girls. She tried concentrating harder, but there was some kind of echo and a buzzing sound in her ears.

Johnny's voice started fading in and out. The people at the table seemed to be changing in size and distance—sometimes looking closer and sometimes farther away. Her stomach grew queasy, then the room started to sway.

She bolted toward the fresh air coming through the screen door of the mudroom. Behind her, Kevin called her name but she couldn't stop. Pushing through the door, she plopped down on the porch steps and put her head between her knees. Taking slow deep breaths, she tried to tame the bilious waves roiling her stomach.

Kevin opened the door and sat beside her. "What's the matter?"

She lifted her head. "I feel sick. I need you to take me home."

"You're probably overheated from dancing. Just sit here for a minute, and you'll feel fine."

"No. I want to go home. I feel awful."

"Okay then." He helped her to her feet.

She still felt nauseous and dizzy on the way to the Caprice. Kevin opened the rear door. "Lie down for a bit and see if it helps you feel better. If it doesn't, I'll take you home."

She shook her head. "I don't think so."

"Please," he said. "I've hardly even had a chance to talk to you."

Jessie got in and laid down. She closed her eyes. The horizontal position did seem to help a little.

Kevin climbed in on top of her. She tried to push him away. "What are you doing?"

He began to kiss her, which only made the nausea worse. She twisted her mouth away. "Get off of me, for God's sake! I'm going to vomit."

He ignored her warning, but she managed to reach behind her and open the door. She writhed and clawed at Kevin to get free, hurt and angry that he wouldn't let her go. He lifted his weight off her as her struggles became frantic. Grabbing the door frame, she pulled herself to the edge and hung her head outside, stomach heaving.

When she finished up-chucking, Kevin tried to pull her back inside. Shocked, she shoved her knee into his chest and scrambled out of the car, smacking hard against the blacktop.

Clambering to her feet, she staggered toward the house. Then everything disappeared.

Her heart began to pound.

A shroud of darkness smothered her, but she could still feel the ground beneath her feet. She spun in every direction, looking for the house... something... *anything*.

A flash like lightning lit the landscape. Everything reappeared in stark black and white. There was no color anywhere. Then everything vanished.

Another flash illuminated the bizarre colorless world.

Taking her bearings during the brief bursts of light, Jessie aimed for the front porch. Every time the area lit up, she seemed to be approaching the house at a different angle. Pulse racing, she stumbled on through the void.

Something clutched at her from the darkness. She gasped and jerked free.

A voice spoke out of the ether. "Where are you going?"

It sounded like Kevin, but not in a material form.

"I-I don't know," she said, trembling. "I can't see!"

"Let me help you." He took her by the arm. "Hold on to me."

She clung to him, trying to make sense of the confusing journey. At last they came to a halt. She heard the creak of a gate. The world snapped back into focus—*and in full color*.

She breathed a sigh of relief. It was reassuring to see colors and forms again, illuminated by the light spilling from the house, instead of the surreal black and white landscape.

Kevin led her through the gate and alongside the pool. An underwater lamp gave the water an aquamarine glow. Cheerful yellow-and-white striped umbrellas topped the patio tables. Whiskey-barrel planters spilled over with red, white, and purple petunias, their powder-sweet perfume mingling with the chlorine odor of the pool.

Jessie could hardly take her eyes off the flowers, she was so afraid they might disappear.

"Would you like to swim?" Kevin asked.

"No," she said, concentrating on the flowers.

Kevin shoved her and she flipped over the edge.

She hit the water, barely able to suck in her breath before plunging completely under. Once submerged, she lost all sense of direction. Millions of rainbow colored bubbles swirled and danced around her. Mesmerized, she watched them until she could no longer hold her breath.

She tried to thrash her way to the surface, but there *was* no surface. Whichever direction she turned, there seemed to be no end to the watery underworld. Her lungs burned. Pains shot through her chest like steely knives. She fought the impulse to inhale, but the fire in her lungs was so excruciating she had to breathe... had to breathe... *something*...

Water burned through her nostrils like acid. She gagged and began to choke. Death had her in its tentacles, then a hand grabbed her arm and pulled her up. Breaching the surface, she coughed out a mouthful of fluid and gasped for air.

"What were you doing down there?" Kevin asked. "I thought you were drowning."

"I was drowning," she managed to croak.

"It's the shallow end. All you had to do was stand up."

"I couldn't figure out which way was *up*."

He helped her through the water and out of the pool. She wandered across the patio and through the gate to the backyard. Kevin caught up and took her by the arm. "You're soaking wet. Take your clothes off so you don't catch cold."

"Yes," she agreed, but stood there zombie-like. She had some vague recollection that it wasn't healthy to wear wet clothes, but she wasn't sure if it was the right thing to do. Her mind felt queer and disconnected.

"Take them off," he repeated patiently. "You don't want to catch a cold."

Sluggishly, she lifted her hands and fumbled with the buttons on her blouse. Her fingers didn't seem to work. "I can't," she said, bewildered. "I don't know how."

"I'll help you then," Kevin said and reached for the buttons.

A strange glow caught Jessie's eye. Across the lawn, she saw a beautiful garden bathed in a radiant light. Turning away from Kevin, she stumbled toward the garden in fascination.

She was almost there when she fell into space, sailing down a deep, deep hole. She was afraid of what might happen when she hit the bottom—if there was a bottom. But when she landed, she bounced and started rolling over and over like a child tumbling in play.

Kevin walked over to where Jessie had fallen. "What are you doing on the ground?"

"I can't get up," she said, giggling. Her head was spinning 'round and 'round. Getting up was impossible.

"That's all right." Kevin knelt and removed Jessie's blouse. Her limbs were limp as a rag doll and she appeared to be almost unconscious. He grappled with the hooks of the bra and yanked it free to expose her tits. Creamy mounds crowned by pointed nipples stood out against her summer tan. His cock throbbed with excitement.

Stripping off her jeans and panties, his gaze traveled to the dark curly triangle between her legs. He began to unbuckle his belt.

Jessie didn't feel connected to herself anymore. She was floating in a peaceful, twilight place. She sensed Kevin above her now, but didn't understand what he was doing.

Pain lanced through her, searing hot.

She heard herself scream and started to struggle. Then, mercifully, it was over.

She fell back into a cocoon of darkness that seemed as deep as space.

Five feet away, standing on a mound planted with purple verbena, a weathered statue of The Virgin bore silent witness.

CHAPTER 4

MYSTERY TO ME

Deep rolling thunder echoed across the hills before dawn, rousing Jessie from her unconscious state. The clouds burst open, stinging her naked body with pellets of cold rain. Lying flat on her back, in a sea of wet grass, she struggled unsuccessfully to comprehend what was happening.

Awakened by the downpour, Kevin reacted quickly. He was up in a flash and yanked her to her feet. Clutching her hand, he dragged her toward the pool house and scurried inside to shelter from the storm.

She began to shiver, and he tossed her a towel. She huddled under it, listening to the drumbeat of rain echo hollowly inside the wooden building. Finally, the downpour slowed and everything became still.

Kevin opened the door and surveyed the pool. An occasional ripple ringed the surface from errant droplets.

Jessie felt uncomfortable standing there completely nude under the towel. She wasn't even sure how she'd come to be naked in the first place. "Where are my clothes?"

"You fell in the pool, remember? Your clothes are all wet."

"Oh," she said, feeling kind of spaced-out. She didn't remember, and it didn't make much sense.

"Wait here and I'll find you something to wear."

Kevin headed out the door.

After he was gone, Jessie undid the towel and began drying herself off. She rubbed her hair and upper body, then bent down to dry her calves and thighs. When she finished, there was blood on the towel.

She stared at it stupidly for a moment, then it occurred to her that she must have gotten her period. How embarrassing to get blood all over someone else's towel.

The door opened and she looked up. Her mind felt alien, her reactions sluggish. It was Kevin. He was dressed in dry clothes, carrying an old college sweatshirt and jeans.

"I'm sorry," she said. "There's blood on the towel."

"That's okay. Here, put these on." He handed her the clothes, stepped back outside, and shut the door.

She pulled the sweatshirt over her head. Getting her arms into the sleeves was like struggling with a Chinese puzzle. With that feat accomplished, she made a stab at putting on the jeans. Balancing on one foot, she tried to insert the other one into a pant leg and almost keeled over. Repeated attempts failed. Finally, the bench along the wall registered on her brain. She sat down heavily and waited for a dizzy spell to pass.

Seated, she was able to pull the jeans on. However, they were far too large. When she stood, she had to hold the waistband up with her hands, and she left the pool house with halting steps.

Kevin was waiting outside. He held out a length of baling twine. "I thought you might need this."

She fumbled with the twine and belt loops, but got nowhere.

"Here, let me." Kevin took the twine from her and threaded it through the loops, then tied it off. He helped her hobble to the car and opened the door.

She sank limply into the seat and leaned back. Her mind was almost a total blank. She vaguely remembered coming to the party. For some reason she must have drank too much and passed out, but that just wasn't like her. She considered asking Kevin about it, but she was too tired to talk.

Her eyelids were so heavy they closed of their own accord.

Kevin drove through the damp gray dawn. He pulled into Jessie's driveway and eased slowly and quietly up to the house.

The dogs weren't out and they didn't bark from inside the house either. Luck was with him.

He shook Jessie to bring her back to consciousness. "Hey, you're home."

She opened her eyes. Kevin jumped out and came around to help her out of the car. She staggered to her feet and clung to him as he guided her up the porch steps.

Kevin turned the handle of the front door. It was locked.

"Shit," he said under his breath.

"There's a key... up on the ledge... under the eaves." She pointed to the spot, trying not to lose her balance.

He felt along the ledge, found the key, and opened the door. Blackjack and Tar Baby stood in the front hall wagging their tails. Jessie began to sway. Kevin scooped her into his arms before she collapsed and carried her over the threshold. He put her down inside and left.

Warm wet tongues industriously plastered her face with slobber, keeping her from veering off into unconsciousness.

"'Nuff, guys, 'nuff," she said in abbreviated doggy-talk. They backed off, looking pleased with themselves.

Jessie crept as silently as possible up the stairs to her room. She had a lot of explaining to do, and she was in no shape to do it. She managed to get in bed without waking anyone and fell into a deep and dreamless sleep.

It was well past noon before the outside world intruded on her consciousness. Her bed felt like a cloud she was floating on. She slowly opened her eyes and lay watching the dance of sunlight and shadow on the ceiling, caused by the wind ruffling the leaves of the tree outside her window.

She had no desire to stir from her bed, but the call of nature soon became urgent. With an effort, she sat up and was startled to see she wasn't in her own clothes. It didn't make any sense. Her mind felt empty and fuzzy, but she tried to conjure up some memory of the night before as she walked down the hall to the bathroom.

The pool.

That was it.

She'd been pushed into the pool at Kevin's party.

Once inside the bathroom, Jessie unfastened the baling twine and the jeans fell down, revealing streaks of blood on her inner thighs. She relieved herself, then reached into the cabinet under the sink to fetch the box of tampons. She fumbled with the lid and pulled one out, then froze. She'd just finished her period a week ago. *Why was she bleeding?*

A rush of hazy, disconnected memories swirled in her mind like crazy quilt pieces. She staggered to her room trying to sort them out. *Water... rainbow bubbles... struggling for air... Kevin helping her... twilight space... then awful, searing pain.*

Kevin had *violated* her!

"Oh no, oh God," she moaned, and flung herself down on the bed. Burying her face in the pillow she sobbed in desolation, quaking and trembling. She felt filthy, degraded to her core, her innermost being defiled. If only it was some horrible dream, but it wasn't. She was still bleeding.

Her life might as well be over. She was ruined; no decent man wanted to marry soiled goods. Even if she found a man willing to marry her, she would never experience the joy of being a virgin bride—and wouldn't her virtue always be suspect somewhere in his mind?

If only she'd listened. Patty was right about the McKenna brothers. But it was too late to change anything now.

Jessie didn't dare tell her parents. They'd call the police, then she'd have to be examined by a doctor. Her father would insist she bring charges and testify. He wouldn't stop to consider her feelings where principle was at stake.

It would cause a huge scandal, and she just couldn't face testifying in front of a courtroom full of people about something so embarrassing, intimate, and shameful. There was the drug angle, too.

She could hear the defense attorney now: "Miss Daniels, didn't you smoke marijuana with the defendant whenever you were out with him? You admit to using illegal drugs. Do you really expect the jury to believe you didn't willingly participate in a sexual escapade? If you were raped, Miss Daniels, why isn't there any evidence that you tried to resist?"

She could say she was drugged, but could she prove it?

She wasn't exactly certain who put the drug in her drink. Even if a test would show what kind of drug it was, the defense would argue she'd taken it willingly. No, it was her word against the McKenna brothers and their friends. Kevin would get off scot-free, and her reputation would be in ruins.

When her sobs slowed, she got up and rummaged through her dresser for an old pack of sanitary napkins. She kept them on hand because occasionally her period got too heavy for tampons alone, but she hadn't used them in a long time. She grabbed some clothes and went back to the bathroom to take a hot shower.

The spray of cleansing water helped soothe some of the turmoil she felt inside, even though she would never feel truly clean again. She was changed and she knew it. There was no going back.

Jessie got out, toweled herself dry, and dressed. She looked at the sweatshirt and bloodstained jeans with revulsion, then balled them up and threw them into the hamper. No one would notice them there for now.

Taking a deep breath to collect herself, she started down the staircase. She wasn't sure how much trouble she was going to be in for coming home so late. But if she was lucky, her parents would never suspect the rest of it.

❦

Liz Daniels was already finished washing up from lunch when she heard her daughter's footsteps coming down the stairs. "It's about time," she said, when Jessie entered the kitchen. "I thought you were going to sleep all day. Would you like a cup of coffee?"

"Yes," Jessie replied, relieved. Her mother seemed to be in a pleasant mood. Maybe things wouldn't go too badly after all.

Sunlight glinted off the auburn tint of Liz's hair as she moved over to the cabinet and took out a cup and saucer. She was a tall, graceful woman who liked to dress well, but today her thick wavy hair was tied back and she was wearing paint-stained shorts and old tennis shoes.

Jessie pulled out a chair and sat at the round maple table. A fresh breeze ruffled the blue and white gingham-check curtains. The matching tablecloth and vase of marigolds gave the room a bonny air, belying how she felt inside.

Liz put the cup and saucer down on the table and returned with the coffee pot. "You must have had a good time last night," she said, filling the cup. "How was the party?"

"Oh, it was okay." Jessie realized that sounded too vague and evasive. "I had a good time dancing."

"Did you swim?" Liz returned the pot to the stove.

"Yes, but Kevin threw me in with all my clothes on so I had to wear some of his home." Jessie spooned sugar into her coffee.

Liz took the cream out of the refrigerator and placed it on the table. "I'm sorry your father and I didn't wait up for you, but we were tired, and we figured you'd be late."

A wave of relief flooded her. "That's okay, Mom."

Liz smiled. "I'm glad you enjoyed the party. I have to go back out and help your father finish painting the trim on the garage. We can talk later. Don't forget your chores."

"Okay, Mom."

Her mother disappeared through the door, and Jessie heaved a sigh of relief. What a break. She was in no mood to talk, and this would give her more time to pull herself together.

A tremor shot through her. Her pocketbook, tote bag and bathing suit were still at the McKennas! She had to get them back before her mother discovered they were missing.

Tomorrow was Sunday, and her mother would notice if she didn't have a purse with her when they went to church. Unlike

Ann, she kept her accessories to a minimum. She had a white pocketbook for spring and summer, and a brown one for fall and winter. Carrying a white purse after Labor Day would rouse as much suspicion as carrying none at all. She hated lying and it wouldn't do much good. She needed her pocketbook for school on Monday—her money, car keys, and driver's license were in it.

She grabbed the phone and dialed Ann. Mrs. Miller answered and said Ann had gone into the city to do some shopping with her grandmother, with plans to stay overnight. She wasn't expected back until late Sunday evening.

Jessie hung up, disappointed. Rick came to mind, but he worked for the farmer next door on Saturdays and wouldn't be available until after supper. If she asked him to go with her to the McKennas his curiosity would be aroused; he'd never stop asking questions.

She had only one viable option. Do the laundry, which was one of her regular Saturday chores, and tell her parents she needed to return Kevin's clothes.

After the laundry was finished, Jessie draped Kevin's jeans and sweatshirt over her arm, grabbed the spare keys, and headed for the car. She called to her parents to let them know she was returning Kevin's clothes. They waved goodbye offhandedly. So far, so good, she thought.

Chapter 5

Through the Looking-Glass

Jessie clutched the steering wheel tighter as she crossed the bridge over the Shadow River. She followed the whitewashed fencing lining the road up to the sweeping lawn where the McKenna farmhouse loomed forbiddingly, shaded by huge maples. Diagonally to its north was a three-car garage with an upstairs apartment for the hired man. The barn, milking parlor and equipment shed bordered the expansive parking area, along with a small house for the herdsman and his family.

She reconnoitered the area, but the grounds appeared as deserted as she hoped during the afternoon milking. She didn't expect anyone to be in the house at this time of day other than Mrs. McKenna, who would probably be preparing the evening meal. Jessie parked as close to the house as possible, then wiped the perspiration from her hands onto her shorts.

Swallowing hard to quell her mounting panic, she got out, draped Kevin's clothes over her arm, then went to the front entrance and rang the bell. She prayed that Mrs. McKenna would open the door before anyone spotted her. Footsteps sounded along the hall, but the lace-covered window made it difficult to see inside.

Johnny opened the door, and her heart skipped a beat.

"Hi, come on in," he said, then turned and yelled up the stairs. "Hey, Kevin, Jessie's here!"

She was too nonplussed to ask for her purse and tote bag, and flee.

"Come on." Johnny led her straight to the kitchen. "Hey, Mom, guess who's here?"

Mrs. McKenna turned. The tangy smell of spaghetti sauce wafted from a pot she was stirring on the stove.

"This is Kevin's girlfriend, Jessie."

Mrs. McKenna smiled. She was a trim, attractive woman in her late fifties. Her once dark hair was tightly permed and streaked with gray. She looked rather quaint cooking in a ruffled apron, shirtwaist dress and pumps.

"Hello, Jessie, I'm Kevin's mother, Maria. It's so nice to meet you at last. I've been wondering who Kevin's been spending all his free time with these days."

"It's nice to meet you, too," Jessie said, trying to act natural. She gave Maria an abbreviated version of the pool incident to explain why she was returning the clothes.

"Go get your brother," Maria told Johnny, then excused herself and disappeared into the laundry room.

Jessie heard the dryer start, then the sounds of Maria putting another load in the washer.

Kevin walked in. "Hey, it's good to see you. What's up?"

She plopped the clothes into his arms with an icy expression.

"Thanks," he said, staring at the jeans and sweatshirt as if surprised to see them. "Um, let's go into the rec-room and I'll fix you a drink."

Jessie followed in Kevin's wake. He closed the French doors behind them, then went to the bar and got out two glasses.

"I don't want a drink," she said through gritted teeth. "I just came here to get my purse and tote bag."

He paused and looked at her. "You sound like you're mad at me."

"I have every reason to be mad after what you *did* last night. I don't ever want to see you again! I just want my stuff so I can get out of here."

She started for the other end of the room. Kevin jumped in front of her. "Hey, I'm sorry about last night. I didn't know you were a virgin—honest—or I wouldn't have done what I did. I thought you were playing around with me."

"Give me a break! Who do you think you're kidding?" she snapped, shaking. "I threw up all over the damn driveway. I almost drowned in your pool. I couldn't even walk straight—and you thought I was playing around with you?"

"I didn't think you were totally messed up. I thought you were playing hard-to-get, that's all."

"That's all?" she exclaimed. "You drugged me!"

"Wait—I didn't have anything to do with that. Mike did it. He said you were just giving me the business."

"And how is Mike supposed to know all this about me?"

"He said he did it with you already—the night you rode home with him from Logan's—so he figured he'd help me out."

Jessie frowned. It wouldn't surprise her if Mike said something like that to assuage his ego, but Kevin ought to know better. She wasn't a tease, and she hadn't come on to him all summer. "I just want my things so I can leave."

Kevin took her by the shoulders. "Wait—please forgive me. I truly am sorry."

"Let go! I don't want to see you anymore."

"If I let you go, you'll never come back. Mike tricked me and I'm ashamed of what I did, but I can't bear it if you won't forgive me."

She tried to pull away but he held fast.

"Please," he continued. "I can't believe I was dumb enough to believe what Mike said. I totally lost my head. What I did was terrible, I know, but you've got to forgive me. I couldn't live with myself otherwise."

Jessie felt a pang of guilt. She was fully aware that God expected her to forgive Kevin, whether she wanted to or not. It was a test of faith, and she knew it. "All right, I forgive you," she said, hoping he'd release her.

"Promise you'll still talk to me."

She shook her head, determined not to see him again.

"Please, I never met a girl like you before. I can't bear to lose you over a stupid mistake. I love you. I'll prove it—just give me another chance," he said, his eyes beseeching hers. "Just agree to talk to me, and I'll let you go."

Kevin appeared so contrite and vulnerable it seemed cruel to deny him all hope. She'd suffered too much rejection herself not to empathize, and she wanted to let him down easy, even though she had no intention of seeing him again and didn't want to talk to him either. Anyway, it was easier just to agree so he would release her. "All right, okay."

Relief washed over his face. "Thank you. You won't regret it." He removed his hands and stepped aside.

She walked to the end of the room and picked up her things by the couch. Kevin opened the door for her, then followed her across the dining room toward the front hall.

Maria spied them as they passed the kitchen. "Did you ask Jessie to stay for supper, Kevin?"

"No, Mom, not yet."

Maria came to the doorway. "Won't you stay for supper, dear?"

"No, thank you."

"Oh, please stay. It's no trouble at all. This is the first opportunity I've had to meet you, and I'm sure my husband would like to meet you too."

"Really, I can't."

"Oh, come on and stay," Kevin urged. "At least call your parents and see if it's all right or not before you say no."

Jessie hadn't a clue how to get out of the invitation without being downright rude. She'd been brought up to be well-mannered at all times. Saying "No" and dashing off went against her conditioning; dissembling and lying were as alien to her as a foreign country. She was stymied.

"All right, I'll call them." She hoped her mother would say no, she'd been out too late the night before, etc. But Liz okayed the supper invitation, sounding pleased.

When Jessie hung up, Kevin offered to fix a drink and led her back to the rec-room. She asked for bourbon and water. She didn't think she could ever drink bourbon and cola again.

Accepting the glass from his hand, she began to wonder how she was going to face Mike over the dinner table. If she hadn't been so flustered, she might have realized that staying for supper to avoid being rude wasn't worth it. She sipped the bourbon gratefully, and it helped her relax somewhat before Maria called them in for dinner.

Jessie's stomach gave a little flip when she saw Mike. Fortunately, he avoided looking at her directly. Johnny entered and took a seat. Everyone said grace, and then began eating. Johnny and Mike started jesting in good-natured fun. It all seemed so normal, like last night was only a dream.

Johnny joked about Kevin finally being snared by love, and Kevin didn't offer any protest.

Jessie saw Kevin's father look at Kevin speculatively. Joseph McKenna had the same handsome, hawk-like features as Kevin, but it was Johnny who had inherited Joe's hazel eyes and light brown hair. Mr. McKenna was so cold and taciturn he made Jessie feel downright uncomfortable. He didn't seem overly pleased that she'd been invited to dinner either.

When the meal was finished, Kevin asked if she'd like to go out on the kitchen porch for a while.

Before she could say no, Maria piped up, "Go ahead, you two," then she began to shoo everyone into the family room to watch TV. Obviously Maria thought she was aiding their romance.

Jessie didn't want to protest because that would seem out of place. She followed Kevin through the door to the porch, and stood beside him while he leaned on the post and made idle conversation. She gazed out over the pool and across the pasture to the Shadow River. The sky above the hills was tinged with the first blush of sunset. At last, she heard Maria finish loading the dishwasher and leave for the family room.

Kevin turned and looked through the window to make sure his mother was gone, then pulled a joint out of his cigarette pack and lit it. He took a drag and held out the reefer.

Jessie shook her head. "I really need to get going."

"And miss the sunset?"

She said nothing and started to turn away.

"Come on, just take one hit," he appealed. "You don't know how nice it is watching the sunset with a little high."

She hesitated. A familiar craving stirred within. She loved the mellow buzz pot gave her. This would no doubt be her last chance to smoke it. What harm could it do?

Kevin's fingers brushed hers as she accepted the joint. She felt a sting of awareness, as though there was some connection between them related to his carnal knowledge of her. Half-embarrassed, she took a drag and passed the joint back. The smoke of the drug began to take effect in seconds, soothing her senses, making the world around her seem richer and more colorful somehow.

Kevin took another hit, then extinguished the reefer between his thumb and forefinger. "Let's sit on the swing."

They rocked slowly while the dazzling display of color waxed and waned across the evening sky. Kevin talked about books, farming and national politics. It was dark long before she noticed.

"I really should be getting home."

"Okay," he said. "I'll walk you to the rec room to get your things.

There were only a few lights on inside. Everyone else appeared to have gone to bed. It felt peculiar walking through the silent house, but farmers had to get up early every day of the week. Weekends were no exception.

Kevin flicked the switch by the door to the rec room, and a light came on over the bar. Jessie walked to the couch and picked up her purse and tote bag.

"Wait a minute," he said. "There's something I need to talk to you about before you go. It's not that late. Let me fix you a drink."

"No, thanks."

"Heck, it's Saturday night. You don't have school till Monday, and it's not my job to get up for morning milking."

"All right," she said, thinking it would sound petty to refuse. She sat on the couch while Kevin fixed the drinks, wondering what he wanted to talk about.

He handed her a whiskey and water, then sat beside her. Hesitantly he began, "I guess I shouldn't ask you this now, but I want you to know how I feel. I want you to be my girl. Will you think about it?"

"No," she said, wary of making a rash commitment, and sipped her drink in silence.

"But I enjoy being with you so much. We get along so well together. We have a terrific time just talking. I've never been in love like this before. Please, just think about it. It means so much to me."

She looked into his eyes, and her heart was touched. If Mike had tricked him, and he truly meant what he said about being in love, then perhaps she should think it over.

Society placed such a high premium on girls remaining virgins until marriage that even date-rape wasn't considered a legitimate excuse. What if no other man wanted to marry her? She'd be forced to live in celibate shame the rest of her life.

What Kevin was proposing was tantamount to an engagement. Heretofore, she'd liked him enough to consider him as a potential mate, and she still found him physically attractive. Besides, what if she was pregnant? It would be foolish to reject him out of hand until she had time to sort things out.

"I'll think about it, but I'm not making any promises."

"Thank you," he said. "It means a lot to me."

Kevin reached for the empty glass in her hand and placed it on the end table, then leaned toward her and kissed her softly on the lips. She felt a flush of warmth and her mouth responded to his.

He drew her closer and kissed her high on the neck, then moved slowly down to the hollow of her throat and into the vee of her blouse. Fire and ice tingled in every pore his lips touched. His hand cupped her breast and his tongue explored her mouth in a probing kiss. For a moment, she thought about stopping him, but waves of pleasure tingled through her body, leaving her breathless and robbing her of reason.

She felt Kevin's fingers fumble with the buttons on her blouse, and unfastened them for him. He traced his lips across the curves of her bosom, making her shiver with desire. She unhooked the bra, burning to feel his hands on her naked flesh. Her nipples hardened under his palms as he caressed the swelling globes of her breasts. A hot sweet ache throbbed between her legs and mounted into a single urge.

She had to have him inside her.

Nothing else could quench the fire.

Chapter 6

Spinning Wheel

Each morning dawned as bright and lovely as the day before; as usual, Jessie awakened to birds singing. She drank in the morning sunshine with her coffee and headed outside to feed the animals with Blackjack and Tar Baby following at her heels. She was greeted by whinnies and moos before she even reached the barn. With a push, the door rumbled open on its rollers. She breathed in the sweet scent of hay and the sun-baked odor of straw.

Jessie couldn't remember ever feeling so on top of the world. The nights spent in the back seat of Kevin's car were like heaven. She was no longer concerned about the dead-end her educational road was coming to. She lived only for the moment.

After filling Blue and Rio's buckets with molasses-coated sweet feed and filling the trough with coarse-ground cattle feed for the Angus, Jessie rounded up her brother and drove off to school in a carefree mood. She wasn't worried about the World War I essay test Mrs. Nelson had scheduled. She'd studied the subject well and had already written a mockup of the required essay.

It was one of the few days that the scheduled time of her first class actually coincided with her arrival on campus, and she walked straight from the parking lot to the classroom. Sunlight streamed through the bank of windows along the wall, and students gathered in various stages of readiness. Most of the girls were already in their seats gossiping with their neighbors, and a group of guys huddled in the back discussing the merits of various cars. On the way to her desk, Jessie noticed Brian Bradley slouched in his seat with a baseball cap pulled down over his eyes. He was either asleep or nursing a hangover.

Mrs. Nelson entered and put her briefcase on her desk. This morning she was wearing a gray pinstripe suit with a ruffled pink blouse, which complemented her salt-and-pepper hair and brightened her sallow complexion. She surveyed the class, checked her delicate gold wristwatch, and cleared her throat.

The girls' chatter stilled, and the guys stopped talking and shuffled to their seats. Mrs. Nelson looked at Brian. "Mr. Bradley, are you with us this morning?"

Brian snapped out of his stupor and adjusted his cap. "Yes, ma'am."

Mrs. Nelson went over the requirements of the timed essay, answered a few questions, and told the class to begin.

Jessie wrote thoughtfully, using the mental outline of events she'd worked up. The hard part was including enough for a superior grade without going over the time limit. Satisfied, she finished with ten minutes to spare. She turned in her paper and left.

In the hallway she felt a wave of nausea and dashed into the nearest ladies' room. She spit up in the sink and turned on the water to rinse it out. She'd only had coffee for breakfast, so it wasn't gross, but she felt a sense of unease. Two girls came in and Jessie exited, heading outdoors. She sat on a bench in the quad and pulled her pocket calendar from her purse to check it. Shock constricted her chest. Four weeks had passed since Kevin's party, and it'd been *five* weeks since her last period!

Oh, God, she thought, *please don't let me be pregnant.*

"You look like you've seen a ghost," Ann said and sat down. "What's the matter?"

"I'm late."

Ann raised her eyebrows. "Have you and Kevin been...?"

"Yes."

"How late?"

"Over a week." She tucked the calendar away.

Ann shrugged. "Just a week or two is nothing to worry about. Heck, if I worried about being pregnant every time I'm late, I'd be a basket case by now."

Jessie's eyes widened. She'd never been the sort to pry, and Ann had always maintained the fiction that she went pretty far, but not all the way.

"Don't look so surprised, and don't worry," Ann said, standing. "I've got to go. We can talk this afternoon."

◦◦◦

A few days later, Mrs. Nelson had the essays graded and ready to hand back. "Before I return your papers, I'd like to share with the entire class the most unusual essay I've ever received on World War I."

Everyone looked up alertly.

"It was written by Mr. Brian Bradley."

Brian smiled. A couple of his buddies whistled.

Mrs. Nelson waited for silence before continuing. "It is also the shortest essay I have ever received, and I quote: 'Some dude shot a duke, and things just went on from there.'"

Howls of laughter erupted around the room. Brian took a bow. Jessie was laughing so hard she had tears in her eyes.

Mrs. Nelson waited for the explosion to vent itself. "Mr. Bradley, did you make any effort to prepare for this test?"

The tall, sandy-haired young man stood politely. "Yes, ma'am, I did."

Mrs. Nelson crossed her arms over her chest. "I find that rather difficult to believe."

"I can prove it," Brian replied.

"How?"

"I knew it was a duke, didn't I?"

The whole class exploded. Even Mrs. Nelson cracked up. When she managed to regain her composure, she looked Brian in the eye. "I want to see you in my office this afternoon."

"Yes, ma'am."

Jessie knew Brian hadn't bothered to study because he was hoping to flunk out. Most guys were in school to avoid the draft, but Brian didn't care one way or the other. His parents believed in higher education; he didn't. That was the whole reason he'd picked Concord. His parents were off his back because it had the word *college* in the title, but he called it "the country club" and was busy having a nonstop party.

Mrs. Nelson handed Jessie her essay back. "Very good work, Miss Daniels. You earned the highest grade overall."

⁜

Time continued to fly by, and Jessie mostly managed to forget she was pregnant. In fact, she was in complete denial.

Patty Jensen stopped her on the way to class one day. "I heard you're still dating Kevin."

"Yes," Jessie said, wishing she would go away.

Patty looked into her eyes. "You blew it, didn't you?"

She winced inwardly, but she wouldn't lie. "Yes."

"So when is the baby due?"

Her mouth opened in astonishment. "How did you know?"

"I was in the ladies' room the other day when you were throwing up," Patty said. "Good luck, Jessie. You're going to need it."

⁜

After Jessie got home from school she took Rio out for a long ride. When she rode she merged into a mystical world, and so far the magic hadn't ceased. Across the fields and through the woods the sights and sounds of modern life ceased. Most of the time she didn't even feel like she was in the same world when she rode through the woods, as though the forest was a portal to some mythical level of existence.

She wondered how long she should wait before telling Kevin about the baby. In health class she'd learned that a large percentage of pregnancies ended in miscarriage, often before a woman even knew she was pregnant, so there didn't seem much point in rushing things. She was confident Kevin would do the right thing and marry her. He'd said he loved her, and he was financially secure enough to start raising a family. The only thing that worried her was what her parents' reaction would be.

Liz was putting a pot of potatoes on to boil when she saw Jessie dismounting at the barnyard gate and decided to walk on out.

When she got there, Jessie was already up in the loft throwing down hay. Liz talked to the steers and scratched one behind the ears. A tabby cat named Tommy rubbed against her legs, purring. She bent to pet him.

Jessie started down the stairs from the loft, and Liz looked up just in time to see her fall. She ran to the foot of the stairs. Jessie was out cold.

"Oh, God," Liz said and prayed. She examined the angle of her daughter's head and neck. Everything seemed to be all right. She checked for a pulse. Finding one, she rubbed Jessie's hands and called her name until her eyes fluttered open.

Thank God, Liz said to herself. "Are you okay, honey?"

Jessie looked up at her and started to speak, but suddenly turned on her side and began to vomit.

This doesn't look good, Liz thought. "Don't get up. Just rest here. I'll go get your brother to help you back to the house."

Jessie began to feel better, so she pulled herself up to sit on the bottom step until her mother came back.

Her mother returned with Rick. Together, they helped her walk to the house. Liz got some ice out of the refrigerator for the lump Jessie could feel swelling on her head. Ignoring her protests, Liz whisked her off to the hospital.

When they reached the emergency room, Jessie sat down to wait while her mother filled out forms. Recently refurbished in trendy shades of orange, gold and avocado, with abstract art prints hung on the walls, the waiting room looked like a hotel lobby. It wasn't crowded, and a nurse came out in short order to escort her to an examining room.

Once inside, the nurse motioned for her to sit up on the examination table, then checked her pulse and blood pressure, making notations on a chart. "Dr. Ryder is going to take a look at you."

Dr. Ryder was a surgeon whom her mother thought walked on water. Although Jessie had heard her mother speak highly of him, she'd never met him before.

A middle-aged, distinguished looking man entered wearing dull green hospital scrubs. His smile lit up warm brown eyes.

"Your mother asked me to take a look at you when she found out I was here. I certainly couldn't pass up a chance to meet you. Liz is the best O.R. nurse I've ever worked with." He shined a light in Jessie's eyes and checked her reflexes. "I want you to tell me what happened as well as you can remember it."

"I fell coming down the stairs from the hayloft."

"Did you slip first?"

"No, I just fell."

Ryder scribbled something on the chart. "Have you ever had blackouts before?"

"No," she said, and he made another notation.

"Do you use drugs?"

Her eyes widened in shock. "What?"

"Have you ever taken LSD?"

She shook her head. "I wouldn't take LSD if somebody paid me to do it."

"All right," the doctor said. He turned to the nurse. "Ruth, call up to Radiology for an X-ray."

Jessie looked at Ryder. "Why?"

"Your mother said you were unconscious and, when you came to, you vomited. You have a contusion on the back of your head, and vomiting can be a sign of a concussion. I want an X-ray to be on the safe side."

"No, I can't have an X-ray."

Ryder raised his eyebrows in surprise. The nurse halted in her tracks.

"Why not?" Ryder asked.

"I might be pregnant."

The eyes of the doctor and nurse met spontaneously.

"I won't be needing you anymore, Ruth."

"Yes, doctor." The nurse diplomatically avoided looking at anyone as she left the room.

Ryder pulled up a stool. "How long have you and your boyfriend been having sexual relations?"

"Seven weeks," she said, mortified.

"Did you use any contraceptives?"

"No."

"How old is your boyfriend?"

"Twenty-five."

"I know your mother well enough to know you've been raised a strict Catholic. You might not know your way around, but your boyfriend is old enough to know better." Ryder shook his head in disgust. "It's too early for a test to be accurate, but it isn't unusual for pregnant women to have blackouts. If you aren't pregnant, and you have any more of these blackouts, you'd better see a specialist."

Ryder paused. "Do you want to tell your mother or shall I?"

"I'd rather you did," she said, relieved.

"Wait here about ten minutes," he said, then left.

Jessie took several deep breaths, but her stomach was still tied in knots. After ten minutes had ticked by, she slid off the table and left to find her mother.

Liz was standing alone in the corridor. She turned and looked at her. "Dr. Ryder says everything is fine. Let's go home." She walked off without another word.

Jessie followed her out to the parking lot. Her mother got in the car, stabbed the key into the ignition, and started the engine. She drove along in utter silence, which was more disturbing than hysterics.

Finally, Liz spoke. "Do you love him?"

Jessie hesitated. She wasn't sure how to answer. In psychology class Father Lawrence had said that passion and love weren't the same thing. She hadn't fallen in love and succumbed to temptation like other girls she knew, but she was almost sure she was in love with Kevin. She was certainly in love with sex. Short of becoming what was commonly considered a slut, she had no choice but to stick with Kevin.

"Yes," she answered.

"Does he love you?"

"I think so."

"Good," Liz said, her voice breaking in a sob. "Then you can get married."

CHAPTER 7

TEARS OF A CLOWN

Driving to school the next morning, Jessie felt elated. At the moment, she was free of any real worries and buoyed by the sensation of being in communion with the great mystery of life. She strolled across the campus to class reveling in the voluptuously feminine creativity of nature.

Jessie remembered a day that she had been out riding Rio through the woods and happened upon an old, unused trail. The entrance was overgrown, so it wasn't surprising that she'd missed it before. It proved to be a difficult trail, tangled with brambles and low-hanging branches. Just when she thought she couldn't stand another briar or snagging branch scraping her skin, Rio broke through into an enchanting emerald space.

A bower of giant walnut trees towered above a grove that was carpeted with delicate grass of luminescent green. The leafy canopy shaded the area from the harsh summer sun, helping to soothe her scratched and overheated skin. Nearby, a stream murmured along its way, cooling the sweet smelling air.

She rode Rio through the grove in awe, intuitively comprehending the pagan veneration of such places. Never before had she seen trees so old. The atmosphere was as sanctified as that of any cathedral. Only a conscious act of will kept her from dismounting and falling to her knees in reverence, so strong was the primeval spell cast by the venerable trees. Her upbringing constrained the impulse to worship creation rather than the Creator—yet there was something about the grove that spoke to her heart.

Abruptly, the present intruded on her reverie. Someone was calling her name. Her mind snapped back into real-time and focused.

Brian hurried up the walkway trying to catch her. "Hi, Jessie, how's it going?"

"Fine," she said. "Hey, you sure had Mrs. Nelson going with that essay of yours. How long did it take you to think it up?"

"It was a spur of the moment thing," he said. "By the way, I'm sorry I haven't asked you out for a long time. I've been kinda busy."

Busy drinking and fishing, Jessie thought, *like that was flattering.*

"Would you like to go out this weekend?" Brian asked.

"No."

His face fell. "Aw, don't be mad at me, Jess. I'm really sorry, honest. Besides, it's Halloween, and the guys and I are working out the details for a great party over at Scott's. Curt has a line on getting an Aerial Flash Bomb, and we're gonna have lots of M-80s."

"I'm sorry, but I can't go out with you because I'm going steady."

"Oh," he said. "Okay, Jessie, see you around."

Brian wheeled and headed back the way he came, bummed-out that he'd blown his chances with the neatest girl he'd ever met. Jessie wasn't a tease like Pam or a hot-pants like Colleen; she was beautiful, shy and mysterious—just the kind of girl he'd like to marry someday. Now some other guy had her all tied up.

He went to the cafeteria and met up with Curt. Together they walked to the parking lot and got into Curt's orange GTO. Screeching his tires for dramatic effect, Curt peeled out of the parking lot and headed at top speed for the liquor store on the outskirts of Mansfield. Acquiring the Aerial Flash Bomb required proper lubrication.

Jessie finished her classes for the day and picked up a cold drink in the nearly deserted cafeteria. She looked around to see if she could get into a card game to kill time until her brother finished football practice, but the only game going involved serious gamblers who wouldn't take kindly to a female of the species intruding.

The weather was too fine to sit around doing homework. She left the building and went for a drive around the countryside. It was a magnificent fall and still so temperate it was amazing. Only a few frosty nights had turned trees everywhere a stunning medley of brilliant reds, oranges and yellows.

The sky was cornflower blue, and the grass once more glowed a rich green because of autumn's cooler nights. Cornfields lay ripe and golden under the Indian summer sun. A crystalline light bathed the landscape, illuminating the colors with such clarity that she ached to capture it on canvas.

Entranced by the spectacular scenery, Jessie lost track of time. A glance at her watch shocked her. She hit the gas, but she was going to be late even if she broke the speed limit all the way to Mansfield. Her brother would be pissed, too.

Once inside the town limits, she slowed to normal speed. The noise of traffic, stink of exhaust, and aromas wafting from fast-food joints reminded her of her childhood in the city. She brought the dark blue Delta 88 to a smooth stop in front of the columned portico that graced the classic brick façade of Archbishop Moore.

Rick was sitting on a bench looking put out. He pointedly checked his watch, picked up his books, and got into the car with a sour look on his face.

"Sorry I'm late," Jessie said.

He sat there stone-faced, ignoring her, not even offering the courtesy of acknowledging her apology.

"Come on, Rick, I said I was sorry. It was such a nice day I went for a drive and lost track of time. It's no fun just doing homework until it's time to pick you up."

Rick turned on her. "Do you think it's any *fun* having your *sister* pick you up from football practice? If we didn't have to feed your stupid horses, Mom and Dad would have given me my own car by now."

"If you hadn't wanted to go to such a pricey college," she shot back, "I'd be in a dorm at the state university and you'd have the car all to yourself."

"Go blow," he grumbled. "Your horses are a big waste of money, and I deserve my own car."

She bit back a retort and they rode home in silence.

***

Putting on her makeup for the evening, Jessie wondered what Kevin's reaction was going to be when she told him she was pregnant. She pictured him being a little overwhelmed at first, but proud to be a father. He was financially secure enough to marry and raise a family. In fact, she wouldn't be at all surprised to learn that he'd already planned to give her an engagement ring for Christmas. She hummed a merry tune as she put on the rose-colored cocktail dress her mother had bought her. It looked wonderful with her black hair and tawny skin.

Kevin took her to Club Roma. It was a glitzy nightspot that featured fine dining, live bands and dancing. The décor favored mirrored walls and faux marble columns. The enormous horseshoe-shaped bar gleamed with polished brass and dark wood. Around the corner a huge parquet dance floor beckoned. Colored lights illuminated couples moving rhythmically to the pulsing beat of a hot local band.

A hostess escorted Jessie and Kevin to the dining room, and led them to a reserved table. The sound of the music was subdued by plush carpet and draperies. Jessie accepted the menu from the hostess and glanced through it.

Kevin placed his menu on the table without opening it. "Have the prime rib. It's the house specialty."

"I prefer steak," Jessie said.

"You really ought to try the prime rib."

"I'd rather have steak."

However, when the waitress came, Kevin ordered two prime ribs, and frowned when Jessie insisted on a Delmonico.

During their meal, couples passing by frequently stopped to greet Kevin and chitchat. He seemed to know people everywhere they went. Growing up in one place and being involved in politics obviously had something to do with it, but he also had the sort of charm that attracted people.

Jessie wished she'd grown up on a farm. Her Daniels ancestors were once farmers who had prospered for generations until they lost their land when their valley's river was dammed to form a reservoir to provide water for the city. By her father's generation they had become city people.

Her father played the saxophone in a jazz band while working his way through college. He met her mother, Elizabeth Blair, on a blind date, and proposed when he realized she was the woman of his dreams. They would have happily remained in the city if Jessie hadn't driven them crazy for a horse.

After an excellent dinner, Kevin took her over to the bar. He quickly spotted some friends of his. "Jessie, I'd like you to meet Wayne and Carol Kramer. They own a dry-cleaning business in Mansfield."

Wayne was short and dapper, and in his three-piece suit looked more like a banker than a dry cleaner. Carol was lanky and tall, with mousey brown hair, and wore a leopard-print dress accessorized with clunky gold jewelry.

Kevin and Wayne were soon involved in a lively debate about extending the water and sewer lines beyond the immediate outskirts of Mansfield.

Carol rolled her eyes, mockingly groaned, and turned her attention to Jessie. "I've been dying to meet you. Wayne and I have known Kevin since first grade and always hoped he'd find a nice girl someday. I had the feeling there was somebody special in his life, but he's been keeping *who* a big secret."

"Oh, um, well..." Jessie trailed off, flustered.

"I'm sorry," Carol said. "I didn't mean to embarrass you. I hope I didn't put my foot in my mouth by saying something I shouldn't have. You do care about Kevin, don't you?"

"Yes, and I'd be thrilled if he cares just as much for me."

"Oh good! This is so great. You're the prettiest girl he's ever dated. I hope he has the guts to pop the question. It would be so nice to see him settled down."

Jessie smiled at Carol's excitement.

"Where on earth did you get such beautiful black hair? I've never seen anything like it. Is it your natural color?"

"Yes," she said, taken aback.

"Really? Damn! I was hoping it was a dye job so you could tell me where to buy the color," Carol said. "Are you Italian?"

"No. I'm part American Indian."

"Wow, part Indian. How exotic."

Jessie found Carol's forthrightness refreshing, once she got used to it. They talked about discrimination against women in the business world, and Carol sympathized with her over the raw deal she'd gotten when her parents decided to skimp on her education to favor Rick. Jessie found Carol an easy person to like. She was elated that Carol approved of her and that Carol couldn't wait for Kevin to propose.

⚮

Kevin drove Jessie home and parked at the bottom of the long driveway. He leaned over and kissed her. She waited for the kiss to end before bringing up the baby.

"I have something to tell you."

"What?"

She hesitated for a second then plowed ahead. "I'm pregnant."

"So get an abortion," he replied coldly.

The world spun crazily and her heart constricted with shock. She stared at Kevin, aghast. "It's our baby! How can you say something like that?"

"Look, I'm sorry you got pregnant. It's my fault. I should have used something. I usually do, but having sex with you was too much fun. I didn't want to spoil it. But if you're pregnant, it's your problem."

Ire heated her blood. "No, it's *not* just my problem. And if you think I'm having an abortion, you're nuts. You're going to be a father whether you like it or not."

"How do I even know it's mine?"

Jessie gasped. *"You son of a bitch!"*

She stormed out of the car and slammed the door. Marching up the driveway, she heard Kevin drive off. What a bastard! What a creep! He wasn't even going to come after her to apologize.

Her parents expected them to marry. What on earth was she going to do? She couldn't possibly face her mother feeling this upset, so she continued past the house and out to the barn.

Rio nickered softly when Jessie entered the barn and flicked on the light. She unlatched the door to his stall and stepped inside to stroke the velvet skin of his muzzle. His golden coat glistened like fish scales, reflecting rainbows in the dim yellow light. She buried her face in his neck. Rio stood there patiently as hot tears dampened his glossy coat.

Jessie moaned in despair. She could hardly believe what Kevin had said. *Abortion?* He was a Catholic too. How could he suggest such a thing? Killing an unborn baby was a terrible sin.

He made her feel like a piece of trash, something used and discarded. He didn't want her, and he didn't want their baby.

Sobs shook her body. If Kevin refused to marry her, her parents would make her give the baby up for adoption. She'd be sent off to live at a home for unwed mothers. That had been the fate of two of her classmates in high school. When the baby was born, she wouldn't even be allowed to see it.

Jessie raised her head and wiped the tears from her swollen eyes. Somehow she had to find the strength to do the right thing, even if it meant having to give the baby away in the end. Steeling herself, she gave Rio a pat, then left the stall and went to the front of the house as if Kevin had dropped her at the door.

Her mother was waiting for her in the kitchen. The only light came from the small bulb over the stove. Blue smoke rose in a lazy spiral from a cigarette in the ashtray.

Jessie stopped just outside the door to the kitchen, hoping the darkness in the hallway would hide the ravages of her tears. "Hi, Mom," she said, trying to sound normal.

"Hello, honey," Liz replied. "How did Kevin take the news?"

"He seemed pretty shocked," Jessie said dully.

"What is he going to do?"

She took a breath. "It's all so sudden. We both need time to think. I'm tired. I want to go to bed."

"Okay, sweetheart," Liz said. "Good night."

"Good night, Mom. I love you," Jessie said, only too grateful that her mother had the tact not to pry further.

CHAPTER 8

PEARLS BEFORE SWINE

Jessie slept through the night as soundly as a child, but in the morning's hazy zone between sleep and wakefulness, when consciousness began to gather focus, her mind churned in turmoil. She was in trouble. Big trouble.

Kevin's demand that she abort the baby had caught her off guard. He'd lied to her all along about being in love, and that hurt intensely, but if he was any kind of man he ought to recognize his obligation to marry her and give the baby a name. It shocked her to think he might not. She prayed he'd come to his senses.

The phone rang after lunch and she grabbed it, hoping it was Kevin. A rush of relief flooded her when she heard his voice. Thank goodness everyone else was out. But the conversation had no sooner gotten past hello, when Kevin bluntly asked what she was going to do with the baby.

"What do you mean?"

"You know—we already discussed it."

"Discussed it? We didn't discuss anything. Are you ready to talk?"

He lowered his voice. "Look, I can't say too much. Someone might overhear."

Her chest squeezed tight with anger. "I'm not getting an abortion. It's illegal and even if it wasn't, I wouldn't have one. If you don't want to marry me, fine. I'll put the baby up for adoption."

"You can't do that! I don't want any kid of mine raised by strangers," he hissed, then abruptly hung up.

She slammed the receiver down in the cradle. *No*, she thought, *you'd rather kill it.*

A half hour later the phone rang again. It was Kevin.

"Why would you want strangers to raise your baby? What kind of mother would that make you?"

"A lot better mother than you are a father. At least then our baby would be alive and have two parents."

"You can't put the baby up for adoption if I say no."

"Well, it's none of your business what I'm going to do, unless you're willing to acknowledge the baby as your child." She hung up.

⚬⚭⚬

Kevin was determined to wear Jessie down. If he wanted to get anywhere in politics, he had to consider public opinion. An abortion could be covered up, but producing a bastard child was a liability. It was in his best interest to have Jessie abort the baby, otherwise he'd have to marry her to forestall any damage to his political ambitions.

A goody two-shoes like Jessie had to be living in dread of her parents discovering her pregnancy, and that was all to his advantage. He continued to phone in hope of wearing down her resistance. When Bill or Rick answered, he just hung up. But one day he got Liz and, thinking it was Jessie, he started to talk.

Liz lit into him. "If you don't propose to our daughter soon, Bill and I will be over to talk to your parents."

There was no getting out of marrying now. His parents would insist that he do the right thing. His only recourse was to put the blame on Jessie by pretending she was nothing more than a gold-digger who'd trapped him with her wiles.

⚬⚭⚬

Kevin rang the doorbell of the Daniels' house and waited with deliberate calm. What had to be had to be. There were worse fates than marrying a pretty girl who was fun to have sex with. When Liz opened the door, he flashed a winning smile and turned on the charm.

Liz's fears vanished like night vapors in the sun. "Jessie's in the barn. Go on out back."

                             ✦

A shadow fell across the sunlight coming through the open door. Startled, Jessie stopped raking and turned around. At the sight of Kevin, anger flickered in her heart. She frowned and leaned on the handle of the rake. "What do you want?"

Kevin smiled. "Is that any way to talk to a man who's come to ask for your hand in marriage?"

She raised an eyebrow. "You aren't the marrying kind, are you? What do you want to marry me for?"

"I've had time to think it over." He gave her an apologetic look. "I've sown my wild oats. I'm ready to settle down with a special woman, and I'd be a fool to let you get away. Besides, it's about time one of us provided an heir to carry on the family name."

Jessie rolled her eyes at that. "What makes you think the baby is yours?" she asked dryly. "I'd just like to know, if you don't mind?"

Kevin laughed. "I knew that all along. I'm the first and only man you ever had. I'd have seen it in your eyes if I weren't."

Jessie looked at him hard. So much for the line about him not knowing she was a virgin before he raped her. Now she knew he'd been playing her for a fool all along. "I'll think about it."

She turned and hung the rake on the wall. Kevin grabbed her arm and yanked her back to face him. "What do you mean you'll think about it?"

Jessie looked him in the eye. "Just what I said—I'll think about it."

She broke away and strode off toward the house.

"Don't think about it too long, Jessie, or I might change my mind," Kevin yelled after her.

She ignored him and kept on walking. Out of the corner of her eye, she saw him stride over to the Caprice. He jerked the car door open, slammed it shut, and revved the engine before peeling off down the driveway.

Jessie shook her head in disgust. He was acting like a spoiled brat who hadn't gotten his way. Well, it served him right. She wasn't about to marry an asshole like him. Resolute, she opened the back door and stepped into the kitchen.

Her mother turned to her anxiously. "What happened?"

Jessie pulled out a chair and sat down, trying to collect herself.

"Did he propose?" Liz asked.

"Yes," she answered flatly.

"Didn't you accept?"

"No."

Liz's jaw dropped. "Why not?"

"I told him I'd think about it."

"What for?"

Jessie looked into her mother's eyes. "I'm not sure what's right."

Liz stared at her, dumbfounded. "Now you listen to me. This isn't the time for that. You should have thought about what you were doing before you went to bed with him the first time."

"But—"

Liz slapped her palm on the table. "The man asked you to marry him. You have no right to bring my grandchild into this world a bastard! If you loved Kevin enough to go to bed with him, then you'd better darnsite face up to your responsibilities as a parent. You phone him right now and tell him you'll marry him."

"But—"

Liz narrowed her eyes. "You aren't going to embarrass me in front of the entire county. You've made your bed, now you're going to have to lie in it!"

Jessie's chest constricted and her throat pinched tight with pain. She sat there immobile, unable to speak, her stunned expression frozen in place. Woodenly, she rose and left the kitchen.

Her whole perception of her relationship with Kevin had altered radically since the night she told him she was pregnant. Now she knew he'd raped her, knowing full well she was a virgin, then seduced her just for kicks. But how could she explain this to her mother if she wouldn't listen?

Although her father knew she was pregnant, how she'd gotten that way wasn't a subject either of them felt comfortable discussing. Even if she could summon the courage to tell him about the rape, she'd never be able to explain why she let Kevin seduce her afterward.

She slumped into the wingchair flanking the fireplace in the living room, and cast her gaze about seeking some form of solace. The ancient Daniels family Protestant Bible was on the bookcase near the sofa. She picked it up and paged through it. Her fingers stopped at a passage at the end of the twenty-second chapter of the book of Deuteronomy:

> *"If a man find a damsel that is a virgin, which is not betrothed, and lay hold on her, and lie with her, and they be found; then the man that lay with her shall give the damsel's father fifty shekels of silver, and she shall be his wife."*

It certainly seemed to cover her situation. While the bride price was a thing of the past, she had been a virgin when Kevin took her. She wasn't betrothed to another, and she was already carrying Kevin's child. No matter her misgivings, her duty seemed clear—and it was the only way to keep her baby.

A few days later, Maria and Joe arrived with Kevin to meet Liz and Bill. Haughty and proud, they acted like they were doing the Daniels a favor. Joe sat grim-faced at the dining room table. He gave Jessie such a stony look, while she served the coffee, she returned to the kitchen to put the pot back on the stove and stayed there.

Bill took a sip from his cup. "I understand that your son has proposed to my daughter."

Joe didn't reply. Maria nodded.

Kevin spoke up. "Yes, sir, I did—and I hope you'll give your consent."

Bill nodded. "My wife and I agree that Jessie should get married as soon as possible, but she's still in college, so the best time would be over the Christmas break. If you get married the weekend after New Year's Day, you'll still have time for a honeymoon before she must be back in school."

"Of course," Kevin replied, "but honeymoons can be costly, and we'll have lots of expenses setting up house. I don't think I can afford to pay tuition, too."

"I'll pay Jessie's tuition. I've asked her to please finish school, and she's promised me she will."

"Whatever you want is fine by me."

Maria piped up next. "Kevin's father and I expect our son to marry in church with a full Nuptial Mass."

Liz stiffened. "We certainly planned on Jessie marrying in church."

"I would hope so," Maria said. "We have lots of friends and prominent acquaintances who must be invited."

Out in the kitchen, Jessie's jaw dropped. She didn't want a big wedding. In fact, she'd hoped for a quiet ceremony at the courthouse as soon as Kevin could procure a marriage license. Then they could pretend they'd eloped.

On Friday, the weather turned cold and gray. Jessie drove to St. Mary Magdalene's late in the afternoon for confession. At that hour the church was nearly empty; most parishioners were still at work or in school. Inside, the stained-glass windows glowed dully, and the atmosphere was dim, hushed, and solemn like the lowering clouds. The murmurs of the priests and penitents in the confessionals were barely audible.

Jessie crossed herself with holy water and genuflected before heading to the next empty confessional. She prayed that the priest would be a visiting confessor, unfamiliar to her, and stepped inside. She knelt, waited for the panel behind the screen to open, then began the familiar litany. Tensing, she told the priest how long it'd been since her last confession.

To her surprise, he didn't seem too perturbed, and she stumbled on, laying bare her sin. Then he spoke to her in a voice that was gentle and compassionate. "How long has this affair been going on?"

"Since the second weekend in September."

"Do you plan on marrying so the relationship can be sanctified in the eyes of God?"

"Yes, Father. I'm pregnant, and my boyfriend has proposed. We'll be married soon."

"Good," he said, and promptly absolved her of all her sins. "Say three Hail Marys for your penance."

Jessie was flabbergasted. No lecture—and only *three Hail Marys*? It was the lightest penance she'd ever received in her life. The worst sin she'd ever confessed before was getting angry at Rick's teasing. She'd never even missed Mass, except once or twice when she was sick.

"Is that all, Father?"

"Yes, you may go, and God be with you."

Mystified, Jessie left the confessional and entered one of the pews to recite the three Hail Marys. She looked up at the large oil painting of Mary Magdalene grieving before the cross of her savior. The painting had always moved her because Mary Magdalene was a sinner's saint, but today Jessie identified with the Magdalene more deeply than ever, for now she, too, had a taste of the scorn directed at fallen women.

Jessie bowed her head and recited her penance, then rose to leave. Glancing at the confessional, she wondered who the compassionate confessor was and why he'd only told her to say *three* Hail Marys.

The first snowflakes were drifting down from the sky, and she paused to button her coat. Just then Patty showed up.

"Hey, how's it going?" Patty asked.

"Not bad," Jessie answered. "I got the visiting priest. He's in the first box on the right side as you go in. He gives really light penances."

"Thanks for the heads-up," Patty said. "Father Martin and Father Gregory are too tough."

A black-winged habit appeared out of nowhere. "What did I hear you say, Miss Jensen?" asked Sister Phillipa, St. Mary Magdalene's organist.

Patty whirled to face Sister. "Um, I was hoping to get the visiting priest."

Sister smiled thinly. "We don't have a visiting priest this week." She fluttered on up the steps into the church.

Maria's sister, Julia, and her husband Hal were so excited when they found out their favorite nephew was getting married they immediately decided to throw a party. They could hardly wait to meet the bride-to-be.

Julia and Hal extended a hearty welcome when Jessie arrived with Kevin at their spotless cottage-style home in Mansfield. Julia was a younger version of her sister Maria and gushed with genuine warmth. Hal was a stout man who exuded hospitality.

He took Jessie's coat and winked at Kevin. "You lucky son-of-a-gun. Where'd you find a doll like this?"

With a sparkle in her eye, Julia led Jessie into the living room and introduced her to the gathered members of the family whom she'd not yet met.

Kevin's oldest sister, Kathleen, was a delicate but ravishing beauty with brown eyes and dark hair like her mother. Her husband, Frank Morgan, was a rusty-haired, lanky, good-ol'-boy who liked stock car racing and pro football. They were both in their mid-thirties and had five rambunctious children. Frank Jr., Billy, Brady and Doug were wrestling and chasing each other around, so all Jessie caught were the names.

Sally, a shy quiet child, was the oldest and the only girl. She seemed to be in charge of entertaining her nine-month-old cousin, Little Charlie. He was the child of Kevin's other sister, Mary Clare, who'd finally managed to give birth after struggling with fertility problems.

Mary Clare was pretty but plump. Like Johnny, her light brown hair and hazel eyes favored her father's coloring. Her husband, Charlie Clark, was a tall, florid man with a blond crew-cut, who was wearing a bowtie and a Madras jacket.

The brothers-in-law cast approving glances in Jessie's direction and congratulated Kevin on his good taste. Maria made an effort to be gracious, but it was clearly a struggle. Joe ignored her completely. Kevin's older sisters were warmly polite.

⚮

Ann washed the last crystal goblet that remained to be cleaned after the bridal shower, and handed it to her mother to dry. Lorna deftly wiped it off with a linen towel. "There's only one reason I can think of why a girl like Jessie would want to get married so quickly, and I know the McKenna boys' reputation!"

"Oh, Mom, can't you just drop it?"

"You know something, don't you?"

Ann was a good liar, but her best lies were for her own protection. Under her mother's probing gaze, her eyes betrayed what she knew.

"So I was right!" Lorna exclaimed. "She's pregnant, isn't she?"

Ann nodded.

Lorna's eyes glittered with malice. "Jessie ought to be ashamed of herself. How dare she have a lavish wedding! Is she going to wear white?"

"Of course."

"I never heard of such a thing!" Lorna huffed.

"What do you want her to do, Mother? Embroider a scarlet letter on her gown?"

"You knew all along, didn't you?"

"Of course."

"I forbid you to take part in this travesty!"

Ann eyed her mother slyly. "If you want me to move out, I can always move in with Mark."

Lorna opened her mouth in rebuke, then shut it. Did she dare suspect... or was this just a ploy for Ann to get her way? "But why would you want to be friends with a girl like that?"

"I owe her one," Ann said, then left and went upstairs.

Rick stunned Liz by refusing to be in the wedding. The number of bridesmaids was set and the gowns were already being altered. Without Rick as a groomsman, the bridesmaids would be short one escort. Liz was forced to break the news to Jessie.

"I don't understand what's wrong with your brother. He won't tell me why he doesn't want to be in the wedding."

Jessie found Rick in the bottom field, shooting his .22 rifle. She watched as he concentrated on the target. He was tall, with wholesome good looks like their father, but his gray eyes and auburn hair came from their mother.

Rick had always been their parents' favorite, and he exploited it to the hilt, but Jessie forgave him his trespasses and loved him like any good sister would. Growing up, Rick had been a relentless tease and was so good at lying to get out of trouble that he usually succeeded in placing the blame on her whenever he got caught. As a result, her parents came to view her as the problem child, not him. She never lied when caught in wrongdoing and always told the truth, even if it wasn't what her parents wanted to hear. Consequently, she bore the reproach for her own as well as her brother's trespasses.

The rifle cracked, and a small hole blossomed in the bull's-eye. Rick lowered the gun. Jessie asked if she could have a turn.

Her first shot hit the bottom of the outside ring. She hadn't practiced for a while, so she was a little rusty.

Rick shook his head. "You're dropping your elbow."

She nodded and corrected her arm position. Her next shot came closer to the center.

"You need to practice more."

"I know," she said and lowered the rifle. "I came down to talk to you about something. Mom said you don't want to be in the wedding, and she doesn't understand why."

Rick took the gun back. "I don't remember anyone asking if I wanted to be in the wedding."

"Well, I'm asking," Jessie said.

"The answer is no."

She stared at him, nonplussed. "Why?"

"I don't want to talk about it," he said and walked off.

"I want to know!" she exclaimed. "This is my wedding. It only happens once."

Rick turned and looked at her for a moment. "How would you like it if your only sister was a whore?"

CHAPTER 9

UNDER MY THUMB

The morning of the wedding dawned foggy and dreary. Thick vapors rose from the melting snow, making the bridal party appear ghostly as they climbed the steps of St. Mary Magdalene's through the swirling mist. Ushers closed the heavy carved doors behind them just as the first strains of "Ave Maria" drifted into the vestibule. The bridesmaids waited in hushed anticipation. Jessie waited in dread. Heart fluttering in fear, she took comfort in the familiar hymn.

Liz gave her a kiss and adjusted her veil, then was escorted by an usher into the church proper to take her seat.

Jessie stood at her father's side, pale and still as marble. The bridesmaids lined up for their cue and began their parade down the aisle. When the last of them reached their places, Sister Phillipa launched into Purcell's "Trumpet Voluntary." The assembled guests rose to attention.

It seemed more like a dream than something real, as Jessie held her father's arm to be escorted to the altar and seal her covenant with fate.

Bill kept his expression neutral as he walked woodenly down the aisle with his daughter. It wouldn't do for the guests to know his real feelings. He was hurt and humiliated to find himself in a position like this. He'd never thought of Jessie as anything but chaste, and he was stunned by her pregnancy. He still couldn't fathom it. Where did he go wrong?

Although Bill didn't put much stock in religion himself, Jessie had always been a deep, different sort of child who seemed sincerely devout. He never imagined that her wedding day would be anything other than an occasion of pride and joy.

From the moment he met Kevin, he could take him or leave him. He was not feeling at all sanguine about the fact that Kevin had seduced his unworldly daughter or that he had to hand her to him until death parted them. Lifting Jessie's veil, he kissed her on the cheek before letting go.

Jessie left her father's side and stood with Kevin in front of the altar. Father Martin began the service. Seeking strength, Jessie looked up at the painting of Mary Magdalene at the foot of the cross.

Kevin stumbled through his vows, promising to "love, honor, and cherish till death do us part."

Jessie swore to love, honor, and obey—as was customary—but cringed inside as she swore to obey. She'd tried to reason Father Martin out of swearing to obey. It was old fashioned and demeaning, but he refused to break with tradition. It was either recite the vows as written in the Missal or no church wedding, and her mother was adamant that there be a church wedding.

After they exchanged rings, Father Martin smiled and said, "I now pronounce you man and wife."

Watching from the pew, Liz wiped a tear from her eye. A sense of relief flooded her. She was absolutely certain it was a match made in heaven.

The newlyweds exchanged a kiss, then faced the crowd.

Sister Phillipa struck up the ringing chords of Mendelssohn's wedding march from *A Midsummer Night's Dream*.

⌒∾⌒

The reception passed by Jessie in a dizzy whirl. There was so much to do from the moment of the opening toast, that before she knew it, it was time for tossing the bouquet.

She picked up the nosegay of white roses and surveyed the cluster of bridesmaids eagerly awaiting the toss.

Of the five, only her friend from Pony Club, Sandy Hanlon, who was blonde and slim and had her pick of boyfriends, was in no hurry to get married.

Ann, however, wanted the bouquet more than anyone. She believed catching it would be an omen that Mark would marry her soon.

The master of ceremonies called for the rest of the single women in the crowd to join the bridesmaids in the center of the floor. When everyone was in position, the drum roll began.

Jessie tossed the nosegay into the air behind her, and whirled to see who caught it. To her amazement, Audrey Reddon adroitly fielded the bouquet. Ann's face fell.

After the ceremonial customs were completed, Kevin escorted Jessie from table to table introducing her to his extended family, who had merely been a blur of faces passing through the receiving line. Both Joe and Maria's parents were deceased, but she met Maria's uncle and aunt, Paul and Helen DeMarco, as well as a confusing array of DeMarco and McKenna cousins.

The rock band, hired at her insistence, turned out to be pretty good. They even managed a few polkas for the older guests. Everyone was having such a wonderful time that it was late before the party ended. Jessie was thoroughly exhausted by the time she was able to change out of her wedding gown into a suit. Kissing her parents goodbye, she drove off with Kevin into the fog shrouded night.

Once Kevin had her on the road, he informed her that his father had insisted he do something useful while away from the farm. They were going to travel around to look at cattle for sale, instead of honeymooning in New York City as originally planned. But Kevin said he'd take her to a ski resort in Vermont after they looked at a few cows on the way.

Jessie found herself slogging through snow and ice at farmstead after farmstead. She hadn't packed the sort of apparel appropriate for rutted farm lanes and manure-laced barns. The roadside motels Kevin chose were often shabby and had lumpy mattresses.

Each day Kevin turned down invitations to dinner from farm wives eager for a bit of company. At first, Jessie was confused by the country custom of calling the midday meal dinner instead of lunch, and assumed they were being invited to the evening meal, which was obviously too long to wait. Kevin always said they'd stop for lunch, but then would find an excuse not to.

On the fourth day, they were invited to stay and eat by yet another farmer's wife. Jessie smelled a mouthwatering aroma coming from the kitchen. Her stomach ached with hunger, and the meal appeared almost ready. She spoke up promptly. "Thank you for asking, Mrs. Neisman."

Kevin shook his head. "I'm sorry, but we can't stay. We have an appointment to look at a bull owned by Amon Harbold's syndicate that I'm interested in getting sperm from."

"But you had a long drive to get here this morning, and Amon's place is five hours from here," Mrs. Neisman said. "That's awfully far to go without a midday meal. You probably won't get there until supper. Why not stay and eat with us?"

Kevin flashed a charming smile. "Thank you, but no. We'll grab a bite to eat somewhere along the way."

Two hours into the drive they still hadn't stopped for lunch. Jessie looked up from the road map she was holding. "I thought you said we were going to stop and eat?"

"No, I never said that," Kevin replied.

"Yes, you did! In fact, you said it the past three days in a row, but then you never stop," she exclaimed. "I'm pregnant. I feel like I'm starving all the time. Enough is enough. I want to know why."

He glanced over at her. "It's a waste of money to feed you. You throw up so much."

Jessie sucked in her breath, shocked by the callousness of his remark. She continued to complain, but he ignored her. In the end, she was forced to beg him for food, then he pretended it was all a joke. During sex that night, and each night thereafter, Kevin used her so roughly that he hurt her.

She considered calling her parents, but she didn't have so much as a dime in her purse for a pay phone, and Kevin watched her like a hawk. When she spoke to anyone too long, he interrupted.

Everywhere they went, people assuming them to be traveling in newly-wedded bliss smiled knowingly and extended felicitations. Jessie forced herself to smile so often that her face hurt.

At last, the days allotted for their honeymoon neared an end. The only ski slope Jessie had seen so far was through the car window. Without warning, Kevin turned back a day early and headed home in one long marathon drive. He refused to stop for lunch. When she protested, he promised to buy her dinner at the most upscale restaurant in Mansfield instead.

Kevin drove right through the center of town without stopping. When she demanded an explanation, he said he wanted to drop off their luggage at the house first so they could enjoy a romantic evening without having to worry about unpacking.

Sighing with resignation, she tried to quell her hunger pangs by sucking the dregs from a can of soda.

Kevin pulled into the driveway of the old house they'd rented just a few miles from the farm. It was situated on a parcel of land with several decrepit outbuildings and gnarled apple trees long past bearing. They'd worked nonstop for weeks before the wedding to make it habitable. It had hand-hewn beams, horsehair plaster walls, and two quaint but unusable fireplaces.

Kevin opened the back door and started to pick her up to carry her over the threshold.

"No, please don't," she protested. "It's too corny."

"Where's your sense of tradition?" he said and lifted her into his arms. He pretended to stagger under her weight. "This is the last time I marry a pregnant woman. You weigh a ton!"

They collapsed on the floor, laughing.

He helped her to her feet, then brought in the suitcases and carried them upstairs. When they were finished unpacking, they walked down to the kitchen. Following Kevin toward the back door, Jessie was surprised when he stopped by the refrigerator and opened it. "There isn't any food in here."

"What did you expect?" she said. "Besides, we're going out to dinner. We can pick up stuff for breakfast at the supermarket on the way home."

He frowned. "But it's your job to keep food in the refrigerator."

"Like I said, we can stop at the store."

Jessie moved past Kevin to get her coat off the rack by the door. He grabbed her by the arm. "There's no point in starting off on the wrong foot. Since you didn't arrange to have food in the house, you'll have to go to bed without supper."

She pulled away. "If this is your idea of a joke, it isn't funny."

"Oh, it's no joke. Now go upstairs to bed."

She tried to get around him, but he blocked her. "Okay, Kevin, I've had enough. Let's just get some food and be done with it."

"Didn't you hear me?" he snarled. "Get upstairs, you bitch!"

Jessie stood her ground, but Kevin began to shout so loudly it hurt her ears. She retreated up the stairs, hoping he'd simmer down if she obeyed. He followed right behind her.

"Take your clothes off and get in bed."

She peeled them off and reached for her nightgown.

"No." He pulled back the covers and pointed to the bed. "Get in."

Kevin stripped off his clothes and slid between the sheets. He squeezed her breasts and pinched her nipples, then mounted her. After he'd satisfied himself sexually, she lay stiffly by his side until exhaustion finally turned into sleep.

Gnawing pangs of hunger awakened Jessie in the middle of the night. She was startled to discover that Kevin wasn't in bed beside her. An uncanny silence brooded in the air. She got up and donned her robe to search the house.

Her footsteps echoed hollowly through empty rooms. The place was deserted, Kevin nowhere to be found. She looked through the window and realized the car was gone. Her eyes burned with tears. All the pent-up fears and emotions she suppressed during the miserable honeymoon rushed to the surface.

It was all some kind of nightmare!

Jessie swallowed hard to quell a sharp pang of despair.

A dissonant and eerie sensation made her skin prickle. Then a palpable malevolence oozed into the atmosphere, raising the hairs on the back of her neck. Panic seized her and she rushed upstairs.

Jumping into bed, she pulled the blanket tight around her body. After the wild beating of her heart slowed, she heard scratching sounds in the attic overhead. She squealed in fright and pulled the covers over her head before realizing it was only mice. Soon she could hear them skittering around the house under the cloak of night.

Too shaken to sleep, she peered intently into the darkness, terrified that the mice might creep under the bedcovers if she relaxed her vigilance.

Shadows thickened menacingly in the corners of the room. A deepening chill permeated the air, as though this world and the Otherworld had merged through the time-space synapse, and a door to the Shadowland had stealthily opened. She had the uneasy sensation that something dreadful lurked in the darkest corner, and that she was its prey.

Fear slithered all over her body. The atmosphere grew denser. Then a form began to emerge from the thickest shadow.

A scream lodged in her throat. Something ghastly was materializing, and she was powerless to close her eyes. Horror gripped her with iron talons. Her teeth chattered like castanets.

Abruptly, a clear thought pierced her terror.

She must be experiencing hysteria. If she didn't fight to stay under control, she might hallucinate a demon image and her mind would slip away into madness.

Clamping down on her teeth, she struggled to control the spasms. Her jaw muscles strained against the paroxysms, aching with the effort, and finally the staccato chatter ceased.

The looming form slowly retreated, and the atmosphere became less murky. The air of evil began to fade, yet the fear wouldn't leave her. She lay there trembling until fatigue mercifully lapsed into sleep.

⚜

Jessie woke with a start, heart fluttering, until she realized it was morning. After last night, she understood how it was possible to die from fear. In fact, she was a little surprised to find herself still alive.

A quick check revealed no mice lurking around the bed.

She pulled on her robe and peered through the window. The Caprice was still gone. The crooked limbs of the apple trees looked stark and forlorn against the pale winter sky. A frigid wind shook the branches and whipped the bleached cornhusks littering the drab brown fields.

The cold wind sucked every bit of warmth out of the old house, and the floorboards were icy underfoot. Jessie slipped on her shoes and dashed downstairs to the phone. She dialed, praying that her mother hadn't already left for work.

It rang twice before being picked up. Her mother's voice never sounded so good.

"Mom, it's me. Thank God you're still there. Kevin's just been awful and—"

"Calm down and catch your breath. I can't understand you."

"Look, Mom, I can't really talk. Please come and get me—I need you."

"Jessie, you're distraught, and you aren't making any sense. It sounds like hysteria to me. I'm sure Kevin wouldn't do anything to hurt you."

"Mom, you don't understand. *Please*, just come!"

"Honey, pregnant women are susceptible to emotional states where the mind blows things out of proportion. Kevin already called me and said you were homesick for the entire honeymoon. He also said you had a panic attack last night."

A chill washed over her. How would Kevin know she had a panic attack last night?

"It's nothing to be ashamed of. It's all hormonal," Liz said. "Now I've got to get to work. We can talk later."

There was a click and the line went dead.

Jessie's head spun with shock. Swaying on her feet, she leaned against the wall for support. Her arm felt leaden as she hung up the receiver. She slid to the floor in a fog.

A cramp twisted through her gut, snapping her mind back into focus. God, she was hungry and dying for a cup of coffee. She needed to find some way to get food.

Home seemed very remote, and she didn't relish the thought of walking far on such a bitter, blustery day. It might be best to knock on the door of the nearest neighbor and ask for assistance, but she didn't have the nerve to do that. There would be too many questions.

Jessie ran upstairs to dress. Instinct warned her to get away from the house as quickly as possible. Just as she finished putting on her clothes, she heard the sound of tires crunching on gravel. She ran to the window, hoping her mother experienced a change of heart.

It was Kevin.

She wanted to hide, but where? There wasn't a stick of furniture upstairs except in the master bedroom. The only access to the attic was through a trapdoor in the ceiling of the empty second bedroom. The back door opened with a squeak.

"Hey, Jessie, are you awake?" Kevin called out genially. "Mom invited us for breakfast. Hurry up and come on down. You must be starving—I am."

There was no escape. Nerving herself, she headed downstairs. She followed Kevin out to the car, tight-lipped and silent. Her throat was too constricted to speak, even if she could have thought of something to say.

Kevin kept up a light-hearted monologue while he drove to the farm, as if the whole past week had never happened.

If Jessie didn't know better, she might suspect she'd imagined everything, but her hunger pangs were real.

The farmhouse was filled with the delicious aroma of frying bacon and eggs. Maria greeted her amiably and began putting the meal on the table. Joe and Mike came in from outside, stripped off their soiled coveralls in the mudroom, and took their seats. Johnny entered, still rubbing sleep from his eyes, and sat down.

It was all Jessie could do to stop herself from digging into the food before they were finished saying grace. Maria plied her with questions about the honeymoon trip, but she gave only brief, noncommittal answers between forkfuls of food.

Jessie watched as Kevin leapt into the breach by relating the merits of the cows they saw for sale before her mood aroused too much suspicion. She was aware that her muteness was having a negative effect on Maria, but she was powerless to do anything about it. She couldn't bring herself to lie and say she'd had a good time, nor could she tell Maria that her son's behavior was despicable.

When breakfast was over, Kevin escorted Jessie out to the car. He pulled out his wallet. "Here's fifty dollars for groceries. You can have the car, but I want to be picked up at four-thirty sharp."

Numbly, she nodded and took the money, then drove around aimlessly, wondering what to do.

Kevin had already undermined her main base of support by persuading her mother that she was unbalanced. She couldn't barge in on her mother in the operating room, and the hospital cafeteria was too public a place to talk. Her mother wouldn't be home from work before four, her father even later, and Rick was useless.

Ann lived nearby and might be at home, but Ann's mother had been scandalized by the out-of-wedlock pregnancy; she wouldn't lift a finger to help. Jessie felt certain that if she confided in any of her other friends, things wouldn't be any different. Her only living grandparents resided in Florida. Her maiden aunt lived all the way in the city; her aunt would not only be at work, she was even more pious than her mother. Her other closest relative, a widowed uncle, taught college in upstate New York.

It wasn't until she got to the grocery store that she realized she'd never planned or cooked a full meal in her life.

Jessie returned home and put the groceries away, then started a load of wash in the old machine in the laundry room, which was built off the kitchen over a section of the back porch. Afterward, she sat down to peruse the cookbook Mary Clare had given her and plan some menus for the days ahead.

When the first load of laundry was finished, Jessie carried it outside to hang on the clothesline. The landlord had never installed a dryer, but luckily the temperature was a little above freezing. After the clothes were all pinned to the line, she put another load in the machine then went upstairs to make the bed.

Jessie returned downstairs to see water cascading across the kitchen floor, gushing from the timeworn washing machine. Dashing into the laundry room, she quickly turned it off.

She tried to reset the machine and make the clothes spin out, but the water came back on and wouldn't shut off. In the end, she had to pull the clothes out and throw them over the rail on the back porch to drain. Annoying as it was to have the washer break down, tomorrow was Saturday; it would give her a perfect excuse to go over to her parents' house.

She grabbed a mop and bucket, and wiped up the floor. When that task was finished, she made a sandwich for lunch and studied the cookbook again. Electing to make a pot roast for supper, she chopped vegetables and browned the meat according to directions. Once she had it simmering on the stove, she lay down on the sofa for a nap.

Jessie awakened to the savory scent of cooking beef. One look at the clock showed she was running behind. She threw the rest of the vegetables into the pot, then collected the still damp clothes from the line. Since there was only one basket, she had to leave the unspun wet ones hanging on the rail. She left dinner simmering and hurried off to the farm.

❧

"What the fuck is this shit?" Kevin exclaimed, looking at the burnt pot roast on his plate.

"I can't help if it's overcooked," Jessie said. "You didn't come out of the barn until half past five."

"I'm not eating this crap!" Kevin pushed his chair away from the table. He grabbed his coat off the peg and slammed the back door on the way out.

❧

In the morning, Jessie collected the frozen clothes from the porch railing and went to her parents' house, anticipating a heart-to-heart talk with her mother.

Liz interrupted her immediately. "I'm not going to discuss anything to do with your marriage. Every couple has things to work out on their own. It's nobody else's business."

"But—"

Liz cut her off. "If you want to visit or do laundry, you're always welcome, but it's unchristian for a woman to speak in any manner that's derogatory of her husband. I refuse to allow you to draw me into complicity with such sin."

A hard lump rose in Jessie's throat. How could her mother be so unfair? She'd listened to Kevin's side, hadn't she? And worse, she'd bought right into his lies. Leaving with the basket of clean dry clothes, Jessie felt naked and abandoned.

⁓

The house still needed a lot of work. It had stood empty for some time and was absolutely filthy when they first saw it. The weeks leading up to the wedding had been spent scrubbing walls, patching plaster, and refinishing the floors. The master bedroom was the only room they'd managed to finish painting before they'd left for their honeymoon. Jessie knew she had her work cut out for her before returning to school.

Picking out the paint colors went reasonably well. By week's end, her cooking had improved and she'd managed to finish two whole rooms. But when she reminded Kevin that she was returning to college on Monday, he argued against it.

"You can get a refund. We could use the money."

"No. I'm going back to school. You knew that before we got married."

"I didn't think you'd do it. It's stupid. You're a housewife. It's a waste of money to educate you."

"That's sexist bull and you know it."

His eyes darkened. "If you don't get a refund, then you'll have to do without a washing machine. The landlord says you broke it and refuses to fix it. I'm damn sure not going to pay for it."

She swallowed hard. "I promised my dad I'd finish school."

"How are you going to get there? I need the car for work."

"I can drop you off at the farm in the morning and pick you up in the afternoon."

"No. It's my car, and you can't use it without permission," he snarled. "Get a refund."

"No," she said, standing her ground.

"Have it your way then—if you can get a ride. But, if you go back to school, you can't use the car for church ever again, and you're not allowed to ask anyone to take you."

Jessie sucked in her breath. Not being allowed to drive the car to church, or ask for a ride to services, was a heavy penalty to incur for going back to school, but she had no intention of backing down. St. Mary Magdalene had multiple Sunday masses so her mother wouldn't notice if her attendance slacked, and thus would be unlikely to offer her a ride. However, she only had to attend Mass once a year to remain a Catholic. She could manage that even if she had to walk.

<hr />

On Sunday morning, Jessie waited until Kevin left the house then phoned her father while her mother and brother were at Mass. She told him it would be a great help to the household budget if she could ride to school with Rick, then drive the Olds up the road to Concord Community. Her father kindly assented.

Jessie expected her brother to pitch a fit, and he did, but after a few days they warmed up to each other. Without telling Kevin, she closed out her small savings account to buy books.

Kevin stopped speaking to her, except to issue orders, and stayed out late every night. But she figured he'd come around eventually. How long could he stay mad over something so trivial?

CHAPTER 10

THROUGH A GLASS DARKLY

Although February had the fewest days, Jessie always thought it seemed like the longest month. The eleven o'clock news was over and, as usual, Kevin had gone out after supper and had yet to return. It'd been several weeks since the argument over school, and he still wasn't speaking to her.

Rising from the sofa, she turned off the television and peered through the window for any sign of a car on the road. An owl perched on the bare bough of an apple tree like a sentinel in the night. Behind it a lucent moon rode high and full in the sky, casting a phantasmal glow over the landscape. Hoar frost lay thick as snow on ground that was as frozen as Kevin's heart.

Jessie yawned. She didn't have the same stamina she'd had before she'd gotten pregnant. Turning out the lights, she went upstairs and was asleep as soon as her head hit the pillow.

A rush of cold air startled her awake as the bedcovers were torn from her body. A dark figure loomed over her. She tried to scream but her throat choked closed with fright.

"Get out of bed, you lazy bitch!"

Recognizing the voice of the apparition loosed the stranglehold of fear on her tongue. "Why? What's wrong?"

Kevin yanked her out of the bed and pushed her across the room toward the door. Ignoring her protests, he dragged her down the stairs and shoved her into the living room.

Heart racing, she spun to face him. He remained in the doorway, blocking the way out. The only illumination came from moonlight slanting in through the windows.

"Who do you think you are, dragging me out of bed?"

"You should be asking what you did to deserve it," he retorted. "I'll teach you not to talk to me like that before the night is through."

She wondered if he was drunk, but there was no telltale slur to his voice.

"When we got married, you swore to love, honor and *obey* me. You'd better see to it that you keep that promise," he said. "Now we can do this the easy way or the hard way—that's up to you—but I will not tolerate disobedience in a wife."

Jessie gave him a scornful look. "I'm not your slave. You owe me a reasonable degree of courtesy and respect."

"I never made a vow to respect you," he sneered.

"Whatever happened to love, honor, and cherish?"

Kevin shook his head. "You don't get that until you deserve it."

"Just what do I have to do to deserve it?" she asked tartly.

"To begin with, you won't talk to me in that tone of voice," he snarled, moving toward her.

Seeing a gap, she made for the doorway. He caught her by the arm and forced her back into the room.

"I am your *master*, and you are to obey me absolutely. When I tell you to do something, you are to do it without question."

"A husband and wife are supposed to be partners," she replied, rigidly controlling her anger and fear. "I don't believe you're superior to me just because you're male and I'm female. I didn't join the Army, and I'm not obeying anyone's orders without question. You are a man, not God."

"That's where you're wrong. I *am* a god," Kevin said eerily. "God, as you understand it, doesn't exist."

"You're wrong."

"No, it's true. Haven't you read H. G. Wells? There are people in this world who were made to be gods—they're born to rule! They know who they are, and I'm one of them. We're as far above ordinary people as ordinary people are above apes."

"You may believe that, but I don't."

Kevin loomed over her. "You'll believe it when the time comes. We always work behind the scenes. It wouldn't be to our advantage for people to know about us yet."

His eyes glittered strangely. Then he spoke in a harsh, rasping voice that prickled her skin. "I *am* one of the gods of this world! Now get down on your knees and worship me!"

"Are you crazy?" she exclaimed. "I will not—it's idolatry. You are a *man*. It's a sin to worship anything but God."

"*Do it!*" Kevin commanded. "I don't want to force you, but I will."

"No!" Jessie cried.

He grabbed her arm and twisted it behind her back. She gasped in pain.

"Get down on your knees," he ordered.

Her muscles burned, her eyes watered, but she wouldn't bend.

"I can break your arm," Kevin said with frightening calm. "To resist is useless."

Fear clutched her heart. The agony in her shoulder made it difficult to speak, but she summoned her courage.

"If you injure me, you'll have to explain it to my father. I will leave you forever, and you'll never know whether you had a son or a daughter."

He wrenched her arm harder. Needles of fire stabbed her shoulder. She stifled a cry and prayed mutely. *God, please help me!*

Kevin's breathing became ragged and heavy. "I guess it wouldn't look too good if I hurt a pregnant woman," he hissed, then let go.

Jessie winced as her arm returned to its normal position. Rubbing her aching muscles, she moved toward the doorway.

"Where do you think you're going?"

"To bed."

"No!" Kevin blocked her way. "You're punished. Go stand in the corner."

"No," she snapped and kept going.

He grabbed her by the hair and twisted it in his fist. "Do what I say."

She gasped, eyes watering with pain. It was impossible to maintain effective resistance. Kevin could hurt her without leaving any marks, and there was no hope of rescue tonight. "All right, let me go!"

He released her.

She walked over and stood in the corner, fighting a rising tide of panic. She had to keep a grip on herself.

Kevin stretched himself out on the sofa. Time drifted by. He didn't say a word.

It was so quiet Jessie could hear the soft ticking of the clock on the mantel. Drafts swirled around her bare ankles, and the floor was as icy as a skating rink. She was dead on her feet. She couldn't stand much longer.

Kevin was obviously insane. The quickest way to get out of the corner might be to humor him. "Please forgive me. I'm sorry."

"That's better," he replied. "Now tell me what you did wrong."

"I don't know," she said, bewildered.

"But you must confess before I can forgive you."

She swallowed the lump rising in her throat. It was like asking for the answer without first telling the riddle. Apparently, he intended to make her stand in the corner until she guessed correctly.

He'd mentioned disobedience. Strictly speaking, going back to school against Kevin's wishes wasn't disobedience, because he'd assented to her father's plans. He hadn't ordered her not to go to school, just made it difficult. She tried another tack.

"I'm sorry I disobeyed you, but I'm not sure what I did wrong. Please tell me so I don't make that mistake again."

He shifted on the sofa. "All right, but just this once. The rule is you must confess first before I can forgive you. You left a coffee cup in the sink. I told you I can't stand that. It should have been washed and put away."

Jessie remembered how he'd nitpicked over the finer points of housekeeping before he had stopped speaking to her. She knew how to keep things clean, but she wasn't fastidiously neat.

"Oh, I forgot. I'll go do that right away," she said, and turned to leave.

"Wait," Kevin said. "That's not all."

"What else?"

"Come here and kneel before me."

Her mouth opened. "But you said—"

"If you want my forgiveness, get down on your knees and beg for it."

The venom in his voice was jolting. There was no way out. Jessie knelt at his feet. "I beg you to forgive me."

"That doesn't sound sincere enough. Do it again."

She tried another appeal, but he rejected that also.

Shivering with cold, it was all she could do not to cry. Then it struck her—maybe he wanted tears. She gave in and let the tears spill down her cheeks.

"*Please* forgive me," she said, sobbing. "I promise to obey you from now on."

Kevin smiled a little self-satisfied smile. "I forgive you. You may get up."

CHAPTER 11

NOWHERE TO RUN

The next morning, Jessie left for school on an emotional rollercoaster, her feelings alternating between deep fear and disbelief. What occurred the night before seemed too bizarre to even have happened. She thought about telling Ann, but it was going to sound so far out Ann might not believe it. Nor was anyone else likely to believe what transpired, least of all her mother.

Kevin's declaration that he was a god was uncanny, and hardly subject to any rational interpretation. A chill ran down her spine remembering the look in his eye. She didn't want to think about it. In fact, her mind didn't want to consciously deal with it at all. As soon as school and interacting with classmates restored some semblance of normalcy, the memory was banished to her subconscious.

❦

After a few weeks, Jessie felt like she and Kevin were getting along better. Of course, she kept everything spotless and tried not to aggravate him in any way. She put off finishing the baby's room, but everything else looked homey and shipshape.

One weekend, near the end of March, the weather took a turn for the better, and she decided to do the laundry at her parents' house instead of using the laundromat in town. She hadn't felt comfortable visiting since the altercation with her mother, but the first hint of spring made her long to wander familiar fields, looking for the signs that herald nature's awakening from winter's death-like sleep. She threw a load in her mother's washer and left for a walk around the meadow.

Jessie had never regretted leaving behind the city and her childhood friends or ballet, art and music lessons.

Owning a horse had been a dream come true. Out riding, it was easy to let her imagination run free. On her horse she felt part of a timeless and transcendent world which she marveled at and pondered over—a world where angels still fought on the side of men to withstand the powers of darkness.

She'd been born a true romantic in an unromantic era, which was one reason she found science somewhat dry and uninspiring. She'd always dreamed of becoming an artist. She'd exhibited some talent as a child, and her parents had encouraged her artistic ambitions, promising to send her to the Art Institute after high school, if she maintained a B average.

Her mother used to buy her paint-by-number sets, with empty numbered patches that resembled a blank uncut jigsaw puzzle. Painting the numbered patches was a tedious task that bore no resemblance to real painting. The only reason Jessie persevered was the promise that she could use any leftover oils to paint something freehand afterward. It took several kits to accumulate enough colors to paint a pastoral farm scene with a chestnut horse in the pasture.

She felt lost, and her only recourse was to endure marriage to Kevin as penance for her sin. Perhaps, if she prayed hard enough, and was good enough, he'd become a better husband.

With a wistful sigh and a prayer for her marriage, Jessie left the meadow and walked to the kitchen door of her parents' house.

Stepping inside, she felt a sharp pang of regret. There was a wall of constraint between her and her parents now, and no way to penetrate it. Jessie inhaled the scent of fresh-brewed coffee and sat at the table.

Liz got out another mug and filled it. "How are things going?"

"Oh, fine," she managed to say in a natural sounding tone. Things were fine compared to something worse, like torture, so it wasn't exactly a lie. Besides, her mother didn't really want to hear anything else.

"Oh, good. I'm so glad you've gotten over the homesickness that spoiled your honeymoon."

Jessie held her tongue and took a sip of coffee.

Liz looked at her thoughtfully. "You know, a wife's first pregnancy is a difficult adjustment for a man to make. Don't think it isn't hard on Kevin, too. You need to help each other through this. It's important to continue to satisfy your husband sexually, even though you'll soon be in your third trimester."

Jessie nodded and continued sipping her coffee.

Liz smiled and got a faraway look in her eyes. "When your father and I got married, I couldn't get pregnant for years. We had fertility tests done, and everything was normal. The doctors were baffled, until one day one of them asked your father how often we had sex. He told them that we'd slowed down a little since we first got married, but we had sex at least once a day and usually twice."

Jessie wasn't comfortable hearing about her parents' sex life, but she knew her mother had spent years praying to the Virgin Mary for a child.

"The doctor told us we were having sex too often to have any children."

Jessie sure wished she'd had that problem. What a great method of birth control.

"A lot of men have their first affair when their wives get pregnant," Liz continued. "Some women just cut them off. Don't make that mistake."

"Yes, Mom," she said, fighting back tears. Kevin went out every night, leaving her to wonder what he was doing, and they hardly ever had sex anymore.

A few days later, Ann stopped by after school. Jessie was elated that one of her friends finally took the time to visit. She led Ann on a tour of the house, showing her the improvements fresh paint and elbow grease had wrought.

The kitchen cabinets were refinished in a glossy barn red, and the walls were painted creamy yellow. A honey-toned pine table, ruffled white curtains, and a multicolored braided rug made the room cheery and welcoming.

Ann sat at the table. "Gosh, the kitchen really looks great compared to when I saw it last. You're so lucky, Jessie. I can hardly wait to get married and make a home for Mark. It would be so much fun to fix up a house."

Jessie ah-hummed noncommittally. "Would you like a soda? I have ginger ale."

"Ginger ale's fine," Ann said. "I'm sorry I wasn't over sooner. We hardly ever see each other on campus anymore, and with Mark and me bowling on two leagues, there's rarely any time to visit. Mom thinks I should be home studying some nights."

Jessie opened a ginger ale and fixed a glass for Ann.

"So how do you like married life?"

She shrugged and poured herself a glass.

"What's the matter?"

"I don't know how to explain it. Kevin and I don't seem to get along like we did while we were dating. He's the man, so his word is law, and I'm supposed to wait on him hand and foot."

"I didn't think Kevin was like that. That stuff went out with the stone age."

"Your parents are like that."

Ann shrugged. "My mother never was with it."

"Mark doesn't treat you that way, does he?"

"No, not really," Ann said. "Gee, I'm sorry to hear you aren't happy. If anyone was made for each other, I'd have thought you two were. What other guy do you know who reads books and can quote Dostoyevsky?"

"Only my cousin," Jessie sighed.

"Well, that won't do you any good, unless you're kissing cousins, and you're not."

Ann got out her cigarettes and lit up. She took a drag, looking thoughtful, then exhaled. "Maybe I was wrong all along."

"What do you mean?"

"Maybe I shouldn't have interfered with you and Mike, and tried to set you up with Kevin."

"Ann, it's not your fault. If I hadn't gotten pregnant the relationship would have died on its own."

"But I thought you two were in love?"

"So did I or I wouldn't have done what I did, but Kevin isn't in love with me and I don't think he ever was."

"Are you serious? You mean it's not just macho garbage screwing up your relationship"

"No," Jessie replied. "I think he might be having an affair. We hardly ever have sex, and he stays out late every night."

"Divorce him," Ann said.

"I haven't even had the baby yet!"

"Have you told your mother?"

"It wouldn't do any good. You know what she thinks about the sanctity of marriage. My parents believe couples should stay together for the sake of the children, no matter what."

Ann flicked the ash off her cigarette into the ashtray. "I'm sorry. I thought Kevin would be better for you. Mike was just playing games."

Jessie sighed. "I thought Kevin was better for me, too."

"You can get a divorce after you have the baby."

"It's against the vow I took."

"Nobody believes in that stuff anymore."

"I do."

"You're still in love with him then," Ann said.

CHAPTER 12

LADY IN WAITING

An elegant invitation arrived in the mail to a fiftieth anniversary party in honor of Kevin's great uncle and aunt, Paul and Helen DeMarco. Paul was Maria's father's younger brother, and theirs was a close-knit extended family. It would be a lavish affair befitting the occasion, and the banquet hall of the Wentworth Inn was reserved for the festivities.

Jessie felt like Cinderella invited to a ball without a thing to wear. She couldn't afford to spend money on a formal maternity dress that would only be worn once. Fortunately, she remembered that her prom dress had been fashioned in an Empire-waist style so it would probably fit over her swollen abdomen.

She phoned her mother, who offered to bring it right over.

When Liz arrived, Jessie removed the plastic bag and took the dress off the hanger. It was a sleeveless gown made of heavy white crepe, embroidered with pale-blue windflowers. Luckily, it looked as good as new. It draped gracefully over her pregnant figure, and she was pleased with the effect.

"I guess you never expected to wear this dress again," Liz said, "but it looks very nice."

On the evening of the banquet, Kevin was surprised to see Jessie in a pretty gown and immediately asked where she'd purchased it.

"This is the gown I wore to my senior prom."

"You must have been the sensation of the evening, going to the prom in a maternity dress."

"You idiot, it's not a maternity dress. The Empress Josephine made this style famous."

"She was married to the Emperor of France, wasn't she?"

"Of course."

"See, I told you it was a maternity dress," Kevin said. "French men are horny as hell. She was just being prepared."

Jessie laughed with delight, touched by his clever teasing. She was warmed by a renewed hope that her prayers would be answered, and Kevin would turn into a real husband. She felt happier than she had in a long time, even though tonight her advanced state of pregnancy would be on display in front of the whole family, her fall from grace painfully in evidence.

⤬

The Wentworth Inn's enormous walnut-paneled banquet room glowed with light. Under the glittering chandeliers, large round tables were draped with gold-colored damask cloths and graced with centerpieces of fresh fruit.

The head table stretched along one end of the hall, adorned with garlands of gilded leaves accented by golden bells. A beautifully decorated ivory and gold wedding cake stood in a place of honor nearby. At the opposite end of the room was a long table arrayed with a tempting assortment of hors d'oeuvres: crab stuffed mushroom caps, mini Beef Wellingtons and Quiche Lorraine, caviar, and various vegetables, dips, and cheeses.

The hall buzzed with the pleasant hum of friends and relatives conversing over cocktails, catching up on the latest family news.

Jessie was making some selections from the hors d'oeuvres display when Aunt Julia came alongside. "Congratulations, dear, I'm so happy for you both."

"Thank you," she said, wondering if Julia was really as delighted as she seemed. "I thought you might be disappointed to see I was already pregnant before the wedding."

"Of course not. Don't be silly," Julia said. "What does it matter? You love Kevin, don't you? That's all I care about."

"I thought it might change how you felt about me. You were so happy over the engagement, and made me feel so welcome and at home. I'm glad this hasn't changed things between us."

Julia put her hand on Jessie's arm. "The moment I met you, I gave thanks to God for giving you to Kevin. He's my favorite nephew and he's like a son to me, since Hal and I can't have any children. I was always worried about Kevin because of the sort of women he dated."

"Oh, I didn't know that."

Julia looked into her eyes. "You're nothing like them. You're intelligent, you're genuine, and you have a good heart. I'm delighted you're having Kevin's baby. He can thank his lucky stars for you."

"It's sweet of you to say that."

Julia's praise lifted Jessie's spirits as she headed back to the family table. Maria and Joe didn't seem at all happy about her being their son's choice. She still felt uncomfortable around them.

Jessie seated herself in the empty chair beside Mary Clare, who was deep in conversation with Kathleen. They paused long enough to greet her, as did Maria, who was talking to Dawn Applegate, Mike's steady girlfriend. Jessie acknowledged their greetings and sat quietly.

Conversation swirled around her like a stream flowing over a pebble, and she thought about Dawn, who was everything Maria hoped for in a wife for her son.

Maria got on well with Dawn and was looking forward to announcing her engagement to Mike one day soon. Dawn was lovely, ladylike, and only too happy to settle down and become a homemaker and mother. She believed making a good match, being a meticulous housekeeper, and raising children was the highest pinnacle any woman could aspire to.

Even though Jessie was already married, she knew Dawn didn't envy her one bit. Dawn would never embarrass the family with a too hasty wedding. Maria didn't know it, but Planned Parenthood took care of that.

Dawn wore Mike's high school ring proudly. He had been disappointingly slow about proffering an engagement ring, but the whole family approved of her and she knew it. Her wedding would be something lovingly planned and savored, a triumphal pageant shared with relatives and friends.

Jessie wished her own wedding could have been like that.

Mary Clare spoke, interrupting her thoughts. "Do me a favor and pick out a bunch of grapes from the centerpiece."

"Which ones do you want?" she asked, puzzled that her sister-in-law didn't wish to select them herself.

"Any kind will do."

Pale-green and wine-red grapes mingled with dusky purple ones in jewel-like cascades. She picked out a cluster of purple grapes tinged with blue-gray frost. "How about these?"

"Those are fine," Mary Clare said. "Now hold them like you're just about to eat them."

Jessie gave her a questioning look, but posed with the grapes in her palm.

"Yes, that's it! Perfect. Now don't move." Mary Clare turned to Kathleen. "Do you see what I mean about that dress and her hair?"

Kathleen nodded. "Yes, I see."

"See what?" Jessie asked.

"You look just like a pregnant goddess!" Mary Clare exclaimed. "Hey, everyone! Look at Jessie. Doesn't she look like a goddess bearing fruit?"

All eyes turned upon her.

Johnny spoke up. "It looks more like she swallowed a watermelon to me."

Everyone burst into laughter. Heat rose in Jessie's cheeks, and she quickly returned the grapes to the centerpiece.

"Johnny, did you fail sex education again last semester?" Kevin quipped.

"Nah, I only have trouble with the written tests. Mr. Burke gave me extra credit for all my hands-on experience."

Everyone burst out laughing again.

CHAPTER 13

TEA-PARTY

J essie flipped through the mail, pausing when her fingers touched a creamy envelope addressed to her in an unfamiliar hand. Inside, she found an invitation to a ladies' afternoon tea sponsored by the Democratic Club.

Without a second thought, she decided to decline. The fact that she was in the latter stages of pregnancy was pretty obvious. She hadn't been quite so large for the fiftieth wedding anniversary bash, and that had been family, not the county social scene. Unfortunately, her decision precipitated a heated argument with Kevin after supper.

He insisted she attend. "You aren't going to insult the club president's wife by declining her invitation. If you look like *that*, it's your own fault."

Jessie's temper erupted. "It wasn't an immaculate conception. You had just as much to do with me looking like this as I did."

"If you'd had an abortion, you wouldn't be as big as a whale, so don't blame it on me."

She blinked back tears, stung by the callousness of his remark.

❧

On the afternoon of the tea, Kevin drove her to the Carlton House, a turn-of-the-century mansion that had been converted to an upscale restaurant. The ballroom, with its magnificent twin crystal chandeliers, had been turned into a banquet hall.

Kevin solicitously introduced her to Virginia Mansfield, the wife of the Democratic Club's president.

Virginia was silver-haired, reed-thin, and elegant in a tailored, lilac-colored silk dress accented with a pearl necklace and earrings. After a gracious welcome and polite small talk, she moved on to her other guests.

Kevin led Jessie toward a pretty redhead in her early thirties, chatting with a stunning black woman. They broke off their conversation and smiled in greeting.

"Jessie, I'd like you to meet Ellen Richardson. She's married to State Delegate Jack Richardson. I was Jack's campaign manager when he won his seat in the House of Delegates."

"And a damn good one too," the red-haired woman said. "It's a pleasure to meet you at last, Jessie. I'm sorry we missed the wedding, but we always go skiing in Colorado during January."

"It's nice to meet you, too," she said, feeling like a frump in her simple maternity dress next to these chic women.

Ellen wore a white dress and jacket trimmed in navy piping. She had on navy and white pumps, and carried a matching handbag. Her remarkable hair was professionally cut and styled.

Kevin turned to the black woman, who looked like a fashion model in her peacock blue, silk-shantung pantsuit and matching hat, accessorized with expensive gold jewelry. "And this lovely lady is Marcella Jones. She's married to Mansfield Town Councilman Leroy Jones."

Marcella smiled. "I'm delighted to make your acquaintance."

"Me, too," Jessie said, sounding gauche in her own ears.

Kevin soon excused himself and headed for the bar.

Ellen turned back to her. "Your hair is absolutely gorgeous, Jessie. I've never seen hair so black before."

"Me either," Marcella said. "It's so long and lustrous."

They made her feel right at home, and she began to think her debut into society wasn't going to be so dreadful after all. She started to relax.

A pallid, heavyset brunette suddenly bore down upon them. The woman exchanged greetings with Ellen and Marcella, and eyeballed Jessie with open curiosity.

"Rosemary, I'd like you to meet Kevin McKenna's wife, Jessie," Ellen said. "Jessie, this is Rosemary Benson."

"Hi, um, how do you do?" Jessie responded.

"Fine, thank you." Rosemary looked directly at her belly. "Are you and Kevin expecting twins?"

"No."

"Didn't you just get married in January?"

"Yes," she replied evenly.

"You look awfully big. What's your due date?"

Marcella and Ellen exchanged glances.

"I'm not exactly certain," Jessie said, hoping Rosemary would drop it.

"Surely your obstetrician told you the month. What month are you due?"

"June," she said, feeling hot and sticky.

Rosemary sucked in her breath. "Well!" she exclaimed, looking disgusted, then turned on her heel and marched off.

Jessie wished she could disappear down a rabbit hole like Alice.

Marcella put a comforting hand on her arm. "It's all right. Don't pay any attention to people like her."

Ellen glared after Rosemary's retreating form. "She probably has sex with her husband and never even breaks into a sweat."

Marcella chuckled. Ellen turned and smiled at Jessie. "Jack and I have been meaning to have you and Kevin over to dinner, but Kevin said you've been so busy with school and fixing up the house you haven't had time."

"Oh," she said, taken aback. *Kevin had never mentioned an invitation to dinner.* "Yes, I have been pretty busy."

"I think it's smart of you to finish school, even with all the work you have to do decorating a home and preparing for a new baby," Ellen said. "Kevin's really proud of you."

"He is?"

Marcella nodded. "Yes. He told me that too."

If so, this was the first Jessie had ever heard of it.

Ellen smiled. "Please come over as soon as you can. We'd love to get to know you better. Call us whenever you're ready."

"I'm sure we'll be able to make it soon," she said. "I'll have the nursery finished any day now."

⁓

Kevin returned to the ballroom as soon as the tea was over, and escorted her to the car. He opened the door for her like a perfect gentleman and helped her into the seat.

"So how did you like Ellen and Marcella?" he asked, after pulling onto the road.

"They're both very nice," she replied, then took a breath and screwed up her courage. "Why didn't you tell me Ellen and Jack invited us to dinner?"

"Our home is not yet suitable for entertaining, and I will not accept invitations which we cannot reciprocate."

Her mouth dropped open. "The house looks nice enough after all the work I did, short of completely remodeling."

Kevin gave her a dirty look. "Your cooking isn't exactly up to company standards."

"We haven't had any yet to find out. Besides, we could always order pizza."

"Try not to be stupid," he sneered.

⁓

Ellen's praise made Jessie feel more confident about her decision to finish school. Kevin's mother and sisters thought it was a waste of time, and told her so. But at least she had a goal to accomplish and normal people to talk to, instead of feeling like a princess locked up in a tower.

As graduation day approached, she was disappointed to learn that Ann and Audrey weren't going to show up for commencement. They were both going on to four-year colleges and decided to have their diplomas mailed.

Kevin refused to attend the graduation ceremony, saying it was ridiculous for a housewife to get a degree. She called her mother to tell her the date and learned that Rick's high school commencement would be held at the same time. Both her parents and grandparents had to go to Rick's graduation; it was his day.

Jessie saw no point in going to commencement alone. Not going would save on the expense of a cap and gown. She decided go to Rick's instead and called to ask her mom for a ride.

"I'm sorry to have to tell you this, honey," Liz said, "but Rick doesn't want you at his graduation. Your condition is a little embarrassing. I'm sure you understand."

"Yes," she said, tears of shame burning her eyes.

❧

The local weekly *Concord Times* came out a few days after graduation. It listed the graduates for all the schools. Concord Community's graduates appeared first, and Jessie's name was listed with honors.

Liz hurriedly placed a call to Jessie. "Congratulations, dear. I'm so proud of you. Why didn't you tell us you were graduating with honors?"

"What difference does it make?"

"*What difference does it make?* How would you feel if your child was graduating with honors and didn't tell you?"

Jessie sighed. "I really didn't know, Mom. I wasn't going to the commencement anyway, so I didn't bother to check." She heard the back door open. "Kevin's home. I've got to go."

Kevin pulled out a chair and sat down, waiting to be served. She handed him a glass of iced tea. He took a long draught then signaled for a refill.

"Hey, why didn't you tell me you were graduating with honors? Mom read about it in the paper."

"I didn't know." Jessie filled his glass again.

"I thought going to school was important to you. Didn't you check your final grades?"

"No."

"Why not?"

"Because nobody seemed to care." She took the meatloaf out of the oven and sliced off a piece for Kevin.

"You mean because I couldn't come to your graduation?"

"You didn't want to come." She spooned some mashed potatoes onto his plate.

"That's not true," he said. "I would've come, but it was so busy on the farm that Dad couldn't spare me."

She finished up in silence. Kevin could hardly expect her to forget the demeaning things he'd said about her graduation, which had nothing to do with whether or not his father could spare him. The Jekyll and Hyde routine really got on her nerves.

CHAPTER 14

THE EYE OF THE NEEDLE

Jessie was bottle-feeding the calves one Saturday morning when an impatient little fellow butted her in the belly. She felt a gush of warm fluid run down her legs. She wasn't sure what was wrong and was terrified that she might be bleeding. Kevin had insisted she take over feeding the baby calves, morning and evening, as soon as school was over. She hadn't been enthused by the idea, but she hadn't thought it might be a risk to the baby—until now.

Every step she took caused more liquid to squish out. She went to the farmhouse and called her mother.

"Don't worry, your water just broke," Liz said. "It happens sometimes. Phone your obstetricians' office. The answering service will get a hold of Dr. Leiberman or Dr. Klein. Whoever's on call this weekend will phone and tell you what to do."

Jessie drove home with burlap sacks covering the seat. Once inside she grabbed some bath towels to put on a kitchen chair while she phoned the answering service.

Dr. Klein returned her call. He asked a few questions and reviewed timing contractions so she'd know when to leave for the hospital. The cramps didn't start until after midnight, but hurt so much by noon she made Kevin take her to the hospital.

When they arrived, she could barely keep from moaning out loud as she waited for Kevin to complete the admission forms. They took the elevator up to the maternity floor. There, Kevin handed her off to a nurse and left for the lounge to relax with a cup of coffee.

The RN gave Jessie a hospital gown and told her where to change. Afterward, the nurse explained that the doctor on duty had to determine her labor status before calling in Dr. Klein.

Jessie inwardly blanched. It had been hard enough getting used to Dr. Lieberman and Dr. Klein examining intimate areas of her body, but now a perfect stranger was going to do it.

The doctor was young, which was somewhat of a relief, but it was terribly embarrassing anyway. She tried to force herself to relax, but had to grit her teeth and clutch the sides of the table to keep from crying out in pain. Sweat beaded on her forehead. When the doctor looked up and saw the sweat, he appeared shocked.

"I'm sorry, I didn't mean to hurt you," he said. "You don't seem to be dilated to any real degree. Are you sure your contractions are strong?"

"Yes." *You ought to feel them*, she thought.

"All right, I'm going to give you the benefit of the doubt." He picked up the chart and made a notation. "You can stay, but it's too early to call Dr. Klein."

The doctor left. A no-nonsense RN in her thirties, wearing a crisp white uniform with her blonde hair pinned-up under a starched white cap, escorted Jessie to the labor ward.

This consisted of a long row of cubicles with curtains that slid across the open ends. Each cubicle contained a hospital bed, a single chair, an IV pole and a blood-pressure monitor. Everything was functional, antiseptic, and cold.

With unsmiling efficiency, the nurse completely shaved her down below, and then administered a two-quart enema that left her groaning in pain. She had to endure ten minutes of agony before being allowed to go to the bathroom. The concurrent bowel and labor contractions left her shaking and covered in sweat.

When Jessie returned to her cubicle, the RN flitted back in. "Dr. Klein's here and will examine you shortly."

Jessie was flooded with relief when the curtain parted to reveal gray-bearded Dr. Klein, wearing his yarmulke. Surely he would give her something to relieve her suffering.

Under his skilled hands, the pelvic exam didn't hurt as badly as before. He murmured something to the nurse, who made a notation on the chart.

"Well, that enema sure did something!" the nurse declared.

It was clear from the RN's attitude that she'd never been on the receiving end of any obstetric procedures.

"It's still too soon to start your epidural, Jessie," Dr. Klein said. "You haven't dilated enough."

"But what about the pain?" she gasped. "It's horrible."

"You can't have anything for pain now if you still want an epidural so you can be awake for the birth. If the epidural is started too soon your labor could stop, necessitating a Caesarean section."

"Okay," she said, terrified of having a C-section, then clenched her teeth as another contraction twisted through her body.

The dreadful cramps continued for hours, wracking her torso until she wanted to vomit.

Off and on, Dr. Klein stepped in to check on her progress, but she still hadn't dilated sufficiently for the anesthesiologist to be called in.

As the hours passed, Dr. Klein became concerned enough to order a pelvic X-ray. The X-ray came back normal, so he ordered a Pitocin drip added to her IV to strengthen her contractions.

If she thought the pain had been awful before, it was even more terrible now. Cramps twisted and contorted her body as if she was possessed by a supernatural force. Only the rails kept her from falling out of bed as she writhed uncontrollably. She felt an overwhelming desire to bang her head on the wall, countering pain with pain, as the dreadful contractions continued to wrench her body.

"Please, *somebody*, help me!"

The RN flew in. "Stop it! Stop it immediately!"

Jessie glared at the nurse and wailed at the top of her lungs. The RN retreated and promptly returned with Dr. Klein. He examined Jessie once more and nodded to the nurse. "Tell Dr. Anderson he can start the epidural now."

Dr. Klein left, saying he had to check on another patient. The wait for the anesthesiologist seemed interminable. Finally, the RN returned with a petite redhead. "This is nurse anesthetist Flynn. She'll start the epidural."

"Where's Dr. Anderson?" Jessie asked, and clenched her teeth as another contraction twisted her torso.

"He had a Caesarean section. He can't come right now."

The RN lowered the bed rails. "Sit on the edge of the bed, Mrs. McKenna, bend your back slightly and stay perfectly still."

The redhead went behind her and started the prep.

Jessie teetered on the edge of the bed as the anesthetist poked at her spine with a needle. With nothing to cling to, she almost fell off when the next contraction wracked her body.

"Sit still or the needle won't go in right," the RN carped.

Jessie moaned and steeled herself against the next wave of pain. She held her breath as another spasm began to stab through her, but it escalated into such agony she cried out.

"Shut up!" the nurse ordered.

Jessie began to sob. It was impossible.

The nurse lit into her again.

Suddenly the curtain parted and a stout, black LPN appeared. The new nurse took one look at the scene and immediately went to Jessie. "I'm here to help you, Mrs. McKenna. Just tell me what the problem is."

"I'm having troub—"

The RN interrupted. "Mrs. McKenna isn't cooperating—"

The black nurse cut her off. "I was talking to the patient."

Scowling, the RN shut her mouth.

Jessie gave the LPN a look of gratitude. "I'm having trouble balancing on the edge of the bed. When a contraction comes, I feel like I'm going to fall off."

"You can hold onto me," the LPN said, then stepped into position.

Jessie took a deep breath to steady herself, then put her arms around the big black woman who filled her with so much comfort. All anybody else had done so far was hurt her worse than she already hurt.

The anesthetist got busy again. Sensing another contraction mounting, Jessie squeezed back as hard as she could with her abdominal muscles, something both the RN and Dr. Klein had forbidden her to do earlier, but it worked.

Dr. John Anderson, a tall angular man in his forties, swept into the enclosure. He looked at Jessie, then at the redheaded anesthetist. "What are you doing with my patient?"

"I'm starting the epidural, doctor."

"Who authorized this?" Anderson asked, and moved to the other side of the bed where he could observe. "STOP!"

"Why?" the anesthetist protested.

"It's *wrong*!" Anderson exclaimed.

"What?"

"Get out of the way, you stupid bitch!"

The redhead drew back in shock.

"Don't move, Mrs. McKenna, or you'll be paralyzed for the rest of your life," Anderson said. "This will only take a moment."

Icy fear gripped her, becoming hot and intense as the seconds ticked on. She couldn't breathe. Her lungs began to burn. She could feel the next contraction mounting and clung to the LPN, straining to remain immobile.

Finally Anderson spoke, "It's okay. You can move now."

Jessie collapsed against the black nurse, sobbing. The LPN hugged her. "It's okay, baby, you made it."

Dr. Anderson addressed the anesthetist. "Get out of here!"

"B-but—" the redhead stammered.

"I have a patient to take care of," Anderson snapped. "I'll talk to you later."

The anesthetist scurried away.

Dr. Anderson turned his attention to Jessie. "Don't be afraid. This won't take long."

Jessie quailed at the thought of starting over. But she knew she couldn't stand anymore pain. Secure in the embrace of the big black LPN, she willed herself to relax.

Anderson was quick, and soon Jessie felt some relief from the pain. Everyone left so she could rest. Eventually, the contractions subsided to a dull throbbing that came and went.

Dr. Klein returned from time to time to check her dilation, and finally said she could be moved to the delivery room.

An orderly arrived to help the RN wheel her bed down the hall. Even with assistance from the nurse and doctor, Jessie found it difficult to move her numbed lower limbs up into the stirrups of the delivery table. Once she was settled, the orderly wheeled the bed out, and Dr. Klein left to scrub.

The RN began to strap Jessie's arms down.

"Is this really necessary?" she protested.

"It's standard procedure," the nurse replied crisply. Uncapping a half gallon bottle of cold disinfectant solution, she dumped it over Jessie's bare bottom, leaving her gasping in shock.

Dr. Klein returned, checked her dilation again, and told her to start pushing with the contractions.

She pushed with all her might, but after a while she began to feel weak and less able to sense the rhythm of the spasms.

Dr. Klein whispered something to the nurse. She left for a moment and returned.

Two men in scrub dress entered the room, startling Jessie.

Who are they? she wondered. *Interns? Residents?*

Then another man walked in wearing scrubs.

Omigod! Four men were looking at her bare bottom. And she thought testifying about rape was going to be embarrassing. If only she knew then what she knew now.

The nurse put her hand on Jessie's abdomen and told her when to push. She could hardly feel the contractions anymore, but she pushed down hard whenever the nurse said to.

Dr. Klein cut the perineum. "Push as hard as you can."

She strained until the small capillaries on her face burst, but her efforts had no discernable effect.

Dr. Klein shook his head. "High forceps," he announced to the men in scrubs before proceeding.

"No!" Jessie cried. *Forceps could be dangerous.*

"I have to," he said. "Your labor has stopped."

Dr. Klein inserted the instrument to grip the infant's skull and pulled with such force that Jessie could feel the intensity of it, if not the pain. The drapes obscured her view, but she felt a sudden release of pressure.

"Congratulations, Jessie, it's a girl!" Dr. Klein exclaimed in triumph.

Moving quickly, the RN suctioned out the baby's mouth and nostrils. The infant cried, taking her first lungful of air in the strange new world. Her skin was bluish-pink, wrinkled, and covered with messy stuff. Jessie suddenly felt faint.

One of the men in scrubs turned smiling eyes upon her. Dr. Klein looked up from suturing and addressed him.

"Congratulations, Mr. McKenna, how does it feel to see your first?"

"I've delivered plenty of calves, doctor, but this is sure something else."

Hearing Kevin's voice, Jessie's eyes widened with shock. He'd flatly refused to attend the birth when she initially brought the subject up and brooked no more discussion on the matter.

Kevin grinned through his mask. "Congratulations, honey."

She was too wasted to care what he said. She felt like she'd just lived through some surrealistic nightmare.

Kevin had to be disappointed that the child was a girl, but that was just too bad. She had no intention of going through this again.

When Dr. Klein finished the stitches, Jessie was wheeled to the recovery room. Shortly thereafter, a young nurse with an angelic face carried in the baby wrapped in pink blankets.

"What are you going to name her?" the nurse asked brightly.

"We haven't decided yet," Jessie said, taking her baby from the nurse, who smiled and walked away.

Kevin had refused to consider any names for a girl child, insisting he was man enough to sire a son to name after his father. He had even forbidden her to think about girls' names.

"Well then," Jessie whispered to her sleeping child, "you're all mine to name."

She tried to think of a name that would suit the baby based on her first impression, but the infant resembled her paternal grandfather more than anyone. Jessie wasn't fond of the name Josephine or of the idea of naming the child after her father-in-law. Hard as she tried, nothing suitable came to mind. Soon the sweet-faced nurse stopped talking to the nurse on duty and returned to take the baby away.

The long labor and anesthesia had taken its toll. Jessie needed a simple formula. She decided to name her baby after the prettiest girl she had known at Archbishop Moore, Laura, and then drifted off to sleep.

❧

When she woke, Kevin was allowed into the recovery room to see her. He was grinning from ear to ear, and bent over to give her a peck on the cheek before pulling up a chair.

"Hey, we have a baby to name, don't we?" he exclaimed. "We never thought of having a girl."

Jessie bristled. Kevin knew perfectly well that he, and he alone, hadn't wanted a girl.

"How about Louise?" he asked.

"No. I want to call her Laura."

Kevin eyes widened. "Well, you'll just have to change your mind."

"No," she replied evenly. "I like Laura."

"I want it to be Louise."

"I don't like it. Pick something else," she said, willing to compromise even though Laura seemed so perfect.

"No, Louise is my favorite."

"But why? Why Louise?"

He smiled. "My favorite girlfriend was named Louise, and I want to name my baby after her."

"You bum," Jessie hissed. "How dare you consider naming our baby after one of your old girlfriends."

"Why not?" he said mockingly.

"Get out!" she snapped. "Get out of my sight!"

Across the room, the nurse in charge rose from her desk and started toward them. Kevin saw her coming and left before she got any closer.

The nurse eyed his retreating form and continued over to Jessie. "Are you all right, Mrs. McKenna?"

"I'm fine," she said, holding back tears until the nurse finished adjusting her pillow and returned to the desk. Jessie closed her eyes and allowed the tears to flow down her cheeks. *Her name is Laura*, she repeated silently, *I won't let you take that away from me.*

⌖

During Laura's morning feeding, Kevin peeped into the room, then strode inside, carrying a floral arrangement of pink roses. He placed the flowers on the table and leaned over the baby, beaming. "I never knew being a father would feel so wonderful."

Jessie regarded his declaration of the joys of fatherhood with a jaundiced eye, but hoped he realized she'd done him a favor by standing firm and refusing to have an abortion. She considered the roses something of a peace offering and decided to forget what he'd said about a certain Louise person being his favorite girlfriend.

Their conversation flowed along—like any happy new parents would have—until Kevin once more brought up naming the baby Louise.

Jessie gave him a frosty look. "I'm not having my daughter named after one of your girlfriends."

"Oh, come on. I was just kidding."

"If that was your idea of a joke, it wasn't very funny."

"I'm sorry," he said, humbly. "I really like the name Louise. Please let me name her Louise."

"No!"

CHAPTER 15

PSYCHOTIC REACTION

Laura Louise arrived home to a peach-colored room with a yellow crib and yellow curtains printed with fanciful, pastel animals. A maple rocker waited on a mint green rug. A dresser, bassinet and changing table completed the room's furnishings.

Jessie had painted the room peach because one night she'd had a dream of herself sitting in the rocker holding a baby bundled in pink blankets. When Kevin protested, she told him she'd chosen peach because it was a neutral color. However, if he preferred blue, he could repaint it himself if he wanted to.

Liz took off work to spend a few days helping out. Jessie wasn't supposed to climb stairs or do much of anything for a couple of days. With a practiced hand, Liz took over the household tasks while modeling the proper techniques of handling an infant.

Jessie struggled to feed and burp Laura. Most of the time the baby spit up the formula she swallowed, except when Liz fed her, making Jessie feel totally incompetent. Jessie felt hot and tense all the time, and the baby was always fidgety and cranky when she held her.

Strangely enough, Laura appeared to be fascinated by her father and quieted right down whenever Liz put her in his arms. Kevin would smile indulgently and tell Liz he just loved being a father. But the minute Liz left in the evening, Kevin ignored Laura and refused to lift a finger. It was all Jessie could do to make it through each sleepless night until her mother returned in the morning.

The first day Liz stopped coming, everything turned sour.

Kevin came home from work at four-thirty and sat at the kitchen table to read the paper, just like he always did. Jessie was getting supper ready when Laura started to whine, and she thought Kevin would pick her up. He rustled the paper and went "Humph."

The baby began to whine louder.

Kevin rustled the paper again. "I think Laura needs her mother's attention."

"Can't you pick her up for a minute? I'm in the middle of slicing vegetables for the salad." She gave a quick stir to the spaghetti sauce simmering on the stove and resumed slicing.

He turned another page. "Don't look at me. You're the one who wanted to have the kid. She's your responsibility."

⁓

Jessie walked the floors with Laura every night, but nothing seemed to help the child sleep. Laura whined and cried incessantly, driving her to distraction. Each day Jessie was dogged by mind-numbing fatigue. She wasn't supposed to do heavy housework until after her six-week checkup, and the house began to show it. Although Kevin took the laundry to the farm for his mother to wash, he did nothing else but complain.

"This place looks like shit. Why don't you get off your lazy butt and do something about it?"

"You know I'm not supposed to vacuum or scrub floors yet. I might start bleeding again. If you want the house to be cleaner, you need to help."

"I'm not doing housework. That's a woman's job," he sneered. "My father never came home to a dirty house while I was growing up."

"I doubt if your father went out every night and every weekend like you do," she said in an icy tone.

"I'm working on Jack's re-election campaign, and you know that has priority," Kevin retorted. "I'd like to have friends and campaign workers over, but I sure as hell can't with the place looking like this."

She knew it was half bullshit. He hadn't bothered to invite anyone over before they had the baby, and she doubted that being the campaign manager for an incumbent member of the state House of Delegates required all that much of his time, even if the delegates did have to run every two years. Kevin had also insisted on coaching summer league softball, claiming Bob couldn't find a replacement.

⚬⚬⚬

Laura's colic continued unabated. She cried because she was hungry, then cried for hours after each feeding because her belly was in pain. The only way to comfort her was to hold her.

Jessie longed to lie down with the baby beside her, but the pediatrician warned her that could be dangerous. She felt more worn out each day. One night she fell asleep in the rocking chair while feeding Laura her formula. Fortunately, the loud crack of the bottle hitting the floor woke her before she dropped the baby.

The next night Jessie was so fatigued, she slept through Laura's cries at every feeding. Kevin had to shake her awake each time. Just before dawn, when Laura started crying again, and shaking didn't suffice, Kevin kicked Jessie out of bed onto the floor.

"You fucking bitch! What kind of mother ignores her baby's cries? Get your lazy ass moving!"

When she tried to stand, her muscles quivered like jelly. Crawling to the staircase, she slid down the steps on her buttocks wishing she could block out the sound of Laura's wails. Jessie grasped the newel post to pull herself to her feet and wobbled into the kitchen to heat a bottle of formula. By the time it was ready, Laura was screaming at the top of her lungs.

Jessie dragged herself up the staircase. The door to the master bedroom was closed. No doubt Kevin had both pillows over his head. Laura was so hysterical when Jessie finally reached the nursery, it actually took a moment for her to calm down enough to drink. After Laura finished the bottle, Jessie changed her and rocked her until she fell back to sleep.

With a sigh, Jessie closed the door, praying Laura wouldn't awaken, and returned to the kitchen. The first golden rays of sunrise peeked through the curtains over the sink as Jessie started fixing Kevin's breakfast.

After six weeks of sleepless nights with a colicky newborn and a husband who refused to lift a finger, Jessie was at her wits' end. She never wanted to have another baby again, and decided to rearrange her scheduled checkup to get Dr. Lieberman instead of Dr. Klein. A devout Orthodox Jew, Dr. Klein wouldn't perform sterilizations. Although the church taught that sterilization or using artificial birth control was sinful, doing so wasn't a mortal sin like adultery, murder or suicide.

Dr. Lieberman brought up the subject of birth control during Jessie's physical before she even asked. She told him she wanted a tubal-ligation, but was shocked to learn she couldn't be sterilized without her husband's permission.

Kevin would never consent. He'd already told her in no uncertain terms that her job was to produce a male heir. Jessie knew she couldn't go on if she had to face the risk of getting pregnant again any time soon. The only recourse was to ask Dr. Lieberman to prescribe birth control pills.

The summer heat and sleepless nights left Jessie so tired she could barely keep up with the regimen of baby care, laundry, cooking and grocery shopping. She was too exhausted and depressed to manage doing the heavy cleaning.

Returning from the supermarket with the baby one day, Jessie was pleasantly surprised to see Mary Clare's car in the driveway. Assuming Mary Clare had stopped by with Little

Charlie to see Laura and chat, Jessie hoped it might be the beginning of a new friendship. She desperately needed companionship and diversion, and could sure use some advice on childcare and housekeeping.

No one was in the car or sitting in the shade of the porch. Puzzled, Jessie turned the handle of the back door and found it unlocked. Perhaps she'd forgotten to secure it, and her sister-in-law had discovered it was unlocked and gone inside to wait.

Jessie carried Laura into the house. The kitchen and living room were deserted. Voices drifted down from upstairs.

She listened for a moment and realized one of the voices belonged to her mother-in-law, who was loudly exchanging critical comments on the state of the house with Mary Clare.

Leaving Laura securely fastened in her carrier, Jessie returned to the back door and slammed it loudly.

The voices fell silent. A flurry of footsteps sounded on the stairs, then Maria and Mary Clare popped into the kitchen.

"There you are, Jessie. Where's my precious Laura?" Maria gushed, then went straight to the infant carrier and began playing with the baby.

Mary Clare followed. "Oh, you're so lucky, Jessie. I'd love to have another baby of my own."

"Where's Little Charlie?"

"We left him with Kathleen."

"Why?" Jessie asked. "I thought you were bringing him to see Laura."

"No," Mary Clare said. "We came over to get the laundry and wash it at the farm for you. Kevin said you could use some help and gave us the key. We didn't realize you'd be home so soon, or we would have waited until you got back."

Jessie found it difficult to disguise her irritation over their snooping, but she held her tongue on that score.

"Thank you. But I did the laundry at my mother's yesterday, and Kevin knows it."

Maria smiled thinly. "How would he know you already did the laundry?"

"Yes, how would Kevin know that?" Mary Clare chimed in.

"He always insists on knowing my plans for the day when I use the car," she said flatly.

Mary Clare shrugged. "We thought you needed help because Kevin said you were so far behind in your housework. We were only trying to do you a favor."

"We're sorry we bothered you," Maria said. "Since there's no laundry we can do for you, we'll leave."

Jessie didn't want them to depart on such an uncomfortable note, and she truly wanted to develop a friendship with them. "Please stay. I'll make some coffee."

Maria shook her head. "I'm sorry, dear, but there's too much to do at the farm to stay for coffee. We don't have time to waste," she said, which clearly implied that Jessie wasted plenty of time or her house would be in better shape.

⟡

The summer dragged on and so did Laura's colic. September brought no relief, neither did October. Jessie had not slept more than four hours at a stretch since June. She felt as if she was held prisoner by a squalling child whose biological clock simply could not connect nighttime and sleep.

Late one afternoon, Jessie heard tires crunching on gravel. Her heart lifted when she recognized Ann's car; Ann must have decided to stop by on her way home from City College. She ran to get the front door before the doorbell could awaken Laura.

"Hey, how's it going?" Ann asked. "Where's Laura?"

"She's taking a late nap," Jessie said, relieved that she'd be able chat awhile without interruption. "So how's school?"

"It's okay." Ann settled into a chair at the kitchen table. "How are things going with you?"

She didn't know how to answer that. Ann could hardly wait to be a mother. It was better to fall back on an old standard. "Well, I don't get much sleep or go out very often."

Ann chuckled. "That's what I thought, so I have a proposition for you."

"What?"

"How about joining my bowling team?"

Jessie's heart sank. "Sorry, but I can't afford league fees and a sitter too."

"Please, one of my team members is quitting, and Laura's old enough for Kevin to watch her for a few hours one night a week."

"I'd really like to, but I don't think Kevin will agree."

Ann's eyes flashed. "If he gives you a hard time about it, tell him to call me."

"Okay, I will. When do I start?"

"Next Wednesday at seven o'clock."

Jessie didn't know what Ann said to Kevin to get him to agree, but it worked. It felt wonderful to get out of the house and spend a few hours away from Laura, but everyone on the team expected her to rave about motherhood. Jessie knew they wouldn't understand if she told them how she really felt.

Even she didn't understand why she couldn't love Laura like other mothers seemed to love their babies. When Laura was awake, she whined and wailed unless she was being cuddled or played with, which left little free time for household chores. Getting anything done required listening to a chorus of Laura's cries. She wasn't the sort of baby to lie in a playpen contentedly sucking on a pacifier for even half a minute. The colic wasn't quite as bad, thanks to a special formula Jessie was able to purchase at the pharmacy, but the baby still wouldn't sleep through the night.

Bowling seemed to help alleviate Jessie's depression somewhat, but the effect didn't last. Kevin allowed her to go, but that didn't stop him from complaining and making her life miserable in general.

As November turned into December, each morning dawned darker than the one before. Every day it just seemed harder to breathe, as if all the air was being squeezed from her lungs while she was sucked into the muddy depths of the slough of despond. Worse, she was afraid she was going to lose her temper one day and harm Laura if she didn't stop crying.

On a gray mid-December morning, Jessie dropped Kevin off at the farm and made the weekly drive to the pharmacy to pick up Laura's supply of formula. Laura wailed the whole way there. After six months, it was enough to drive anybody nuts.

Laura's cries continued to ring in Jessie's ears on the way home. She felt a compulsive urge to stop the car and toss the baby out. Jessie gritted her teeth. Would the crying never stop?

The cloudy day only deepened her melancholy. Leafless trees lined the road like bars of living iron. She felt hemmed in, unable to escape the prison her life had become. Concentrating on the trees, she tried to block out the baby's squalls.

A pall of exhaustion swept over her, as dizzying as too much alcohol. The car swerved as her hands slipped on the wheel. She clasped it tighter. *What would it do to the human body to hit the trees doing forty? Would death be quick?*

She was locked into a loveless marriage from which the only true release was death, according to Catholic doctrine. To remain faithful to her vows, she must endure all without complaint. To fail, she'd been told, was to be unfaithful to God. *But was God even real?*

He hadn't answered her prayers for her marriage.

She'd hoped Kevin would stay home more often after Jack won reelection the first week of November, but nothing changed.

Would Kevin miss her if she died? Not really.

He might mourn her from the shock, but that's all. Everybody would feel sorry for him raising a baby alone and fall all over themselves to help out.

Jessie twisted the steering wheel to follow the road as it made a steep downhill turn. At the bottom of the hill, the road curved sharply to the left through the woods. If she accelerated, the car would be doing sixty when she got there. All she had to do was go straight and her misery would be over.

She stomped on the gas pedal and the car surged into high gear. In a few seconds she'd be at the point of no return. After that she'd never make the curve. In the moment just before impact, she'd pray for forgiveness.

A baby's cry startled her.

"Oh my God!" Jessie exclaimed and slammed on the brakes.

With a screech of burning rubber, the Caprice fishtailed sideways and skidded to a halt.

Heart pounding, she turned to look behind her. How could she have forgotten Laura was still in the car!

Jessie offered a silent act of contrition and drove the last mile home profoundly shaken. She couldn't remember where she'd come from or why she was even on the road.

Pulling up to the house, she parked close to the back door and took Laura straight up to her crib.

Jessie staggered back down the staircase and collapsed on the floor. Trembling all over, she sobbed in despair. What was wrong with her? She'd almost killed her baby! She was losing her mind, and she knew it. Looking up, she cried out to heaven, "God, please help me! Please don't let me go insane!"

If she lost her mind, Kevin would have her carted away to an asylum. It wasn't all that hard to have someone committed, and no one would believe her if she told the truth about Kevin.

Jessie wept until she had no more tears, then crawled into the living room and pulled herself up on the sofa. She sat rigidly still and stared fixedly at the windowpane-pattern the sunlight cast on the carpet, until she saw nothing at all.

When at last she came to herself, something about the room seemed queer.

She wondered what was wrong. Nothing seemed out of the ordinary, yet she felt totally creeped out. She glanced at the pattern of sunlight on the carpet. When she'd entered the room the sun's rays were shining in through the east windows. But now the pattern was reversed. The rays were slanting in from the *west*!

Her mind spun in confusion. She couldn't have been sitting there all day. Laura hadn't even cried for a bottle.

The clock on the mantle began to chime. The dial said four p.m.! Jessie jumped up and ran into the kitchen, praying that Laura would stay asleep long enough to get dinner started.

⁕

The next morning Jessie awoke to the alarm clock jangling in her ears. She was too disoriented by the noise to understand what was happening until Kevin growled, "Turn off the fucking alarm."

She leapt out of bed to switch it off. Rubbing the sleep from her eyes, she suddenly realized why waking to the ringing alarm had seemed so confusing. Laura hadn't woken her first with her cries. It had been six months since Laura had been born, and she'd finally slept through the night.

Jessie headed into the bathroom to brush her teeth. After she was finished, she reached into the medicine cabinet to get her birth control pills. She opened the lid of the container and paused. She couldn't remember if she'd taken a pill the day before. She'd have to check the date on the prescription label to figure it out, and read the instruction insert to find out what to do if she hadn't.

She found the box under the sink and read the brochure. In the warning section, one of the side effects listed was depression. She didn't recall Dr. Lieberman mentioning that.

Jessie stared at the sleek plastic container on the sink. What did she need the Pill for anyway? Kevin hardly touched her.

What if the Pill had contributed to her suicidal feelings? Yesterday, she'd almost killed herself and her baby.

One by one, she popped the rest of the tablets through the foil backing and flushed them down the toilet.

In a matter of days her energy level soared. She went on a marathon house cleaning spree. Kevin was so happy to see the whole place sparkling, he invited Wayne and Carol to dinner.

It turned out to be quite an enjoyable evening. Wayne raved over the Chicken Divan Jessie served. Carol gushed over the baby and the house.

"I know how hard it is to paint a house from top to bottom, and redo all the floors. It's hard to believe you managed all that while being pregnant and finishing school."

Kevin was so witty and charming all evening, Jessie could hardly remember why things had seemed so dark for so long. This was the man she'd fallen in love with, and she wanted him badly. After seeing Wayne and Carol off, Kevin closed the front door, then turned around and gave her a peck on the cheek.

"Thank you," he said. "I didn't know you knew how to make Chicken Divan. It was great."

Delight rippled through her. She looked into his eyes and slid her arms around his neck. "If you thought the chicken was good, I've got something you'll like even better."

Chapter 16

Dairy Princess

Jessie felt certain she was pregnant again by the time her first wedding anniversary rolled around. It was too early for a pregnancy test, however, she was sure it happened the night they'd had Wayne and Carol over for dinner. Kevin assumed she was still on the Pill, but she had needed him so badly that night she went ahead and took the risk. He disliked condoms, and she didn't like them either. They weren't as reliable as the Pill, and intercourse just didn't feel as good.

If she had to pay the piper, so be it. Kevin wanted a son and she wouldn't be off the hook until she produced one. Being a mother seemed more of a blessing now that she wasn't depressed.

❦

A few days before the anniversary, Liz showed up with the top of the wedding cake which she'd been storing in her chest freezer.

"Are you and Kevin going out to dinner on the big day?" Liz asked, handing over the cake box.

"I don't know. We haven't discussed it."

"Well, let me know whether or not you need me to baby-sit."

❦

Jessie brought the subject up with Kevin over supper that evening. "Mom offered to baby-sit so we can go out to dinner on our anniversary, if you want."

"To be honest, I'd prefer a home-cooked meal with a little wine and candlelight," he said. "It's not like we have the money to eat out."

She felt a sharp pang of disappointment. A couple's first anniversary was supposed to be special. She'd hoped he'd planned on taking her out to dinner.

Kevin could hardly be considered frugal, given how many nights a week he went out. He claimed he had to belong to a lot of clubs and attend so many meetings because of his future political ambitions. She didn't like it, but there wasn't anything she could do to change things. Perhaps she should just be happy she'd have him all to herself.

⚮

On the morning of the anniversary, Jessie was in high spirits anticipating a romantic evening ahead. She cleaned and polished for hours so everything would gleam with a fresh sparkle. Laura was in a good humor and Jessie flew through her tasks, humming as she worked.

For the finishing touch, she shined the silver candlesticks Kathleen and Frank had given them as a wedding present, placed them on the dining table, and put tapers in them. Then she started preparing the special menu she'd planned from the cookbook Mary Clare had given her: roast tenderloin of beef, twice-baked potatoes, and green beans with almonds.

Savory aromas filled the kitchen at four-thirty, making her mouth water. Everything was timed to serve at five on the dot, the time Kevin always insisted that dinner be served. However, by five-thirty there was still no sign of him.

Jessie poured herself a cup of coffee, turned the oven back as low as she could, and kept an eye on the roast. At six, she turned on the television news and tried to stay calm. After all, something might have gone wrong with the equipment or a cow might be sick.

By seven, the candles were still unlit, and the roast remained in the oven. She was too angry to eat even one morsel of the overcooked food, and kept watching television with an eye on the clock.

At eight, she put Laura to bed. Around nine, she brewed another pot of coffee. She drank some, then left her cup and saucer on the counter in case she wanted more. When the eleven o'clock news came on, Kevin still wasn't home.

Jessie was determined to stay up until he walked in the door so she could find out where he'd been. She tried to hang on longer by propping her head up with a pillow and watching the late movie. In spite of her resolve, she drifted off to sleep.

The jangle of keys unlocking the front door woke her.

Kevin sauntered into the living room.

Jessie stood to face him. "Where have you been all evening?" she asked, straining to maintain a civil tone.

He grinned. "Where do you think?"

"If I knew, I wouldn't be asking," she said. "You told me you wanted a home-cooked meal for our anniversary. I assumed you'd be here to eat it."

"I never said that."

Indignation burned in her breast. "Yes, you did. You told me you wanted me to cook dinner instead of going out."

Kevin smiled slyly. "I never said I'd be here to eat it."

Jessie sucked in her breath, thunderstruck by the premeditated malice of his actions. She struggled to get a grip on herself. "Do you mind telling me where you've been?"

"Of course not, since you've asked so nicely. I'm glad to see you've learned something," he said. "I went out to dinner with some friends to celebrate my anniversary."

"I thought you didn't want to go out. That's why you told me to cook."

"No. I just didn't want to take *you* out. I told you to cook so you'd have something to eat." Smirking, he turned and headed for the kitchen.

She hurried after him, ready to give him a piece of her mind.

Kevin spoke before she had a chance to say anything. "Why is the table still set for dinner?"

"Because you never came home to eat it," she snapped.

"Didn't you eat?"

"No, I've been waiting for you."

"How foolish," he said. "You've wasted all the food."

"No, you did!"

Kevin grabbed her arm, twisted it behind her back, and shoved her against the counter. With his free hand he pointed to the empty cup and saucer. "What's this?"

"A coffee cup," Jessie gasped.

"Why hasn't it been washed and put away?"

"Because I wasn't sure I was finished needing it," she said, heart hammering.

Kevin relaxed his grip. "All right, but from now on I expect you to wash the cup and put it away every time you use it."

"That's ridiculous."

"That's an order. Now take care of it," he snarled, then released her and walked away.

"Okay." Snatching the cup and saucer, she hurled them against the wall. They splintered in a ricocheting burst. "Satisfied?"

He turned and looked at her with amusement. "What did you do that for? Now you just have a bigger mess to clean up."

"You son of a bitch!" She grabbed the overcooked roast out of the oven and threw it at him. He dodged through the doorway just in time. The roast smacked into the wall and the pan clattered to the floor, leaving behind a greasy black smear.

Kevin popped back through the doorway and laughed, then ducked out when a plate sailed at him. Burning with rage, Jessie pulled open all the cabinets and threw whatever came to hand. Cups, saucers, bowls and plates cracked against the wall and splintered into pieces. For good measure, she opened the refrigerator and smashed the wedding cake on the floor.

Breathing heavily, she surveyed the destruction with glee.

Kevin peeked around the door and eyed the wreckage. "Be sure and clean up before you go to bed."

Glaring, Jessie turned on her heel and marched out the back door, slamming it behind her. She ran about a quarter mile, seething with anger, before the cold hit her.

She kept moving, but began to shiver. The temperature was somewhere in the teens, too frigid to stay outside without a coat much longer. Her parents' house was too far away to try to make it in the bitter cold. She considered spending the night in a nearby barn, but decided against it. If the farmer had dogs, it might be dangerous to wake them, and sleeping in an itchy pile of hay or straw wasn't appealing.

Sighing with resignation, she trudged back to the house.

It was dawn before she had the kitchen cleaned up. One bowl, two plates, and two coffee mugs had survived intact, enabling her to serve breakfast.

Kevin sat down and surveyed the skimpy place setting. "You're lucky enough china survived to eat on because you aren't allowed to buy anymore."

She scooped some fried eggs onto his plate and said nothing. Up to now he'd only gotten away with his bad behavior because her mother refused to hear a word against him. Surely her mother would side with her this time and offer her refuge.

❧

Jessie heard tires crunching on the gravel of the driveway just as she was setting the table for supper. Her mother let herself in without knocking. "Hi, honey. I thought I'd stop by to see what Kevin gave you for your anniversary."

Sniffing at the aroma of fresh coffee wafting through the kitchen, Liz opened a cabinet to fetch a cup and saucer. All the shelves were bare. Frowning, she opened another cupboard. It, too, was empty. The remaining cabinet held only a single cereal bowl. She glanced at the table. It held two dinner plates and two coffee mugs.

"Your grandparents gave you a full china service for twelve as a wedding present. What happened?"

"Kevin said he didn't want to go out to dinner for our anniversary," Jessie replied sourly. "He said he wanted a home-cooked meal with wine and candlelight."

"I know, you told me. So then what?"

"He never came home to eat it."

"Well, I guess I understand why you lost your temper. I suppose there's no point in asking what he gave you for a gift."

"He didn't get me anything. He told me he went out to dinner with friends."

Liz crossed her arms over her chest. "So what brought this on? You must have done something to make him mad."

Shocked, Jessie sucked in her breath then sputtered, "I didn't do anything! I tried to tell you he's mean to me most of the time. He's done awful things. Once he—"

"Stop right there!" Liz snapped. "I'm not going to listen to an hysterical diatribe against your husband. You know perfectly well you aren't a very good housekeeper, and you probably did something to upset Kevin."

Jessie's jaw dropped.

Liz continued lecturing. "It's a woman's responsibility to keep her husband happy. You're married for better or for worse. If I were you, I'd try being a better wife and see if Kevin doesn't become a better husband."

❧

Her mother took pity on her and bought her a set of cheap china at the Goodwill store. But it was a week before Kevin finally came home for supper in a good mood. Relieved, Jessie asked him how his day had gone.

"The herdsman quit today because Dad refused to give him a raise. I'm going to need you to help me with milking until we find a replacement."

"I don't understand. You still have another hired hand—Cletus—not to mention your father and Mike and Johnny."

"The herd's so large it takes two men to handle the milking while Cletus drives the cows in, otherwise we'd be milking all day. Normally, Dad only milks when one of us has a day off. You and I'll do the morning shift, so Dad won't have to get up at four-thirty every day, and Dad and Mike will take the afternoon shift."

Jessie gave him a sullen look. "I have housework to do and a baby to take care of all day. Why can't Johnny do it?"

"Johnny doesn't want to be a farmer. Mom and Dad swore that if he finished high school, he wouldn't have to milk cows."

"I don't see what the big deal is, if he's asked to help out for a few weeks. Besides, he *hasn't* finished high school."

"My parents don't want to do anything to jeopardize the chance of Johnny graduating this year. Mom can watch Laura."

"I'm not milking cows, and that's final," Jessie said.

"You'll do as I say!" Kevin exclaimed and stomped out of the house, slamming the door behind him.

⚬⚭⚬

Returning after midnight, Kevin quietly opened the back door and slipped into the house. He crept silently up the stairs and entered the bedroom. For a moment, he watched his wife sleeping peacefully. A wash of moonlight spilled through the curtains, revealing the steady rise and fall of her breast.

He closed his eyes and breathed deeply, savoring the almost sexual excitement of what he was about to do. The stupid bitch had no idea who she was dealing with. He bent over his wife, grabbed her thick long hair and yanked her out of bed.

She screamed and flailed in panic.

He twisted his grip tighter. "Shut up!"

Pulling her to her feet, he shoved her across the room and hauled her down the staircase.

Eyes watering with pain, Jessie tried not to stumble in the dark. Kevin dragged her into the living room, then spun her around to face him.

When she saw Kevin's eyes the blood drained from her face. Illuminated by the moonlight, his irises and pupils looked inhuman, almost reptilian.

Kevin spoke in a harsh rasping voice, "How dare you try to defy me! *I am your master.* By your own oath, you must obey me. If you ever defy a direct order again, I'll slit your horses' throats."

Transfixed by his preternatural eyes, she was powerless to speak and powerless to turn away. *What in God's name was he?*

"Do you *understand*?" he hissed.

Her heart stuck in her throat.

"Answer me."

His terrible eyes bored mercilessly into hers. She felt so strange. The air was getting misty.

"ANSWER ME!" Kevin shouted.

"Y-yes," she stammered. Hearing a roaring sound like a waterfall in her ears, she fainted.

Jessie woke to bone-numbing cold. The bedroom was filled with fog and a lingering menace. Trembling, she clutched the blankets closer.

She blinked rapidly and the fog began to dissipate, but the unnatural chill remained. The mist might be some sort of waking dream, but why did she feel so afraid? Her mind felt fuzzy and disoriented, and something else was weird.

Kevin's side of the bed was empty.

The clock on the dresser showed half-past eight. Kevin had never let her sleep in before. What would have induced him to forego breakfast?

Laura started to whine. Jessie got up to warm a bottle.

A peculiar lethargy affected her all day. Her mind felt hazy and sluggish. She had no recollection of the day before, not even what she'd cooked for dinner. It was almost as if a portion of time had disappeared.

When Kevin came home for supper, goose pimples prickled her skin. She couldn't bear to look at him and avoided making eye contact. Her pulse raced while she served him. She sat down to eat in silence.

Kevin paused between forkfuls and said, "The man who milked the cows quit. Mike and my father are taking the afternoon shift, and I'm going to need your help for morning milking."

"What about Laura?" she asked, feeling a strange sense of déjà vu.

"My mother can watch her."

∽

Jessie rose at four a.m. to make up bottles of formula, and pack up diapers and a slumbering Laura for the short ride to the farm. She passed the sleeping child over to Maria when they reached the house, then Kevin gave her a set of overalls and boots to wear that were far too large. She covered her hair with a scarf and followed him out to the free-stall barn.

It was an enormous building filled with three-sided stalls bedded in sawdust. The open plan allowed the cows to roam at will—choosing to sleep, chew cud, or socialize as the spirit moved them. Most were sleeping deeply. A few lifted their eyelids and peeked through long lush eyelashes before quickly closing them again, feigning slumber.

The paths between the stalls were filled with manure, which emitted a foul odor that stung Jessie's nostrils as her rubber boots squished through it. It was her job to wake up the sleepy-headed Holsteins and herd them into a chute which funneled them through a door into the milking parlor.

This proved to be an arduous task. All of the black and white cows looked alike, and there were few volunteers. In the maze of open stalls, it was difficult to keep the cows that hadn't been milked separated from those that had. Although the air was freezing, Jessie had a hard time staying alert enough to keep an eye out for truants sneaking out of line.

When most of the cows had been milked, and those remaining were getting anxious to relieve their swollen udders, she saw the McKennas' elderly hired-hand, Cletus, shoving his way through the cows clustered in the doorway to the milking parlor.

Jessie breathed a sigh of relief, grateful to see another human being amid the alien sea of bovines.

Cletus was a simple old country Negro who'd never known anything other than farm work in all his born days. He could neither read nor write and didn't even know the year in which he'd been born. Kind brown eyes twinkled out of his weather-beaten face, muffled against the bitter January cold.

"Mornin', Miz Jessie," he said. "Kevin wants you in the milking parlor now. I'll finish driving in the herd."

Pushing past the remaining cows, Jessie managed to squeeze through into the parlor. She clambered over the iron railing and down into the sunken corridor which paralleled the milking stalls.

Kevin acknowledged her with a nod and pointed at the first enclosure. "This is the prep stall where the cows' udders are washed before moving along to a milking machine." He handed her a pair of rubber gloves, then indicated a bucket hanging on a bracket by the stall and told her to take out the sponge. When she grabbed hold of it, a pungent medicinal scent filled her nose.

Kevin pulled a lever that opened a gate allowing the next cow in line to enter the prep stall. "Wash the udder, and then wait until there's an empty milking stall before sending the cow down the line to me."

Kevin pulled another lever to release the forward gate so the cow could travel down the aisle to an empty stall. He hurried along the sunken corridor to close the aft gate behind the animal and pen her in, then showed Jessie how to attach the milking machine to the cow's udder. It grabbed the teats with a sucking sound. When the milk flow stopped, Kevin demonstrated the proper way to empty the rest of the udder by hand.

"Why do you do that?" she asked.

"It prevents problems and helps the cows produce better."

By the time the last Holstein was milked, Jessie was falling over from exhaustion. "Can I go now?"

"No, the milking parlor has to be washed down."

Kevin flushed the lines, then dragged out the power hose and showed her how to use it. He disappeared into the dairy.

❦

Maria had breakfast on the table when they finally reached the farmhouse. Pausing in the mudroom, they stripped off their boots and coveralls. Jessie removed her scarf. Her hair was sweaty and stunk like manure. Kevin got to the bathroom first. After he emerged, she went in to scrub her hands and face clean. When she finished, there was only one place left at the table, and it was right between Kevin and Mike.

After everyone said grace, Maria began passing around the platters of food. Kevin filled his plate, salted the eggs, and began discussing the morning's output of milk with his father. Mike reached past Jessie for the salt, brushing his arm across her breast.

She leaned away reflexively, a hot flush of embarrassment and irritation sweeping through her.

"Excuse me," Mike said with a guileless expression.

But she knew he had rubbed his arm against her breast deliberately and in a way no one else would notice.

⚮

Jessie told Ann about Mike's stunt during bowling Wednesday evening.

Ann laughed. "Boys will be boys. You've got to hand it to Mike, though. He's got some balls, rubbing your breast right in front of Kevin. Do you ever wonder how good Mike is in bed?"

"Ann!"

"I just asked. There's nothing wrong with fantasizing a little."

"I never thought about it," Jessie said, hoping no one overheard.

"Come on, seriously?"

"Honest."

Ann chuckled. "You just kill me sometimes."

She rolled her eyes. Sometimes she didn't get Ann either.

⚮

Jessie became so proficient at milking that Cletus returned to his old job of herding the cows. However, the early milking took a toll. Pregnancy drained Jessie's energy reserves, and the house soon began to show it. Every time Kevin complained, she looked him straight in the eye and asked how much longer it was going to take to hire another herdsman.

Kevin woke up with the flu one morning. "Damn! I feel like shit. Call the farm and tell Mike to take my place."

Mike grumbled but he had no choice. He was late getting to the milking parlor and arrived scowling. "Why haven't you started milking?"

"I'm not about to start the machinery without an experienced hand to depend on if a cow freaks out." She began her work at the prep stall and assisted at the two nearest milking stalls. Mike was in such a foul mood he barely spoke. She figured he was pissed because he'd be stuck milking night and day until Kevin was well enough to work.

Occasionally Mike brushed against her when things got hectic. They had to hurry past each other in the narrow corridor to attend to a milking machine malfunction or a cow getting upset, so it didn't come across as sexual. Nevertheless, she remained on guard. Toward the end, the pace slowed. Mike pulled a pack of cigarettes from his pocket. "Would you like a smoke?"

"No, thanks," she said, keeping her distance.

"Suit yourself." Mike lit up, took a deep drag, and blew the smoke toward her.

She fanned away the fumes, studiously concentrating on the cows.

Mike took another drag and moved closer. "Do you know why farm boys are such horny guys?"

Jessie ignored him.

"It's because we play with all these big tits every day," he said and snickered.

CHAPTER 17

BABYLON FARM

Shortly after Kevin's bout with the flu, Joe announced at breakfast that he'd hired a new herdsman. Jessie breathed a sigh of relief. "When does he start?"

Joe frowned as if she'd spoken out of turn. "His name's Bert Daugherty and his wife's name is Doris. They'll be here in about a week."

"Good," Kevin said. "I can hardly wait to get back to milking in the afternoon."

"No way," Mike said. "I'm keeping the afternoon shift."

"Like hell!"

Joe held up his hand. "That's enough. You'll both do as I say. Mike's done the morning milking enough years, he can keep the afternoon shift for now."

Kevin scowled and Mike grinned.

Jessie concealed her delight. She wouldn't have to have breakfast ready until Kevin was finished milking. If she was lucky, Maria would continue to feed him at the farm.

Kevin spoke up. "Dad, the landlord's been after me to buy the house, but he wants too much money for it. I'm not sure what we should do. I haven't been able to find another place close by to rent."

Joe allowed that might be a problem. He looked thoughtful for a moment. "Well, you mother's been after me to retire."

Kevin's eyes widened in surprise.

"Semi-retire," Joe said. "I'll help out three days a week so everyone in turn can have a day off."

Jessie did the math in her head. Three days meant Kevin, Mike and the new herdsman got one day a week off. Cletus was apparently too far down the pecking order to merit one.

Maria smiled indulgently at Joe. "If you truly want to semi-retire, we could buy a house in that new development on the outskirts of Mansfield. Otherwise, you'll never get away from the barn."

"Your mother's right, and if we move to town Kevin can move back here to stay on top of things."

"B-but I can't handle all the cooking and cleaning for Mike and Johnny," Jessie stammered.

Joe gave her a dirty look.

"She's right," Maria said. "It wouldn't be fair. I'll do the boys' laundry and cleaning. Since the office is right next to the family room, we could turn it into a kitchen and open up the wall between them. The boys can cook for themselves."

"That's a good idea," Kevin said. "We can build an office attached to the dairy, and it'll be easier to keep the records."

Everyone nodded in agreement except Jessie. She wasn't happy about the idea of living with her brothers-in-law. However, her mother was stuck feeding the horses and had been asking about the feasibility of moving them to the farm.

<hr />

That evening, Kevin informed Jessie that he expected her to freshly paint all the rooms in the small house reserved for the herdsman and his wife. "It has to be finished in a week's time. Mom will watch Laura."

He handed Jessie the list of colors that Doris Daugherty had chosen, and sent her to the hardware store for paint. Jessie didn't mind the job. She was a good painter and it was a break from Laura's constant fussing. She never understood how Maria managed to keep Laura so content in the playpen, until one day she discovered a piece of hard candy in Laura's mouth.

Jessie confronted Maria, explaining that it was dangerous, and asked her not to do it again. But Maria didn't take it very well.

Maria and Joe found a house they liked in the new development and bought it immediately. The day they moved out, Kevin informed Jessie over supper that they only had forty-eight hours to move their furniture to the farm.

"That's an awfully short time frame. What's the hurry?"

"I don't want to waste money paying the April rent."

"Could Mike help us out by doing the morning milking on moving day?"

"No, and I'm not asking. I expect you to handle the move."

"Some things are too heavy for me to lift," she protested.

"Then ask Rick. Isn't he home from college for spring break?"

Rick bitched, saying it wasn't fair unless one of Kevin's brothers lent a hand, and agreed to assist only if Johnny would too. Jessie hated to go begging to Johnny. He refused just as she expected. Finally, he gave in to her pleas and offered her a deal. "I'll help, but only if you write my history term paper."

"But that's cheating!"

"Come on, Jess. Mom and Dad are really going to be pissed off if I flunk high school again. You scratch my back, I'll scratch yours."

"Okay, okay," she said, resigned.

After the guys moved the furniture to the farm, Jessie took a box of odds and ends up to the attic for storage.

Fortunately, there was a full staircase leading to the attic and a landing at the top. She opened the attic door, wrinkling her nose at the stale smell. Dust motes swirled in the dim beams of light coming through the grimy windows. Cobwebs trailed from the rafters, floating with ghostly life in the draft coming up the stairs. Mouse droppings littered the floor, along with the desiccated bodies of dead flies and wasps. Cartons of forgotten junk mingled with pieces of forlorn furniture and an old steamer trunk.

Jessie put the box down and went over to investigate the trunk. Like Pandora, she couldn't resist opening the lid. The pungent scent of camphor rose from layers of tissue shrouding crinolines and brightly colored dancing dresses. Underneath those, she discovered a pink poodle skirt from the fifties. No doubt the apparel belonged to Kevin's sisters.

Closing the trunk, Jessie turned to go but accidentally knocked over a cardboard carton. A cigar box tumbled out and flipped open, dumping a packet of letters in the dust. The rubber-band disintegrated, scattering them across the floor. They were all addressed to Kevin in a feminine hand.

Jessie scooped them up and tried to put them back in their original order, based on the postmarks. Curiosity compelled her to open a few and read them. They were all from a girl named Louise. The very last one was a "Dear John" letter rejecting Kevin's marriage proposal. Jessie felt a pang of sympathy for him. The Louise he pined for didn't have the nerve to turn him down face to face, but at least she'd escaped marrying him.

⌒∽⌒

Kevin pushed his plate away, signaling that he was finished eating, and mentally assessed the number of seconds it took Jessie to jump up and remove it. Her alacrity was gratifying.

"If those horses of yours are going to stand around eating their heads off, they're going to have to be of some use."

"I don't understand," she said. "What would they do?"

"You could ride out to round the cows up for afternoon milking, instead of me having to do it on the tractor."

"I don't want to. I have to take care of Laura."

"It's an order. I'll stay inside and watch Laura."

Jessie rolled her eyes and sighed. Laura always took a nap around that time, otherwise Kevin wouldn't have come up with the scheme.

Well, at least she'd get to ride every day—even if rounding up cattle wasn't her idea of fun.

The cows were even less enthusiastic about evening milking than morning milking, and the pasture was large, with plenty of thickets to hide in. At first, Rio wasn't quite sure what to do and neither was she. They'd get half the group moving in one direction and the rest would take off in another. But before the week was out, Rio knew every cow in the herd. All Jessie had to do was give him his head and hang on tight while he scrambled through scrub and brambles to chase the truants home.

Jessie was glad Rio turned out to be such a good cowpony. The horse looked forward to their daily duels with the cows, but she missed her afternoon naps. Dogged by fatigue, she found it impossible to keep the farmhouse up to Maria's impeccable standards. This provided rich fodder for gossip among the McKenna women.

Once a week, Maria arrived with Mary Clare to clean Mike and Johnny's rooms and do their laundry. They kept up a running conversation as they worked and seldom paused long enough to say more than hi. They never stayed for coffee, claiming it wouldn't be fair to Kathleen, who was dutifully minding Little Charlie over at her house, so he wouldn't interfere with their work.

Maria and Mary Clare never offered to help Jessie with anything, and the mother-daughter chitchat only served to remind her of how lonely she was. Her own mother couldn't spend much time with her, and her friends were in college or working.

One evening, Jessie came downstairs after putting Laura to bed and discovered Mike and Dennis cleaning a pound of marijuana on the kitchen table. She stopped in her tracks, dumbfounded.

Mike was lighting a joint he'd rolled to smooth out operations. The pungent scent of marijuana smoke filled the air. He took a drag and held out the reefer. "Care to join us?"

"No," she said and turned to leave.

Dennis followed her with his gaze. "Man, what a nice ass."

"Yeah, but her tits aren't that big," Mike remarked.

"All you need is a handful," Dennis said.

Jessie ignored their comments and kept walking. She was glad the new kitchen was almost completed. But while they'd soon be out of her kitchen, any real privacy was a thing of the past.

Dennis was in and out so often he practically lived there. Johnny's good friends, Dave Walker and Jimmy Fremont, came over frequently to smoke pot. On weekends, noisy parties kept her up late, and the only difference between the farmhouse and a brothel was that the girls weren't charging money for sex.

One night, a drunken couple staggered into the master bedroom and almost got into bed with her. She ordered them out and locked the door. Thankfully, the nursery was only accessible through the master bedroom, otherwise she'd have to worry about people fornicating in there.

Later that night, she was awakened by the sound of fists pounding on the door. Wondering if a partygoer had gone berserk from drugs, she clutched the blanket closer, pulse racing. The pounding became so violent, she feared the doorjamb would splinter and the latch would give way.

"Open the door, goddammit," Kevin shouted.

Shaking, she scurried to unlock it.

Kevin shoved her aside and stomped into the room. "If I ever find the bedroom door locked again, I'll break it down."

A few days after that episode, Jessie developed an itchy, flaky rash. It soon became so irritating she called her obstetricians' office and was able to get an appointment with Dr. Lieberman.

When Lieberman learned she was pregnant, he chided her for not coming in sooner. After he examined her and she mentioned her sleep deprivation, he diagnosed the rash as stress-related and prescribed Valium, along with a salve he said would be safe to use during pregnancy.

Jessie took the Valium as directed until the rash went away, then decided to stop using it. The artificial balm it conveyed was too surreal.

A few weeks later, she found herself tossing and turning for so long, she decided to give in and take a Valium just to get some sleep. She'd left the pills in the first-aid cabinet in the kitchen the last time she used them. Normally she avoided going downstairs once dressed for bed, but tonight she was desperate. She threw a light robe over her nightgown and headed down the stairs.

The door to the family room was closed, but a thin line of light gleamed underneath. She moved quietly along the hall to the kitchen and opened the cabinet to get her pills. She was relieved to see they were still where she'd left them; there were so many other drugs flowing through the house, Valium probably wasn't worth stealing.

She downed a pill with some water, then washed and dried the glass and put it away. She flicked off the light and walked down the hall to the staircase.

The door to the family room flew open and banged against the wall.

Mike emerged gripping a beer bottle by the neck. He leaned on the doorjamb and eyed her appraisingly. "What have we here?"

She froze like a deer in a spotlight. An icy tremor snaked along her spine.

Swaying, Mike took a swig from the bottle. "Hey, Dennis, come here and look at this."

Dennis staggered to the doorway. He looked at Jessie and took a pull on his beer.

Prickling with fear, she stared at him and clutched her robe closer just above the bulge in her abdomen.

"Nah," Dennis said, shaking his head, then stumbled back into the family room.

Mike's mouth curved into a sly grin. He laughed wickedly.

Jessie ran then, as if released from a spell, and fled up the staircase, heart pounding. She slammed the bedroom door closed and locked it. Shaking, she jumped into bed and wrapped herself in the covers like a protective shield.

Mike might make a lewd jest at her expense, but her pregnancy wasn't so far advanced that her body lacked all allure. There was no telling what Mike might do while intoxicated if he lusted after her. Thank God, Dennis said no.

What if he'd said yes?

Jessie stared at the door. She wasn't sure who to fear most: Mike or Kevin? Steeling herself, she rose and unlocked it.

Sandy Hanlon drove her yellow Volkswagen up the driveway of the McKenna farm, hoping to find Jessie at home. On the seat beside her was a box with two dog bowls, a leash and a brush. A large bag of dog food sat on the floor. Sprawled across the back seat was an enormous shaggy-haired hound.

Parking in the shade of a tree, she left the windows down, commanded Dusty to stay, and got out of the car. She climbed the steps of the front porch and rang the doorbell.

Jessie answered the door. "Sandy! It's so nice to see you. Come on in."

Sandy followed Jessie down the hall into the kitchen. Over coffee they reminisced about Pony Club.

"I'm qualified for my 'A' rating now," Sandy said. "I sure missed riding with you in the team competitions last year."

Jessie sighed. "Well, after Laura was born I was too busy. I even had to give up playing softball all last summer."

"It doesn't look like you'll be playing softball this summer either."

"No, but I still bowl with Ann every Wednesday evening. Luckily the league will end for the summer break before I get too big to bend over, or I'd have to pay for a substitute."

"That's good," Sandy said and sipped her coffee. "I don't suppose you've heard my brother's wife left him?"

"Oh no! What happened this time?"

"Drugs again," she said with disgust. "Pierce had to put the house up for sale because he and Meg couldn't make the mortgage payments. Meg said it was the last straw and left. Nobody really blames her."

"What's Pierce going to do?"

"Mom and Dad begged him to go back into rehab, and he agreed in hope of winning Meg back."

"Gosh, it's too bad about Meg, but I'm glad Pierce is going for treatment."

"That's why I'm here. I need your help."

"Oh, what can I do?"

"It's Pierce's dog. He's a Scottish Deerhound. They're huge, and Mom's been scared to death of dogs since she was bitten by one as a child. Anyway, we were hoping you'd give him a home. Pierce's rehab will take a while, then he'll have to live in a halfway house, and there's no telling how long it will be before he'll be back on his feet."

Jessie didn't know what to say. She missed Blackjack and Tar Baby, but Kevin hated pets. She saw hope brimming in Sandy's eyes. How could she let her down? "Is the dog safe to have around children?"

"Yes, he's just great with kids."

"Okay, I'll take him. What's his name?"

"His registered name is Moon Dust, but Pierce calls him Dusty for short. Come on outside and I'll introduce you."

A homely, shaggy face poked out of the window of the Volkswagen. Sandy opened the door and Dusty jumped out, wagging his tail. He looked like an enormous, incredibly hairy greyhound. Dusty was certainly friendly, but he'd probably eat her out of house and home.

"Let's take him into the house," Jessie said, wondering how pissed off Kevin was going to be when he came in for supper.

Once the dog was settled, Sandy thanked her and left.

Watching through the window, Jessie saw Mike come out of the barn and head for Sandy's car. He stopped her before she got in and began chatting her up. Sandy came back inside all excited, saying Mike had asked her out on a date. Jessie tried to warn her about his reputation, but Sandy said not to worry. She'd be careful.

⁓

Kevin removed his boots and coveralls in the mudroom. He headed for his seat at the table and stopped in his tracks. "What the hell is that?" he exclaimed, pointing at the giant hound lying on the braided rug by the woodstove.

Dusty raised his head and looked at Kevin. Jessie swallowed the lump of fear that rose in her throat. "Sandy's brother is going into rehab. Mrs. Hanlon's terrified of dogs, so they can't keep him. Sandy was desperate. I couldn't say no."

Kevin frowned. If he sent the dog back, he'd look like a creep, which would be bad for his public image. "All right, he can stay, but he sure as hell isn't living in my house. Get him out of here—now!"

⁓

Cletus walked to the house to fetch his supper tray and spied the huge hound in the backyard. He knocked politely and waited by the door. When Jessie handed him the tray, he asked what kind of dog it was.

"He's a Scottish Deerhound."

Cletus looked flummoxed. "I ain't never heard tell of them kind of dogs, Miz Jessie."

"Me either, until today. His name's Dusty. My friend Sandy needed somebody to take him. Kevin won't let him live in the house. I hope he doesn't mind sleeping in the barn."

After Cletus finished his supper, he took some leftover meat scraps down to the yard. Squatting, he put the scraps on the ground and waited.

Dusty eyed him curiously and then walked over.

Cletus watched as he gobbled the beef down. When Dusty was finished, he sniffed the grass for more, then began to lick Cletus' hand. Tentatively, Cletus reached out and stroked the dog's head. He seemed like a friendly enough beast.

"Come on, Dusty, follow me. You can sleep on my couch."

The next morning, Bert asked Cletus about the huge hound following him to the barn.

"He be Miz Jessie's new dog. His name's Dusty."

"That's an awful big dog. What kind is he?"

"Miz Jessie says he's a Scottish Deerhound, but I don't rightly know what that be."

"What's the matter with you, Cletus? Them there dogs as hunt deer in Scotchland," Bert replied, pleased that he'd one-upped his co-worker with his astuteness.

When Kevin wasn't around, Jessie let Dusty into the kitchen so Laura could coo over him and feed him crackers. She always slipped him out the door before Kevin saw him. In the afternoons he ran along when she rounded up the cows.

One day Jessie let Dusty inside as usual and went over to the cabinet to get some crackers. The screen door slammed in the mudroom. Pulse racing, she looked for a quick way to hide the dog. Kathleen marched in and a cool wave of relief flowed over her.

"What's this I hear about you rounding up the cows on horseback? Is it true?"

"Yes."

Kathleen stared at her. "Are you out of your mind? What if you fall? You might have a miscarriage!"

Jessie knew she couldn't disobey Kevin's orders, and Kathleen's remark put her on the defensive. "I'm a good rider, and it's the only time I get to ride my horse."

"Even the best riders can fall."

"*Me* fall off *my* horse?" Jessie laughed. "Not a chance."

"If you won't listen to reason, I'm going to tell Kevin to put a stop to this." Kathleen spun and strode out to the barn.

❧

When school let out for the summer, Kathleen began bringing her kids over to swim. Jessie welcomed the idea at first, thinking she and Kathleen would spend time getting to know one another better while the kids were swimming. But Kathleen acted like Jessie was supposed to be a built-in lifeguard service. She dropped Sally and the boys off then went on her merry way.

It was impossible to keep Frank Jr., Billy, Brady and Doug out of mischief, but Jessie's complaints fell on deaf ears. Between the heat and the extra kids to clean up after, it was shaping up to be another miserable summer.

Near the end of June, a record-breaking heat wave blanketed the state for nine straight weeks. By the end of August, the baby had grown so large Jessie could hardly breathe. It seemed like the summer and the pregnancy would never end.

Late one afternoon, in the first week of September, a cold front came sweeping through, sending temperatures plunging thirty degrees in only a few hours. After Jessie finished washing the supper dishes and putting Laura to bed, she stepped into the master bath and showered off the accumulated sweat of the day. What bliss to feel clean and cool again.

A refreshing breeze blew through the windows as the outside temperature continued to drop. Jessie put on a long, floral, muslin dress that she'd bought at the hippie shop, then applied makeup and curled her hair. Feeling like a new woman, she headed downstairs.

The guys were all out for the evening. It was nice to have some peace and quiet instead of enduring a raucous party, but it was lonely not having anyone, particularly a caring husband, to talk to. Although she would have liked to settle down with a good book, she hadn't had a chance to get to the library. Going anywhere was just too exhausting.

She switched on the TV and the canned-laughter of a sitcom filled the void. Settling herself on Maria's gold brocade sofa, Jessie rearranged the pillows until she felt comfortable. Her body ached with Braxton-Hicks contractions, her feet hurt, and her diaphragm was compressed. She could hardly wait for the baby to come out just so she could breathe.

Before long, the house grew noticeably chilly. Now that she'd gotten comfortable, she was reluctant to rise and close the windows. But the TV show following the sitcom was so stupid, she forced herself to get up and change the channel.

A knock sounded at the front door, startling her.

Jessie walked into the hall and froze.

Through the lace-covered panes of the door, she saw the profile of a man illuminated by the eerie yellow glow of the porch light. He was a total stranger.

Fear raced along her spine. Why would a stranger show up at an out-of-the-way farm late on a Friday night?

The doors were never locked, and she was too heavy with child to run and lock them all now. There were several ways for the stranger to get inside if he wanted to, and she could see him peering through the curtain. He already knew she was home.

Nerving herself, Jessie opened the door.

There were actually two men on the porch. The one who'd knocked was medium height with shoulder-length dark-brown hair. He was wearing an Australian bush hat and a plaid flannel shirt open halfway down his chest, revealing a mat of curly hair. His faded jeans were stuffed into metal-studded motorcycle boots.

His appearance was hardly reassuring; he looked like he might have a knife hidden in one of his boots.

The other man was younger and taller. His sandy hair was neatly styled and just brushed the collar of his shirt. He wore a camel-colored sport jacket, brown slacks, and low-heeled brown leather boots.

He was a very handsome man.

The dark-haired fellow spoke first. "Good evening, ma'am," he said, inclining his head slightly and touching his fingers to the brim of his hat.

The handsome one stood there quietly studying her.

They weren't exactly Tweedledee and Tweedledum, but they were certainly an odd combination.

Jessie suppressed a bubble of laughter. "I'm sorry, but the men are all gone. Who did you come to see?"

"We came to see you," the dark-haired man replied.

Her mouth opened in surprise.

The dark-haired man smiled. "I'm Tom Hamilton, and this is Sam Leland."

The handsome one inclined his head, but remained silent.

Tom continued the introduction. "We're friends of Kevin's. We just got in from the West Coast and heard he was married. So we came over to see what kind of woman could hold Kevin long enough to get him to the altar."

Tom and Sam looked at each other, then back at her. "We didn't expect you to be so pretty and so... so pregnant," Tom stammered.

Sam smiled. "Pregnant women have a special kind of beauty."

Jessie hardly knew what to say.

"Come on, Tom, stop staring," Sam chided. "We've already taken up enough of the lady's time."

"Good night, ma'am," Tom said, touching his fingers to the brim of his hat. Then, as one, they turned and walked away.

Mystified, Jessie closed the door. *You meet the most unusual people among Kevin's friends*, she thought, and went upstairs to bed.

CHAPTER 18

THE PARALLAX VIEW

The contractions that plagued Jessie earlier woke her around midnight. When the cramps became too uncomfortable for her to remain in bed, she went downstairs. After thirty minutes of escalating labor pains, she decided to start calling the local bars to see if she could locate Kevin. She had no luck, but left messages at each establishment saying Kevin needed to call home.

At last the phone rang. Jessie picked up the receiver with a sense of relief, thinking it was Kevin, but it was Mike.

"Is something wrong with the cows?"

"No. I'm in labor, and I don't know where Kevin is."

"I'll see if I can find him," Mike said and hung up.

Jessie paced, timing her contractions with increasing anxiety as the hours passed. The phone rang again, but it was only Mike checking to see if Kevin had shown up. By four a.m. the contractions were coming too fast to wait any longer. Jessie reluctantly dialed her parents' number.

Mike walked in a few minutes later and volunteered to stay with Laura until his mother could come over in the morning.

Kevin arrived shortly after that. "What the hell do you think you're doing phoning bars all over the county leaving messages for me to call home? Do you have any idea how bad that looks?"

She narrowed her eyes. "Do you have any idea how bad it looks to have to call my parents to take me to the hospital, because it's after four and you weren't home?"

"You called your parents? You stupid little fool, how dare you embarrass me by not waiting until—"

The sound of a car door slamming cut short Kevin's tirade. He greeted her parents warmly. "I'm sorry Jessie bothered you, but since Mike's volunteered to stay with Laura, why don't you come with us to the hospital."

Jessie's parents stuck to innocuous small talk during the drive, and asked no embarrassing questions. She was a little surprised that they didn't ask Kevin why he'd been out so late with a pregnant wife near term. But they were polite people, and probably thought it wasn't appropriate to discuss something like that on the way to the hospital.

Jessie had specifically asked for Dr. Lieberman to handle the delivery this time. He was a bit more progressive than Dr. Klein.

After her previous experience with the perils of anesthesia, she had decided to opt for natural childbirth. Kevin volunteered to stay with her. She suspected it was only for show because he wanted to impress her parents.

Her suspicions were confirmed as soon as the nurse left.

"It'd better be a boy this time," Kevin said. "You know, in some cultures, a man can divorce his wife if she doesn't produce a son."

"You creep!" she gasped out between contractions. "How can you say something like that, when I'm going through agony to bring your child into this world?"

He chuckled. "I like seeing you in pain. It was all Eve's fault anyway. That's why God punished women with pain during childbirth."

"Get out! I'm not listening to anymore of this!"

Kevin laughed. "No. I'm having too much fun."

"I said get the *hell* out!"

A nurse pulled back the curtain. "Sir, I'm going to have to ask you to leave. It's important to keep the patient calm during labor. It's... er... getting rather loud in here."

Kevin nodded and followed the RN out. Her next words floated clearly back to Jessie. "I'm sorry, sir, they just get like that sometimes."

When the nurse returned, Jessie asked if her mother could stay with her instead.

"It's not standard procedure. I'll have to ask Dr. Lieberman's permission."

Jessie glared. "Then you'd better get going."

Liz arrived a few minutes later. "Kevin said he couldn't stand seeing you in so much pain, and I'm not sure I can either. You don't have to be a martyr—it's the twentieth century, you know. If it gets too bad, promise me you'll take something."

"Okay, Mom." But labor progressed normally this time. Despite the pain, Jessie remained in control.

When she was moved to the delivery room, she still had to put her feet up in stirrups. The nurse put a wedge-shaped board under her back and a pillow under her head. She felt far more comfortable than she had delivering Laura.

The contractions were just as agonizing, but this time Jessie could put her full strength into the effort when the doctor told her to push. She could feel the baby sliding backwards after every squeeze—the angle was wrong with her legs up—but each time the baby moved further forward than backward.

Jessie turned deep inside herself as she rode the painful waves of contractions. She felt Lieberman inject a local anesthetic to prepare for the episiotomy, but she was too far gone to object. The rhythm quickened and the pain dimmed as a strange altered state enveloped her. In her final efforts, she became dissociated from the sterile room.

She was floating in space. She was the Earth. She was Nature herself bringing forth life by the power of the Creator.

With a burst of amniotic fluid, the baby slid out and was caught by the doctor.

"Congratulations, Jessie, it's a boy."

But she knew that already because God had shown her in a dream, just like He had with Laura.

Jessie was up in the clouds, miles high. So this was it, *this* was what it was all about. *What a rush!*

"Congratulations, Mr. McKenna, you have a son."

"Thank you, Doctor," Kevin said and stepped into Jessie's line of sight, causing her to crash from the high. If she'd known someone had sent for him, she'd have had him removed.

Liz beamed at her. "Congratulations, honey."

The nurse carried the baby over for Jessie to see. Pink and lively, the infant regarded her with an expression of wonder. Jessie smiled back.

There was no long stay in the recovery room this time. She wasn't wiped out from the anesthesia, and they took her straight to her room. Her parents and Kevin were allowed in as soon as the nurse had her settled. Jessie didn't really want to talk to Kevin, and he soon left for a smoke with her father.

The nurse brought the baby in for his first feeding. Jessie had been considering breastfeeding and broached the subject.

Liz looked nonplussed. "What do you want to go to all that trouble for? You'll never have any time to yourself. Women of my day praised God for baby formula. Besides, it's just so... *primitive.*"

The RN passed over the bottle and Jessie took it, too intimidated to try nursing in front of her mother's disapproving gaze.

Kevin insisted on calling their new baby Joseph after his father. Given her father-in-law's coldness toward her, Jessie wasn't thrilled with the idea. However, she had no choice but to go along.

A few days later, Jessie was discharged from the hospital with Joey. Silently cursing Dr. Lieberman's decision to do an episiotomy, Jessie gritted her teeth and tried not to cry out when the car hit bumps on the rough country roads. She sighed with relief when they finally reached the farm.

Kevin took Joey from her arms so she could get out of the car, then handed him back. Jessie thought Kevin was going to carry in the baby stuff but he walked straight to the house.

Maria, Joe, Mike and Johnny crowded into the mudroom for their first glimpse of the baby before Jessie could get him into the house proper. Everyone extended congratulations to Kevin. After a cursory look at Joey, they chattered on, heaping praise on Kevin, who basked in their attention.

It irritated Jessie that they were ignoring the baby, while acting as if Kevin had produced him single handedly. She couldn't move into the house proper because they were blocking the way. A wave of fatigue swept over her, and she began to feel light-headed. Her father-in-law was the closest person to her. She extended the baby toward him.

"I've carried him for nine months already, wouldn't you like to hold him now?"

Joe looked startled. Jessie pushed the baby into his arms and hurried outside to suck in fresh air. Once her dizziness passed, she got the baby things out of the car and took them inside. Everyone had moved into the kitchen, and Maria was holding the baby. Jessie put Joey's bottle in the fridge, then carried Joey into the living room where the bassinet was set up near the sofa. To her surprise, Mike followed along.

"Congratulations," he said, catching up to her side. "It looks like you did all right."

"Thanks," she replied, touched by his sudden solicitude.

Mike moved around to the far side of the bassinet. Too late, Jessie realized that the scooped neckline of her dress afforded him a generous view of her bosom as she laid the baby down. Mike stared at her breasts with such naked lust, Jessie almost blushed.

"I'd sure like to suck on one of those," he said.

She drew in her breath, too stunned to come up with a tart put-down. He stared into her eyes then nonchalantly walked away.

Maria brought Laura downstairs when she woke from her nap.

"Hi, sweetie," Jessie said, eager to hold and reassure the child she'd had to leave behind. Laura ran to the sofa and scrambled onto her lap. After a hug and kiss, Jessie gently put her down. "Mommy missed you, honey, but Mommy's tummy's sore. Nonna will pick you up and show you your new little brother."

Maria lifted Laura onto her hip and took her over to the bassinet. "Look, Laura, see baby?"

Laura eyed her new brother with amazement and reached out to touch him. "Be-be," she said, but Joey slept on.

"Baby's sleeping," Maria said. "Mommy needs to rest too. Nonna's going to take you to the kitchen and fix you lunch."

Liz came over to relieve Maria in the evening, and was planning to stay overnight for a few days. Jessie was glad because she felt more comfortable having her mother there. At bedtime, Kevin started upstairs and Liz had to remind him to carry Jessie up the steps.

Jessie was hurt that Kevin hadn't remembered she wasn't supposed to climb up or down stairs for a few days. But when he picked her up in his arms, she felt an unexpected surge of desire. She didn't know why she still found him so attractive; the way he treated her, half the time she couldn't stand him.

When Jessie woke in the morning, Kevin was already gone. Liz had taken care of the baby through the night and brought her a steaming cup of coffee.

"Aren't you glad you decided against breastfeeding and were able to get a good night's sleep?"

"Yeah, kind of," Jessie said. "But it's got to beat warming up a bottle in the middle of the night and lugging baby bottles everywhere you go, then worrying about keeping them sterile and the extra formula cold until you need it—or the baby getting colic."

Liz rolled her eyes. "You can take all this back to nature stuff the hippies started too far. If you breastfeed, you can't go anywhere. After all, you can't whip a boob out in public and feed the kid. Besides, you're living with your brothers-in-law. Do you want to stay in your room all day?"

Jessie sighed. "You're right."

Liz nodded. "Now enjoy your coffee while I go find Kevin to carry you downstairs."

After an inordinate amount of time passed, Mike appeared in the bedroom doorway.

Jessie's mouth opened in dismay. "Where's Kevin?"

"He's harvesting out in the field. Your mom asked me to carry you downstairs. I told her I'd be happy to oblige."

No doubt, she thought, but she was hardly in a position to refuse his help.

Feeling next to naked in her long satin robe, Jessie summoned what poise she could muster and walked over to Mike. She hesitated before reaching up and putting her arms around his neck. He lifted her into his arms and her milk-laden breasts pressed against the hard muscles of his chest. It was difficult not to think of what he dreamed of doing. Her feelings were suddenly confusing.

⁂

Liz soon had to return to work, so Maria obligingly took over. Jessie preferred having her mother around but Maria was more familiar with running the farmhouse, and Jessie was grateful for her help. It was a relief not to have to handle the full brunt of caring for a newborn and a toddler, as well as all the cooking and housework.

Kevin acted like a changed man. Perhaps her prayers were finally being answered. He stayed home and played with Laura in the evenings, and talked baby-talk to Joey. Home life took on a similitude of domestic bliss. But, much to Jessie's disappointment, Kevin reverted to his old habits as soon as his mother stopped staying overnight.

Thereafter, Mike began to linger at home in the evening and played with Laura while Jessie fed Joey his bottle.

Jessie was grateful for Mike's company and felt safer when he was around. She hadn't forgotten the fright she'd experienced the night Tom Hamilton and Sam Leland showed up on the doorstep. Nevertheless, she was surprised that Mike was taking such an interest in the children and said so. He told her he was looking forward to having a wife and children someday. Guiltily, she wondered what it would be like to be married to Mike instead of Kevin. It would certainly be nice to have a husband who stayed home in the evenings and played with the children.

❧

Jessie's spirits were high as she drove herself to the six-week checkup scheduled with Dr. Lieberman. She could hardly wait to have sex again after the enforced abstinence she'd endured the past few months. Although she wasn't sure why, she still found Kevin arousing and hadn't given up hope for her marriage.

The warm breeze made it hard to believe October was already here, but the day promised to be a hot one.

The checkup showed she had healed properly from giving birth and it was safe to resume marital relations. She drove home in a buoyant mood admiring the rich reds and bright yellows of the autumn leaves arrayed against a perfect blue sky.

Just as she was putting the finishing touches on lunch, Kevin walked into the kitchen. "How'd your checkup go?"

Jessie picked up a pitcher to pour him some iced tea. "Dr. Lieberman said everything is fine, and we can start having sex."

"What do you mean *we?*" Kevin said. "I never stopped having sex."

Her grip tightened on the pitcher and she put it down slowly, feeling strangely disconnected. She stared off into space, too stunned by the callous nature of his revelation to speak.

Kevin chuckled. "I don't know what you're going to do for sex, but good luck." He turned and headed for the back door.

Jessie grabbed the pitcher and hurled it toward him, as he disappeared through the doorway to the mudroom. The pitcher crashed against the doorframe and exploded, just as Kathleen's husband Frank was about to step into the kitchen.

He jumped back. "Holy smokes! What did I do to deserve that?"

Jessie glared at him, chest heaving, too angry for words.

"Okay, I'm leaving—I'm leaving," Frank said, then turned and spoke to Kevin, who'd been hiding off to the side. "No wonder you didn't go in there."

The screen door slammed behind Frank, and Kevin peeked into the kitchen. "Make sure you don't forget to clean up the mess," he said. "If I were you, I'd get to it right away."

He left, whistling a merry tune.

Jessie regarded the slush of tea and glass marring the once spotless floor with resignation. Too bad she'd missed hitting Kevin—it would have made cleaning up the mess worthwhile. But she'd never forget the look on Frank's face, and knew he'd be telling the tale for weeks to come in bars all over the county.

That evening, Jessie put the children to bed feeling irritable and depressed. Kevin was taking a shower in preparation to go out, and she couldn't even pretend it might be for a farm organization meeting or civic function.

She went downstairs wondering what to do about it.

The heady scent of marijuana filled the hall. Johnny and his friends, Jimmy Fremont and Dave Walker, were in the family room smoking pot with Mike and Dennis.

"Hey, Jess, come in and join us," Johnny called through the open door as she started past. Dennis smiled and waved her inside. She hesitated, then went in. What else did she have to do this evening? Getting high might take some of the pain away.

Dennis held out the reefer. "Here, babe, take a hit."

Mike watched Jessie as she took the joint from Dennis and inhaled. This was the first time the ice princess had stepped into the den to smoke dope, and he reckoned the odds of a thaw were starting to shift in his favor.

A couple of hits made Jessie feel better, but she didn't want to smoke too much. She left and headed upstairs in a pleasant glow. Maybe she could seduce Kevin before he was fully dressed.

She entered the bedroom and saw that Kevin was still in his underwear. He pulled a shirt out of the closet. She walked over and ran her fingers up his back.

"Get away from me," he said, pushing her aside. "I know what you're trying to do."

She retreated to the rocking chair in the corner. Kevin quickly finished dressing. He turned to leave, then paused and looked back. "You're too fat. If you want to have sex with me, lose ten pounds."

Jessie jumped up and slammed the door behind him. *Too fat? Lose ten pounds?* She didn't weigh that much. In fact, she thought she looked pretty damn good after having two kids right in a row.

Jessie plopped on the bed, angrily kicked off her shoes, and started to undress. She might as well get ready for bed. She stripped off her bra and panties, then reached for the skin cream and propped her leg up on the bed to smooth it on. Catching a glimpse of herself in the mirror, she paused to look.

Her belly wasn't perfectly flat anymore, but it wasn't bad. She could work on that and be back to normal in no time. Her skin was still beautiful—not one stretch mark and not an ounce of cellulite. Her muscle tone was good. She might weigh a little more, but her breasts were bigger, too.

Jessie went over to the full-length mirror and analyzed her body closely. She'd overheard Jimmy and Dave saying she was a real fox, and she didn't think Dennis would find anything wrong with the figure reflected in the mirror.

She thought about the way Mike looked at her the day she'd come home from the hospital. She cupped her breasts in her hands and began to massage them like she knew he wanted to. It was a good thing there were so many people in the house tonight, otherwise she might do something rash.

CHAPTER 19

DARK SIDE OF THE MOON

Mike pulled one of Kevin's beers out of the refrigerator and popped the cap. He took a swig and headed for the family room, wearing a cocky grin.

A tingle of desire shot through Jessie as he passed by. *God, he's beautiful!* The way his hair curled on his neck, the texture of his skin, the supple movement of his muscles—all of these, and more, took her breath away.

Nothing but a man could quench her burning desires. The fact that Kevin was keeping her at arm's length was driving her crazy. She'd fallen in love with sex more so than him; otherwise she never would have married. Everyone was getting some but her.

No matter how exhausting her daily routine, at night her body's sexual privation left her restive and unable to sleep. She lay in bed imagining what would happen if she walked down the hall to Mike's room. She told herself it was incest, taboo, *verboten*, but it didn't stop her from fantasizing about it.

Jessie resolved to lose ten pounds before she did something she knew she'd live to regret. She cut back on food drastically and performed callisthenic exercises daily. Fortunately, Kevin started having sex with her before her resolve completely crumbled. It took the worst edge off her lust for his brother. Even though Kevin's use of her tended to be sporadic, it gave her renewed hope that their marriage would work.

❧

The holidays rolled around, and Jessie's spirits brightened at the prospect of attending a party at Kathleen and Frank's. She could dress up a bit and spend time with Kevin while he was on his best behavior. If she was lucky, they might get home early enough to make love.

When they arrived at the party, Kathleen was already ensconced in the kitchen with her girlfriends and Mary Clare. Charlie was manning the welcoming committee with Frank, and fetching drinks for new arrivals from the kitchen.

Mike showed up without Sandy, and Jessie was disappointed that she wouldn't have a friend to talk to. Johnny arrived accompanied by his new best girlfriend, Traci.

After introductions, Kevin gave Johnny a conspiratorial smile. "So now we know why you've been so busy lately," he said, making the petite brunette blush.

The bell chimed, and Frank opened the door to Tom Hamilton. "Hey, glad you could make it! Come on in and let me get you a beer. Where's Sam?"

"Sam sends his regrets," Tom said. "He had a prior engagement."

Jessie felt a twinge of disappointment. The moment she saw Tom walk in, her heart lifted at the prospect that Sam was coming too. He'd been so charming the night they first met; she'd never forget how good he made her feel when he said pregnant women had a special kind of beauty.

Kevin and Mike went downstairs to play pool. Frank brought Tom a beer and they started talking football with Dale and Bubba, the husbands of Kathleen's friends.

Charlie was monopolizing Johnny and Traci, so Jessie decided she might as well fix herself another drink.

Inside the kitchen, a matronly brunette and a blonde with a bouffant hairdo were sitting at the table chatting with Kathleen and Mary Clare.

Kathleen took a sip of her drink. "Has anyone seen this month's *Playgirl*?"

The blonde shook her head. "No, but I'd sure like to. I heard the centerfold was something else."

The heavyset brunette giggled. "LuAnn, you'd better not let Dale catch you looking at another man's cock!"

"Maybe if I saw more of Dale's, I wouldn't have to," LuAnn said, and the others burst out laughing.

Jessie finished fixing her drink and turned to leave.

The brunette whispered something to Kathleen.

"Wait, Jessie," Kathleen said. "Let me introduce you to my friends, Ruby and LuAnn." The brunette nodded and the blonde inclined her head. "Jessie's married to my brother Kevin. They had their second child less than four months ago."

LuAnn looked incredulous. "You're kidding, right?"

"No."

Ruby's eyes widened. "Ooo la la, I didn't look that good after my first, much less the second."

Mary Clare shook her head. "How do you do it, Jessie? It's not fair. Nobody has the right to have two babies so close together and still look as good as you."

"Mary Clare!" Kathleen exclaimed. "Don't be rude."

"I'm not being rude. I'm green with envy, and I'm not afraid to admit it. Besides, it's a compliment to have someone envy your figure—isn't it, Jessie?"

She was amused by Mary Clare's frankness, but felt uncomfortable about being the center of attention.

"Come on, tell me how you did it."

Jessie shrugged. "Diet and exercise."

"What kind of exercises? Show us some."

"Not now."

"Please," Kathleen appealed, "we all want to know how you did it."

Anticipation filled their eyes, as if she held the key to a wonderful feminine secret. There weren't any men in the room and she was wearing slacks, so a demonstration wouldn't be indecent.

"All right," she said and began with a simple exercise, then performed a more difficult one.

Mary Clare groaned in exasperation. "I couldn't do that in a million years. How can you expect me to put my leg up alongside my head?"

"You asked me to show you what exercises I did."

"Show us something else."

"Okay," she said. "This one's for firming your buttocks." She knelt and demonstrated each move slowly. "It'll seem hard at first, because you're really using your muscles, but it's easy to learn."

The women started to giggle. She thought they were laughing at the exercise, then realized they were looking past her toward the dining room. She scrambled to her feet and turned around. Tom was standing just inside the doorway.

"Wow," he said. "So that's how you manage to look so great."

She flushed, mortified, then picked up her drink and walked out. Tom followed on her heels.

"I'm sorry," he said. "I didn't mean to embarrass you. I know it's rude to stare—I-I just couldn't help myself," he stuttered. "You're... you're so... so put together. I could really go for a girl like you."

"Thank you," she replied, feeling uncomfortable. "Excuse me, but I need to talk to Traci."

Jessie hurried off to the family room.

Johnny and Traci were standing just inside the doorway talking to Charlie. They hadn't managed to get away from him yet. Unable to enter, Jessie leaned on the doorjamb. She smiled at Traci. "How long have you and Johnny been dating?"

"Just since homecoming, but I've known him since I made the cheerleading squad my sophomore year."

Jessie wondered if Traci's parents knew how old Johnny was. In the lull, she could hear what he was saying to Charlie. "That's one fine bowtie you got there, brother-in-law. I'd sure like to get me one."

Charlie swelled with pride. "You can't buy 'em like this anymore."

"I didn't think so," Johnny said, winking at the girls.

Jessie sensed someone coming up behind her. A warm male body pressed against her back. Mike spoke, "I've been admiring that bowtie myself. It's a damn shame you can't get 'em anymore."

Jessie wasn't sure what to do. She couldn't move away from Mike without stepping right into Traci's face, but having Mike so close was disturbing.

Traci picked up the thread of conversation. "I like those new high-waisted jeans that are in style, don't you?"

"Yes," Jessie said. Mike leaned into her, pushing her tight against the doorjamb. The sharp edge bit into her shoulder, but she tried not to let her discomfort show.

Traci chattered on. "I bought five pairs at the mall the other day. The department store was having a terrific sale—"

"Coming through," Frank hollered, and everyone moved at last.

With a sigh of relief, Jessie moved to the couch and lit a cigarette to steady herself. A few seconds later, Mike sat beside her. "Can I bum a smoke?"

"You have your own in your pocket."

"I want to try your brand."

She smoked nonfilters which he didn't like, so the innuendo wasn't lost on her—though no one else in the room was likely to get the salacious implication. But if she refused, it might attract undue attention.

She slipped a cigarette out of the pack and passed it over.

Mike smiled, then grabbed hold of her hand to light up off of her own cigarette. That rattled her.

Looking into her eyes, he took a drag then exhaled. "It's better than I thought. I think I might switch to your brand from now on."

Pressing his thigh against hers, he took a few more puffs, grinning slyly, then stood and walked away.

In the days that followed, Jessie couldn't get Mike's pass off her mind. More than once she caught herself opening the bedroom door to start down the hall, but turned back before it was too late. She was wary of the dark side of Mike's character. She couldn't trust him not to stab her in the back.

Wayne and Carol Kramer were throwing a big New Year's Eve party to show off their new home. Jessie was looking forward to going and even bought a new dress to wear—on clearance, it was a steal.

New Year's evening, however, Kevin went out right after eating dinner. Although the party wasn't starting until late, and would probably last until morning, Jessie was piqued.

At least she didn't have to worry about picking up the sitter—the girl's parents had offered to drop her off at the appointed time. Kevin didn't return until after Jessie had the kitchen cleaned up and the children bathed and ready for bed. He insisted that she allow Laura to stay up past her bedtime, even though the sitter was not there yet to mind her, and Jessie needed to get dressed.

She tried to make Kevin see reason. Just because he said he wanted to be with Laura, didn't actually mean he'd keep a close eye on her. Kevin had refused permission to install a child-safety gate on the stairs. With Laura now toddling about, Jessie spent many anxious hours each day standing guard over her. But Kevin insisted that Laura remain downstairs with him.

"Don't let her out of your sight. You need to watch her like a hawk. I don't want her trying to climb the stairs and falling."

"I said I'd watch her," Kevin retorted.

Jessie carried Joey upstairs and put him in the crib, then showered. After donning her bra, slip and panties, she put hot rollers in her hair and applied her makeup while they did their work. She snagged a nail in her hair as she undid the rollers.

Damn! She looked at the nail. It was split, and the polish on the rest of her nails was chipped. She really ought to redo all of them. She got the bottle of nail-polish remover and sat down on the bed next to the nightstand to rub off the old polish with a tissue. A glance at the alarm clock showed there wasn't enough time to paint her nails. Deciding to leave them natural, she filed the broken one smooth and hurried into the bathroom to rinse off the acetone-based remover.

A quick swig of mouthwash and an artful finger fluff of her hair, and she'd be ready to slip into her new dress. Jessie walked into the bedroom and froze.

Laura had the bottle of nail-polish remover to her lips. Her face contorted as the burning liquid registered on her tongue, and she let out a wail of pain.

Jessie rushed to grab the bottle from her hands, screamed for Kevin, and scooped Laura into her arms. But it was Mike who ran up the stairs.

"What's wrong?"

"Laura swallowed nail-polish remover. I need you to call the poison control center. The number's posted on the inside of the medicine cabinet in the kitchen. Tell them that she swallowed nail-polish remover, and ask them if I should make her vomit."

Mike ran downstairs. Moments later he rushed back up. "What brand of nail polish is it? The guy needs to know."

"It's polish remover. Make sure you're clear about that— chemically there's a big difference. Use the extension in here."

Laura continued screeching at the top of her lungs. Jessie took her out into the hall so Mike could hear better. Her heart raced knowing every wasted second might count. She did her best to comfort the squalling child without success.

Kevin finally made it upstairs to see what was going on, and tried patting Laura on the back to no avail.

Mike hurried out of the bedroom. "The guy needs to know what brand it is."

"It doesn't matter—chemically they're all the same. It's acetone, just tell him that."

Mike returned almost immediately. "Look, I think you better talk to him."

Jessie handed Laura over to Kevin and rushed to snatch the phone. "Hello. This is Mrs. McKenna. My daughter just swallowed acetone. I need to know if I should make her vomit or give her milk."

"Exactly how much did she drink?" the man asked.

"Listen, we don't have time for this. Look up acetone and tell me if I should make her vomit!"

"It says here you should make her vomit. Do you have any syrup of Ipecac on hand?"

"No," Jessie replied and hung up. Racing back to Laura, she told Kevin to bring her into the bathroom and hold her over the sink, head down. "What are you going to do?"

"Make her vomit." Jessie squeezed Laura's mouth open so she could thrust her finger down Laura's throat.

"Jesus, what are you doing to her?" Kevin exclaimed, pulling Laura away.

"For God's sake do as you're told, and let me do what I've got to do."

"Do as she says, Kevin," Mike ordered.

Jessie had never been so grateful to anyone in her life, as she was to Mike for his support at that moment. She shoved her finger down Laura's throat until Laura gagged and vomited, then did it once more for good measure.

Jessie threw on an old dress, then they rushed Laura to the hospital. The emergency room was crowded, and Jessie did her best to comfort Laura while Kevin filed out forms. Jessie was furious with him for failing to watch Laura properly, and angry at herself for not putting the bottle of nail-polish remover away. At last, a nurse escorted them to an examination room. But the wait for a doctor seemed interminable. When he finally arrived, he asked a lot of seemingly pointless questions, and Jessie was silently freaking out at the time being wasted. Then the doctor ordered an X-ray of Laura's lungs. Another long wait. Jessie counted her blessings that she'd made Laura throw-up before leaving the house. It was no small feat to get Laura to hold still long enough for the X-rays to come out.

Laura's lungs turned out to be clear. But, just before she was released, a nurse gave her syrup of Ipecac, and Laura vomited all the way home. Although it was mostly dry heaves, the child was miserable and bawling her eyes out.

The sitter was there when they arrived home, and Jessie explained the situation. She took Laura into the upstairs bathroom to rinse her mouth and clean her up for bed.

Kevin came in to see if Laura was all settled, and told Jessie to get going so they could still make it to Wayne's before midnight.

"You can go if you like, but I'd rather stay here in case Laura needs me," she said, wondering how anyone could go to a party after a near tragedy had threatened their child.

"We're both going. Wayne and Carol are expecting us, and I have no intention of disappointing them because of your carelessness."

"*My* carelessness? What about yours?"

"The children are your primary responsibility, not mine. When something like this happens, you have to take the blame for it. Now get dressed so we can leave right away."

"No! I'm not going! And, yes, the children are my primary responsibility, not your friends' party. I'm not leaving Laura with a babysitter after what she's been through."

Kevin grabbed Jessie by the shoulders and fixed her with his eyes. "I'm ordering you to do it! Do you *understand* me?"

She froze in fear, paralyzed by what she saw in his eyes. Her will to resist seemed to evaporate. "Y-yes," she stammered.

Kevin left her then. She wanted to run to Mike and beg for his protection, but fear still gripped her. Besides, she doubted Mike would champion her cause now that Laura was out of danger. Why would Mike defy Kevin without anything to gain for himself?

Heartsick, Jessie pulled her new, slinky, orange dress out of the closet and slipped it on. Once the gossip about this evening's events made the rounds, everyone would be calling her a cat for a mother—and Kevin would somehow escape any blame.

Once the holidays were over, the dull brown fields, bare gray woodlands and dreary skies depressed Jessie's spirit. She felt trapped in the gloom of a twilight world. The force of gravity seemed to have increased two-fold. It was all she could do to make it through the day, and the lonely evenings were interminable.

After dark, the atmosphere of the house became ominous. It felt like some mysterious presence was hovering there, watching her night after night. Peculiar noises made her jump. No matter how often she told herself it was just the house contracting in the frigid temperatures, she couldn't shake the feeling that something else was present.

Every now and then she thought she heard footsteps. The skin on the back of her neck would crawl, but when she looked around there'd be nothing there. She began to wonder if she was going crazy. Maybe sexual frustration could drive you insane.

Once she heard a thump in the attic. Mice, she told herself, but her heart raced with fear.

Spending night after night in the eerie old house with the men gone was nerve-wracking. It was hard not to imagine scary things. She almost missed the rowdy parties that had petered out now that the weather had turned foul.

One February evening, she was downstairs reading a book when she heard the sound of footsteps tapping down the attic stairs. The hair stood right up on her head.

What if a stranger had gotten into the house?

She was sure she hadn't imagined the noise this time. Footsteps on uncarpeted stairs made a distinct sound.

Slipping off her shoes, she hurried to the kitchen for a carving knife, then ran on tiptoe up the stairs. Warily, she entered the master bedroom and opened the door to the nursery.

Laura and Joey were sleeping peacefully.

Taut as a bowstring, Jessie held her breath and listened for any unusual sound. She waited for what seemed like an eternity but heard nothing abnormal, only the soft rhythmic breathing of her children. She exhaled slowly and listened again. Still nothing.

Easing out of the nursery, she closed the door quietly, then exited the master bedroom, and softly shut the door behind her. She checked the other bedrooms, turning on lights, opening closets, and peering under the beds. Nothing there either.

The staircase leading to the dark landing of the attic loomed forbiddingly. She'd definitely heard footsteps on those stairs. The hallway and staircase going to the first floor were carpeted, and wouldn't have produced the crisp tip-taps she'd heard. Slowly, she crept up the stairs.

Hearing a sharp creak, she froze and held her breath. She'd forgotten the fourth step squeaked. Stealth was pointless now. She strode up to the landing, threw open the door, and flicked on the light switch, heart pounding. She scanned the area, but the dust and dirt appeared undisturbed.

What if someone had gotten past her?

She hurried back down to check on the children, pulse racing. The nursery was undisturbed, and the children slept on.

Jessie listened intently once more, but sensed only the ordinary vagaries of the house. She started to relax, and then the fourth step to the attic squeaked.

She rushed to lock the bedroom door and slept with the knife on the nightstand next to the bed.

Jessie woke to pale wintry sunshine and immediately checked to see if the knife was still there; it was right where she'd left it. Kevin hadn't broken the door in, which meant that he hadn't come home last night. He frequently failed to come home before morning these days, but she figured he was out in the barn milking—that was one task he had to be home in time for. Dressing quickly, she went downstairs to warm Joey's bottle.

When Kevin came in for breakfast, she told him about the footsteps she'd heard on the attic stairs.

"You must have imagined it."

"But I didn't. I was reading a book, and the hair stood right up on my head."

"Then maybe you need to see a shrink." He gave her a contemptuous look, finished eating in silence, then left for the barn.

Johnny staggered in, yawning and rubbing his eyes. "Man, the coffee smells good. Mind if I have a cup? I'm running late for work."

"Go right ahead," Jessie said. "By the way, I need to ask you something, but it might seem strange."

Johnny took a swig of coffee. "So shoot."

"I'm beginning to think this place is haunted."

"Why's that?"

I've been hearing footsteps at night after everyone's gone out, and I know I'm not imagining things."

"You sure about that?" he asked, eyes twinkling.

"Yes, I am! So please tell me if you know anything about the house ever being haunted."

He shrugged. "The ghost must be getting restless again. Don't pay it any mind. It never hurt anyone—just walks around." He drained the cup and went away chuckling.

Jessie wasn't sure if he was amused because the ghost had frightened her or if he was stringing her along.

She continued to sleep with the knife in the drawer of the nightstand and was almost desperate not to be left alone in the house. Although the brothers went out nearly every evening, Mike usually left later than the others. There was one sure way to make him stay and, sooner or later, resisting temptation would become impossible given her stressed state of mind.

Standing in the check-out line at the grocery store that week, Jessie impulsively reached over and picked up *Ms. Magazine*. She read through it when she got home. Perhaps she should consider getting a job. She might find life more fulfilling and, at the very least, it would get her out of the oppressive atmosphere of the house. Maybe she could pay Mary Clare to baby-sit.

The next day, Jessie started answering the classified ads. When Kevin came inside for lunch, he caught her on the phone with a potential employer. He grabbed the receiver and slammed it back in the cradle. "What do you think you're doing?"

"I'm looking for a job."

He gave her a disgusted look. "You already have a job."

Two days later, Maria and Mary Clare showed up to clean, and Maria cornered her.

"Kevin said you were applying for a job. What's gotten into you? Don't you love your children?"

"Of course I do, but I need more than that."

Mary Clare looked askance. "Don't you realize nothing can replace a mother's nurturing in a young child's life? There's time to do anything you want later, but children are only small for a little while. They need you."

For all her feminist leanings, Jessie knew Mary Clare was right. She could hardly explain to anyone the real reason she wanted a job. Almost anything was better than teetering on the edge of mental illness or adultery. If she heard the footsteps again, she didn't know what she might do.

A week later, Kevin announced that he was going to the Daytona 500 with Frank, Bubba and Dale. Jessie knew it was the end of the line. She couldn't possibly resist temptation if she was left alone in the house with Mike.

She tried to cajole Kevin into taking her with him, but he refused. When she discovered Kathleen, LuAnn and Ruby planned to accompany their husbands, she talked Maria into baby-sitting and convinced Kathleen and her friends to appeal to Kevin on her behalf.

Out-maneuvered, Kevin finally gave in.

The warmth and sunshine in Florida buoyed Jessie's spirits. She had a lot of fun at the car races. Although she saw more than enough to be concerned about Kevin's penchant for gambling, she returned home rested and feeling much better about life.

The following week, odd anonymous calls started coming.

For the first few days, Jessie attributed them to rude people dialing the wrong number, or associates of Mike and Johnny hanging up when a female answered. But the calls continued day and night, almost exclusively during times when Johnny and Mike were most likely to be absent, so she soon ruled that out.

Sometimes she'd be changing a diaper or bathing the children and had to put up with the ringing until she could safely get to it. It was nerve-wracking to rush to answer the phone and hear nothing but breathing, and then the hollow echo of an open line, knowing someone was enjoying her torment.

She couldn't leave the phone off the hook without incurring Kevin's ire. Everyone who knew them dialed the house number. The new phone line in the dairy office was meant for business; but Kevin spent little time in the office, consequently the tractor supply store, feed store, and other farmers called the house. At night, the house phone had to be operational in case someone spotted the cows out or the barn on fire.

One Sunday night, Kevin happened to be home when the phone began ringing around nine. Jessie cringed and waited for Kevin to get it. He gave her a sour look.

"How long is it going to take for you to answer that?"

Dread filled her, but she forced herself to pick up the receiver. Relief washed over her at the sound of her mother's voice. "Hi, honey. I'm sorry to call so late, but I have some bad news. Your father had to be rushed to the emergency room."

"What?" Icy fingers of fear clutched her heart. "I'll be right over."

"No," Liz said firmly. "It's too late at night. Your father had a heart attack this afternoon, and we've been here half the day. He's in his own room now and sleeping peacefully, so there's no point in you coming over."

"I'm coming anyway," she said, going numb at the thought that she'd almost lost her father.

Seeing his wife pale and hearing arguing, Kevin grabbed the phone. He spoke to Liz, listened a moment, then nodded. "I agree it isn't necessary for Jessie to go to the hospital."

When she started to protest, he took away the car keys.

Distraught, she ran upstairs and threw herself on the bed sobbing. What if her dad died? What if she didn't get a chance to say goodbye? She cried herself to sleep, worried sick about him.

The first thing in the morning she phoned her mother, anxious to get to the hospital and see her dad.

"And what will you do with Laura and Joey? Young children aren't allowed in," Liz said. "Your father will be released today anyway. Wait until he's home and had some rest, and feels up to visitors."

When Jessie finally got to see her dad, he looked almost normal. Except for the phone call in the night, and the fact that he wasn't at work, she wouldn't have suspected he'd been ill. But the specter of death had touched him, and the tenuous nature of life had suddenly become overwhelmingly real.

The anonymous phone calls got so bad, Jessie told Ann about them at bowling.

"Harassing calls are illegal. Report them to the telephone company. They can trace the calls and put a stop to it."

Jessie did as Ann recommended. Unfortunately, the phone company needed Kevin's authorization—and Kevin flatly refused to grant it.

Day after day, the phone rang incessantly, well into the night. If she didn't answer it, it kept ringing until she did.

Her nerves were worn to such a frazzle she was forced to start taking Valium again. One morning, after she took her regular dose, she still felt edgy. By ten, she was so tense she needed to take another pill; by noon, she needed another. An hour later, she felt so tense and restless she took one more.

Jessie put the children down for their naps, hoping to get a little rest herself. Then the phone began to ring again. She'd had six anonymous calls already that day; once it had rung almost twenty times before she finished changing Joey's diaper. She lifted the receiver and heard breathing, then nothing. She was so upset she took two more pills.

Afterward, she sat on the floor and began to weep. All she wanted was peace—blessed peace. Her life was nothing but dirty dishes, dirty laundry, dirty floors, dirty diapers, crying children and ringing phones.

Her husband didn't love her and probably never would. How long could she go on without committing the mortal sin of adultery? Was there even any point in trying to go on?

⁓

Ann sped down the road that passed the farm on her way home from class at City College. On impulse, she slowed and turned into the driveway. It'd been a long time since she'd seen Jessie's kids, and Mark had something else to do that evening.

She parked near the back door and went inside. Jessie was sitting on the floor crying.

Ann rushed to her side. "What's the matter? Is your father sick again?"

Jessie shook her head.

"Is something wrong with one of the kids?"

She shook her head again, then burst into fresh tears.

"Come on," Ann said. "Let's get you off the floor, sit down with some coffee and talk about it."

"No. I'm too sad. Leave me alone."

"*Please* tell me what's the matter!"

"Kevin d-doesn't love me," Jessie sobbed. "Kevin d-doessn't looove me." She started laughing hysterically.

Maybe she's drunk, Ann thought. "Wait here. I'll be right back." She rushed to the barn to find Kevin. He was running silage into a feeder. "Kevin, there's something wrong with Jessie."

"I can't leave now. Go stay with her until I get there."

Ann dashed back to the house, afraid it might have been a mistake to leave Jessie alone. She yanked open the door and flew through the mudroom into the kitchen. Jessie was standing at the sink with a glass of water to her lips and an open bottle of pills. Ann snatched the bottle off the counter.

"How many did you take?"

Jessie ignored the question. "Give them to me, Ann. I need them. Dr. Lieberman prescribed them for me."

"No. First tell me how many you took."

She lunged for the bottle. Ann dodged and raced for the bathroom in the mudroom. She dumped the pills down the toilet and flushed.

Jessie began to sob. "Damn it, Ann, why did you do that? I need them! I have to have them!" She turned away, weeping.

Kevin came in a few minutes later, and Ann breathed a sigh of relief. "Jessie was hysterical when I arrived today, and just now she tried to swallow a whole lot of pills. You'd better call a doctor."

"No. We should try to find out how many pills she took first. How many did you take, Jessie?"

She stayed mute and eyed him warily. Inside, she felt very small, and Ann and Kevin seemed very large, like they were the grown-ups and she was a child. Ann was her friend, but she didn't trust Kevin.

"Please tell us," Ann pleaded. "We only want to help you."

"Kevin will punish me," Jessie said in a little-girl voice.

Baffled, Ann looked at Kevin.

"She's out of it. It's the pills talking." He turned to Jessie. "I love you, honey. Why would you think any such thing? I just want to help you. I can call the doctor, but I won't have to if you'll just tell me how many pills you took."

Panic seized her. What if the doctor thought she was crazy? What if he didn't believe her about the ghost and the anonymous calls? "Please don't call the doctor. I didn't mean to do it. I was just sad."

"Why were you sad?" Ann asked soothingly.

"'Cause Kevin doesn't love me."

He countered quickly. "Jessie, I know you think it's tough being home alone most of the time with two kids. I'm sorry I haven't helped you more. I didn't realize it was having this effect on you. I'll try to cut back on my commitments from now on and spend more time with the kids. But you know I love you. I'll prove it. I'll buy you anything you want, just name it."

Her befuddled brain tried to comprehend this twist. "A car... a car would be nice. I could get out more."

"No problem. I should have thought of that."

Ann smiled. "See, Jessie? Now, how many pills did you take?"

"Maybe eight or nine, starting from this morning."

Ann gave Kevin a worried look.

"It's okay if they were spread out over the day," he said. "I'll get Jessie upstairs to bed so she can sleep it off."

In the morning, Jessie woke feeling refreshed. Kevin came in for breakfast in surprisingly good humor. He didn't seem at all angry about the episode the day before.

"Let's go car hunting this weekend, Jessie. Call Kathleen and ask her to baby-sit."

They found a gold Grand Prix at a fair price. It was only a year old, was air-conditioned, and had a great stereo sound system. Kevin had it registered in both their names.

Well, at least it was half hers, anyway.

The ghost quieted down and the phone calls slacked off, but suddenly Kevin turned on her again.

"Damn it, Jessie," he said, kicking a toy out of his path. "Why isn't this place ever straight? It never looked like this when my mother raised us."

"I do the best I can. Besides, I doubt you noticed whether or not your toys were put away when you were little."

He glared back. "From now on I expect this house to be in perfect order at all times. I want the newspaper brought up at exactly four-thirty every day and put next to my plate."

"That's absurd. I've a baby to take care of and a toddler running around. Besides, the paper doesn't always come on time."

"I did not ask for your opinion. You'll do as I say. And one more thing—from now on I expect you to sleep in the nude."

She tossed her head. "I'll sleep as I please."

"I'm not giving you a choice," he snarled, fixing her with his eyes.

She shrank from what she saw there. Just as quickly what she saw was erased from her conscious mind. She knew she had to obey, and she did, but if pressed, she could hardly explain why.

She was uncomfortable sleeping in the nude, and she had trouble getting to sleep the first few nights. She ran herself ragged keeping the toys picked up and trying to remember to fetch the newspaper before supper was on the table. She waited on pins and needles on the days the paper was late, hoping it would get there in time. Then, one day, it didn't.

She checked twice before Kevin came into the house, but the newspaper still wasn't there. She put food on Kevin's plate then served herself. Just as she picked up her fork, Kevin stood and yanked the tablecloth off the table. Glassware and china clattered to the floor and cracked into pieces.

Jessie stared at Kevin, flabbergasted. "If you're trying to imitate a stage-act tablecloth trick, you need to practice more. The idea is to pull the cloth off without disturbing the place-settings," she said dryly.

"I wasn't doing a trick. I'm sending you a message."

"What kind of message is that?"

"The newspaper wasn't next to my plate, like it's supposed to be."

⁂

The anonymous calls began again. Jessie cringed every time the phone rang. One afternoon it began to ring at quarter past four. She winced and picked it up; it was Aunt Julia.

"I just got home from work and read the article about Kevin in the *Concord Times*. Tell him I said congratulations."

"For what?"

"Congratulations on the announcement of his candidacy for County Commissioner."

"Oh," Jessie said, scrambling for words. "I didn't realize it was in the paper already, but I'll tell him you called."

As soon as Julia hung up, Jessie ran to the paper box. She pulled out the *Concord Times* and scanned the front page. There it was in black and white. The bastard hadn't even told her.

Kevin came in for supper a short time later and reached for the newspaper nonchalantly.

She gave him a dirty look. "Why didn't you tell me you decided to run for office before informing the local paper?"

He scowled. "It's none of your affair what I choose to do with my life."

"It *is* my affair. I have to put out and be put out if you're running for election. You promised to cut back on your commitments and spend more time at home with the children. How are you going to do that if you're campaigning?"

"You've always known I wanted to be a politician. Two of the commissioners are retiring. Jack advised me to jump on it. I can't afford to miss an opportunity like this."

"The least you could have done was told me yourself, instead of waiting for me to find out from the newspaper."

"You lost that privilege a long time ago. If you were the kind of wife you should be, things would be different."

"What's that supposed to mean?"

Kevin opened the paper. "If you want to be treated like a real wife, all you have to do is deny God and bow down to me."

CHAPTER 20

SOMEBODY TO LOVE

Kevin's ten-year high school reunion was scheduled for the weekend immediately following the *Concord Times'* announcement of his candidacy. Former classmates who kept up with the news would have something to talk about—and those who didn't soon would.

Jessie was nervous about attending Kevin's class reunion. She'd been too busy to go shopping for something stylish to wear, so the rose-colored cocktail dress would have to do. Worse still, she was now a candidate's wife.

❦

The Carlton House banquet hall was festooned with Mansfield High's school colors. Groups of smartly dressed people sipped cocktails and chatted, while others helped themselves to the buffet arrayed along the far side of the room.

Jessie's stomach churned as she gazed over the sea of unfamiliar faces. How was she ever going to succeed as a politician's wife? She hadn't a clue how to chitchat or make small talk with strangers.

With a sense of relief, she saw Sam Leland enter. He had an attractive blonde on his arm, wearing a very revealing dress.

A number of heads turned in their direction.

Tom Hamilton trailed in their wake. In concession to the occasion, he wore a sport jacket and slacks, but retained his worn bush hat and motorcycle boots.

Kevin greeted Sam and Tom, then turned his attention to the blonde. "Leave it to you, Sam, to be escorting the fairest lady here tonight."

Jessie winced. It was a nice compliment to bestow, but not right in front of one's wife.

Something flickered in Sam's eyes and was gone. "Let me introduce you. This is Mandy Everett. She was a freshman when we were seniors."

Kevin smiled. "It's a pleasure to make your acquaintance. I can't imagine how I missed noticing a beauty such as you in high school."

Sam's jaw tightened. "Mandy, I'd like you to meet my good friend Kevin McKenna and his lovely wife, Jessie."

Mandy extended her hand. "It's so nice to meet you at last. Sam talks about the two of you all the time."

Sam smiled. "Jessie, why don't you and Mandy find us a table and get better acquainted. Kevin and I'll get your cocktails. What would you like?"

After Sam took their orders, they found a table and sat down. Mandy pulled out a pack of cigarettes and offered Jessie one.

"Thanks," she said and took it. "How long have you and Sam been dating?"

Mandy's eyes brightened. "Just since last November. I still can't believe my luck."

Jessie gave her a quizzical look.

"I suppose you don't know." Mandy lit her cigarette, took a puff, and exhaled. "All through high school, Sam was every girl's dream lover. With his looks and his charm, he had the cream of the crop to choose from. It wasn't long before he was hot and heavy with Candace Mansfield. She was the envy of everyone. She had it all—wealth, beauty, and Sam Leland. Everybody expected them to get married right after college."

Jessie took a drag on her cigarette. "So what happened?"

Mandy shrugged. "Nobody knows. Tom came back from Vietnam and finished technical school, then he and Sam left for California together."

"I didn't know Tom was in Vietnam. I guess I never thought about it. Kevin got some special farmer exemption. What about Sam?"

"Apparently Sam just lucked out, but Tom volunteered right out of high school and joined the Army Rangers. He was real gung-ho then, although I heard he never talks about anything that happened over there. He still carries a knife in one of his boots, though."

"That's funny," Jessie said. "The first time I met Tom and Sam, they scared the hell out of me. I was home alone with my fourteen-month-old baby when they showed up one night. The moment I saw Tom, I thought he had a knife hidden in his boot. I was afraid he might be dangerous."

"Tom's actually kind of sweet and a bit shy."

Just then Sam and Kevin returned with the drinks.

"Who's sweet and shy?" Kevin asked.

Mandy arched an eyebrow. "Certainly not you."

⁓⁓

Every weekend Jessie attended as many social events with Kevin as he could locate in the county, ranging from church suppers and country dances to more formal civic organization affairs. She was spending more time with Kevin than ever before, but they had no family life to speak of. Campaigning was tedious and the regimen exhausting, requiring her to burn the candle at both ends. And warmer weather meant grass to mow and a pool to keep clean. Trying to keep the house perfectly neat at all times, while managing such a hectic schedule, wasn't easy, but she was improving.

Sam and Tom often came to the farm to target-shoot and knock back a few beers. If Sam learned there was a rock band performing at any of the events Kevin and Jessie were attending, he usually asked to accompany them.

Oddly enough, Sam never bothered to bring Mandy or any other date along.

Mandy had become friendly with Jessie and invited her on shopping trips, so she knew Mandy was still Sam's lover. Jessie wondered why a single guy would prefer to accompany a married couple to dances and never bring a date of his own.

Nevertheless, she was thankful for her good fortune. Sam was just as charming as he was good-looking, and his presence served as a buffer from Kevin's habitual criticism.

She'd almost forgotten how it felt to be treated like a lady, and Sam's courtesies were a balm to her scarred psyche. He opened doors for her, lit her cigarettes, and made certain she never lacked for refreshments. However, he studiously avoided any other familiarity.

As perfect as Sam's manners were, he ignored the conventional courtesy of asking her to dance at least one dance. It wouldn't have seemed so remarkable, except for the fact that he always asked other married women in Kevin's circle of acquaintances. Kevin was too busy trolling for votes to bother dancing with her, so she spent most of her time feeling like a third wheel and envying Sam's partners.

Kevin had a habit of making her dance with dirty-minded old men with whom he hoped to curry favor, and she hated it. She was tempted to go ahead and ask Sam to dance, just to be able to get out on the floor with someone under the age of fifty who wasn't squeezing her during the slow dances. Sam was a marvelous dancer and having him as a partner would be a pleasure, but perhaps too much of a pleasure. The possibility of Sam coming along on a night out was the only thing she looked forward to anymore.

Jessie put Laura and Joey down for their naps, wishing she had time for a nap herself. There was something scheduled for the evening, just like every other weekend night for the past six weeks, but at least Kevin hadn't needed her any earlier in the day. It was almost the end of May, and she had to finish the flowerbeds. It was important that the garden look appealing if anyone supporting Kevin's candidacy should drop in.

Putting a packet of seeds in her apron pocket, she went out to the kitchen porch and picked up the flat of petunias she'd bought at the nursery, along with a few gardening tools. She stepped off the porch and began to walk across the patio to the backyard, then noticed Johnny and Dennis sitting at one of the umbrella tables near the pool. They waved her over.

Jessie approached the table. Dennis gave her a welcoming smile. When she saw what he was doing, she stopped dead in her tracks. Dennis was holding a tablespoon over a wooden match, liquefying a whitish substance. A glassine packet of white-colored powder lay on the table.

Johnny had a tourniquet on his arm and a syringe ready. "Hey, Sis, wanna do some heroin?"

She stared back at him, horrified.

"How about it?" he continued.

"No, thank you," she said, once she found her voice.

"Oh, come on," Dennis urged. "Try it, you'll like it."

"No," she snapped, and strode off. Of course she'd like it— that was the trouble. Heroin was the last thing she needed.

Dennis and Johnny looked at each other and laughed.

Ignoring them, she pushed through the gate into the backyard. The focal point of the garden was the statue of the Virgin Mary. Jessie knelt and removed last year's dead flowers from the mound, then planted it with red and white petunias from the market packs. After that, she moved to the end of the annual border where she'd run out of marigold and zinnia seeds the day before. Scraping up the soil, she opened a packet of cosmos. The label depicted a variety aptly named *Sunset,* which sported red and orange, daisy-like blooms on tall purple stems.

She sprinkled the seeds over the earth and covered them with dirt. Thunder rumbled in the distance as she gathered up her tools. Dark clouds quickly obscured the sun. Scattered drops of rain began to fall, and she hurried into the house.

Just as she finished washing up in the laundry room sink, the phone started to ring. *Damn!* she thought. *Won't that creep ever give up?* She'd already had nine anonymous calls that day. Praying it wasn't another, she braced herself and picked up the receiver. "Hello?"

"Hey, Jess, it's me—Kevin. I had a little trouble with the Grand Prix, and I'm running late. Sam found me broken down, and he's taking me to the rest of my appearances. The car's being towed to Keller's garage, and he's going to take a look at it."

"Okay," she said. The fact that Kevin had taken her car because it was air-conditioned had irked her, but it was a hot day. She hoped the problem wasn't going to be expensive to fix.

"Sam said he'd like to come to the dance tonight and offered to drive, but I'm running at least an hour behind."

"That's nice of Sam. Thanks for calling." She hung up the phone feeling a flush of delight. Sam was coming!

By early evening the rain tapered off. Jessie went ahead and picked the babysitter up at the originally scheduled time. It would be much easier to get ready with Suzy minding the children, instead of trying to keep an eye on them herself.

Humming a merry tune, she pulled her new red gown with the white ruffle trim from the closet and slipped it on. With a little effort, she managed to zip it up on her own and went over to the full-length mirror to see how it looked.

The sweetheart neckline was low-cut and a little more daring than she was used to, but Mandy said it was perfect. Red was certainly her color, and the matching bolero jacket, also trimmed with white ruffles, would come in handy now that the rain had cooled things off.

Hearing the sound of an engine, Jessie went to the window and saw Sam's white and gold Cutlass coming up the lane.

She took one more look in the mirror. Yes, the dress was flattering indeed. A secret part of her hoped that Sam would like it, too.

She went downstairs and found Sam and Kevin in the kitchen, kidding around with the sitter. When they finally eased up on the girl, Jessie began going over her instructions.

A wild neighing started up outside.

"Sounds like something's wrong with your horse," Kevin said.

Jessie hurried outdoors. Rio was running frantically along the fence of the small pasture bordering the driveway. Half the dairy herd was ambling across the lawn toward the road. She dashed back inside to tell Kevin.

"Get Cletus and Bert," Kevin said, and rushed out the door with Sam.

She knew Bert and Doris had already gone out for the evening, so she made straight for Cletus's apartment over the garage. He was already coming down the stairs, with Dusty at his heels, to check on the commotion Rio was making.

"Cletus, the cows are heading for the road."

"Don't worry, Miz Jessie, we'll get 'em. That Rio, he's a smart one. You'd best try to calm him down."

Cletus scurried off with Dusty, and Jessie walked across the driveway, getting as close to the fence as the paving would allow. The grass was still wet from the rain, and she didn't want to ruin her shoes. "Easy, boy," she said to the horse.

Reassured by her soothing tone, he soon returned to graze with Blue, although he kept raising his head to keep an eye on the action.

Jessie returned to the house to finish going over the list of instructions with Suzy.

Kevin stormed into the kitchen moments later. "What are you doing in here, Jessie? Get back outside and help us with the cows!"

She looked at him in astonishment. "I can't chase cows dressed like this."

Kevin shoved her toward the door. "Move!"

"No! Cletus and I have to round the cows up by ourselves often enough. Three men should be able to do it without my help."

"You lazy bitch," Kevin growled. He grabbed her arm and twisted it behind her back.

Suzy stood there gaping.

Kevin forced Jessie through the mudroom. Once he had her outside, he hurried off to help head the cattle up the lane into the barnyard. She stayed where he'd left her and made a pretense of shooing-on the returning cows as they walked past. When the bulk of the herd was safely in the barnyard, she went back inside the house.

Kevin stomped into the kitchen a few minutes later, tracking clods of mud all over the floor. Sam paused to wipe his feet on the doormat and gingerly sidestepped Kevin's muddy tracks.

Jessie regarded the soiled floor with irritation. Kevin should have removed his shoes in the mudroom. That's what it was there for.

He pulled out a chair and sat down. "Come here and take my shoes off, Jessie. I want you to clean them."

She stiffened.

Her first impulse was to tell Kevin to drop dead, but she clenched her teeth and said nothing. She knew she had to obey, something deep inside compelled her, though she wasn't sure why.

Bracing herself, she untied the laces and removed the shoes, careful not to get any of the filth on her dress.

Kevin got to his feet as she headed to the laundry room to rinse the shoes off in the sink. "How about a drink, Sam?"

"Sure. I'll have a bourbon and water."

Kevin poured the drinks, and they left for the living room.

Jessie scrubbed furiously at the shoes. "Suzy, can you please mop up the floor? We're already late for the dance as it is."

When the shoes were finished, Jessie took them out to the living room. Sam and Kevin were seated on the sofa together, sipping drinks and joshing with one another. She placed the shoes on the floor at Kevin's feet and turned to leave.

"Wait, I want you to put them on."

She halted. Stone-faced, she turned and knelt at Kevin's feet.

Sam looked amused and openly eyed her cleavage.

Jessie finished tying the laces and stood up. She put her palms together and bowed in the Oriental fashion.

Sam chuckled.

Kevin seemed to think Sam was laughing at her, but Jessie could tell he appreciated the contemptuous nature of her theatrical gesture.

She turned on her heel and strode off.

Still laughing, Sam rose and followed on her heels.

She snatched her evening bag from the kitchen table and walked to the car.

Sam caught up to her side and opened the door. After she was settled in, he closed the door, walked to the driver's side, and climbed in.

Too choked with anger to speak, Jessie feared Sam might think she was angry with him also. She struggled to overcome the painful constriction in her throat. "Please excuse me, but I'm upset."

Sam nodded. They waited in silence for Kevin. He took his good old time in coming, too.

Jessie didn't utter a word on the way to the dance.

When they arrived at the hall she remained mute, but dutifully followed Kevin and Sam to the bar. It was located in the short leg of the new L-shaped addition that wrapped around two sides of the building.

Kevin turned to her. "What would you like to drink?"

Still too angry for words, she didn't bother to answer.

Kevin ordered her regular and handed it over. Leaving her under Sam's watchful gaze, he left to find a table.

He returned, shaking his head. "It's packed solid. I couldn't find any place to sit."

The bartender pointed toward the long leg of the addition. "Sir, there's lots of empty tables around the corner."

The area around the corner was deserted. Midway along the wall was a closed set of doors, inset with glass panels, providing access to the dance floor from the new section.

Jessie followed Kevin, with Sam bringing up the rear, and seated herself at the table Kevin indicated. She pulled out her cigarettes and Sam immediately offered her a light.

Kevin began a conversation with Sam, but when he tried to include Jessie, she ignored him. After a few minutes, Sam excused himself and headed for the dance floor. Kevin turned to Jessie. "Why won't you talk to me?"

She looked past him, staring off into space. Frowning, he stabbed out his cigarette and left.

Jessie listened to the muted music echoing from the hall. No one drifted through the doors leading to the dance floor, and the bar was around the corner, out of sight. She was glad no one she knew saw her sitting there, because she was in no mood to talk. She lit another cigarette. Letting her thoughts drift, she called to mind the details of a recent dream which she'd found disturbing.

As dreams went, it had begun pleasantly enough.

She was riding Blue along familiar fields and trails, when they crested a ridge and entered a valley she'd never seen before.

The lovely valley was bisected by a crystalline stream. Pastel water lilies floated in pools formed by the meandering waters. Golden fish flitted along the stream's pebbled bottom as she rode Blue across the valley to the mouth of the cave from which it emanated. Large rocks obscured most of the opening, so Jessie dismounted and left Blue to graze while she surveyed as much of the cave as she could without actually entering. Satisfied, she turned back to her horse.

Blue was gone.

Jessie quickly scanned the valley. It was empty. Maybe he'd wandered over the hill. She trudged to the top, expecting to find him grazing on the other side. She reached the summit and froze in her tracks. Nothing was as she remembered it. The landscape was as alien as a foreign country, and her horse was nowhere to be seen. A hollow feeling came over her.

She turned around and scrutinized the valley once more. There was still no sign of Blue. Jessie shivered, even though it was a warm day. She had no idea in which direction home lay.

Strangely, she felt drawn to the cave and started walking toward it. She sensed that if she followed the stream to its source, she would somehow find her way home. But entering caves alone was dangerous, and she balked at the idea.

Contemplating the landscape, she began to see it with different eyes. The valley had an uncanny, almost mesmerizing sort of charm. Suddenly, she felt desperate to get away. She clambered over the rocks and ducked inside the cave.

It appeared to be an ordinary cavern, and she followed the stream for a long way before the passage narrowed. The ceiling sloped lower and lower, until she was walking bent double. The air seemed to be getting warmer, and her unease grew. Weren't caves supposed to be uniformly cool?

As the tunnel continued on, she was forced to crawl on her hands and knees. Although the cold stream flowed on beside her, the atmosphere grew so hot it was stifling. Sweat trickled between her breasts. Abruptly the stream dipped underground, and the passage narrowed into a nearly impassable crevice.

The tunnel appeared to widen farther ahead, and she thought she saw a faint glow.

Swallowing her fear, she tried to squeeze her body through the narrow opening. It was so tight she could hardly breathe. Rocks pressed in all around. Blood began to pound in her head.

She was stuck.

Panic gripped her in hot and cold waves. Fighting for every breath, she tried to push herself backwards without success. Her head spun. She gasped for air but couldn't fill her lungs. A roaring sound echoed in her ears. She was passing out—if she did, she knew she'd die there.

Jessie pushed against the rock with her last ounce of strength. Abruptly, the stone just seemed to release her.

Heart pounding, she scrambled backwards until she could stand, then wheeled and fled to the mouth of the cave. She clambered out and collapsed on the ground, panting for air.

The sky swirled above her. Her head slowly stopped spinning. When the dizziness had passed, she climbed the hill and confronted the unknown territory. She could detect nothing familiar in the alien landscape. The valley and land around it appeared to be under the spell of some dark enchantment. She knew she would remain captive forever, unless she could find the source of the stream and somehow emerge on the other side of the cave.

She walked back to the entrance and stood there, trying to summon the nerve to go inside once more.

And there the dream had ended with that terrible fear in the pit of her stomach.

Jessie stubbed out her cigarette and got up to get another drink.

The dream didn't seem too difficult to figure out. Since the day she married Kevin, she'd felt trapped in some bizarre microcosm with no easy way out. However, she had the strangest sensation that the symbolism went deeper.

Returning to her table, she glanced toward the closed doors which led to the dance floor. Sam was standing on the other side watching her through the glass panels. Their eyes met and held briefly.

She sat down facing the same direction as before so that Sam was out of her line of sight. She wondered how long he'd been watching her and to what purpose. It wasn't like him to play the wallflower, and he never lacked for dance partners.

Maybe Kevin had asked him to spy on her?

Sam, however, made no attempt to disguise his surveillance when she looked him in the eye. He wanted her to know he was watching, but why?

Deep in thought, she lit another cigarette, rhythmically inhaling and exhaling. Just as it was finished, Ellen Richardson came around the corner.

"Jessie! What are you doing back here all alone? Come inside and sit at our table—there's room."

"Thank you." She stood then glanced back, just in time to see Sam melt into the crowd of dancers.

꧁꧂

Among the couples seated at the Richardsons' table were Leroy and Marcella Jones, but Jessie didn't know anyone else. Ellen started to make introductions. Before she even finished, Jessie began to forget which names went with which faces.

Marcella looked over and smiled. "I didn't realize you were here until now."

"Kevin had trouble finding a table when we arrived. I was out in the annex."

Leroy pushed his chair away from the table and stood. "I was just about to leave for the bar. Can I bring you something to drink?"

"Thank you. A gin and tonic will be fine."

Jessie managed to fumble her way through some small talk. Thankfully, the conversation soon began to flow over and around her. She lit a cigarette and scanned the room, looking for Sam. He was dancing with a blonde. Kevin was nowhere to be seen, and Jessie hoped it would stay that way.

When the music ended, Sam walked over and asked Marcella to dance. She nodded and Leroy smiled indulgently.

Sam helped Marcella to her feet, offering his arm as they headed for the dance floor. The band began to play, and Marcella swayed sensuously to the music in her slinky black dress. Sam's eyes followed her every move, and Jessie squelched a pang of jealously.

Kevin suddenly materialized at her side. "I need you to make the rounds with me and meet some people."

He escorted her from table to table, outwardly courteous and affectionate. She met the two retiring county commissioners and their wives, the mayor of Mansfield and his wife, several businessmen and their spouses, assorted Democratic Party officials, and the county coroner. The whole process was excruciating, but she feigned good cheer and interest.

Pausing at yet another table, Kevin said, "Jessie, I'd like you to meet Dr. Herman Gross and his wife, Dorcas."

Dr. Gross, as his name implied, was a large man—and not only large, but grotesquely fat. His wife, by contrast, was diminutive and sweet voiced. She engaged Jessie in polite conversation, which provided some distraction from the crude comments Gross made to Kevin about every woman within sight.

As Kevin bantered with Herman, Jessie caught glimpses of Sam dancing with the other wives at the Richardsons' table. At last, Kevin said his farewells and led her back to their party.

Ellen was on the dance floor with Sam. When the music ended, they walked back to the table, chatting like old friends.

Jessie squelched another stab of jealousy.

Sam helped Ellen into her seat. "Thanks for letting me borrow your wife, Jack."

"My pleasure."

Jessie was certain Sam would ask her to dance this time. He'd already danced with every other woman at the table. She looked into his eyes.

Kevin stood abruptly. "I'm sorry to have to cut this short, but we need to be getting home."

Jack glanced at him, surprised. "Heck, Kevin, the night is young and the party's just begun. Come on and stay awhile."

"Sorry, but I told the babysitter we'd be home long before now."

This was news to Jessie, but she couldn't contradict him outright without causing a scene.

Ellen made an appeal. "Can't you just call the sitter?"

"No, her parents are expecting her."

Sam gave Kevin a look, then shrugged. "Well, it was certainly wonderful meeting all of you. Good night, everybody."

A round of goodbyes ensued.

Kevin helped Jessie out of her seat—probably to ensure she left with him—and promptly headed for the parking lot.

She said nothing on the ride home. Sam helped her out of the car without waiting for Kevin to do it. After that night, she found Sam's eyes meeting hers more and more often.

CHAPTER 21

LIFE IN THE FAST LANE

Jessie wasn't looking forward to spending the evening at the Knights of Columbus dance. The music would be too old fashioned for her taste—something her parents would like, not her. She would probably be the youngest person there, and she dreaded having to mix with strangers for hours. She closed her eyes and took a deep breath to quell the stress she felt inside.

The entrance doors opened onto a wide corridor paralleling a large hall with a dais for the band. A multifaceted, mirrored ball was suspended above a dance floor which was ringed by round tables covered in red cloth. Each had a lighted, glass-ensconced candle for the centerpiece.

With a stab of annoyance, Jessie noted the buffet had already been served and only a few scattered leftovers remained.

Kevin could never seem to be on time for anything.

They wound their way around the hall in a circuitous route, so Kevin could exchange greetings with everyone he recognized, and finally arrived at Ellen and Jack's table.

Ellen smiled warmly as she greeted them. "Kevin, Jessie, I'm so glad you made it. Let me help you get acquainted with everybody." She proceeded to make introductions all around, beginning with Tony and Inez Patero. Tony owned a car dealership in Mansfield, and his wife was on the school board.

The conversation at the Richardsons' table was lively, but Jessie found it difficult to join in. Pleading hunger, she excused herself and headed for the buffet.

She put some raw vegetables and a few leftover shreds of cold meat on her plate. Kevin came over, picked up a dish, and forked up some congealing green beans. "I don't know why you can't be more like Ellen. A man can really go far in politics with a wife like her."

Jessie looked him in the eye. "She's more than ten years older than I am. She's had a lot of practice. I hardly know a soul in this room."

"That's no excuse," he said and walked away.

His criticism left her feeling more inadequate than before—and with even less taste for the tedious evening ahead. Kevin routinely praised Ellen and urged Jessie to emulate her: the perfect wife, homemaker and mother.

Jessie had never been a social butterfly, and she doubted if she had it in her. Besides, Ellen's twin girls were thirteen and old enough to be a real help around the house.

Returning to the table with her miniscule rations, she ate the meager fare and lit a cigarette. Soon the lights dimmed and the band struck up a number. Couples all around the room rose from their places and headed for the dance floor. The glittering ball slowly revolved, bespeckling the dancers with ephemeral sequins of light.

Kevin circulated and Jessie chain-smoked, hoping against hope that no old geezers would ask her to dance. Kevin came back to the table.

"There's someone I want you to meet. Come with me."

Her heart sank. As she suspected, that someone turned out to be a man in his late sixties who was just dying to dance with her.

The fellow escorted her into the midst of the other dancing couples, and squeezed her so tightly that her breasts were crushed painfully against his chest.

Nauseated, she struggled to block the ugly memory that was rising into her mind. The geezer rubbed his hand across the back of her brassiere. His breathing got heavier. "I could really go for a woman like you. Your husband's a lucky man."

Jessie wanted to scream and wrestle herself away, but Kevin had warned her against offending a potential voter.

Perspiration oozed from her skin and she could hardly breathe. Ignoring everything but the music, she prayed that the band would stop soon.

Finally, mercifully, it was over. As soon as the fellow loosened his grasp, she pulled away and marched back to the table. She saw Kevin at the edge of the dance floor wearing a sly grin and gave him a frosty look. The old man went straight to Kevin, shook his hand, and thanked him heartily.

With a sigh of relief, Jessie savored the cool air drying the sweat on her neck and shoulders. God, she hated dirty old men. She sat at the deserted table, trying to compose herself, and picked up the glass in front of her. The ice had melted and the drink was watery.

Jack sat down beside her and smiled.

She smiled back, his presence lifting her spirits. She'd always liked Jack and enjoyed his company. Tonight he was wearing one of the new, light-colored, vested suits that had just come into vogue. His brown hair was styled fashionably long, but not so long as to appear too radical.

"How are you doing, Jessie? I haven't had a chance to talk to you yet."

"I'm doing fine." She reached for a cigarette.

Jack whipped out his lighter and lit it for her.

She inhaled deeply, savoring the calming effect the tobacco smoke had on her nerves. "Thank you."

"My pleasure." He slid his hand under the table and stroked her thigh.

For a moment she was shocked, but his touch felt strangely comforting after her recent ordeal. Jack was notorious for chasing women, but he probably didn't mean anything by it.

His hand froze, and his gaze fixed on the opposite side of the table. Jessie glanced over and saw Kevin standing there.

Jack withdrew his hand slowly, careful not to make any hasty or abnormal movement, and shifted in his seat as if he was merely assuming a more comfortable position. He looked at her. "Can I get you a drink?"

"Yes, thank you. I'd like that."

Jack got up and left. Kevin's gaze followed him, but he said nothing. Jessie didn't think Kevin saw anything he could be sure of, but he definitely seemed suspicious.

Ellen returned to the table and a normal conversation ensued. If Ellen had noticed anything, she didn't show it.

When Jack returned with the drinks, he and Kevin talked to each other as if nothing untoward had happened.

Jessie wouldn't dream of causing Ellen pain by letting things get out of hand with Jack. Unfortunately, there were plenty of other women who were only too willing to fool around with him. Ellen couldn't always disguise the hurt in her eyes.

*

The lights came on, and the band began packing up their instruments. Jessie was relieved to be leaving at last. To her dismay, Tony Patero and his wife, Inez, invited everyone at the table to stop by their house for a nightcap. Jack politely declined, but Kevin eagerly accepted, even though Jessie knew he could tell she was dead on her feet. In fact, on the way over to the dance, she had pleaded with him not to stay too long.

Inside the Pateros' rambling ranch house, the men headed for the family room, and the women gathered in the kitchen. Inez was a small, thin woman who was as meticulously groomed as her house. It was apparent that her housekeeping bordered on the fanatic—not even a crumb escaped her notice.

Jessie struggled to stay awake while the women discussed their last bridge game and friends she didn't know. Stifling a yawn, she said she needed another drink and headed for the family room. At least the men would be talking politics, which was something she could follow.

Tony was manning the bar. His tie was gone and his shirt unbuttoned far enough to reveal the dark hair on his chest. Gold rings flashed on his hands as he gesticulated to punctuate a humorous anecdote. Bonhomie and liquor flowed freely, but soon the men's group began to break up, as wife by wife, the men were rounded up and headed home, until only Kevin and Tony remained at the bar.

Inez collected empty glasses and used ashtrays, and returned to the kitchen.

Tony waved Jessie over to a bar stool, giving her figure an appreciative glance as she sat down. "What can I fix you to drink?"

He served up a gin and tonic, smiled, and lit her cigarette with a flourish. Then, in a lowered tone appropriate to the subject, he began to fill them in on the latest scandal in Mansfield.

"We've got a real problem on our hands with the most popular teacher at the high school. You know who I mean—I won't name names."

Kevin nodded.

"He's gotten another one of his students pregnant. She's the daughter of a bank vice president. Unfortunately, the parents couldn't press charges because she's over sixteen. The principal ought to take disciplinary measures, but he's afraid it might lead to a riot on campus."

"No doubt," Kevin said.

Tony took a drag off his cigarette. "The family made overtures, but you-know-who refused to consider marrying the girl. Her parents had to make her get an abortion. But what else could they do under the circumstances?"

"I agree," Kevin said. "Luckily some sense prevailed on the Supreme Court in Roe versus Wade."

"Yeah, I know what you mean," Tony said. "Anyway, things are really out of hand at the high school. Parents who are in the know don't want their daughters in this teacher's class."

Kevin nodded and took a sip of scotch.

Tony glanced furtively toward the kitchen. "I'm not opposed to premarital sex, but this guy ought to stick to women his own age."

Jessie knew exactly which teacher Tony was referring to. Last fall, the guy made a pass at Sandy Hanlon's sister. He was a handsome blackguard with movie-star looks. He espoused a popular liberal agenda, and the students considered him one of their own, standing up against the establishment. Lacing his classes with humor, he revealed some of the spicier aspects of history, making what could be a boring subject come alive.

He was the most exciting teacher at Mansfield High in more ways than one.

For several years now, it was rumored that he'd had affairs with attractive female students under the guise of tutoring them for better grades, but this was the first time she'd heard of him getting them pregnant as well.

The whole thing was sickening—a pretty girl preyed on by a popular teacher who fed her romantic dreams. She probably never gave a moment's thought to the consequences, except to think they'd lead to a trip down the aisle with a sexy guy who had a respectable job. Instead, the poor kid was hauled off to an abortion clinic to have the child of her lover cut out of her— rape in reverse.

The girl was just as much a victim as her unborn infant. Everyone she loved and trusted had rejected the essence of her. All they wanted was the pretty shell. Her lover couldn't have cared less or he would have married her. He was too busy living the *Playboy* myth. Her parents were too busy living a social myth. They were wealthy by the world's standards, but they sacrificed their grandchild to avoid social scandal.

A wave of nausea twisted Jessie's stomach as she thought of the butchered baby and violated soul of the girl. *God help us,* she thought, *is this what we've become?*

CHAPTER 22

HEAD GAMES

Mike hung up the phone in the dairy office and rose from the desk. He hated ordering supplies and keeping the books. Lately, he seemed to be shouldering more and more of Kevin's responsibilities, but Kevin was too busy campaigning to handle the business end of the farm operation these days.

In an hour and a half it would be time to start the afternoon milking, so this was as good a time as any to take a break. Mike turned off the desk lamp and left. Before heading to the house, he paused for a moment and surveyed the farm.

Overhead, cotton clouds scudded across a bright blue sky, and fields of wheat billowed in waves like an inland sea. Acres of rich green corn sprang from the earth, and hay was drying in wind-rows ready to be baled. He was filled with a sense of accomplishment as he contemplated the fruit of his labor.

Mike walked to the house whistling a tune. He was looking forward to a cold drink and seeing his sister-in-law. She'd be alone, except for the children, who would be napping upstairs.

When he entered, Jessie was fixing herself a glass of iced tea. She turned and smiled. "Would you like some?"

"Sure," he replied, then watched her appraisingly while she got out another glass and filled it. He assumed a neutral expression when she turned to hand it to him.

"Thanks." He took a long swallow. "It's just what I needed."

"You're welcome."

"By the way, could you come into the family room for a minute? I need your advice on something."

"Sure." Jessie followed Mike down the hall. She was surprised he valued her opinion enough to ask her advice on anything. But the sexual attraction was so strong she couldn't resist spending a little time with him, and just talking wasn't a sin.

Mike sat on the couch, so she seated herself in the chair opposite him and waited expectantly. He studied the glass in his hand, seemingly at a loss for words.

"What is it?" she prompted.

He looked up. "Well, I have a real problem, and I was hoping you could help me with it." He paused. "Uh, the thing is, I like my brother's girl, and I'm pretty sure she likes me too. But I don't know what to do about it."

Jessie wondered if Mike was thinking of dumping Sandy because he'd become infatuated with Traci, but she was afraid to come right out and ask. "Is Johnny in love with her?"

"No," Mike said flatly

"Are you certain?" Johnny and Traci had been dating hot and heavy, although she wasn't sure Traci was his only girlfriend. "He's your brother. You have to respect his feelings, too."

"Yes, I'm certain. She's a great girl and she's just wasting her time with him. He's just stringing her along. I really care about her, and I'd treat her a lot better than he does."

"Then I think you should let her know what's going on."

He shook his head. "No. I couldn't speak against my brother. It wouldn't be right."

Jessie took a sip of her tea and thought for a moment. "So just tell her you like her. If Johnny's stringing her along, she'll see the light sooner or later."

"I can't."

"Why not?"

"It's against the rules."

She lifted an eyebrow. "I didn't think there were any rules in this house."

"Kevin and Johnny almost killed each other over a girl once," Mike said, shaking his head sadly. "We had to come up with some rules, and we all agreed not to hit on each other's girls. So I can't tell her myself."

"I see." Traci was so sweet, Jessie disliked the idea of Johnny using her. "I could tell her for you."

"No. She has to figure it out on her own, or it wouldn't be within the rules."

Jessie eyed Mike curiously. *Why bring the subject up at all if the rules precluded any outside assistance?* "Well, I don't know what else to suggest, but good luck."

He leaned forward and looked directly into her eyes. "Do me a favor and think about it. You're pretty smart. If you come up with anything, be sure and let me know."

"Okay." She got up to leave.

Mike leaned back, clasped his hands behind his head, and smiled.

His smug grin made Jessie think twice as she left the room. A self-satisfied smirk made no sense if he was simply seeking her advice about an infatuation with Traci. Then it hit her. It was the phrase "my brother's *girl*" that had thrown her off. She'd automatically assumed Mike meant Traci. But technically it could just as easily mean herself. Kevin was his brother also.

Jessie stopped in her tracks.

The whole thing had been a come-on specifically calculated to avoid infringing the rules.

Mike's timing was perfect. The children were napping and no one else was in the house. There was plenty of time to fool around before afternoon milking. Bert would prep the milking parlor and Cletus would round the cows up in the back pasture.

Jessie thought of Mike's muscled chest and felt a surge of heat between her legs. It was awfully tempting to turn around and give him what he wanted. But she had her vows to consider, and she didn't want to betray her friend Sandy.

Country music filled the main hall at the county fairgrounds, and couples were energetically dancing on the concrete floor. Jessie sat alone at a table, holding a plastic cup of draft beer, trying to pretend she was having a good time. Frank and Charlie were jigging up a storm with Kathleen and Mary Clare. The band was Carla Snyder and the Country Spiders. They were mediocre at best, and presumably came cheap.

Jessie had survived several dances with lecherous farmers of Kevin's acquaintance and prayed there'd be no more. She thought about Mike's clever come-on and almost wished she'd taken him up on it. A lot of middle-aged men who hit on her complained that their wives didn't like sex. She wasn't that kind of woman, and not getting enough was driving her nuts. However, she remembered Mike's smug grin, and resolved to hold out as long as she could.

At the moment, she couldn't take any more of the music. She got up and went outdoors. Kevin wouldn't miss her for awhile. She lit a cigarette, took a drag, and surveyed the area. Several people were milling around just talking—nothing threatening there. Then two dudes wearing cowboy hats and boots got out of a pickup and approached the entrance.

Jessie looked at the ground to avoid making eye contact, but they stopped right in front of her. She pretended not to see them, but they didn't move away.

"Hey, pretty lady, what are you doing out here all by your lonesome?" the tall thin one with a mustache asked.

She tried to ignore him, but he repeated the question.

"I just needed some air."

The shorter fellow spoke up. "How about joining us inside for a spin on the dance floor?"

"No, thanks. My husband wouldn't like it."

The dude with the mustache eyed her. "Now don't pull my leg, darlin'. No husband in his right mind would let a doll like you stand outside all by herself."

"Yeah," the short one said.

Mr. Mustache winked. "Looks more like you had a fight with your boyfriend. Forget him. I'll be happy to show you a good time."

"Me too," Shorty added, looking hopeful.

"Sorry, fellas, I'm not available." She held up her left hand, flashing her wedding ring.

Mr. Mustache grinned. "Tell you what, babe, divorce the scum and let me show you what a good time really means."

Jessie sensed someone come up beside her.

"These fellows bothering you?" Tom asked.

Shorty scowled. "Heck, no, we was just askin' for a dance. Who the hell are you anyway?"

Tom pulled a knife. "Does this answer your question?"

Mr. Mustache's eyes widened. "I reckon so."

Shorty nodded, and they both started backing away.

Tom grinned. "Guess they didn't want to dance too bad after all."

"Thanks," Jessie said. "It was kind of you to come to my rescue."

"Anytime," he said and sheathed the knife.

The following night, Kevin took Jessie to Club Roma to mingle and troll for votes. He trolled. She sat at the bar chain-smoking and drinking.

There was only so much small talk she could manage in one evening, and she'd already exhausted her repertoire. She stared at her drink pensively. Would all this drinking turn her into an alcoholic? She hoped not.

She didn't think she was addicted. She only drank because she felt out of her depth in social situations, and because of her sexual frustration. There was only so much masturbation could do, and she needed to sleep at night.

"A penny for your thoughts," a familiar voice said.

She turned and looked into Sam's eyes.

"Well?" he asked.

She hadn't a clue what to say. God knows she couldn't tell him the truth. Her mind scrambled to come up with something.

His gaze probed her eyes. "If a penny's not enough, how much will it cost me?

"Um, nothing. I was just lost in space listening to the band."

Sam smiled. "You really like music, don't you?"

"Yes, I do."

"I have this terrific Pink Floyd tape I just bought for the car. Do you have any of their albums?"

"No, but I'd like to."

"Why don't you come out to my car and I'll play the cassette for you. It's nice to hear something through before you buy it."

Jessie hesitated but only for a moment. Kevin probably wouldn't like it if she left the club with Sam for awhile, but the offer was too tempting to refuse.

"Okay," she replied.

Sam chatted with her companionably as he escorted her to the Cutlass. "So what kind of music do you like best?"

"I like all kinds. My father's a jazz musician, but I like rock 'n' roll more than anything."

Sam opened the car door for her with athletic grace. Once she was settled, he climbed into the driver's seat.

Being alone with him made her feel as awkward and tongue-tied as a teenager with a crush. He leaned toward her. A wave of heat tingled through her body and her breasts grew taut.

Sam reached past her and opened the glove compartment. He pulled out a cassette and popped it into the tape player. "I know you'll love this. You're the kind of person who would."

He smiled into her eyes. For a moment, she thought he would make a pass as the music began to play.

The opening strains of the instrumental were stirring, but totally unfamiliar. Sam leaned back into his seat. Jessie felt a stab of disappointment. Perhaps she'd misread the look in his eyes.

She concentrated on the melody, the better to resist temptation, and pondered what the musical selection might reflect about the man beside her. The song ended only too soon, and she hoped the next composition would be just as intriguing.

Sam abruptly reached out and turned the tape off. "All right, we can go back inside now."

Jessie gave him a questioning look but he avoided her eyes. She waited for him to come around and open the door, puzzled as to why he suddenly seemed vexed. She got out and faced him squarely.

"Thanks for letting me hear the tape."

Sam said nothing. He turned and walked toward the club in absolute silence.

Bewildered, she followed at a decorous pace.

When Sam reached the entrance, he stopped and held the door for her, but kept his gaze averted.

Jessie started past him, then halted and looked directly into his eyes. They were cool and distant.

She turned her face away, wondering what she had done to offend him.

CHAPTER 23

IN THE HEAT OF THE NIGHT

The night was hot but not too humid, and Jessie wished she could be out in it, walking over the hills, and gazing at the stars. Ever since the day she first moved to the countryside, she'd found it entrancing. It was almost as if she'd entered a magic kingdom, a place where one might still glimpse the corn goddess strolling in the moonlight. Unhappily, however, she was stuck at another boring party at Kathleen and Frank's.

She'd been sitting in the kitchen with Kathleen, LuAnn and Ruby for an hour now. The gossiping women bored her silly, and she was already on her third drink.

Mike and Sandy hadn't arrived yet. Johnny hadn't brought a date because he and Traci recently had a falling out. And Tom and Sam sent word earlier that they weren't coming.

Jessie had hoped to see Sam. She longed for some clue as to what offense she had given him at Club Roma. It wouldn't have surprised her if he made a pass when he took her out to the car and, truth be told, she wished he had. But he hadn't, and she couldn't understand why he suddenly acted so cold and aloof. She was afraid he had avoided coming to the party because he knew she'd be there.

The atmosphere in the kitchen was claustrophobic. Sealed windows shut out the trilling of insects and rustle of leaves. An air conditioner hummed in tandem with the dull conversation.

Jessie excused herself and headed to the basement where Kevin and Johnny were playing pool along with Frank, Bubba and Dale. There was no chance of her getting into a game. They were betting money, so she wouldn't be allowed to do anything except watch. Still, it was better than hanging out in the kitchen listening to gossip about people she didn't know.

When she reached the bottom of the stairs, Kevin took a shot on the eight ball and scratched.

Frank chuckled with glee. "Okay, Kev, pay up."

"Heck, Frank, let's make it two out of three and see who wins. The pot will be bigger," he whined.

"Nope. Pay up. We pay each game. Everybody agreed."

"Come on."

"Pay up, Kev," Frank said. "Who wants to take me on next?"

Just then Mike walked down the steps followed by a long-legged, big-breasted brunette. She was wearing skin-tight jeans and a halter top that tied in front. All the males sucked in their breath. Jessie stared at Mike in shock. *Where was Sandy?*

Frank could hardly take his eyes off the woman's tits, but then he remembered he was winning money at pool. "Any takers?"

"Not me," Bubba said. The other guys shook their heads no.

"How about Tonya here?" Mike said. "Would you like to play my brother-in-law, Tonya?"

"I don't know how to play pool, Mike."

"That's okay, puss, we'll teach you."

Frank smiled. "That's right, honey. You'll do just fine. Let's start out by showing you how to hold the stick."

Kevin held out his stick. "You can have mine."

"You can have my stick anytime, too," Johnny quipped.

Tonya smiled at Johnny and took Kevin's.

Mike showed her how to position her hands. She bent over to take a shot. Male gazes fastened on her cleavage like metal drawn to a magnet. Mike eyed the butt crease exposed by Tonya's hip-hugger jeans and licked his lips. The cue ball wobbled about, randomly tapped a few other balls, and stopped.

"Oh darn," Tonya said. "Look how bad that shot was. I'm just awful."

"Not from what I could see," Kevin said.

Mike grinned. "You're doing just fine, pussy. Do it again. I'm sure you can get a good shot off if you try."

"Yeah," Frank said. "You could get a good shot off of me just by holding my stick."

Jessie gagged on her drink. Things were getting too lewd to hang around any longer. She went upstairs to find something to eat.

Unfortunately, Ron Meyers, a short balding friend of Frank's, found her at the buffet in the dining room. He gazed longingly at her figure, then struck up a conversation. She tried to disengage herself, but Ron wouldn't stop talking.

"By the way, Jessie, there's something I've been meaning to ask you. You're Kevin's wife, so maybe you can tell me."

"What?" she asked and inwardly groaned.

"I've known Kevin for a long time and I like him a lot, but I just can't understand how a man like him can hang around with those guys in that crazy motorcycle gang."

She knew which club Ron was referring to. In fact, several of the guys had stopped by the farm showing off their bikes.

"Maybe he just likes motorcycles."

"That's not what I mean. I mean the kind of guys they are."

She wondered what he was getting at. There were two biker's clubs in the county, a semi-respectable one and the self-dubbed "Wild Bunch." Kevin had known most of them since high school. "I don't know anything except that they're wild."

"You mean you don't know?"

"Know what?"

"They're all homosexuals."

Her eyes widened with astonishment.

Ron looked chagrined. "I see you really didn't know," he said and excused himself.

Jessie hardly noticed Ron leave. She drained the drink in her hand and stared off into space. She'd never heard of any straight guys who liked hanging out with homosexuals. Did that mean Kevin was bisexual?

⚊⚊⚊

Before long Tonya and Mike trooped upstairs and left, but another three hours passed before Kevin was ready to leave. When they finally got home, Kevin stretched himself out on the sofa. Luckily Suzy was baby-sitting and had her own car now, so Jessie didn't have to drive her home.

After Suzy left, Jessie went over and knelt next to the couch. She thought Kevin might want her since he hadn't gone straight up to bed. He'd gotten pretty excited over Tonya at the party and might actually want to have sex.

When she kissed him, he pushed her away. "Leave me alone. I'm too tired."

Too drunk, Jessie said to herself. She gave him a disgusted look, then went upstairs to the bedroom and stripped off her clothes. She was so angry that if Mike had been home, instead of out with that woman, she'd throw herself into his arms without a second thought.

However, the rational part of her mind had to thank providence that he wasn't there. Rationally, having sex with Mike was all wrong—and not just because he was her brother-in-law. Mike was deadly, even though he made her feel alive.

The master bedroom was on the wrong side of the house to catch a breeze, and the heat of the day hovered inside. She got into bed, but sleep eluded her. After tossing and turning for half an hour, she threw on some clothes and went down to the kitchen to fix herself a drink. It was impossible to keep booze in the rec room bar. It disappeared too fast.

Jessie walked outside to the pool. The water shimmered under the moonlight, placid, lovely, and alluring. It was a perfect night for a swim, and there weren't any freeloaders hanging out at the house for once.

She checked to be certain no one else had come home, then went into the pool house and disrobed. She wrapped a towel around her body and walked over to the pool. She took one last look around, then dropped the towel and slid in.

There was nothing between her skin and the soothing caress of liquid. The water felt soft and sensuous, and she luxuriated in wonderful new sensations. She'd never really had a chance to swim without a suit before; it was risky because of the number of people normally hanging around, and you never knew who was going to show up.

It felt marvelous gliding through the water like a dolphin, and she wished she'd tried it sooner.

Feeling much calmer, she swam to the center of the pool and turned on her back to float. Overhead, the spangled depths of space stretched on into infinity. Cradled by the languid water, she soon felt so detached from her body that she might have been the planet itself, instead of a separate being on its surface.

Watching the twinkling stars, she contemplated the paradox of a world filled with so much beauty, yet flawed by so much evil. Of course, to have free will at all presupposed a choice between good and evil. And there were the legends of the fall. Had there truly been a mythic choice so destructive that it altered the nature of Nature itself?

At length, with a sigh, she backstroked to the end of the pool where she'd left the towel. When she reached the edge, she turned her back to the house—just in case anyone else had come home—and boosted her bottom up on the rim. She reached back and felt for the towel. After wrapping it around her body, she got up and headed for the pool house.

"Good evening," a voice said out of the darkness.

Jessie froze in her tracks.

Mike was sitting in one of the lounge chairs.

A flush of embarrassment swept through her—*he'd seen most of her body naked*—but she met his gaze evenly, angry at being spied on. The air between them sizzled. She felt a flash of heat that left her tingling. If he made a move toward her, she knew she couldn't resist.

Mike let his gaze travel slowly over her body, then looked back into her eyes. He didn't bother to rise, and he didn't speak. Obviously he was waiting for her to come to him.

It would be so easy to give in, so easy to let the towel drop and go to him—so easy to satisfy animal lust.

But she wasn't going to play his game. She knew he didn't really care about her or respect her.

Jessie lifted her chin and strode off to the house. Kevin lay snoring on the sofa. She went straight upstairs to the master bedroom and locked the door behind her.

CHAPTER 24

SUSPICIOUS MINDS

Johnny rolled up the driveway in his Dodge Challenger. He ambled indoors through the mudroom and strolled down the hall toward the family room. He paused when he noticed Jessie in the living room doing her exercises, and stepped closer to ogle.

Jessie broke off when she sensed someone watching her.

"Don't stop," Johnny said.

"I was finished." She got up and walked past him to the kitchen. He turned and followed.

Jessie checked the pots of tea steeping on the counter. They were cool enough now to transfer into pitchers. She lined up a few and began to fill them.

"Hey, fix me a glass," he said.

"All right." She reached into the cupboard and took out a couple of glasses.

He came over and leaned on the counter. "I have a question I've been meaning to ask you."

"About what?"

"Sex."

She rolled her eyes. "You've got to be kidding."

"No, I'm serious."

She stared at him, incredulous. "*You* want to ask *me* a question about sex? Come on. It's got to be a joke, right?"

Johnny shook his head. "No, I'm serious. It's about women. I figured you could tell me the answer."

Sure he was baiting her, Jessie sliced a lemon and squeezed a section into each glass without responding. He gazed into her eyes disarmingly. "You see, men don't really know how women feel about some things. I was hoping you could help me out."

She wondered which girlfriend he was having trouble with now. "Okay, I'll try. What's the question?"

"Do women ever get hard-up?"

"What kind of question is that?" she asked, taken aback.

"I really need to know—honest. It has me puzzled, and I was hoping you could tell me."

"Of course they do." She stirred some sugar into the tea.

"Nah, I don't believe it," Johnny said, shaking his head. "Women don't need it like men do."

Jessie grabbed some cubes from the icemaker and dropped them into the tea, then handed Johnny a glass.

"If women didn't need it, the population explosion would be a non-issue overnight. No woman in her right mind would put up with the male ego just to keep on having kids."

He took a swig of tea. "No, I say you're wrong. Women don't need it like men do."

"Maybe they don't need it as much as men do, but they still get hard-up."

"I don't believe it."

"Why?" she asked, and took a sip of tea.

He looked into her eyes. "Because you never come to my room."

Jessie choked on her drink.

Johnny grinned and drained his glass in one long swallow.

"Thanks for the tea." He put the glass on the counter and walked away singing the lyrics to "Time Is On My Side" by the Rolling Stones.

She slammed her glass on the counter. "Fuck you!"

Johnny turned back to face her. "Anytime, Sis, any time."

He swept his gaze over her body, smiled like the Cheshire Cat, and left singing the same tune.

Mary Clare arrived all by herself that week to do the guys' laundry and cleaning. "Mother couldn't come today. She's too busy getting ready for the Sodality social," she said, in response to Jessie's query, then went to work like a whirlwind, without pausing to say another word until she was through.

"I can hardly wait for Friday night," Mary Clare said, after she put the dust mop away. "I made a new dress to wear."

"That's great. What does it look like?"

"I'm not telling. I want everyone to be surprised. Mother hasn't even seen it."

Mary Clare picked up her purse to leave. "You should learn to sew, Jessie. It's amazing how much money you can save on clothes. Think how much better it would be for your family budget."

She stiffened. "I'm sure it would, but I don't have time to learn at the moment."

"Well," Mary Clare huffed. "I was just *trying* to be helpful. See you Friday night then."

She turned on her heel and marched off.

Ten minutes later the phone began to ring.

Jessie's heart drummed in her chest. She'd already had six anonymous calls before Mary Clare arrived. Pulse racing, she picked up the receiver. "Hello?"

Breathing, then hollow silence was all she heard in reply.

She banged the receiver onto the cradle. The phone hadn't rung once while Mary Clare was there. Wasn't it strange how nobody else got the calls? And Kevin still refused to do anything about it.

The phone started ringing again. Her heart began to pound. She picked up the receiver. "Hello?"

There was no response.

Jessie slammed the receiver down and pulled the phone directory out of the drawer. She found the number and dialed.

"Mansfield Pharmacy," a female voice answered. "How may I help you?"

"Hi, this is Jessie McKenna. I need to get my tranquilizer prescription refilled, but I lost the bottle, and I don't know the prescription number."

"That's no problem, Mrs. McKenna, I'll just have the pharmacist look it up in the files. It'll be ready in an hour."

❦

Jessie arrived at the Sodality social prepared to be bored all evening. It was a bring-your-own-bottle affair. Kevin had whiskey, but she would have to do without gin and tonic. The only mixers offered were cola and ginger ale.

Mary Clare caused a brief moment of excitement when she walked in wearing her homemade, hot-pink satin dress. Maria praised it lavishly, as did Kathleen. Jessie feverishly wracked her brain to find something complimentary to say. The dress accentuated Mary Clare's figure problems, and the color looked terrible with her mousey, light-brown hair.

"Well, Jessie, what do you think?" Mary Clare asked, still preening.

"I've never seen such fine seam-work. You can't even tell it wasn't professionally made."

"Of course you can't tell that—I've been sewing since I was twelve. Don't you just love the color?"

"Oh yes," Jessie said. Strictly speaking it wasn't a lie. Hot-pink looked nice on some women.

After dinner, a gray-haired ensemble carried their instruments to the dais and warmed up. Johnny and his date immediately got up and said their goodbyes. Jessie wished she could leave too. She hated having to dance to the kind of music they were sure to play. Her grandfather had tried to help her learn the steps to various dances when she was young, but he was too tall, and Rick didn't lead properly. After her grandparents moved to Florida, she managed to escape anymore lessons. Most of the men who squired her around the dance floor, squeezing her, weren't into fancy footwork. She much preferred rock 'n' roll.

Joe turned to Maria. "Would you like to dance, Momma?"

Maria smiled. "Of course, Poppa."

Joe gave her his arm and escorted her to the dance floor.

Right after that, Mike walked into the church hall with a stunning blonde on his arm.

Frank gave a low whistle. "Would you look at that."

Kevin nodded. "That boy sure knows how to pick 'em."

Mike approached the table with a smug grin on his face. "Good evening, everybody. I'd like to present Miss Lynette Carter."

The males of the family immediately fell all over themselves to impress her. Lynette flirted as effortlessly as she breathed and played them like a maestro. She was no virgin, you could see it in her eyes; the looks she favored the men with were all too knowing.

Jessie watched her performance, intrigued.

Lynette took male worship as her due. Though her overt flirtation with every male at the table appeared to annoy Mike, she didn't seem to care.

Kevin couldn't take his eyes off of her. "Are you in college, Lynnette?"

"Yes. I just finished my junior year at the University of Virginia."

"That's a great school," he said. "Thomas Jefferson founded it."

"Yes. I'm surprised you knew. Mike didn't."

Kevin smiled. "That's Mike for you. But he's smart in his own way. He did well in anatomy."

Lynette's eyes widened. "Really? I didn't know Mike went to college."

"He didn't. He used the home-study method."

Lynette gave a ladylike chuckle.

Mike scowled as his brothers-in-law guffawed.

Kevin grinned. "So what are you studying, Lynette?"

"Literature. I just got through with the Russian authors."

"Who did you enjoy the most?"

"Tolstoy."

Kevin nodded and took a drag off his cigarette. "Tolstoy is terrific. Which did you like better? *War and Peace* or *Anna Karenina?*"

"Oh, *Anna Karenina.*"

"Me too. Tolstoy's characterization of Anna was brilliant."

Mike frowned and drained the drink in his hand. "I hate to interrupt such an illuminating conversation, but Lynette and I are expected someplace else tonight. So, if you don't mind, we have to get going."

"Of course not," Kevin said. "It was a pleasure meeting you, Lynette."

She fluttered her lashes. "It was my pleasure, too."

Mike's expression was thunderous. Jessie suspected he was going to get a taste of his own medicine. Poor Sandy would be heartbroken when she found out Mike was two-timing her, again.

Saturday morning, Kevin finished milking the cows then drove over to Jack's place. The Rotary Club was having a big breakfast, and he and Jack were going to be making joint appearances all day long at every function they could find. Jack was a popular politician, and his public support was essential if Kevin hoped to stand out among the competition.

There were two spots open on the county board of commissioners, and Leroy Jones was in contention for one. He was popular on the town council and name recognition meant a lot. Kevin congratulated himself on cultivating a good rapport with Leroy, but Jack had the broadest base of support among the electorate. The more the public identified him with Jack, the better his chances would be.

Kevin rang the bell. Ellen opened the door. "Good morning, gorgeous," he said, then gave her a peck on the cheek.

She smiled warmly. "Good morning to you, too."

Jack grabbed his suit jacket and gave her a goodbye kiss. "See you tonight, sweetheart. I'll pick you up for the dance around seven, after we get Jessie."

He pulled the Lincoln out of the garage, and Kevin climbed into the passenger seat.

Jack backed out of the driveway and accelerated up the road. "We've got a shit-load of events to attend, but it's the last two weeks before the primary. If you pick up enough support today, you'll beat Bud Hanks and Dwight Ayers. Leroy's a cinch to win the other seat on the party ticket, and he'll bring out the black vote. That should help tip the scales in your favor."

"I hope so," Kevin said.

"I told Joan Harris you're with her on the women's liberation thing, so watch what you say around her. She pushed to get the state Equal Rights Amendment on the ballot this fall, and she has a large constituency."

Kevin chuckled. "The only thing I want to see liberated on women is their panties."

"I'm with you there, buddy, but you gotta do what you gotta do," Jack said. "Party officials would prefer someone older to run against the Republicans in the fall. I had to pull some strings so they'd hold off endorsing anyone in the primary, but I told them you've got what it takes."

⚜

At the end of the day, Kevin and Jack were running almost an hour behind by the time they got to the farm to pick up Jessie.

"Hi, beautiful" Jack said, and gave her a kiss on the cheek. "Sorry we're a little late."

She smiled. "No problem. Things were a bit hectic with the kids. I haven't been waiting long."

"No man should keep a lady waiting—certainly not one as pretty as you," Jack said. "By the way, that's a lovely dress you're wearing, but it's too long."

Her mouth opened in dismay. "Oh, no, I thought Ellen said she and Marcella would be wearing long dresses tonight."

"They are, but they don't have legs like yours," Jack said and winked.

Kevin frowned. "We're already late. Let's go."

He marched out to the Lincoln and opened the door to the back seat for Jessie, then climbed into the front with Jack.

Jessie lit a cigarette and listened while they talked. She always enjoyed their repartee. It was fascinating to observe how well Kevin related to other people when he couldn't relate to her at all.

Jack's tone of voice suddenly became conspiratorial. "I had a meeting with Susan Sanders last week to try and get the endorsement from her organization."

"How did it go?" Kevin asked.

"Good. I got it."

"That's great. I'm glad to hear it."

"Great tits, too," Jack said. "How about you, Kevin? Did you get any yet?"

Kevin stiffened. "Not now," he said in a low voice.

"Why not?"

Kevin nodded toward the back seat.

"Oh, come on," Jack said. "How was it?"

"My wife's in the back seat," Kevin hissed.

Jack peered into the rearview mirror and caught Jessie's eye. He grinned. "It's okay, Jessie's cool."

Kevin's jaw tightened and he got a peculiar look on his face.

Jessie figured Kevin had been suspicious of her and Jack since he caught Jack with his hand on her leg at the Knights of Columbus dance. And, by saying she was cool, Jack had given him even more reason to suspect something might be going on. However, Jack had just made certain that she knew Kevin was running around, and Kevin was in no position to throw stones.

It was actually tempting to consider having an affair with Jack. He was a handsome man, and couldn't afford to be named co-respondent in a divorce suit. He was only in it for the sex, and sex was what she needed. But what she wanted was for Kevin to become a decent husband.

And she would never betray Ellen—never.

Frankly, she didn't understand why Jack couldn't keep his hands off other women. It was breaking Ellen's heart, and none of the broads he jumped into bed with had the class she did.

⁂

On the morning of the primary election, Jessie was a little nervous when she took up her position at the Belleville poll to hand out Kevin's campaign literature to the voters. She was uncomfortable about greeting strangers and trying to get them to take Kevin's brochures.

Around nine, Ann arrived to keep her company. Jessie got her first look at the engagement ring Mark had given her. "Wow! It's gorgeous."

Ann smiled wanly. "Yeah, but guess what?"

"What?"

"Mark's parents want him to go to graduate school. They're offering to pay for it—on one condition."

"Oh no! I hope it isn't what I think it is."

Ann nodded. "They want us to put off getting married— and I'm pissed, really pissed. Mark and I both have our bachelor's degrees, and we can both start working full-time."

"Then why doesn't he stand up to his parents?"

Ann sighed. "Mark said it made good economic sense, and maybe that's true, but I'll bet his parents are hoping he'll meet somebody else in grad school and dump me."

"Right. If they can afford to send him to graduate school, and they liked you, they'd do it whether he got married or not."

"Exactly, lots of graduate students are married. But we both know they don't like me, and Mark's taking them up on the offer. So just to make him jealous, I got a job as a cocktail waitress."

"Good for you. Man, I bet that blew his mind."

"Yep. He can't stand the thought of guys flirting with me all evening, but that's just too bad," Ann said. "And guess which well-known politician came in the other night with a woman who isn't his wife?"

"Jack?" Jessie whispered.

Ann nodded.

Just then a convertible plastered with Jack's campaign signs cruised through the parking lot playing the "1812 Overture" over a loudspeaker. Jack and Ellen sat in the back together, waving at the crowd. They made a handsome vibrant pair, and many of the voters waiting in line waved and cheered.

Concord was a county with traditional values, and Jessie wondered what the voters would think if they knew the truth.

CHAPTER 25

LONG HOT SUMMER

Marcella called to congratulate Jessie on Kevin's win. "Isn't it wonderful that our husbands will be on the ticket together? Leroy and I have always liked Kevin so much, and we weren't sure he was going to make it."

"Yes, I know he was afraid Dwight Ayers would beat him."

"Honey, if it wasn't for you, Dwight more than likely would have."

"What do you mean?"

"You improved Kevin's image so much, by picking out his wardrobe, he really looked sophisticated and stood out from the crowd. Ellen and I think it was just the edge he needed. Even Jack said so."

Jessie was warmed by the compliment, but somewhat ambivalent. It felt good to be the wife of a winner, but the rest of the summer and most of the fall would be spent campaigning. They'd have no home life to speak of. Still, maybe Kevin would finally realize they made a good team.

Mike asked Jessie for riding lessons so he could impress Lynette by inviting her to the farm to go horseback riding.

Jessie started Mike on Blue, and it was obvious he had enough natural aptitude to become a decent rider. She felt a pang of regret that things had gotten so fouled-up when they first met. Despite his bad-boy attitude, he did want a wife and children someday, and he liked horses.

Lynette had a good seat and nice hands, so Jessie really didn't mind her riding Rio. But she had to squelch a pang of envy every time Mike and Lynette rode off together. However, as long as Lynette was showing up regularly at the house, Jessie was privy to many of their quarrels. And quarrel they did.

Mike fumed because Lynette refused to date him exclusively, and it drove him crazy whenever she went out with someone else. He roared like an angry lion, banging doors when they argued or slamming down the phone whenever Lynette declined a date.

If things weren't volatile enough, the anonymous calls kept on coming, and Kathleen's children were there almost every day. The farm was Dennis's second home, and Johnny's friends Dave Walker and Jimmy Freemont were frequently there smoking pot. On weekends Jessie wiped up vomit, swept up glass from broken beer bottles, and rescued patio furniture from the pool. It wasn't easy being a perfect housewife under the circumstances, but she was improving.

Besides taking care of the house and children, she mowed the grass, washed the Grand Prix, and cleaned the pool every week. She became such a fanatic about keeping everything spotless, and in order, that she often forgot to eat, and lived on caffeine in colas and coffee for energy. At night, she drank wine to wind down—and if she couldn't sleep, she took Valium.

It'd been some time since Johnny had invited her to smoke any pot, and her craving for it was growing. She never intruded on the male sanctum of the family room unless invited to do so. In the past, the invitations had been fairly frequent when Dave and Jimmy were over to play cards, and she wondered if Johnny was mad at her because she'd gotten angry at his joke.

She decided to ask him outright if he'd sell her some pot.

"Nope," Johnny said. "I won't."

"Why not?" she asked, afraid he was still peeved.

"Because it's against the rules."

It wasn't the answer she expected. In fact, it seemed nonsensical. "I don't understand."

Johnny crossed his arms over his chest and looked at her. "Kevin told me not to sell you any pot if you ever asked me. But I'm a nice guy, so from time to time I'd get you high for nothing. Only you aren't very appreciative."

"Come on, Johnny, give me a break. I'm sorry I got mad at your joke. Kevin won't know if you sell me some."

He shook his head. "You come to my room and we'll work something out."

Jessie rolled her eyes. "Never mind."

"Aw, come on, Sis. Give me a break. I'm getting hard up."

"I don't believe it."

"Why not?"

"Because you never come to my room," she said, playing off the punch-line of his jest. It was too good a riposte to pass up.

Johnny chuckled. "Oh, no, I couldn't do *that*."

"Why not?" she asked, her tone dripping with sarcasm.

"It's against the rules," he quipped, grinning. "But you come to my room, and I promise I won't tell."

"Forget it."

Johnny shrugged. "Suit yourself."

He turned and walked out of the house. Jessie heard the car engine revving, then Johnny peeled off down the driveway.

So he hadn't been joking about wanting her to come to his room. Obviously the immorality of having an affair with a sister-in-law didn't seem to bother Johnny or Mike one bit. All they appeared to care about was being caught in technical violation of the rules they had agreed on. While the regulations made sense in so far as they pertained to girlfriends, what sort of brothers would think it was okay to screw their sibling's wife right under his nose? And why were they so concerned about obeying the rules of the brotherhood, yet so cavalier about violating a far more sacred one?

Jessie was sitting in the rocker by the wood stove, feeding Joey, when she heard the screen door to the mudroom open and shut. Lynette tapped on the frame of the doorway leading into the kitchen.

"Do you mind if I come in?"

"No, of course not."

Lynette walked over and looked down at Joey. "He's cute. Mike said he wants one just like him."

"Yes, he told me he wants to be a father someday."

Laura shyly showed Lynette her stuffed toy rabbit.

"Oh, I love bunnies. They're so cuddly and soft."

Laura nodded and hugged the velveteen rabbit, then went back to play with the toys scattered on the rug.

"I'd like to have children someday," Lynette said, "but not anytime soon. I'm having too much fun to settle down and be a housewife."

"I don't blame you," Jessie said. "Take your time. Find the right guy."

"Oh, I am. And I'm not sure Mike's the right guy. He asked me to marry him, but I turned him down. Now he's furious with me."

Poor Sandy, Jessie thought, *she was going to be devastated to learn Mike had proposed to Lynette—whether she'd turned him down or not.* "So that's what he's been so angry about all week."

"I told him there were other guys just as handsome as him who wanted to date me, and some of them have a lot more money. So why should I tie myself down?"

"I agree," Jessie said.

"You haven't seen a gold, engraved cigarette lighter lying around, have you?"

"No, I didn't, but look around if you like."

"Thanks." Lynette left the kitchen and began searching through the downstairs rooms. She returned empty-handed.

"I'm positive I left it here. I called and asked Mike, but he insisted I hadn't, only I don't believe him."

"If you want to check his room, it's okay by me."

Lynette looked relieved. She nodded and went upstairs. A few minutes later she returned with the lighter.

"Thanks, Jessie. My parents gave it to me for my birthday."

"You're welcome."

"Please don't tell Mike I was here."

"No problem." Jessie wondered how Mike would react when he found the lighter missing. But if he said anything, she had the perfect out. With so many druggies showing up on the weekends to party, anybody could have taken it.

❧

When Mike asked Jessie if Lynette had been there, she lied without a qualm. After a heated argument with Lynette over the phone, Mike took off for the ocean with Johnny.

If it wasn't for the anonymous phone calls, it would have been a relief to have them gone. But Kevin was out every night, often not returning until dawn. At last, in the wee hours of the morning near the end of the week, Jessie heard car doors slamming, and Mike and Johnny staggered upstairs to crash in their rooms.

Later that day, Jessie was upstairs putting away the laundry, when she happened to glance through one of the bedroom windows, and noticed something moving in the back seat of Mike's lime-green Barracuda. As far as she knew, Mike and Johnny were still asleep. Maybe one of their buddies had been too wasted to get out of the car and make it up to the spare bedroom.

It looked like a long-haired blond-headed person. Probably Dave Walker; he had real long hair. But when the car door swung open, a bare-breasted woman fell halfway out of the vehicle.

Jessie dashed downstairs and hurried toward the back door. When she entered the kitchen, she saw Mike sitting at the table drinking one of Kevin's beers. He glanced up.

"Mike, there's a naked woman hanging out of your car!"

"Oh, *that*. Hell, I forgot all about her."

"Well you'd better do something. I don't think she can walk. I'll help you bring her into the house."

He took a swig of beer. "Why should I bring that scumbag into the house?"

Anger flashed through her. She hated hearing that term applied to women. "For one thing, someone driving by the farm might see her hanging out of your car, bare-breasted. Besides, she's probably hungry and thirsty, too."

"So what?" he sneered. "I don't want her in my house. She's just a tramp I picked up on the highway."

"Why did you bring her there then?"

"To *fuck*, what else?"

Jessie's jaw dropped.

Mike laughed. "You didn't think I was going to give her a ride for nothing, did you? I'm not a good Samaritan. She's spaced out on drugs anyway. When I'm ready, I'll take her back to the highway."

Jessie narrowed her eyes. Discussion was useless. She started for the door.

"Where are you going?"

"To help her out of the car and bring her inside for some lunch."

He leapt to his feet and blocked her path. "No, you're not! I won't have that trash in the house."

Jessie looked at him defiantly. "She's a human being! How can you have sex with a woman, then say she isn't good enough to have in the house?"

Mike's expression grew thunderous, but she was determined not to back down. She stared into his eyes without flinching. He was close to violence and she knew it, but she held his gaze waiting for a sign of weakness.

The blonde staggered through the mudroom door, abruptly ending the duel of wills. Mike looked away first, turning to the blonde who was now wearing a halter top and jeans.

"Would you like a beer?" he asked genially.

"Thanks, I could sure use one."

He opened the refrigerator and handed her one of Kevin's beers.

Jessie turned around and headed back upstairs to finish putting away the laundry. She didn't understand Mike at all. Lots of pretty girls were only too happy to have sex with him, and Sandy would take him back in a minute if he dumped Lynette, yet he wasn't averse to picking up what he himself referred to as tramps for sexual gratification. On the other hand, he couldn't stand the thought of Lynette making it with other guys.

As the summer wore on, Mike continued to stew over Lynette, and Ann kept Jessie informed about whom Lynette was seen with around town. Mike had always been in the habit of coming into the kitchen and grabbing pitchers of iced tea instead of brewing his own, but now he made snide remarks when he did.

"Getting any lately?" he'd ask rhetorically. "Must be boring playing with yourself."

It stung, but Jessie tried her best to ignore him. If she had any kind of sex life with her husband, Mike wouldn't seem so tempting, but to a starving person, any meal looked good.

The phone continued to ring off the hook. It was so bad that even Valium didn't help anymore. She called the telephone company again and broke down in tears talking to the customer service rep.

"Ma'am, there's nothing we can do without your husband's permission. The phone is listed in his name."

"Please, I beg you. Isn't there any way to stop this harassment?"

"Well, you could purchase an athletic coach's whistle and blow on it into the phone. But it has to be a professional whistle or it won't be loud enough to do any good."

"Oh, thank you. I'll buy one right away."

She hung up, put the kids in the Grand Prix, and headed for town. The proprietor of the sporting goods store looked at her like she was a little kooky, but sold her an Acme Thunderer. She could hardly wait to get home and try it.

Returning to the car with the kids, she was shocked when she turned the key and the Grand Prix wouldn't start.

"Damn!" She didn't know much about cars, but opening the hood and jiggling all the wires seemed like a good place to start. After a few tries, the engine finally came to life.

When she got home, she took a locket off a chain and hung the whistle around her neck. She had to be careful lest she abuse some poor farmer or feed dealer, but when someone called and didn't speak up promptly after "hello," they got blasted. She used it five times in two days.

Considering the number of anonymous calls she normally received, there was definitely a reduction in volume.

A few days after she bought the whistle, Sam strolled into the kitchen nonchalantly. "Hi, Jessie, how have you been?"

She looked at him in surprise. She hadn't seen him in ages. "I'm fine. And how are you?"

He smiled. "Good, and even better now."

"Who are you looking for? I know you didn't come here to see me," she said ruefully.

"How can you be so sure?" he asked, a twinkle in his eye.

Jessie said nothing, remembering how peeved he'd been the night he'd taken her out to his car.

Sam moved closer. His gaze dropped to her bosom and lingered. "What are you wearing that thing around your neck for? To blow the whistle on some poor guy who can't resist your charms?"

"No," she said, amused.

He studied her eyes for a moment. "How do I know you're telling the truth?"

She looked directly into his eyes... gray eyes that she could get lost in forever. "I'd always tell you the truth."

A fleeting change came over his face, then he seemed to recollect himself. "Okay, seriously, why are you wearing a whistle around your neck?"

"It's to blast the anonymous caller who's been harassing me."

"I guess I'll have to stop calling you now, if you're going to damage my hearing."

"Oh, Sam, I know it's not you."

He grinned mischievously. "How can you be so sure?"

"Oh, quit kidding."

"Seriously then."

"Because you couldn't possibly know every hour of the day when I'm home alone and when I'm not. Often I'll be right in the middle of changing the baby, and the phone will ring twenty times before I pick it up. It happens all the time at night, too. The calls wake me up so often, I hardly get any sleep. It's frightening, and I want to scream every time I hear the phone ring, but nobody else gets the calls." She paused and drew breath to voice her suspicions. "It has to be someone in this house, or a conspiracy directed by someone in this house."

"You're right," Sam said, catching her completely off guard. His jaw tightened and his eyes darkened. "It's gone far enough. I'll see that it stops."

She stared at him in shock, her thoughts all ajumble. *If he had the power to stop it, why had he let it go on at all? And what the hell was going on, anyway?*

Sam gazed into her eyes, seemingly debating whether to say more. Just as he opened his mouth to speak, Mike walked in.

"Hi, Sam. How about a beer?"

"Sure," he said, and followed Mike to the family room.

CHAPTER 26

RUNNING ON EMPTY

Just before sunrise, Kevin pulled into the driveway. He walked into the house and quietly climbed the stairs. His wife was asleep, naked under the sheet the way she was supposed to be. He stripped to his briefs and pulled the sheet off Jessie, exposing her nude body to a sudden rush of cool predawn air.

She jerked awake with a startled look in her eyes.

"Get up. I want to talk to you."

"What's the matter?" she asked, thinking there was an emergency.

"I want a divorce."

"I don't understand." Her mind was still foggy with sleep, but she automatically rose as ordered and faced him. Something in Kevin's eyes made her feel embarrassed by her nakedness.

"It's real simple," he said. "I want a divorce. I'm tired of being married to you. You leave, disappear, go anywhere. I don't care where."

"What the hell is that supposed to mean?"

"It means you leave. Laura and Joey stay here, where they belong. They'll have all the advantages my family can provide."

"You must be nuts if you think I'm going to disappear and leave Laura and Joey with you. They're babies—they need their mother."

"You? You're a lousy mother. They'd be better off without you," he said with contempt. "Besides, I can make you do what I want."

She frowned. "How?"

He smiled slyly. "I figured it all out tonight. If you don't do what I say, I'll put a contract out on one of the members of your family."

"Are you crazy?"

"No, of course not. It's the best way to get what I want. I'm tired of waiting around for you to commit suicide."

Jessie sucked in her breath, feeling hollow inside. The anonymous calls, nitpicking, and unreasonable demands all made sense now—a cruel sick sense.

"I can't believe this. I've done everything you asked. I've tried so hard to be a good wife. Isn't that enough? I'll let you have all the girlfriends you want."

Kevin shook his head. "No, it isn't good enough. Your attitude is wrong. It's just a game with you, like taking a test and getting a perfect score. You've never humbled yourself."

He stepped closer. His eyes seemed to change, becoming almost reptilian. "You still haven't proved that you love *me*, only me!"

"You mean worship you," she said, swallowing the lump of fear rising in her throat. "If you're really going to put a contract out—why not have your hit-man kill me and put me out of my misery?"

"The police would suspect me right away. Besides, I was fond of you once, and you are the mother of my children."

"I'll go to the police myself."

Kevin chuckled. "No one will believe you. That's the beauty of it. You're a nobody, and my family is well-known around here."

She glared at him. "I have no intention of leaving without my children."

His eyes narrowed. "Do what I want. If you don't, someone in your family is going to die. How do you think your parents would feel if it's Rick?"

She stared at him, aghast.

"Think about it, Jessie. I'll give you a few days," he said, then climbed into bed.

Heart pounding, Jessie stood there frozen for several seconds then threw on some clothes and hurried downstairs. She was shaking all over when she reached the kitchen. Taking slow, deep breaths, she tried to get a grip on herself.

She lit a cigarette with trembling hands, then started a pot of coffee. When it was ready, she poured a cup and sipped, deep in thought. She didn't want her brother to die, but she couldn't leave her kids without putting up a fight.

There had to be something she could do. Grabbing the phone book, she thumbed through the yellow pages' listings for attorneys wondering which one to pick. The first attorney she dialed happened to have an opening that afternoon. Unfortunately, her mother was already at work and she couldn't ask Kevin's sisters to baby-sit. Mrs. Hanlon, Sandy's mother, came to mind. She'd been a housewife her entire marriage so it was worth a shot.

When Nancy Hanlon answered, Jessie told her she'd lost a filling overnight and the dentist said he could take her that day due to a cancellation. Nancy said she'd be happy to watch the kids at her house for a few hours.

An elderly secretary with permed silver hair asked Jessie to take a seat, then picked up the receiver of the desk phone and pushed a button. "Mrs. McKenna is here, Mr. Dickerson."

The door to the inner office opened and a middle-aged, balding man appeared. He wore a three-piece, charcoal-gray, pinstriped suit. "Please come in, Mrs. McKenna."

He helped her into a chair, then seated himself behind his desk. He picked up a pen and leaned forward in his chair. "How may I be of service?"

Jessie took a deep breath and began her story. He didn't believe her. She could see it in his eyes, which spent more time looking at her legs than her face.

When she finished, he put down the pen—which he had yet to use to write anything.

"Mrs. McKenna, your husband's threats shouldn't be taken seriously. People say all kinds of things when they want a divorce. But if you want a divorce, I'll be happy to take your case."

"I'm Catholic. Divorce is out of the question. I just want a legal separation and custody of my children."

Dickerson shook his head. "There's no such thing under state statute. If you want to be legally separated, you must file for divorce first. Now what grounds do you have?"

Jessie regarded him with a mixture of disdain and hopelessness. "You mean *besides* the death threat?"

"Even if your husband did make a threat—and I'm sure he's only bluffing—we can't go into court with that. It's just your word against his. We need real grounds, something juicy, like adultery. Has Kevin ever committed adultery?"

"Of course. He's even admitted it."

"Great. Now when was that?" he asked, grabbing the pen and holding it poised above the yellow legal pad.

"Last October."

His face fell. "That's too long ago, unless he swore not to do it again and you recently caught him in the act."

"I'm afraid that isn't the case, Mr. Dickerson. My marriage vows precluded me from filing for divorce or failing to perform my wifely duties, merely because of adultery. But Kevin trying to bully me into disappearing, by death threats against my family, is something I cannot endure."

Dickerson rolled his eyes in exasperation. "Look, Mrs. McKenna, forget the death threats. That dog don't hunt, and your husband knows it. And since you knew your husband was committing adultery and continued having marital relations, you effectively gave your consent. All you can do is file for divorce based on irreconcilable differences."

"What does that mean?"

"You can get a divorce, but it'll take three years, and your husband will fight you tooth and nail for custody. You need to count the cost before you begin."

"I thought my husband was obligated to pay the expenses?"

"What I mean is that Kevin McKenna is a man to reckon with in this county. It'll get down and dirty, and you'd better not have any skeletons in your closet he can exploit. He's free to commit adultery, because you gave your tacit consent, but you aren't. And if you do, he can divorce you in no time flat and get custody handed to him on a silver platter."

"B-but I only put up with it because of my religion. He doesn't deserve custody of the children. He's never even acted like a father, except in public for show."

"The law's the law, and given the situation, if I were you, I'd file for divorce immediately. Talk to your parents. You're going to need them to provide you with a place to stay, until a court can rule on temporary custody and spousal support, since your in-laws own the farmhouse."

In a state of turmoil, Jessie drove to Mrs. Hanlon's to get the kids. Afterward she drove to her parents' to wait for her mother to come home.

When Liz arrived, she looked surprised to see her waiting in the kitchen. "What's up?"

Jessie briefly described Kevin's demands, but left out the death threat as counterproductive.

"I can't believe this," Liz said. "It sounds like Kevin's been imbibing too much on the campaign trail. Asking you for a divorce is ridiculous."

"He didn't *ask* for a divorce. He wants me gone, period. I consulted an attorney to protect my rights. He advised me to file for divorce immediately, and I need a place to stay."

Her mother held up her hand. "No more talk about divorce. Remember your vows. I'm going to have a talk with Kevin this minute and straighten everything out."

Liz snatched up her purse and drove to the farm fuming, then marched straight into the house to confront Kevin. He was filling a glass with cubes from the icemaker.

"I understand you asked my daughter for a divorce. What's this all about?"

Kevin recovered quickly. "Oh, um, not exactly. I really just meant a separation or something. We aren't getting along, the house is always a mess, and there's the strain of the campaign. I was angry, and I just lost my temper."

"Well, Jessie thought you wanted a divorce. She saw an attorney this afternoon."

Kevin stiffened. He hadn't anticipated that. "But my whole family's Catholic. I'd never ask for a divorce."

Liz looked relieved. "I think it's about time you two went to marriage counseling, don't you?"

"Yeah, we should go, but I'm right in the middle of campaigning. There just isn't time, but I'll try to be more patient, and I promise we'll go as soon as the election's over."

Just then, Jessie walked in with the children.

"Hi, honey," Kevin said smoothly. "Look, I'm sorry for what I said. I was just blowing off steam. I didn't think you'd take it seriously."

Jessie turned to her mother. "He sounded serious to me."

Kevin assumed a contrite expression. "I didn't mean it the way it sounded. I lost my temper, that's all. I should have listened to you before about marriage counseling. Laura and Joey are too important not to work things out."

Jessie eyed him warily.

Liz smiled brightly. "See, Jessie, I knew it was all a misunderstanding. When people have marriage problems, the fault's usually fifty-fifty. You both need to acknowledge your shortcomings, forgive each other, and turn over a new leaf."

Jessie didn't think Kevin's about-face was genuine, but she had no idea what to do. Visiting her grandparents in Florida was out of the question; they didn't believe in divorce either, and they lived in a one-bedroom senior-citizen high-rise. Her maiden aunt had recently married so "visiting," even for a few days, would be awkward. And she doubted that her pious aunt would support the idea of divorce.

She needed to get away, even if it was only temporarily. She felt lost in a fog, and the bottle of Valium was looking awfully tempting. Who on earth could she turn to?

Uncle Eric?

Her mother's brother was a distant figure who taught college in upstate New York. From time to time he'd lent them his beach house in Avalon, New Jersey, for vacation. Although he and his late wife were intelligent and likable people, they'd little time for a distant niece and nephew. They'd always been thoroughly wrapped up in their only child, Garrett.

Uncle Eric was fifteen years older than her mother, and Cousin Garrett was off to college before Jessie turned nine. Although they'd dutifully spent every other Christmas with Grammy and PopPop, while Jessie was growing up, the last time she'd seen Garrett was at his wedding ten years ago.

Jessie picked up the phone and dialed information. She asked for the number at her uncle's beach house. Jotting it down on a scrap of paper, she said a quick prayer and dialed.

The phone rang and rang, but finally someone picked up. "Hello?" said a familiar voice.

A vision of Uncle Eric's stooped figure leaning on his cane popped into her mind. She could almost smell his pipe smoke. After a few pleasantries, she asked if he'd mind if she came for a visit.

"By all means. Bring your husband and children. You can have the place to yourselves. I'll stay at my house near the college and get some things ready for the fall semester."

"Actually, I need a little vacation away from parental and wifely duties, if you know what I mean, but maybe my friend Ann would like to come."

Uncle Eric chuckled. "Bring as many friends as you like."

After ringing off, Jessie phoned Mary Clare and Kathleen to try to arrange for baby-sitting Laura and Joey. It took a little arm twisting—she had to lay a guilt trip on Kathleen about all the free lifeguard services she'd provided for her kids. But between Mary Clare and Kathleen, she had most of it covered. And if she could just get her mother to baby-sit Friday night and Saturday, she could stay at the beach for a full week.

Next she called Ann, who jumped at the chance to loll on the beach and work on her tan. "I'll get somebody to cover my shifts next week."

⚬⚬⚬

Jessie drove over to speak to her mother personally, rather than phone. Liz reacted coolly to the idea just as anticipated.

"I told you at the beginning of the campaign that I'm not running a baby-sitting service. I work hard, and I want to spend all my free time with your father."

Jessie sighed. "I know, Mom, but I really need a break. I'm exhausted. It's a long way to Avalon, and I don't want to drive home in Friday afternoon traffic."

"You know I don't like to bend my own rules," Liz began, then took a real look at her daughter. The stress of the campaign and two active toddlers was obvious. She was too thin, and Liz hoped it wasn't a sign of something worse.

"I don't understand you girls these days, always dieting. You can overdo it, you know. You're starting to look flat-chested. It's not like you had any extra to spare. Try to eat more."

"Mom, when you were growing up, fuller figures were in fashion, but not now."

Liz looked her straight in the eye. "People who are alcoholics usually don't eat much. That's one of the first symptoms. You'd better watch out or you're going to be in trouble."

When Jessie pulled up to her uncle's beach house early Sunday afternoon, Ann was amazed.

"Wow! Right on the beach, too," she exclaimed. "What does your uncle do for a living?"

"He's a college professor. He teaches English."

"How can he afford this?"

"My late aunt was a school teacher and made a lot of money investing in real estate. My cousin Garrett is an only child and will inherit this one day."

"Some people have all the luck," Ann said, and got out to unload the suitcases. Jessie found the spare key and unlocked the door. The house smelled of pipe tobacco, comforting in its familiarity.

She directed Ann to the guest room. They stowed their gear, donned bikinis, and grabbed two sodas from the cooler, then headed for the water. After a few hours of surf and sun, they returned to the house and ordered pizza.

The next morning, Jessie and Ann did some grocery shopping then prepared for a day of basking in the sun. Jessie perused the bookshelf in the living room trying to decide what to read first. She picked out *Catch-22*.

"Why do you even read books like that?" Ann asked, and grabbed one of Garrett's wife's romance novels to stuff in her beach bag.

"I want to learn things and be well-read."

"Take it from me, everything you need to know about life you can learn by watching soap operas."

Jessie chuckled. "So what do you think? Should I divorce Kevin or not?"

"I told you to divorce him over two years ago."

"But what can I do? I've never had a job. I don't have any money. My parents won't help, and I have to wait for a judge to rule on spousal support to afford an apartment."

"You're really in a jam then." Ann shook her head. "It's funny how life works. All I wanted to do was get married, but my parents made me go to college. All you wanted was to go to college, and your parents pulled the rug out from under you."

⦿

The ocean's timeless rhythms soothed Jessie's jangled nerves. Tanned and rested, she drove home in a pleasant frame of mind. She dropped Ann off, and then decided to stop at the farm before heading to her parents. It would be easier to unload the car before picking the kids up, and her mother had agreed to feed the children their dinner.

Jessie was shocked to find them already home, with one of the sitters, Betsy, minding them.

Why weren't they still at their grandparents?

Kevin was storming around the house.

"What's going on?" Jessie asked. Betsy gave her a frightened look.

Kevin glared. "Come upstairs."

Puzzled, she followed.

Inside the bedroom, he closed the door and turned on her. "It's about time you got home! What the hell were you doing at the ocean all week instead of being here taking care of your responsibilities?"

"Trying to get arrested for soliciting," she deadpanned.

His jaw dropped. "What?"

"I was hoping they'd put me in jail so I wouldn't have to come home to you."

He gave her a dirty look. "Get dressed. We don't have all night."

Kevin started to leave then halted in his tracks. He turned and stared. "What did you do to your skin?"

She looked down at her arms and legs, then back at him. "I got a tan."

"But you're dark enough to pass for a Negress. How did you get so *dark*?"

"I'm part American Indian."

"Damn!" he exclaimed. "That's almost as bad."

Jessie regarded him with disdain. "I feel sorry for people like you, Kevin. I thought you truly liked Leroy and Marcella."

"That's politics."

She sighed. "Where are we going?"

"What do you care?" he snapped.

"I need to know what to wear."

"The Carlton House—wear something long." He walked out and slammed the door.

Jessie took a quick shower and hurriedly fixed her hair. She opened the closet, pulled out the red dress with the matching bolero jacket, and smiled at the memory of Sam roguishly ogling her cleavage. She slipped into it and managed to shimmy the zipper up the back without any trouble. That was unusual, but she didn't think any more about it until she looked in the full-length mirror and did a double-take.

The dress hung on her like a flour sack. She couldn't believe her eyes. How on earth had she lost so much weight without noticing?

She couldn't be seen in public like this. She rummaged through the top drawer of her dresser looking for some safety pins, then called downstairs to the sitter. "Betsy, can you come up here for a minute?"

When Betsy entered, she asked her to gather the bodice in the back and pin it. Betsy's handiwork would be concealed by the jacket.

⁓

When Jessie arrived at the Carlton House with Kevin, a large crowd was gathered inside enjoying cocktails. Hors d'oeurves were lavishly arranged on strategically located tiered tables. Waiters strolled among the guests, pausing at intervals to proffer scrumptious morsels on silver trays.

Kevin spotted Marcella the minute they entered, and walked over to greet her. He offered to get some drinks. Marcella said she was fine. Jessie asked for a gin and tonic. He nodded and left for the bar.

Marcella turned to Jessie. "You look gorgeous, dear. Red is the perfect color for you, and I've always loved that dress. Now tell me how you got that tan."

"I needed a break, so I spent the week at my uncle's beach house."

"That was smart. With the campaign heating up, you'll be running nonstop from now to November. It was so thoughtful of Kevin to let you go to the ocean. Aren't we lucky to have such wonderful husbands?"

She was spared having to reply because Ellen rushed up gushing. "Ooo! You're really looking good, Jessie. I wish I had skin like that. I'm jealous. How do you do it?"

"I asked her the same thing," Marcella said, changing gears smoothly. "But the truth is, you're too white, Ellen. You know that."

They burst out laughing together, then resumed chatting, their conversation light-hearted and amusing. From the outside looking in, Jessie thought, they were three attractive women supporting their husbands in public life. Two of them hid their personal pain very well.

CHAPTER 27

LADY IN RED

She'd walked down the staircase the same way a hundred times before. Catching a glimpse of her reflection in the mirror over the hall table, Jessie paused for a moment. She was wearing an off-the-shoulder scarlet gown with a fitted waist and floor-length full skirt that swirled around her. Her raven hair flowed loosely down her back in long shimmering waves. A black and white cameo strung on a satin ribbon graced her neck.

She continued her descent, but halted again when she noticed Mike standing by the family room door. His gaze was expectant, almost hypnotic, and she knew exactly why he was there.

Mike smiled as he watched Jessie resume her progress down the stairs. She'd kept him waiting long enough. Scarlet was definitely her color and suited to the occasion.

Confidently, he awaited her approach.

Jessie hesitated, fully cognizant of the danger, but her body yearned with a desire that compelled her to move toward him. She reached up and put her arms around Mike's neck, pressing her breasts against his muscled chest. He bent his head, hungrily seeking her mouth, and pulled her closer. Kissing her deeply, his hands caressed her body, arousing exquisite sensations that made her ache for the feel of him inside her.

Darkness whirled around her as she surrendered herself.

She struggled against losing consciousness.

Her mind screaming now, she twisted violently in protest.

Flinging off the tangled sheets, she sat bolt upright in bed, pulse racing and heart pounding madly. Panting and frightened, but now oriented to her surroundings, she fell back onto her pillow and waited for her pulse and breathing to return to normal.

The dream had seemed so real it was difficult to believe she was still in her own bed. Walking down the staircase felt the same way it always had: the same pull of gravity, the buoyancy of her hair as it flowed behind her, and the soft give of the carpet under her feet.

The only incongruent note had been the dress. She'd never owned one like it, but she recognized the cameo as one that belonged to her grandmother before being passed to her mother.

Jessie's breathing finally evened out, and she rose from the bed. When she reached for her summer robe, something odd caught her eye.

The door was open!

Blood drained from her face. She sat down weakly, feeling faint. *Had some person come into the room during the night?*

The door had been closed when she went to sleep. She had to keep it shut because Kevin insisted she sleep in the nude, and anyone coming up the stairs could see right into the bedroom.

She got up and looked through the window to check for Kevin's car. He wasn't home yet. She wondered who might have opened the door.

Jessie dressed and peeked in on the children, then checked the guest room. It was empty.

She went downstairs and started a pot of coffee deep in thought. Something was going on she didn't entirely fathom.

It wasn't hard to figure out the dream though. She was close to the edge, and she knew it. God only knew what depths of depravity she would fall into once she took that step into darkness with her brother-in-law.

She was afraid Mike would resort to blackmail, once his appetite was sated. But she was even more afraid of herself.

Mike didn't understand what a dangerous game he was playing. He had no idea what she was capable of; she had a terrible temper. Didn't the saying go: "Hell hath no fury like a woman scorned"?

⚭

The day wore on interminably. It was breathlessly hot, and static hummed in the air. Jessie prevailed upon Bert's wife, Doris, to watch Laura and Joey for a little while and drove out to the liquor store. She couldn't get to sleep unaided tonight, and she couldn't afford to be awake if Mike returned home alone.

Lightning split the air on the ride back, and rain cascaded from the brooding sky in a blinding downpour.

A cool wind rushed across the countryside in the wake of the drenching rain, dispelling the pent-up heat of the day. The dark clouds sped away, and the sun shone with a renewed sparkle.

After cleaning up the supper dishes and getting Laura and Joey off to bed, Jessie carried a bottle of wine out to the patio and poured a glass. She strolled the length of the pool, then paused to gaze pensively at the tendrils of mist rising from the Shadow River as twilight faded. She began to sing. The lyrics were all about betrayal and unrequited love.

When it was fully dark, Jessie headed back inside. She poured another glass of wine, then went to the stereo and put some records on to play. She was grateful that Mike hadn't stayed home tonight. If all went as planned, she would soon be relaxed enough to glide up to bed in a pleasantly inebriated fog.

She heard a vehicle pulling into the driveway and tensed. Two car doors slammed and she relaxed a bit. Then the screen door of the mudroom creaked, and she heard a male and female voice conversing.

A moment later, Mike escorted a buxom, bleached blonde into the living room and breezily introduced her as an old and dear friend.

Jessie had never met any old, dear, women friends of Mike's before. The blonde looked about Kevin's age, but her body was already running to fat.

"Excuse me a minute while you two get acquainted," Mike said. "Cindy's interested in looking over your record collection. Why don't you show her some things?"

Cindy smiled warmly as Mike walked away. "I hope you don't mind the intrusion, but Mike says you have a terrific collection and I'm really into music."

"What kind do you like?" Jessie asked politely, irritated at being imposed on.

"Not the type you're playing now. Can you put on something else?"

Jessie took the record off and stiffly walked to the cabinet where the others were stored.

Cindy followed. "Do you have 'Stairway to Heaven'?"

"I have all of Led Zeppelin's albums." She stashed the record, then waved at the alphabetized assortment on the shelves and backed away. "They're filed together, it's on number four."

Cindy rummaged through the covers. "I don't see it here."

Jessie shrugged. "Someone might have borrowed it."

"Darn. Mike said he thought you had it, and I especially wanted to hear it. Can you double-check for me?"

Jessie searched through the cabinet. "Sorry. Whoever took it hasn't returned it yet."

"Well, I guess I'll have to pick something else. But the light isn't very good here. Why don't you bring some albums over to the sofa so we can sit down and go through them?" Cindy seated herself on the couch.

Does she think I'm her personal handmaid? Jessie huffed to herself. Grabbing an armful of albums, she placed them on the coffee table.

Cindy gestured at the spot beside her on the sofa. "Show them to me, one at a time."

Annoyed, Jessie sat down and picked up an album. She cringed as Cindy leaned in close, rejecting one title after another, then began touching her on the hands as they flipped through the covers. Jessie was already feeling quite uncomfortable when Cindy suddenly cuddled up to her.

Repulsed, Jessie jumped to her feet. Recollecting her manners, she tried to cover up for any apparent rudeness. "Would you care for a glass of wine?"

"Certainly," Cindy replied, regarding Jessie speculatively as she headed for the kitchen.

Returning, she handed Cindy a glass of wine then deliberately sat in a chair on the opposite side of the room.

"Have you decided which album you want to hear?" she asked, wishing Cindy would just pick one and get it over with.

"You have so many good ones it's hard to choose something. We haven't finished looking through them all together. Why don't you come over and help me decide?"

Jessie pressed deeper into the chair. "I really think you can do that yourself. My taste isn't likely to be the same as yours."

"I see," Cindy remarked, and took a sip from her glass. "Thank you for the wine. I like it."

Mike strolled into the room and sat in a chair near Cindy. "So, how are you two getting along?"

"Fine," Cindy answered, "but we couldn't find any music we enjoy in common."

Mike gave her a peculiar look and took a swig of beer.

Jessie glanced from one to the other, wondering what the look meant.

Cindy smiled reassuringly. "I'm a Gemini. What Zodiac sign were you born under, Jessie?"

"Libra."

"Ah, the scales."

"What kind of scales?" Mike inquired. "Fish or reptile?"

Cindy rolled her eyes. "Libra's symbol is the Scales of Justice."

Mike looked at her sardonically and drained his beer in one long swallow. "Come on, Cindy, let's go."

"Nice meeting you," Cindy said, and headed into the family room with Mike.

Jessie carried the empty wine glasses into the kitchen, then gathered the dirty ashtrays and washed everything in the sink. She dried the glasses and put them away, then returned the ashtrays to the living room and switched off the lights. She started for the stairs, but stopped in her tracks at the sound of raised voices coming from the family room.

"Not tonight, Mike, please. I'm tired. I've been on my feet all day. These straight jobs are murder."

"You're not getting off so easy. You know me better than to think that."

"Come on, stop it, you're hurting me," Cindy pleaded. "Some other time, but not tonight—*please*. I'll do you anytime for free, you know that."

"I want it *now*," Mike said harshly, "not some other time. All the trouble I went through to bring you here, you'd better do something to make it worth my while."

"Let go of me," Cindy begged. "I just can't do it tonight."

"I'll break your arm," Mike said in a flat hard voice.

Jessie drew in her breath, shocked at Mike's viciousness. But what else did Cindy suppose Mike brought her to the farm for, if it wasn't to have sex?

"Okay—all right," Cindy gasped. "Let me go. I'll do it!"

Jessie was sorry Cindy was being bullied into doing Mike, but she swallowed her anger and continued upstairs. Cindy wasn't that pretty, and likely not whom Mike would prefer tonight, but there was no way to help Cindy without compromising herself.

The next day dawned sunny and breezy with low humidity. A gentle wind blew, and Jessie's spirits were high as she flew through her household tasks. If only she could feel like this all of the time.

After serving Kevin his lunch and giving Cletus his tray, she took the children out into the backyard to play. Laura hopped and skipped from flower to flower. Joey tried to eat the marigold petals.

Dusty appeared. Jessie helped Laura toss the ball for him. After he had enough, he lolled on the grass contentedly.

When the children tired of the garden Jessie took them inside for their naps. Once they were both asleep she went down to the kitchen and washed the lunch dishes. Just as she picked up a towel and began drying a plate, the screen door banged in the mudroom.

Startled, she turned toward the sound.

Mike stormed into the kitchen looking so wild-eyed and furious, she almost dropped the dish.

"Just what is it with you?" he snarled, advancing.

Her heart leapt into her throat. There was no mistaking the rage in his eyes or violence coiled in every muscle. *What could she have done to upset him so?*

Mike loomed over her, breathing heavily.

She stared at him mutely, frozen with fear. Time seemed to stand still. The only sound was Mike's heavy breathing.

Abruptly he turned and left. The screen door slammed in his wake.

Jessie sagged against the counter and took a deep breath.

What the hell was wrong with him?

He just got laid last night, didn't he? What was he so angry about?

CHAPTER 28

A KNIGHT ERRANT

Jessie was polishing the china cabinet when she heard the front door open. Footsteps paused near the family room, then headed down the hall to the dining room.

"Good afternoon, my lady," Jimmy Fremont said and bowed. "Is Johnny home?"

She looked at him, bemused. "I'm not your lady—Lisa is. Johnny already left. He won't be back until supper."

"I'll come back later then," he replied, but adjusted his glasses and continued to linger.

Jessie liked him better than any of Johnny's other friends. Jimmy was relatively unspoiled and cute in an unprepossessing sort of way. He had curly brown hair, thick-lashed brown eyes, and a few freckles. She wondered what it would be like to kiss him—but she was married, and he was Lisa's.

"Why did you call me 'my lady'?"

The question seemed to throw him for a second. "It's just what I call you, sort of like a nickname."

"But why?" she asked, puzzled.

Jimmy shrugged and looked sheepish. "It's short for what the guys call you."

"What do the guys call me?"

"Lady Willpower."

Jessie regarded him quizzically. "Why do they call me *that*?"

Jimmy looked chagrinned. "I'm not supposed to tell you."

"Please," she implored, her eyes beseeching his. "If you don't, I'll die of curiosity."

"I guess I can tell you, but promise you won't tell anyone I did."

"I promise."

"It's because..." He stopped and looked at her ruefully. "I'm not sure how to put this. I can't say it nicely."

"That's okay. Please tell me anyway."

"It's because you don't screw around."

She gazed at him, bewildered. "Married people aren't supposed to screw around."

"Yeah, but the guys can't understand why you don't, living here with Johnny and Mike like you do. We know Kevin doesn't... um... Kevin isn't here very much," he finished lamely.

"Mike said you must be a lesbian, but I never believed that. He said he could prove it and started taking bets. Then he got some bisexual prostitute, who recently retired 'cause her pimp got blown away, to come here and test you. She said you definitely weren't a lesbian, and Mike lost a lot of money."

Jessie chuckled. The strange episode now made sense. Mike was not only furious because she'd failed to respond to his come-ons, he'd also lost a substantial sum of money.

Jimmy looked at her with admiration. "The other guys call you Lady Willpower. But I don't call you that. I just think of you as a lady."

Touched, she could have kissed him on the spot. But she didn't dare—not because Jimmy would be offended, but because she knew only too well the forces that could be unleashed under the circumstances. She wasn't certain she would constrain herself to a sisterly peck on the cheek, and she had no desire to lead into temptation an earnest young man who had just expressed his faith in her character.

"If there's ever anything I can do for you, Jessie, just let me know," he said.

"There is something you can do for me."

"What?"

"Would you go into town and buy me some pot?"

He stared at her like she was crazy. "But you're Kevin McKenna's wife!"

"What's the matter? Are you worried about my reputation?"

"No, but I don't understand why you want me to score for you when you're married to him."

"What's that got to do with it?"

"Well, you're Johnny McKenna's sister-in-law."

"So?"

"Johnny's one of the biggest pot dealers in Concord County. I buy all my dope from him. He can get you a lot better stuff than I can, wholesale."

It was Jessie's turn to be dumbfounded. She knew Johnny did drugs and heard he dealt some on the side, but she never suspected he did it big-time, although that would explain how he could afford all of the drugs he took, including the heroin.

"Kevin's giving me a hard time. He won't let Johnny sell me any pot, and Johnny isn't going to give it to me. If you could help me out, I'd really appreciate it."

"Hey, no problem. I'd be happy to do that for you," he replied sympathetically. "How soon do you want it?"

"Tonight, if you can swing it."

"Okay, I'll do my best. If you see Johnny, tell him I'll catch him later." Jimmy turned to go.

"Wait! I'll get you some money."

"No," he said, shaking his head. "Pay me back when I bring it. I don't know what I'll be able to find on the street today."

❧

Jessie glanced at the clock for the tenth time. She was running out of strategies for dealing with the temptation of slipping down the hall to Mike's room, and she was going to need something better than wine and Valium to prevent that tonight.

She wasn't even sure why she'd held out this long, until Jimmy reminded her. The incident with the prostitute showed beyond a shadow of a doubt what she was in for. Mike didn't want her because he desired her, or even because having sex with her would be fun. He wanted her to crawl to him, and he would delight in humiliating her once he'd used her. Apparently her sex life was the subject of gossip and speculation. The guys knew that Kevin had been keeping her on short rations all along.

Jessie had loved marijuana from the first, and the booze and Valium routine was wearing thin. It wouldn't matter how good the stuff was that Jimmy could get, just as long as it got her high. Now that she was beginning to dream about Mike, she was afraid that she might start walking in her sleep.

⁂

Jimmy returned at four o'clock.

"I'm real sorry I couldn't do any better than this, but it sounded like you wanted it by tonight."

Jessie heaved a sigh of relief. "It'll be fine. I really appreciate you doing this for me. Thank you."

"Anytime," he replied.

She smiled at him. Then, on impulse, she stepped closer and gave him a kiss on the cheek. He deserved his accolade.

Jimmy flushed pink. "Wow!" he exclaimed and adjusted his glasses. Then he bowed gracefully. "*Au revoir*, my lady."

As Jessie watched him go, she envied Lisa. What a lucky girl to have a fellow as nice as him.

⁂

After Kevin left for the evening and the children were asleep, Jessie filled a pipe with marijuana and took a deep drag. It was pretty rough tasting stuff, but it got her high all right.

The next morning, her mouth watered as she fixed her weight-gain staple: peanut butter on toast. It was the first time she didn't have to force herself to eat it, since the night Betsy pinned her into the red dress.

CHAPTER 29

A QUESTION OF BALANCE

A week later, the icemaker malfunctioned. Kevin said he'd ask Sam to take a look at it, when he had a chance, so they wouldn't have to pay a repair man to come out unless it was necessary.

Jessie's heart leapt at the thought of seeing Sam again. The anonymous calls had stopped the day after he'd promised to put an end to them. Although she couldn't be certain whether it was Sam or the whistle that was the actual effective agent, she preferred to give credit to Sam. After all, he'd volunteered to stand up for her and that meant a great deal. Maybe, just maybe, he liked her a lot, too.

The evening that Sam arrived, Kevin and Mike were already gone. Johnny was in the family room talking on the phone with a girlfriend.

First, Sam took a look inside the refrigerator, then headed for the cellar to investigate. In short order, he returned upstairs. "It's fixed. You should have ice a little later tonight."

"Thanks," Jessie said, relieved that there wouldn't be an expensive repair bill. "It was awfully nice of you to come all the way out to fix it for us."

"It was no trouble. It was just an air block in the line. Come downstairs and I'll show you what Kevin should do if it happens again."

She followed Sam down to the basement, wrinkling her nose at the musty smell. He walked over to the spot where the waterline from the icemaker fed into the cold-water pipe.

Jessie stopped a few feet away, feeling uncomfortably warm being so near Sam.

"Come closer or you won't be able to see."

She hesitated. It was true she couldn't quite see everything from where she was standing, but all Sam needed to do was explain what she needed to tell Kevin.

Sam looked at her expectantly.

She moved closer and gazed at the pipes in the ceiling, then looked into his eyes. The tick of time seemed audible. She resisted the urge to kiss him.

His eyes flickered. "See which pipe I mean?" he said, then grabbed one overhead. "All you have to do is shake it."

On impulse, she stood on tiptoe and reached up to touch the pipe. It crossed her mind that she could just pretend she lost her balance and cling to Sam to steady herself. If he took her in his arms to kiss her, she'd know for sure he wanted her, but a cheap trick wasn't her.

If Sam wanted to have an affair, he'd have to make up his own mind. She wasn't going to throw herself at him like some boy-crazy girl.

She jiggled the pipe. "This one?" she asked coolly.

The look he gave her in return was unfathomable, if not decidedly chilly.

"Yes, that one," he said dryly.

She could tell he was piqued, and she almost felt like saying she was sorry. *What are you going to do?* she asked herself. *Apologize for not kissing him or apologize for wanting him to kiss you?*

She let go of the pipe, then turned and walked upstairs. Sam followed and left the house without saying another word. The Cutlass growled to life and roared off.

That night she lay in bed, restless from longing, and berated herself for being a fool. Why hadn't she taken advantage of the situation and just thrown herself at him? Was acting like a lady really so important? And how much longer did she actually think she could hold out against Mike?

If you know you're going to fall, she thought, *wouldn't it be better to fall for Sam?*

CHAPTER 30

BLUE MOOD

"How much do you want me to take off, an inch or an inch and a half?" Lucy asked, as she busied herself combing out Jessie's wet hair."

"At least a foot."

Lucy's hand froze in mid-stroke. Her eyes widened. "Are you serious?"

"Yes," Jessie said, chuckling.

"You haven't let me cut more than two inches a year off your hair since you were thirteen."

"Kevin's holding a fundraiser for the campaign, and I want to look chic and sophisticated." She reached for her purse and pulled out a magazine picture. "Here's a photo of the style I want and the cutting instructions. It's called *Gypsy*."

"I can hardly believe you're going to let me cut it!"

Lucy set to work, shearing off a lot more than a foot, especially around the sides where the cut curved up to frame Jessie's face. It just brushed her shoulders in the back and was layered all around

Jessie ruefully regarded the cloud of hair surrounding her feet.

"No sighing now. The style looks great on you," Lucy said. "There's enough hair on the floor to stuff a pillow, and I just might in memory of the occasion."

Jessie handed her a big tip and headed outside to the Grand Prix. When she turned the key in the ignition nothing happened. "Damn!"

It was freaky because it didn't happen all the time. Groaning, she climbed out and opened the hood. Jiggling the wires didn't seem to help. She went back inside to ask Lucy for assistance.

"How long have you had this trouble?"

"Off and on all summer. The car will go for weeks without a problem then it'll do this."

Lucy wiggled the wires while Jessie turned the key in the ignition. The car started right up.

"Thanks for the help."

"You're welcome." Lucy closed the hood. "It's probably a bad solenoid. You ought to get it fixed."

"I'll tell Kevin. Our mechanic hasn't been able to figure it out, and he thinks I'm crying wolf."

⚬⚋⚬

Early on the evening of the fundraiser, Jessie went upstairs to get dressed. Kevin walked into the bedroom.

"I expect your behavior to be above reproach tonight. No pot—understand—and don't drink too much either."

"Yes," she said, giving him a sidelong look. *So he knew.*

While she would like to smoke some marijuana before the start of the evening, she certainly knew better. Obviously he didn't like not having her under his complete control, and he couldn't figure out how she was getting the pot.

Jessie put on her new black and white dress. The scooped neckline of the white bodice set off her bosom, and the princess-line cut defined her waist, then flowed into a wide black skirt. It was perfect for dancing, but she knew her chances of being asked by a man under fifty were slim to none. Still, having a rock 'n' roll band should save her from the worst.

⚬⚋⚬

When she and Kevin arrived at the hall, Kathleen and Mary Clare were bustling around putting the final touches on the decorations. Jessie made a brief inspection and thanked them profusely for all their trouble. They had been only too happy to attend to the details, and she was grateful that she hadn't had to shoulder additional responsibilities.

Jessie took up her post next to Kevin by the door to greet arrivals. Over an hour passed before they were free to take a break. Jessie sat down at their table with a sigh, only too glad to have a drink and a cigarette at last. Greeting so many people was an ordeal for a shy person like herself. She needed something to soothe her taut nerves.

She smoked several cigarettes, going slowly with the drink, and listened to the music. The band was excellent.

Jessie had suggested a rock 'n' roll band when Kevin sought her advice in staging the fundraiser, and she was glad he was forced to hire one despite his initial objections. Once he discovered the only bands available on the date they'd reserved the hall were Carla Snyder's Country Spiders and a hot new local rock group, he prudently opted for the better musicians.

Although she was supposed to be the hostess of this party, she felt more like Cinderella. Her table was deserted. Kevin was making the rounds. She noticed Sam and Jack asking other women to dance, but they were both avoiding her. The latest dance looked like a lot of fun, but they were the only men who knew how to do it well.

Johnny and his friends left at intervals to go outside.

Jessie wished that she could join them for a hit off a joint. She took a deep drag on her cigarette.

Charlie sat down, interrupting her thoughts. He was sporting a Madras jacket and a fresh crew cut. Regarding her somberly, he spoke. "Who died?"

"What do you mean?" she asked, bewildered.

"Well, you're the hostess of this wonderful party, but you're the only one who doesn't seem to be having a good time."

"Oh, I didn't realize it was that obvious."

"So what's wrong?"

"No one has asked me to dance," she said, giving him the simplest explanation, since anything else was off limits.

He laughed. "Is that all?"

"I love dancing," she said wistfully.

"Well, that's easy enough to fix. Let's dance."

The band struck up The James Gang's "Funk 49."

Charlie was one of those people who danced to a different drummer. It was a real effort to pretend they were partners. Jessie preferred to interpret the music as it moved her, and it was awfully tiring to try to keep pace with Charlie. For all she knew, this would be her only dance tonight. The song was too good to waste, so she decided to let herself go.

Charlie stopped and watched her with frank admiration.

"I'm not in your league," he said, when the song ended, and walked away.

Stymied for the moment, Jessie decided to get some more ginger ale to mix another drink back at the table. To keep costs down, the bar was only serving beer and set-ups. She was almost there when a stranger approached.

"May I have a dance?"

She cringed.

He was a dark-haired man of about thirty-five, around six feet tall, wearing a navy-blue suit. His face was too hard-edged and masculine for her to find him initially attractive. He was close-shaven, but the shadow that remained indicated he had a heavy beard.

It would be impolite to refuse his request. She nodded and he offered his arm. The gesture surprised her because it was so seldom used among her peers.

Thankfully, the band was into a rollicking number when they reached the dance floor. Jessie moved away to pick up the beat, but the man caught her by the wrist to restrain her.

"No," he said. "That's no way for a man to dance with a woman."

She looked at him, nonplussed. This was rock 'n' roll, and the tempo was too fast to slow dance to.

"Do you know how to waltz?"

"Are you serious?" she exclaimed, then laughed. "You must be joking."

He ignored that and contemplated her for a moment. "How old are you?"

"Twenty-one."

"I thought so. Look, I'm sure I could teach you. Will you try it?"

She didn't want to dance with him, period, but it was her duty to be cordial. "Yes, but we can't waltz to rock 'n' roll, and I don't think the band knows any waltzes."

He appeared thoughtful for a moment. "I think I know a song the band can play that we could waltz to, one I'm sure you know."

"Oh, what is it?" she asked, curious.

"'Nights In White Satin' by the Moody Blues."

"Really? How would you do that?" she replied with an edge of sarcasm. The Moody Blues might be a perfect description of her mental state, but she had never heard of waltzing to them.

"I'll show you. Give me your right hand and put the left one on my shoulder."

Inwardly she blanched, but it couldn't be worse than anything she'd endured before. She gave him her right hand and rested her left one on his shoulder.

He put his arm around her waist and drew her closer, holding her firmly. Reflexively, she stiffened.

"Relax," he said, looking into her eyes.

She was going to have to calm down. He surely had no idea of her antipathy to being held by someone she didn't know, and he wasn't holding her so tightly that it hurt, like so many other men.

"Now I want you to move in the direction you feel me taking you. Understand?"

"Yes."

"Okay. Ready? One, two, three..." he said, moving to a waltz he hummed along with the steps. "Relax, you're too stiff, and you aren't following my lead."

Dancing with the band playing the wrong rhythm wasn't easy. Jessie tried to loosen up.

The stranger continued his instructions until he judged that she was following his lead in a passable manner.

"I think you're doing well enough to dance to the music. Why don't you ask the band to play 'Nights In White Satin' now."

"Me?" she gasped.

Looking her directly in the eye, he replied firmly, "You are the hostess, Mrs. McKenna. I'm sure the band will be happy to play it for you."

There was something in his tone that brooked no dissent.

Jessie was glad to get away from him. She could feel the tension draining out of her body as she skirted the dance floor and the distance between them increased. Stopping at the foot of the stage, she waited for the band to finish their song.

The nearest guitarist leaned down to hear her request.

"Could you play 'Nights In White Satin'?"

He smiled. "Sure. It's one of my favorites."

Jessie walked slowly back to where the man waited. Nerving herself, she let him take her in his arms as the band began to play. She wondered what he was thinking and why he had asked her to dance, and immediately realized that was a mistake. The lyrics of the song expressed the passionate sexual love of a man for a woman, giving the impression that he'd rather have her in bed than on a dance floor.

Everything she sensed about this man told her that he wanted her, and her tension steadily increased. She should be blocking out thoughts and concentrating solely on the music. Suddenly she had a vivid mental impression of being naked under him, his weight pressing down on her body. She lost her concentration and fell out of step. "Oh, I'm sorry."

"That is a tricky part in the music," he said. "It wasn't written for a waltz."

She managed to pick up the rhythm again, but maintaining natural eye contact was impossible after that, and she kept her eyes lowered.

"Look up at me, please," he said. "You can't dance properly looking down."

She tried, but looking at him only made things worse. She started freezing up.

"Relax and follow me," he said soothingly. "I'm leading you, remember?"

She could hardly breathe. Sweat was breaking out on her skin.

"You have too much natural rhythm to be this stiff. Is something wrong?"

"No—yes," she said, opting for honesty over politics.

"I'm sorry," he said in a softened tone. "I wouldn't want you to feel uncomfortable. If dancing with me is bothering you, we can stop."

"Yes, please."

He came to a halt and released her.

Jessie stepped back and took a deep breath to recover her composure. The air felt refreshingly cool on her damp skin. Finally, she could look him in the face again.

"Thank you for the dance," she said, hoping she hadn't offended him too much.

The corner of his mouth curved into a smile. He looked into her eyes and shook his head. "No," he said, "thank *you*."

Her eyes widened in surprise.

He inclined his head, then turned and walked off the dance floor.

The fact that he had noticed her discomfort, and had been kind enough to end it, said something for his character. She'd never danced with a man before who cared how she felt when he held her. She was almost sorry she didn't know him better and wouldn't get the chance.

What she needed was a stiff drink.

Jessie returned to the table, mixed a strong highball, and lit a cigarette, wishing it was a joint. Kevin appeared and sat next to her.

"Who were you dancing with?"

"I don't know," she said, annoyed.

"What do you mean, you don't know?" he exclaimed. "You ask the band to play 'Nights In White Satin' while you dance with some guy, and you expect me to believe you don't even know who he is!"

"I never saw him before in my life. Why don't you ask him, if you don't believe me?"

Kevin gave her a penetrating look, but said no more because Leroy and Marcella were approaching.

"My compliments on the music, Kevin," Leroy said. "I don't know where you found this band, but they're terrific. Marcella and I are having a great time."

"It's such a pleasure to attend an event where we can enjoy ourselves like this," Marcella added. "A lot of the bands we've had to listen to during the campaign weren't very good musicians. We want to thank you for this wonderful evening."

"Oh, don't thank me. It was Jessie's idea. I have to give credit where credit is due."

Jessie was astonished that Kevin had complimented her for once.

⚬⚮⚬

The band packed it in at two a.m. Kathleen volunteered to go to the farm with Jessie and cook a big breakfast at Kevin's request. He had failed to mention his intentions earlier, and most of the bacon and sausage was frozen. They hurriedly thawed the sausage in warm water and made up half-frozen patties to fry. When the guests arrived, Jessie took orders for the eggs. After a nightcap, however, most people excused themselves and headed for home without eating.

Kathleen and Frank left as well. Kevin said he was too tired to eat and went into the living room to put his feet up.

Tom ate as though he had a real appetite. Sam made a gallant effort, but his weariness was obvious.

Jessie sat at the table sipping a cup of coffee. She was too worn out to eat but she savored being near Sam, sitting in companionable silence as if they were old friends.

He put down his fork and smiled into her eyes. "You look pretty shot." His gaze held hers, the weariness in his eyes no longer evident. "It was sweet of you to cook all of this after such a long day. It's delicious. I'm sorry I can't do it justice."

Warmth filled her as she basked in his visual embrace.

Tom glanced up from his food. "It's great. Thanks a lot," he said, inadvertently breaking the spell.

Sam stood. "We really should get going, Tom. We've kept our lovely hostess up late enough for one night." He gazed into her eyes once more. "Thank you for the marvelous evening and a wonderful breakfast, too."

"You look too tired to drive safely. You're both welcome to stay here. There's a guest room with two beds."

"Thank you, but no. We really must go," Sam said. "Don't worry, we'll be all right. If I didn't think I could drive safely, I wouldn't do it. We've imposed on your hospitality long enough. Come on, Tom."

"Good night, Jessie," Tom said. "Thanks again."

"Goodbye, and please be careful."

She gazed longingly after Sam as he and Tom left the kitchen. A moment later the engine of the Cutlass roared into life. Aching with fatigue, Jessie rose and began cleaning up, praying silently for their safety. When the kitchen was spotless, she glanced at the clock and sighed. Laura and Joey would be waking up in less than two hours.

CHAPTER 31

NEVER-NEVER LAND

They arrived home before midnight for once, and Jessie was glad. All of this political socializing was getting tiresome. It would be a relief when the campaign was finally over.

There was a car parked next to Mike's that belonged to Dennis, but no other strange vehicles cluttered the driveway, which pretty much ruled out a rowdy party disturbing her sleep tonight.

She followed Kevin into the house through the back door, and immediately sensed a dissonance in the atmosphere. The kitchen was empty. The dining room and rec room were dark. A lamp was lit in the living room, where the sitter would normally be watching TV, but it was deserted and the television was turned off. *Where on earth was Betsy?*

The family room door was closed, and Jessie couldn't hear a TV or anyone talking in there either, but a line of light gleamed under the door.

"Betsy?" Jessie called, low enough not to wake the children. The door to the family room opened. Mike came out.

"She's upstairs with Dennis."

"What?"

Kevin came down the hall to find out what was going on.

"She's upstairs with Dennis," Mike repeated.

"I want her back down here, now!" Jessie declared. "You go up there and tell him that."

"I'm not going up there," Mike said. "He's busy. I'm not going to stop him."

Jessie stared at Mike, aghast. Betsy was only *fifteen*.

She couldn't believe he'd let this happen in the first place, and now he was refusing to stop it. "Kevin, do something!"

"I'm not doing anything either." Kevin grinned at Mike.

"You scum!" Jessie rushed upstairs to the guest bedroom. Halting just outside the door, she knocked sharply. "Dennis, stop this minute! Do you hear me? I want her out of there immediately or I'm coming in with a knife!"

She ran back to the kitchen and grabbed a carving knife.

To save Betsy any worse embarrassment, she lingered in the downstairs hallway and listened to see if they were coming out on their own.

At the sound of footsteps, she returned to the kitchen and put the knife away.

Betsy entered a moment later, looking shame-faced.

Jessie turned and walked out to the car without speaking. Betsy followed and climbed in. Jessie drove her home slowly, trying to think of what to say.

Betsy broke the silence first. "Please don't tell my parents. I'm really sorry. I'll never do it again. Honest."

"Was this the first time you did this?"

"Yes, ma'am. I swear," she said, on the verge of tears. "Please don't be angry."

"I'm not angry with you. I'm mad at those bastards."

"I'm sorry, Mrs. McKenna, but I just couldn't help myself. Dennis is so handsome. He always comes into the living room to talk to me when I baby-sit. He kids around with me. I fell in love with him."

Jessie sighed. If Betsy had been attractive, it would be easier to understand why a man like Dennis would go after her, but she was thirty pounds overweight and not well-favored.

"Dennis is only beautiful on the outside. Inside he's spoiled and corrupted. Having you didn't mean anymore to him than drinking a six-pack or smoking a joint. You got him high for a little while, that's all. Don't waste your time on men like him, or Mike, or Kevin," she said bluntly, hating to be harsh, but the kid needed to face reality.

Betsy gave her a puzzled look. "I don't understand. Why would you say that about your husband? He married you and you're so pretty, he must love you."

"Oh, Betsy, everyone knows that we *had* to get married. It doesn't matter how pretty you are. Save yourself for a man who truly loves you. A lot of them will say they do, but if they're honest, they'll certainly be willing to take you to the altar first. I'm not saying that a man couldn't fall in love with you the other way, but you can get into a lot of trouble trying to find out. It's just not worth the risks. Promise you won't do this again."

"I promise."

Jessie pulled into Betsy's driveway and paid her. "I can't let you baby-sit for me again. It's not because I'm mad at you—it just wouldn't be safe for you to come to my house. I'm only sorry I didn't realize that before."

"I understand." Betsy opened the car door to get out. "Thanks for not telling my parents. I think you're a nice lady, Mrs. McKenna. Good night."

"Good night." Jessie watched until Betsy was safely inside the house. Suddenly the irony of the situation struck her. Betsy had already been harmed—the only thing left was to hope the poor kid wasn't pregnant.

Dennis had calculatedly used his good looks and charm to take advantage of the girl. No matter how willing she had been, it was a callous act.

And having sex with a girl under sixteen was also statutory rape. Dennis had broken the law, and Mike let him do it.

Jessie returned to the farmhouse determined to have it out with Dennis right then and there. She went straight to the family room and opened the door without knocking.

Mike was alone.

"Where's Dennis? I want to talk to him."

"It's too late. He's already passed out." Mike rose from his seat, yawning. "I think I'll hit the sack myself. Don't forget to do the sheets in the guest room tomorrow."

"You S.O.B.!" Jessie spat. "Why the hell can't you keep yourselves under control?"

"Don't get on my ass about it," Mike retorted. "I wasn't balling the girl."

"You act like animals. What am I supposed to do for babysitters if you can't control your friends? I have to be out three and four nights a week with the campaign. And now I can't, in good conscience, ask a teenage girl to baby-sit! What if the newspapers got hold of this? Then what?"

"I didn't think of that," he said, then immediately dodged responsibility. "The girl was asking for it. It wasn't like Dennis raped her or something. I wouldn't let him do *that*."

"No. You wait until they're over sixteen," she retorted.

"That's not a nice thing to say," Mike said, giving her a cold, hard look. "I wouldn't talk that way if I were you."

Her stomach clenched, but she stared Mike directly in the eye. She knew exactly what he'd do to her if Kevin wasn't home, but she had no intention of allowing him to intimidate her. His eyes locked with hers in a burning test of will.

It was Mike who blinked first. "Don't forget to wash the sheets," he sneered, covering up for his defeat.

"The sheets can stay on the bed until hell freezes over. I'm not touching them! If you want them washed, do it yourself."

Turning on her heel, she marched upstairs to bed.

Kevin was already fast asleep.

It was late morning before Dennis put in an appearance.

Jessie was sitting at the kitchen table having a cup of coffee when he walked in, pulled out a chair, and sat down.

She ignored him.

"Aren't you going to offer me a cup of coffee?"

She looked him in the eye. "I'll offer you a piece of my mind. Who the hell do you think you are screwing the babysitter while my husband and I are out?"

"Aw, come on, Jess, don't be mad at me," he said with a Peter-Pan smile. "I was getting hard-up, and she was asking for it. It was only natural."

"Don't you ever ask them how old they are first? She's fifteen. You're ten years older than she is. You should be ashamed of yourself."

"Well, she didn't look it."

"I don't care what she looks like. She's my babysitter. My husband is in the middle of an election. It's statutory rape in this state, for God's sake!"

"Now how was I supposed to know *that*?" he said, smirking.

"Don't you give me that shit, Dennis!" Jessie snapped and got up from the table.

Dennis grinned as she took her cup to the sink and rinsed it. "Man, I sure would like to give it to you."

Anger shook her.

Suddenly she felt reckless. She wanted to get back at him for what he did to Betsy. *Why not call his bluff?* If worse came to worse, she'd get out of it somehow.

She turned and faced him. "All right. Let's go."

Dennis sat up in his chair. "Are you serious?"

"If that's what you want. Let's just do it and get it over with. Leave my babysitters alone."

"But I can't fuck *you*!"

"Why not?" she asked sarcastically. "You don't seem to have any trouble doing it to little girls—or aren't you man enough to handle a real woman?"

Dennis shook his head. "It's not that. You could make a man out of anybody. I'd love to ball you, but I'm too young to die."

Jessie burst out laughing. "Dennis, I'm a woman, not a Black Widow spider."

"Anybody can see that," he said, eyeing her figure. "*Kevin* would kill me, though."

"What do you mean? Kevin doesn't care about me. He'd like to get rid of me."

"I'm not in the inner circle, so you're off limits," Dennis said. "I can't screw you without permission. A *fuck* ain't worth dying for."

She raised an eyebrow. "Who is in the inner circle?"

He shook his head. "I can't tell you that."

"I want to know." She moved toward him.

Dennis looked at her nervously. "They'd figure out it was me. I gotta go. See you later." He jumped up and ran out the back door.

Jessie poured herself another cup of coffee, pondering the significance of what Dennis had said.

What was the inner circle? And who was in it?

Johnny and Mike for sure. But if Dennis wasn't in it, that left out Jimmy, Dave, and assorted others.

Was it just the McKenna brothers?

❧

Kevin came in for lunch at noon. He sat at the kitchen table and took a long draught of iced tea.

Jessie spooned some vegetables onto his plate. "I want you to talk to Mike and Dennis, and tell them that the sort of behavior they exhibited last night will not be tolerated."

Kevin frowned. "Aren't you overreacting? It was just boys being boys. What's the big deal?"

If she couldn't appeal to Kevin's moral conscience, she could always try expediency and ambition. "You almost lost the election last night. Isn't that a big enough deal? Betsy is terrified of her parents finding out, but what if they do and decide to press charges? How's that going to sound in the local paper right before the election?"

"I didn't think of that."

"Either you get them to agree that the babysitters are off limits, or I'll have to stop campaigning."

"I'll take care of it. It won't happen again."

Jessie smiled. Kevin would be too afraid of losing the election not to lay down the law. But if Betsy hadn't begged her to keep things under wraps, she would have been only too delighted to testify in court against all of them.

It puzzled Cletus to no end when he spied a whole set of sheets in the dumpster. He decided to discuss the phenomena with Bert during the afternoon milking.

Bert went to see for himself, then returned and said the sheets weren't worth saving. There was already too much garbage on top by then.

When Cletus went to the main house to fetch his supper tray, he mentioned the curiosity. "Why would anyone throw away sheets, Miz Jessie? They's always good for rags."

"That's a good question," she said, struggling to keep a straight face.

The next morning, around nine o'clock, the phone rang. Jessie anxiously picked it up, hoping it wasn't a phone call from Betsy's mother. She didn't want to deal with a distraught diatribe no matter how justified. However, she had no choice but to answer the phone in case it was a farm-related call.

"Hello," Jessie said, trying to sound pleasant, but there was no response. She heard a click and figured it must have been a wrong number.

An hour later the phone rang again. "Hello," she said, but again no one spoke. She heard a click as the caller hung up.

It wasn't the exact same M.O. as the anonymous calls she'd gotten during Kevin's harassment campaign—usually the caller kept the line open—but she was getting freaked out and pissed.

The phone rang again at eleven.

"Hello," she said. "I don't know who this is, but I'm sick of you calling and hanging up. The next time it rings I'm taking the phone off the hook. So if you have anything to say, you'd better say it now."

"Oh, ah, sorry," a masculine voice replied. "Um, is Kevin there?"

"No, but he's normally home for lunch about noon."

"Okay, I'll call back then. Tell him I need to talk to him. It's important," the guy said and hung up.

Kevin showed up for lunch early, and Jessie gave him the message.

"What's the guy's name?" Kevin asked.

"I don't know. He hung up before I could ask, but he said it was important."

Kevin hurriedly finished his meal and rose to leave.

"Aren't you going to wait for that guy to call back?"

"I'm too busy to wait around. If he calls get his name."

Jessie shrugged and began clearing the table. The phone started ringing. She grabbed the receiver.

"Is Kevin there?" the man blurted out before she could say hello.

"No, you just missed him."

"I told you to tell him it was important!"

"I did, but he said he didn't have time to wait."

"Time's running out. I guess I'll have to tell you then. There's a warrant out for Johnny's arrest. Tell him to get the hell out of town."

Jessie hung up in a panic, wondering whether she'd be able to get hold of Johnny before the Sheriff's deputies caught up with him.

A few minutes later, Johnny pulled up the driveway. He strolled into the kitchen and plucked one of Kevin's beers from the fridge.

"Johnny, some guy called and said there's a warrant out for your arrest!"

"Fuck!" He grabbed the phone and dialed up a friend of the family with a hunting cabin in another state, then hurriedly packed a duffle bag and left.

Jessie raced around checking to make sure Johnny hadn't left any drugs lying out, wondering if the warrant would entail a thorough search of the house. In less than a half hour, a deputy sheriff rolled up the lane.

He got out of his cruiser and rang the front doorbell.

Jessie wiped her sweaty palms and opened the door.

"Good afternoon, ma'am, is Johnny McKenna at home?"

"No, sir, he isn't here."

"I have a warrant for his arrest. Do you mind if I take a look around?"

"Not at all, come on in," she said, feigning more calm than she felt.

The deputy looked into every downstairs room, but didn't ask to go upstairs. He apologized for any inconvenience he might have put her through and left.

Sighing with relief, Jessie walked back into the kitchen and froze. Growing amongst the herbs on the kitchen windowsill was a straggly marijuana plant that had sprouted from a seed Johnny planted as a joke. Jessie grabbed the pot and stashed it under the kitchen sink, pulse racing.

Thank God the deputy hadn't seen it. He could have arrested her.

A knock at the mudroom door made her jump. The deputy was back!

He asked if he might come in and look around once more. She nodded and let him in. He walked straight over to the windowsill and stared at the herb pots, then turned and looked into her eyes.

She met his gaze evenly.

"Thanks again, ma'am," he said, then touched his fingers to the brim of his hat and headed out the door.

Jessie sagged against the counter, feeling faint.

CHAPTER 32

ELECTRIC LADYLAND

The following Saturday found Jessie in high spirits. She was looking forward to spending the evening at Club Roma. The band performing was supposed to be good, and there was always the possibility that Sam might show up.

Her makeup turned out perfect, and her hair couldn't have looked better. Humming, she pulled her favorite dress out of the closet, a floor-length white gown printed with tiny red rosebuds. The sensuous material reminded her of whipped cream, and she slipped into it with a sigh of pleasure. The back of the dress was cut low enough that she managed to zip it up without any help. She didn't like asking Kevin for assistance.

The gown had spaghetti straps and wasn't designed to be worn with a bra. It fit beautifully now that she'd gained back the weight she'd lost over the summer.

Jessie started to pick up the jacket to the ensemble, then paused to look in the mirror. If the reflection she saw didn't give Sam a rush, nothing would.

It was tempting to skip the jacket. However, the gown alone was just too revealing—and she had never dared to wear the dress without it.

The long-sleeved, hip-length jacket was designed with narrow stripes of rose, gold, and lavender, alternating with rows of the same tiny red rosebuds printed on the dress. The jacket was striking, but covering the dress made it seem almost modest. She doubted it would cause a man to do a double-take.

Kevin was congenial on the drive to the club. Moments like these still gave her hope that their marriage would succeed—if only he wanted it to. And if Kevin didn't want the real thing, a marriage of convenience could be civil with just a little cooperation. The thought of divorce remained anathema to her because of the children, and because she was Catholic.

The club was crowded but they managed to find two seats at the bar, next to some acquaintances of Kevin's, and ordered drinks. Jessie exchanged a few pleasantries and was content to sit and listen as Kevin charmed the couple. They soon left for dinner and were quickly replaced by others in Kevin's circle.

Jessie tried to lose herself in reverie, drinking gin and tonics, and smoking one cigarette after another. She was bored silly and sick to death of politics. Restless, she decided it was time to leave the bar and check out the band.

Excusing herself, she left her seat and walked beside the mirrored wall leading to the dance floor. The ultraviolet light made her dress glow with a rainbow of iridescent colors. When she reached the dance floor the band launched into a cover of "Venus" by Shocking Blue. Jessie loved the song, but felt out of place standing there just listening. She didn't want to hang around too long for fear some stranger would attempt to pick her up.

Returning to the bar, she was startled to see Sam in Kevin's place. Her breath caught and her pulse quickened.

Sam was staring at her as though transfixed.

She halted in her tracks, captivated by his gaze, and wondered what he suddenly found so fascinating.

A cigarette burned unheeded between Sam's fingers as he contemplated Jessie, still dazzled by the vision he'd seen under the black light. Illuminated by the ultraviolet spectrum, she seemed like a goddess come to earth. "I should come to the farm more often."

Jessie looked at him, her thoughts bittersweet. "What difference does it make? You don't come to see *me* anyway."

"More's the pity," he replied, and stubbed the useless cigarette out in the ashtray.

She slid onto the bar stool next to him with liquid grace. Opening her evening bag, she pulled out a pack of cigarettes. Sam immediately picked up his lighter.

Jessie leaned toward him for the light, revealing an enticing amount of bosom. She took a puff from the cigarette and exhaled before looking into his eyes.

Sam's eyes held hers for a moment, then his gaze traveled over her body. He sucked in his breath and turned his face away, shaking his head as though in disbelief.

"I must have been blind," he said, and looked back into her eyes.

Jessie returned Sam's gaze evenly. Looking into his eyes in this communion was heaven. She wanted to touch him, trace her finger along the curve of his cheek. Only the fact that they were in a public place, kept her from slipping into his arms.

They were so intent on one another, time ceased to exist.

"Is this a private conversation?"

At first, Kevin's voice simply registered as an unwelcome intrusion from a world that had become irrelevant.

Jessie saw a shadow veil Sam's eyes. He gave her a look of certain knowledge that they were one in their desire, then turned and smiled at Kevin.

"Hi, Kevin, we were wondering where you were."

"I just got tied up," he replied, looking from one to the other. "You know how it is."

Sam shifted off the bar stool. "Here, you can have your seat back. I was just leaving."

Kevin tried to catch his eye, but Sam evaded him.

"It was nice talking to you, Jessie." Sam's gaze sought her eyes once more before he moved to go.

Kevin frowned. "I'll catch you later, Sam, but I need to talk to my wife right now."

Kevin sat on the bar stool next to her and looked directly into her eyes. She didn't try to avoid his gaze and returned his probing look serenely.

"So, what were you two talking about?"

"Nothing much."

"I guess you didn't have to talk," he replied shrewdly.

Ignoring him, she stubbed out her cigarette with the same calculated calm she would exhibit facing a dangerous animal and pulled another one out of the pack. It was unfortunate that Kevin had seen them, but it couldn't be helped.

He gave her a dirty look. "I don't want you wearing that dress in public again. Do you understand?"

"Go to hell," she replied coolly, and struck a match into flame.

The bartender had been observing the situation with interest and chose that moment to intervene.

"Would you like another drink?" he asked Jessie.

"No, she would not!" Kevin exclaimed, turning on the bartender. "She's already had too much. Don't serve her anymore."

The bartender backed off. Kevin scowled at Jessie and stomped off in the direction Sam had taken.

Jessie watched Kevin disappear into the crowd and continued smoking, savoring the effect of tobacco on her system. The nicotine was calming, but she wished she could have a drink. She certainly hadn't had too much alcohol. But she didn't have any money in her evening bag.

To her surprise, the bartender put a gin and tonic in front of her. He was a nice looking guy not much older than herself. She gave him a questioning look.

"It's on me," he said. "I like the dress."

She smiled at the compliment. "Thank you."

Grinning, the bartender nodded and returned to work.

Jessie sipped her drink, wondering how long she'd have to wait before Kevin was ready to leave.

His jealous reaction surprised her. Why did he care how she looked at Sam?

Kevin made it plain that he despised her, and he had other women as often as he pleased, so something else must be bothering him. But what?

She knew exactly what Johnny and Mike expected from her, and it wasn't chastity. Indeed, except for her religion, there was no reason to remain faithful if Kevin only had sex with her occasionally. He scorned their marriage vows and scorned her religion; if she succumbed to adultery, it would be a triumph on his part.

Jessie never thought it would come to this, but she couldn't exist in a loveless, degrading, and sexually unsatisfying continuum. She was falling apart, and she had no intention of becoming an alcoholic if she could help it.

She wanted life, *real life*, and sex was something she couldn't live without. If she'd been capable of being a nun, she would have joined a convent long before she met Kevin. And if she didn't have an affair, she was going to wind up killing Kevin or committing suicide.

She'd already made up her mind that she'd rather be eternally damned than give Kevin the satisfaction of killing herself. Murder, suicide and adultery were all dishonorable. But adultery, being the least permanent of the mortal sins, was the most easily repented, and a lot easier to get away with than murder.

She'd been in love with Sam for a long time. She wanted to touch him and feel his skin on hers. Just thinking about it made her shiver with desire. She'd been possessed against her will and held captive by passion, but she had never given herself to a man before.

Still, she couldn't afford any illusions.

Sam belonged to the inner circle. He never would have asked her to listen to a tape in his car alone, if he didn't. He hadn't taken her out there just to hear the music—and he knew

Kevin too well not to be aware of the risks if they did anything else.

Dennis had been afraid when she came on to him. Sam, however, had expected her to do something and was aggravated when she didn't. Apparently, Sam was free to have her as long as he abided by the rules of the inner circle. She wasn't precisely sure what those rules were, but she could guess.

Jessie took a drag on her cigarette. She had disappointed Sam before, but she had no intention of disappointing him again.

Chapter 33

Twilight Zone

Jessie closed the door to the master bedroom, filled a pipe from her stash of pot, and lit up. She opened the window while she smoked the bowl, and looked out at the night. There was a crisp autumn chill to the air and frost every morning now. The leaves were colored brilliantly, although the darkness had turned the trees into black silhouettes against the night sky.

After she finished the pipe, she turned the exhaust fan on in the connecting bathroom while she got ready for bed. Kevin would be none too pleased if he came home and smelled pot. He was already peeved because she'd started wearing a nightgown again, and she didn't want to give him an incentive to ferret out her stash.

Once the bedroom and bath were aired out, she switched off the bedside lamp and slid under the covers.

Later, something roused her from a deep sleep.

She wasn't sure what had disturbed her. It was dark in the room and she was still alone in the bed, which meant that Kevin hadn't come home yet. Glancing toward the door, she noted that the density of the darkness indicated it was still closed.

She rolled over to assume a more comfortable position.

A prickly sensation came over her. *She knew she wasn't alone.* Then she saw it.

Hovering near the ceiling, on the far side of the room, was a swirling cloud-like being with a jagged visage and eyes that glowed like burning coals.

Her heart skipped a beat, her breath caught in her throat.

Oh my God!

She blinked quickly, hoping the apparition was just a dream.

The phantasm remained.

She slid her fingers along the edge of the blanket, feeling the silky coolness of the satin binding and warmth of the fuzzy wool. If she was dreaming, would she really feel the material so plainly? She bit down hard on her tongue, wincing at the pain, and tasted the coppery flavor of blood.

Now she knew she wasn't dreaming!

Her body went taut, muscles locking so rigid it hurt to breathe. Every nerve screamed out the need for flight, but she was paralyzed stiff.

The entity hovered in the air, watching and waiting, like something from the Twilight Zone that had come to suck her into the Shadowland.

Mute with terror, she silently prayed for help.

Immediately, a thunderous voice boomed: "EVERYTHING WILL BE ALL RIGHT."

Had God answered or the entity? The words seemed to echo in her ears, and she couldn't tell where they came from.

The monster continued to hover in a revolving spiral, the scrutiny of its burning orbs dreadful to behold.

Jessie's teeth began to chatter. The strain of facing the immortal was almost more than she could bear. Her quivering mind would soon slip away into madness.

She struggled to clench her jaws shut and stop the clacking of her teeth. But she couldn't shut her eyes. Mind shrieking, she made a last ditch attempt to will her hands to move.

She managed to cover her face with the blanket and fervently prayed not to die. Time ticked tensely on, but she dared not lift the covers to see if the entity was gone. She lay stiff as a corpse, waiting desperately for dawn.

Something heavy bore down on her, pressing on her face, smothering her with its weight. Writhing in terror, she clawed at the predator, fighting frantically for air.

Light lanced into her eyes like a laser, blinding her with pain. The entity had overwhelming powers. She knew it meant to kill her now.

Abruptly, cool air flowed into her lungs. She gasped.

She could *see* and she could *breathe*. The light was morning, and the beast was only the blanket. Glorious sunshine streamed through the windows, and the awful apparition was gone.

Jessie climbed out of bed, weary from the exhausting night. Her jaw ached. She massaged the sore muscles with her fingers, wondering where Kevin was. He had never come to bed.

She heard one of the children stirring in the nursery and opened the connecting door. The scent of baby powder lingered in the atmosphere. The warm sweet smell of young children filled the room.

Laura was still asleep, looking like an angel.

Joey lay uncovered, happily chewing on a stuffed toy in his crib. He reached for his mother as soon as he saw her. Jessie picked Joey up and hugged him close.

He babbled happily as Jessie carried him to the changing table. His diaper was only wet this morning.

⌒∞⌒

During the long hectic day, Jessie tried not to think about the phantom in the night. But when she started to get ready for bed, she was struck cold with fear.

Kevin was out, and neither Mike nor Johnny was home.

Jessie bathed and put on her nightgown with every lamp and light fixture lit. In the end, she didn't have the nerve to turn them off. Although she was exhausted, she couldn't sleep a wink. Her nerves were just too tense.

Weary of the agitation, she rose from the bed and headed for her stash of pot. She put a large pinch of grass in her pipe and reached for the matchbook, then paused. *What if the pot had something to do with the specter materializing?*

It wasn't supposed to make people hallucinate, but what if it made her vulnerable to certain supernatural forces? Did she dare chance it? She never wanted to see a thing like that again!

She wanted sleep, needed it badly, and marijuana had always helped before, but now she was afraid to do anything that might be linked to the being appearing.

After a moment's hesitation, she flushed all the marijuana down the toilet. Heading back to the bed, she remembered there was something else that might help her, something she had neglected for a long time.

Jessie knelt beside the bed and began to pray.

She was close to committing adultery with Sam. Kevin was hardly ever home at night, and Mike was still waiting for her to break down and come to his room.

The Voice said everything would be all right, but what would be all right?

Was it all right to commit adultery if you thought you were in love? Was it a sin if you just couldn't live without sex anymore? Would Kevin come to love her if she only had enough faith and remained chaste?

"Oh Lord, please give me the strength to be true," she pleaded. But it took all the will she possessed to offer up an earnest prayer for her marriage.

CHAPTER 34

ELECTION DAY

Ellen and Jack extended an invitation to the McKenna family, as well as Kevin's campaign workers, to the "victory" celebration they would be hosting at the country club on election night.

Jessie was delighted. Partying at the country club, while listening to the election returns, would be a lot of fun, and it would save her a ton of work besides.

Kevin immediately nixed the idea. "It would be crass to take advantage of the Richardsons' hospitality instead of hosting a party for our own campaign workers at the farm."

"Don't you think our campaign workers would prefer the country club, with a live band and dancing, to anything we could do here?" Jessie appealed.

"That's not the issue. I want you to plan a buffet for around thirty-five people."

Jessie ran herself ragged cleaning the house and preparing all the food in advance for the party Kevin wanted to host. She'd be busy at the polls at least half the day and wouldn't have time to cook everything from scratch.

Kevin went over the polling assignments the night before the election. "I want you at the Rendale Middle School, Jessie."

"What time were you planning on scheduling me?"

"I want you there all day."

"All day?" she exclaimed. "Don't I get any relief?"

"I don't have enough campaign workers to go around," he replied brusquely. "As my wife, I expect you to do everything within your power to help me win this election."

"But what about Jack's people? We're supposed to hand out brochures for him, too. Can't he send someone to relieve me for awhile?"

"Look, I told Jack I'd take care of the poll in Rendale. Besides, if you wanted help, you should have recruited Ann or somebody from your family."

"Ann just got a new job. She has to work. My parents have to work, too, and my brother's away at college."

"If you didn't recruit any help, that's your problem. I want you at the Rendale Middle School—from the time the polls open at seven a.m. until they close at eight p.m. After that, I want you to wait around for the preliminary ballot count."

Jessie stared at him in consternation. "Are you serious?"

"Yes. It's important to know the preliminary count."

"What about the party?"

"My mother and sisters can handle that."

Election Day dawned clear and sunny, and unusually mild for November. Jessie waited for Mary Clare to arrive with Little Charlie and baby-sit Laura and Joey. Mary Clare was half an hour late and apologized profusely. Jessie didn't mind. It was just less time she'd have to spend standing around at the poll.

She took her time driving to Rendale, admiring the beautiful countryside along the way. She pulled into the school parking lot and parked far away from the building.

It was already eight a.m. so the before-work rush was over.

Two campaign workers were dutifully manning their posts. One of them was in his early thirties and introduced himself as Adam Kirkland. He was working for the Democratic candidate for state senate. The other fellow, Lemuel Brown, was in his fifties and working for Leroy Jones.

Jessie passed the time in amiable conversation with both of them, but around mid-morning Adam asked her a pointed question.

"Shouldn't you be driving around from poll to poll making appearances with your husband?"

She was rattled by the query and furious with Kevin, but she didn't dare allow herself any outward expression of emotion. "My husband considers Rendale a critical post, and he doesn't have enough campaign workers to go around."

Adam remained unconvinced. "That's no reason not to have you make a few appearances with him at other polls."

Jessie ignored his comment and kept smiling at the voters. She was glad when representatives of some of the other candidates arrived. Adam and Lemuel were relieved by replacements at noon.

The pace picked up considerably during the lunch hour.

Around six, Adam returned with a fresh supply of campaign brochures. He conducted a brief conversation with the fellow he was relieving, then turned his attention to Jessie.

"I can't believe you're still here."

Pretending she hadn't heard his remark, she smiled warmly at the passing voters and continued handing out campaign literature. She was tired of covering up Kevin's mistreatment of her, but she couldn't speak out against him in public.

Near closing, the stream of voters thinned to a trickle, and Adam turned to her once more. "Your husband didn't send you relief once today. I'll be damned if I'd treat my wife that way. If I were you, I'd have left long ago."

Finally the doors to the poll closed, and campaign workers piled into cars to leave. Jessie said goodbye to Adam.

He looked into her eyes frankly. "You're a good sport, Mrs. McKenna, but you're too good for the man you're married to. You can tell him he didn't get my vote today."

Jessie nodded numbly. There was nothing to say.

She waited an age for the preliminary ballot count and wrote down Kevin and Jack's totals. On aching feet, she crossed the parking lot and got into the Grand Prix. Kevin had chosen to ride around in the Caprice because of the high visibility the convertible afforded.

Jessie started the car and turned the stereo up high. She was so angry, it was all she could do to drive the speed limit through Rendale. Kevin might have needed her to man the poll all day, but the least he could have done was send her relief for one meal.

Once she passed the town limits, she stomped on the accelerator and red-lined the Grand Prix down Route 32. Luckily there were no police patrolling the highway, and the extreme speed helped relieve her fury.

When she turned off onto the back roads leading to the farm, she slowed to down fifty. It was a little risky to travel country roads so fast, but she knew every twist and turn by heart, and was alert for other headlights.

Pulling into the driveway, she was surprised to see so few cars. Perhaps Kevin had asked most of his poll workers to stay for the preliminary ballot counts. Some of the polls were even farther away than Rendale, and she'd been driving very fast.

Maria and Mary Clare greeted her cheerfully as she entered the kitchen. Laura ran up and Jessie hugged her. Maria carried Joey over. "Kiss Mommy good night, it's bedtime for you two."

Jessie kissed them. "Nighty-nite, sweethearts."

Maria carried Joey off. Mary Clare followed, leading Laura and Little Charlie up to bed.

Kathleen and Frank were in the living room chatting with Bubba and Ruby. Joe was tuning the radio, searching for election coverage.

Kevin wasn't home yet, and Jessie hoped he was still standing outside a poll somewhere waiting for the count.

She poured herself a drink and went over to the buffet to fix a plate of food.

Mary Clare returned downstairs and entered the dining room. "The Swedish meatballs are great, Jessie, and the shrimp fondue is out of this world. You'll have to give me the recipe."

"I will. Actually, they're both in the cookbook you gave me at my bridal shower," she said warmly. "I want to thank you for taking care of everything here today."

"Oh, it was no trouble. I'm just glad I could do something to help Kevin."

The sound of a powerful engine coming up the drive rumbled in from outside. Jessie went into the kitchen and looked through the window to see who was there. It was Sam.

Her heart leapt with delight.

Sam and Tom came in through the back door. They greeted Jessie and Mary Clare genially, then headed straight for the buffet. Jessie fixed them drinks while they filled their plates, then they all joined the small group in the living room.

Joe turned on the radio. Desultory conversation waxed and waned as the station sporadically reported results. As the election returns poured in faster, the room began to buzz with excitement. When a precinct reported a victory for Kevin or Jack, everybody cheered. If it was a loss, they moaned.

Jessie was soon caught up in the fever. She noticed Sam studying her reactions, and he smiled into her eyes.

She tried to avoid looking at Sam too often. It was terribly risky but hard to resist, considering what had happened the last time they'd seen each other.

With seventy percent of the precincts reporting, the station announced a landslide victory for Jack. Next, Kevin and Leroy's Republican opponents conceded.

Everyone shouted in jubilation.

"This calls for a toast," Sam said.

Everyone went into the kitchen to refresh their drinks and toast Kevin in absentia. He still hadn't put in an appearance. It was starting to look bad.

Frank spoke up. "Where the hell can Kevin be?"

While the family discussed the non-appearance, Jessie slipped back into the living room and Sam followed.

"Congratulations," he said, catching up to her.

"What for?" she asked, mystified. He'd already congratulated her and her in-laws on Kevin's win.

Sam looked into her eyes. "You are now one of the first ladies of Concord County, and indubitably the fairest of them all."

A thrill went through her, but she felt flustered.

She wanted to be the fairest of them all, in Sam's eyes, but it was hard to believe that he really cared for her. She hadn't seen him since that night at Club Roma, when he'd gazed at her with such passionate desire. The magic of that moment hadn't faded for her, but Sam was too worldly a man for her to think it still held the same magic for him.

She regarded him wordlessly, unsure how to respond, then heard the sound of another car engine coming up the driveway.

"Hey, it's Kevin," Tom called out.

Sam held her gaze a moment longer, then turned and walked back into the kitchen.

Jessie lingered in the dining room so she could watch Kevin's performance through the doorway, but not be readily noticeable. The polls had been closed for hours now, and he was only just arriving at his own victory party. She wanted to see how he'd manage to excuse such rudeness.

Kevin walked through the back door accompanied by an attractive brunette. No one acted as if his behavior was untoward. He accepted congratulations all around then introduced the brunette to everyone, explaining that she had been of great assistance to his campaign.

The woman seemed to be charmed to meet his parents, and they thanked her effusively for her efforts on Kevin's behalf.

Jessie wondered what poll the brunette had worked all day wearing high heels and a pretty dress. More than likely Kevin had picked her up at Ellen and Jack's party, after she got off work as someone's private secretary and waved a few leaflets around at a poll.

Kevin asked the woman if she wouldn't like something to eat. She nodded. Kevin pointed toward the dining room buffet, and Jessie quickly moved back out of sight.

The brunette poured herself a glass of punch from the sideboard. Next, she picked up a plate and selected some raw vegetables and Swedish meatballs. Just as she turned to leave, she noticed Jessie in the far corner and walked over to introduce herself.

"Hello. I'm Karen Blackburn, and you are?"

"I'm Jessie McKenna."

"Oh, another of Kevin's sisters. Pleased to meet you."

Jessie looked her straight in the eye. "No, I'm Kevin's wife."

Karen's jaw dropped. "I'm sorry. I didn't know Kevin was married."

Jessie said nothing. She spied Sam standing in the doorway, watching the tableau.

"Excuse me, but I think I'd better leave." Karen put her plate down on the dining room table and headed for the kitchen. Jessie saw her glance at Sam as she went by, and noticed an odd look pass between them.

Karen walked up to Kevin and touched his arm. "I need to get home."

He promptly said his goodbyes and escorted Karen out to the Caprice.

Sam gave Jessie one last look and walked back into the kitchen. "I'm going to call it a night, too. Congratulations again on Kevin's victory, Mr. and Mrs. McKenna. Good night, everyone."

Tom hurriedly said goodbye and followed Sam through the back door.

Jessie suppressed the impulse to rush out after them. She had Laura and Joey to think of; she couldn't afford to be rash.

Kathleen and Frank soon left, along with Bubba and Ruby. Maria and Joe went off to the guest bedroom. Mary Clare offered to help clean up, but Jessie made up the sofa and told her to get off her feet and go to sleep.

Jessie finished cleaning the kitchen, then went into the living room and collapsed in an armchair near Mary Clare. She had to rest her legs a minute before climbing the stairs.

Mary Clare was still awake and started to chat about Kevin's victory.

Jessie made polite noises in response, but her thoughts turned to Sam. She wanted desperately to be with him, but she knew she had to wait; the risk of going to him now was just too great. Too bad her children had been born into an unhappy home, instead of a happy one like Mary Clare's.

"I wish I could leave the children with you and just go away," Jessie said, not realizing she'd spoken out loud.

When Mary Clare probed further, Jessie scrambled to cover herself by saying she was dissatisfied with being just a housewife and had been raised to aspire to other things. She wished things could have been different and that her children could have a mother who was as maternal as Mary Clare.

"You're the best mother I know—better than I could ever be."

Kevin slipped into bed at dawn. Jessie didn't bother to ask where he'd spent the night—or with whom.

CHAPTER 35

WICKED GAMBIT

All morning long, Jessie was torn between shock and anger over the fact that Kevin had walked into their home with another woman, and did so right in front of his family. The knowledge he had other women didn't bother her too much anymore, but he'd crossed a line that even the worst of philanderers ordinarily honored.

When Kevin came in from the barn for lunch, he behaved as if everything was normal. Since nothing had ever been normal, it was just par for the course.

"Hey, how'd you like to go out to dinner Thursday night," he asked, "as a little reward for all the work you did during the campaign?"

"Sure," she said, surprised. *Maybe it was a peace offering.*

"Call a sitter and choose any restaurant you like."

༄

Thursday afternoon, Jessie skipped lunch so she could consume extra calories at dinner without having to worry about her weight. She decided to strip and wax the kitchen floor while she had the children down for their naps.

She removed her wedding rings and put them in a jar of jewelry cleaner to soak. She wanted the diamond to sparkle at its best tonight.

Her stomach grumbled but she ignored it.

Waiting for the floor to dry, she drank a soda and smoked. When it was safe to walk on, she put the table and chairs back and went upstairs to get Laura and Joey.

Suzy arrived promptly at five o'clock to mind the children, so Jessie had time to shower and dress at leisure.

It was after seven before Kevin showed up. He immediately offered an apology. "I'm really sorry for being late. I was tied up."

Jessie suppressed a hunger pang and smiled. "That's okay. As long as I don't have to cook, I can't complain."

When they reached the car, Kevin opened the door for her—something he hadn't done in a long time.

"Thank you," she said.

Kevin got in and started the engine. They drove toward Route 15, companionably making idle conversation. When they reached the intersection, Kevin stopped to wait for a break in traffic.

"Where would you like to eat?"

"Neptune's Den," she said. "I feel like having seafood."

"Okay, but we need to stop at Argento's first."

"Why?"

"I promised a friend I'd meet him there before we go out to dinner. He wants to personally congratulate us both on my victory in the election."

She sighed. Once they got inside Argento's bar, they'd be lucky to get out in less than an hour. She knew Kevin and how he liked to talk. "Do we have to?"

"I didn't know it would be this late when I told him we'd stop by. He's probably been waiting for some time now. It would be rude not to show up, and he did me a lot of favors during the campaign. It won't take long. I promise."

Jessie resigned herself to the inevitable. She would pass on Neptune's Den altogether, but Argento's restaurant didn't have lobster on the menu. Since she had a craving for lobster, she'd just have to wait and see if Kevin kept his word.

They parked in Argento's lot, and Kevin escorted her to a table inside the nearly empty lounge.

Their cocktail waitress, Mia Donato, hurried over to take their order. She was looking attractive as usual in the white peasant blouse, black laced-bodice, and short red skirt of her work uniform.

The long-haired bartender, Lonnie, prepared the drinks, and Mia brought them over to the table. Jessie took a sip of her gin and tonic and looked around. A man in his forties sat at a table flirting with a girl half his age. The only other patrons were two men at the bar, deep in conversation, who seemed to have no interest in anyone else.

"Do you see your friend anywhere?"

"No. But he said he'd be here." Kevin lit a cigarette and tossed the match into the ashtray.

"You were pretty late picking me up. Maybe he left already."

"I doubt it. He said he'd be here."

"If he isn't here by the time we finish our drinks, let's just leave. You can always tell him you're sorry we missed him the next time you see him."

"I'll decide when we're going to leave," Kevin said coldly. "I don't want to hear another word out of you."

His words hit her like a slap. "Why are you talking to me this way?"

"Don't you understand *English*? I told you to keep your mouth shut."

"I'm entitled to some explanation," she retorted, hotly.

"You want an explanation—I'll give you one. I'm sick of you. It was all I could do to be civil to you during the campaign, but I managed because winning was important to me."

Kevin blew smoke toward her. "Now that the campaign is over, I don't even want to hear the sound of your voice. I'll give you permission to speak to me again when you've earned it, by perfect obedience to my wishes. Each time you forget and speak without being spoken to, the longer it'll take."

Jessie stared at Kevin, dumbstruck.

Giving her a look of disdain, he picked up his drink and headed for the bar.

She just couldn't win, could she? Kevin had set her up and she'd fallen for it.

He probably only promised to give their marriage another chance because he found out she had gone to a lawyer. He must have figured it would look bad if she filed for divorce in the middle of the campaign. But what was he up to now?

Mia came over. "Are you ready for another drink?"

"Yes, thank you. Can you bring me some pretzels or breadsticks with it?"

"Sure."

Mia returned with the drink, but no food. Jessie gave her a questioning look.

"Kevin said not to spoil your appetite."

The honeymoon treatment again. At least the piano player was good, and listening to him helped pass the time.

Mia kept the drinks coming.

Jessie saw Jack and Ellen enter the lounge. They spotted Kevin at the bar and went over to join him.

After a while, Jack got up and came over to the table. "How are you doing, Jessie? I just noticed you over here. I haven't seen you since before the election."

She wasn't sure how to reply. Jack had to know that Kevin attended the victory party at the country club without her, but she assumed Jack was trying to be diplomatic.

"I'm doing fine. Congratulations on your re-election."

"Thank you," he replied. "And thanks for all the work you did to help my campaign. I couldn't have done it without you and Kevin."

"All the credit should go to Kevin. I didn't do that much."

Jack furrowed his brow. "You stood at a poll for twelve hours handing out my campaign literature along with Kevin's. I'd call that a big help. I didn't have to station any of my people there. I ought to do more than just give you a word of thanks."

"That's true. You should ask me to dance," she said wryly.

He laughed. "You've got me there. I'll dance with you anytime you like. Come on, let's go."

Jack went to the piano player and told him to take a break, then went to the jukebox and selected some songs they could rock to.

They danced several of the latest dances together, something Jessie had been dying to do for months instead of being squeezed to death by dirty old men.

Jack seemed amazed by her ability. "I never knew you were so good. We'll have to do this more often."

Unfortunately, he and Ellen had other places to go and soon took their leave.

Jessie returned to the table, and Mia brought her another drink. She finished it, then decided to risk asking Kevin if they could leave. Steeling herself, she walked over to the bar.

Kevin gave her a stony look.

"I'm tired," she said. "Can we just go home?"

"No. Now give me your car keys."

"Why?"

"You broke the rule of silence. But I'm willing to give you another chance to shape up and be the wife I know you can be. It's just a test of obedience. You'll get the keys back."

She shook her head and turned to walk away.

Kevin caught her arm. "Wait—think about Laura and Joey," he said, playing his trump card. "You know how important it is for children to grow up in intact families. I'm willing to keep you on as my wife—all you have to do is cooperate. Now please hand me the keys."

Her heart twisted. How could she refuse if there was any hope of preserving their marriage for the sake of the children?

She opened her purse and handed Kevin the keys.

⟡

The crowd in Argento's bar began to thin. By now it was obvious Kevin had no intention of buying her dinner, and she still couldn't get a pretzel out of Mia.

Kevin came over to the table. "There's someone here who wants to meet you. He's a good friend of mine, so I want you to be nice—very nice—understand?"

"Why?"

"He did me a lot of favors during the campaign, and I owe him. He's in a position to do me even more good in the future. He's retired from the service and now acts as a consultant to the military. Try to be charming for once, will you?"

She followed Kevin to the bar. He introduced her to a man with blue eyes and hair so gray it was almost white. The man kept himself in good shape, but he had to be in his mid-fifties, or maybe even sixty. She wondered if he was the man who had spoiled her dinner.

"Jessie, I'd like you to meet Howard Townsend. Howard, this is my wife, Jessie."

"Good evening," she said, but didn't offer her hand.

Howard studied her figure openly, then smiled. "I've been looking forward to meeting you for a long time. Having met you, I can only say that I regret not having made your acquaintance sooner."

She was already sorry to have met him.

Kevin grinned and walked away.

Howard indicated the bar stool next to him. "Please sit down. Let me buy you a drink."

"Ginger ale will be fine."

"Hey, bartender, give me another and bring her whatever she's been drinking."

"No, please don't," Jessie told Lonnie. "I really don't want any more alcohol."

Howard frowned. "Bring the lady what she was drinking."

Lonnie gave him a sideways look, but complied.

Jessie idly fingered the stir stick while Howard talked. Thankfully, he spared her any details about his career. That kind of talk could be a drag.

"I like my line of work because it allows me to travel to different countries a lot. Have you ever traveled abroad?"

"No."

"Would you like to?"

"Of course, if I ever get a chance." She sipped the drink to be polite.

The conversation about his travels dragged on. It might have been interesting, but she didn't feel comfortable being near the man. She was dying for a smoke, but she was trying to avoid giving him the opportunity to offer her a light.

Howard pulled a cigarette out of a pack on the bar and lit up.

The scent of tobacco undermined her resolve. She opened her purse to get out her cigarettes and matches.

"Allow me." Howard picked up his lighter.

It would be rude to ignore his offer, and Kevin had told her to be nice, although she had no intention whatsoever of being charming. She accepted the light and inhaled deeply, trying to avoid eye contact. Howard was looking at her in such a lascivious manner it was unnerving.

He leaned over and squeezed her thigh, then slid his fingers down to her knee. "You have good muscle tone. I like that. Kevin tells me you ride."

Revulsion swept through her. She found Howard as repulsive as the grocer who had molested her at age thirteen.

"Take your hand off my leg!"

"All right." He reluctantly removed his fingers.

Jessie stubbed out her cigarette. "Excuse me," she said and got up to leave.

Howard grabbed her arm. "Where are you going?"

"Really, sir," she snapped, "a simple 'excuse me' should suffice."

His grip, already painful, got tighter. "I want to know."

"A lady shouldn't have to spell it out."

"Oh, ah, okay," he said and released her.

Jessie headed toward the ladies' room until she saw Howard turn around to talk to the bartender. She slipped back into the lounge by another door and hurried over to Kevin, who was surrounded by acquaintances at the far end of the bar.

She tugged on his sleeve. "I need to talk to you—*now*."

Kevin moved out of earshot of his friends. "What is it?"

"That man is coming on to me pretty strong. He already put his hand on my leg. I can't stand him. I want to go home."

"No."

"Please, let's just go home."

"No. I told you to be *nice* to him, and I mean it. If he wants to put his hand on your leg, let him."

"No!" she exclaimed, appalled. "How can you ask me to do something like that?"

"If you don't, I'll reconsider keeping you on as my wife. Now go back there and do your job."

Crushed, Jessie walked woodenly back toward Howard. At the moment, even Howard didn't seem as despicable as Kevin. She sat on the stool next to the man and mutely stared at the surface of the bar.

"What's the matter?" Howard asked.

Her throat was too constricted to speak.

"Bartender, bring her another drink."

Jessie fought for control. "No," she managed to croak.

"Okay, at least you have your voice back. Look, Kevin isn't worth it. He's too young, too much of a hotshot to appreciate a woman like you. He doesn't even know how to treat you." Howard smiled. "Now me—I'm an older, wiser man. I know class when I see it. Come with me. I'll take you all over Europe. You'll love it."

"I couldn't do that. I have too many obligations at home. Besides, I love Kevin," she said, cringing at the lie, but desperate to put the man off. If Kevin treated her with a modicum of decency, she *would* love him still. "I only wish he loved me. I won't just walk out and leave my family."

"Have another drink," Howard said. "Let's talk about this."

Jessie shook her head. "No, please. I can't drink anymore. I haven't eaten since breakfast. If I have another, I'll get sick."

"What do you mean, you haven't eaten? Doesn't Kevin feed you?"

"He told me he was taking me out to dinner, but I haven't eaten yet."

"Good God! Why didn't you say something sooner? I'd have bought you dinner. Let's go to the dining room and see if we can still get you something to eat."

She followed Howard into the restaurant section. He pulled out a chair at the nearest table, helped her sit down, then signaled a waiter. "I'd like two menus."

"I'm sorry, sir, the restaurant is closed."

"Can't we get anything?"

"Only from the bar."

Howard ordered drinks. "Can you bring some breadsticks or pretzels with our drinks?"

"I'll have to check on that, sir."

"You should have something to eat in a few minutes," Howard said when the waiter left.

"Thank you," Jessie said, relieved.

"You know, we can go somewhere else to eat. It doesn't have to be here. Hey, I've got an even better idea. Let me take you to the Virgin Islands tonight. You can get a snack on the plane, and we can be there in a few hours."

She rolled her eyes. *What kind of man expected her to leave her husband and children, and fly off to the islands?*

"You don't believe me, do you?" Howard asked. "Okay, I'll prove it." He reached inside his jacket, pulled out a leather credit card case, and flipped it open. It was filled with high-end credit cards. "See—believe me now? I'll take you anywhere you want to go. Come on, what do you say?"

"No," Jessie said flatly.

"Quit playing games. It's a great act, but it's wearing thin."

She looked at him like he was crazy. "I don't know what you mean."

"Playing hard-to-get, that's what I mean. I'm a nice guy, and I'm offering to show you a good time, but you keep turning me down. You've made your point. Now cut the crap and let's get on with the deal."

"What deal? I don't understand."

"Your price. How much do you want? Just name it, I'll pay it—you'll be worth it."

"Excuse me, I'm leaving." She stood to go.

Howard grabbed her and shoved her back down on the chair, just as the waiter appeared with their drinks.

"Are you all right, Miss?" the waiter asked. "Is this man bothering you?"

"No, I'm *not* all right. Please get my husband."

Howard backed away, but the waiter continued to eye him warily. "What's your husband's name?"

"Kevin McKenna."

"Wait," Howard appealed. "Let's talk."

Jessie shook her head. The waiter headed for the lounge. Howard sat down with annoyance. "Why do you keep pretending to be Kevin's wife?"

"Because I am."

"But we both know that's not true. You aren't even wearing any rings."

She looked at her left hand. "I forgot them. They're sitting at home in a jar of jewelry cleaner. I always put them in there when I wax the floor. I really am Kevin's wife."

"Quit lying. I've met Kevin's wife—she's a blonde."

Jessie's eyes widened with surprise. Kevin sleeping around was one thing, but passing another woman off as his wife?

And what was he anyway? A pimp on the side? And now this idiot thought she was a *hooker*?

Just then, Kevin came up to the table.

"Hey, a waiter said I was wanted in here. How are you two getting along?"

Howard gave him a disgusted look. "It's this broad of yours, Kevin. I wish you'd straighten her out. You romance them too much. She refuses to leave you, and she keeps on insisting she's your wife."

"Oh, that's because she *is* my wife."

Howard scowled. "I've met your wife, remember? Now how much do you want for this one? I'll make it worth your while, but I'm in a hurry."

"This is my *real* wife," Kevin replied, grinning.

Howard's eyes widened. He looked at Jessie and back at Kevin, then stood.

"You know, Kevin, I used to think you were smart, but I was wrong. You're nothing but a damn fool!" he said and walked out.

CHAPTER 36

DAZED AND CONFUSED

Livid, Jessie stood and left to get her coat. Kevin followed in her wake.

She grabbed her coat off the hanger in the cloakroom and put it on.

"Where are you going?"

"I'm leaving."

"No, you're not. I have all of the keys to the car, and I'm not ready to go yet."

"I'm leaving if I have to hitchhike." She walked out the door and headed across Argento's parking lot toward the intersection up the road.

Kevin ran after her. "Okay, let's just get in the car."

"I'd rather hitchhike."

"Don't do anything stupid, Jessie. You can get hurt doing that."

"What's it to you?"

"Look, I don't want to get into an argument out here. It's cold and it's late," he said, then softened his voice. "Get in the car so I can take you home. It's better than winding up in a ditch with your throat slit."

Jessie paused. It was freezing, and all she really wanted to do was go home.

She turned and followed Kevin to the car. He opened the door for her. She gave him a glacial look as she got in.

Kevin started the car and pulled out onto the road. At the traffic light, he turned left and headed home. He drove for several miles without Jessie uttering a single word. The humming of the car's heater echoed in his ears.

"I'm sorry about what happened tonight. It was all a misunderstanding."

"Don't even speak to me," she shot back. "I don't want to hear it."

"Be reasonable, Jess. It was just a mistake."

"A mistake? Was it a mistake that we went to Argento's instead of Neptune's Den? Was it a misunderstanding that we were supposed to be going out to dinner—and I still haven't had a thing to eat? Save it, Kevin. I don't want to hear it."

He drove awhile before trying to talk to her again. "What are you going to do?"

She didn't reply.

Her silence was irritating. "I asked you a question, and I want an answer. What are you going to do, Jessie?"

"It's none of your business. From now on I'm going to do whatever the hell I want to do, whenever the hell I want to do it."

"You're going to have an affair, aren't you?"

There was only silence in response, so he tried another tack. "I know you're going to. I can tell. Why don't you answer me?"

"You already know the answer."

"Yes, but I don't know *who*. Who is it, Jess? I want to know."

"Guess," she replied flippantly. If he hadn't figured it out by now, she still had a chance to protect Sam.

"No. I want to hear it from your own lips."

"Why? I'm not going to tell you."

"I want to know which of my friends is ready to betray me. There's no point in being suspicious of the wrong person. Tell me who it is."

So he can't figure out if it's Sam or Jack? And that meant he never even considered the possibility of one of his brothers having an affair with her in violation of the rules.

Sam was the only one she cared about, certainly not Jack. But either way, Kevin obviously thought he had everyone under his control, and now he was beginning to realize his control was slipping. Amused, she began to laugh.

"What's so funny?" he asked. "Why are you laughing?"

It was time to give him something to think about, but she was chuckling so hard she couldn't talk.

"Stop it, damn it!" Kevin ordered. "Tell me who's going to betray me."

It was just too funny, especially now that she knew how to throw him off Sam's track.

"Tell me *why* you're laughing," Kevin demanded.

"You're asking the wrong question."

"What do you mean?"

"You should be asking *how many* would betray you." She rolled with mirth. It was so hilarious she had tears in her eyes.

Kevin's jaw clenched with rage. His hands gripped the steering wheel in a stranglehold. He pulled into the driveway and screeched to a halt just outside the mudroom door.

Jessie watched his actions with detached, albeit drunken amusement. "Pay Suzy," she said, then went straight upstairs to change out of her clothes and fall into bed.

Although she was exhausted, she was too drunk to sleep, but pretended to be passed out when Kevin climbed into bed.

Her guts felt queasy, then the room started to spin. She fought for control, regretting that last drink. Her stomach began to roll. She pushed off the covers and started to rise.

Kevin stirred. "Where are you going?"

"To the bathroom."

"No, you're not! You aren't going anywhere. You're punished."

"But I'm going to vomit!

"Stay where you are."

Jessie got up and ran downstairs. She went straight out the front door and threw up off the porch.

Kevin must have stopped to put on some pants because he wasn't right behind her. She hurried to the car, hoping he'd left the keys in the ignition like he usually did.

It was locked.

She headed for the mudroom, hoping to grab the spare keys off the hook in the kitchen, but saw a figure moving around inside. There was no way to open the mudroom door and get to the keys without being caught.

She had no choice but to head for her parents' place on foot. There was no telling what Kevin might do if she returned to the house. She didn't relish the thought of slipping through barbed wire fences and wading the icy river in bare feet. The only alternative was running to the road and using the bridge.

Ducking below window level, she scurried along the side of the house, then peered around the corner to see if the front was clear. Kevin was standing in the middle of lawn, scanning the area. *If he was outdoors, who was in the kitchen?*

She gauged the distance between herself and Kevin and the road. If she ran fast enough, she just might make it. She took a deep breath and started across the lawn.

Suddenly, Kevin turned and stared at her. She froze in her tracks.

His eyes had no irises or pupils. Sickly-white orbs glowed from the sockets.

Her heart stopped and her blood ran cold

He looked like some kind of zombie.

"Come to me," Kevin said in a rasping voice that lifted the hairs on the back of her neck.

She stood there petrified, unable to move or draw breath.

He raised his arms, stretching his hands toward her. "Come to me."

The specter of a night long buried rose into her mind—a night when preternatural eyes had stared into her own, leaving her mesmerized with fear.

"You *must* obey me! I have power over you," he growled, then began to advance.

"No!" she screamed and bolted.

The Kevin-thing sprinted after her.

Jessie was ahead of it until she got to the road.

When her bare feet smacked the pavement, she gasped and recoiled in pain. Each stride stung like a slap across the face. Grit and gravel pricked her feet like needles. Cramping muscles stabbed her side. She couldn't maintain her speed. Eyes watering, she labored for breath in torment.

A stone bruised her heel, jarring her off stride. She staggered and almost fell. Righting herself, she lurched desperately toward the bridge.

An arm snaked around her neck from behind.

She screamed and clawed at the Kevin-thing's face, but he wrestled her to the ground. "You aren't running away from me, you bitch! You're coming home right now!"

Yanking her to her feet, he forced her along the road to toward the farmhouse.

Feigning submission, she waited until he relaxed his grip then took off. He caught her, threw her to the ground, and dragged her across the lawn to the house.

Mike stood in the doorway with the light on. Kevin managed to haul Jessie onto the porch, but she grabbed for a post and held on for dear life. She wasn't going back into that house.

Kevin tried to pry her fingers loose.

"Do you need any help?" Mike asked.

"Not yet," Kevin said, then punched Jessie in the eye.

Stars swirled across her vision, and she lost her grip on the post. Kevin grabbed her as she fell, and Mike helped him carry her inside.

"Keep a guard on her," Kevin said to Mike. "I need to call someone." He disappeared into the family room to use the phone.

The only person Jessie thought Kevin could be calling was his buddy Dr. Herman Gross. The lustful way Gross looked at her made it obvious he wouldn't mind fucking her. Kevin was probably counting on his help to get her drugged and pacified, then committed. And she could guess what the bribe would be.

Her only hope was to escape from Mike, lock herself in the kitchen, and phone her parents.

She relaxed every muscle, and Mike loosened his grip.

"Why do you always let Kevin boss you around? Why don't you think for yourself?"

"He can't boss me. I know how to think for myself."

"You're obeying without question. If you don't even know what's going on? How do you know you're taking the right side?

Mike frowned and relaxed his hold some more. "Okay, then tell me what's going on."

Jessie jerked free and fled down the hall to the kitchen. She slammed the door closed and locked it, milliseconds before Mike reached it. He rattled the doorknob to no avail. Jessie dashed to lock the other doors before either of them could run out front and around to the back of the house. She grabbed the phone and dialed frantically. It rang three times before being picked up.

"Mom! It's me, Jessie! I need you to come right away!" She burst into sobs and slid to the floor in a heap, the phone clutched to her chest. She clung to the receiver like a lifeline, crying uncontrollably, until she heard a knock and her mother's voice at the door leading into the mudroom.

Jessie pulled herself to her feet, hung up the receiver, and unlocked the door. With anxious expressions, her mother and father hurried into the kitchen.

"What's wrong?" her mother asked.

"Kevin tried to hurt me—he punched me in the eye!" Jessie exclaimed, her voice hoarse from weeping.

Kevin knocked on the door leading into the kitchen from the dining room. "Let me in. We need to talk."

"Don't let him in!" Jessie cried.

"I want to get to the bottom of this." Bill unlocked the door and waved Kevin inside. "Jessie said you hit her in the eye. What's going on?"

"That isn't true," Kevin countered. "We had a fight over her drinking. Jessie got drunk and hysterical, and I slapped her to bring her out of it."

"No, that's not what happened!" Jessie interjected. "We were supposed to go out to dinner, but Kevin made me stay at Argento's bar, drinking for hours, without any food. He was hoping I'd get drunk, then he tried to sell me to some man he knew! The man walked out on the deal when he found out I was Kevin's wife. When we got home, Kevin tried to punish me so I ran. I was trying to escape!"

Kevin shook his head. "Why would I do something like that? It's absurd. She's drunk and irrational."

"What actually happened?" Bill asked.

"During the campaign, Jessie's drinking got out of hand. And she made a public spectacle of herself tonight in Argento's. A guy I knew helped me get her into the car. She got hysterical because we had to manhandle her a bit. When we got home we had a big fight. I told her the drinking had to stop. She spit at me and said nobody was going to tell her what to do, screeching at the top of her lungs. I was afraid she was going to wake the children. I slapped her to bring her to her senses.

She ran out the front door in her nightgown and ran toward the road. I had to stop her before anyone driving down the road saw her. If a scandal involving my wife got into the papers, it would ruin my political career. I was desperate to get her back inside. She fought me like a wildcat. I had to drag her across the lawn to the house."

"I see," Bill said.

"No, Daddy, it's not true! He's lying!" Jessie sobbed.

"Honey, you're drunk. You probably misinterpreted what happened."

"No! Kevin's lying! I swear. You've got to believe me!"

"Calm down," Liz interjected. "You're hysterical. I'm sure Kevin didn't mean to hurt you. But what was he supposed to do? You've got no business getting drunk out of your mind and running down the road."

Jessie moaned. "You don't understand. Please, you've got to believe me."

"You need to go to bed and sleep it off, honey," Liz said.

"That's right," Bill said. "I think we're done here. Your mother and I need to get up early to go to work. Don't ever do anything like this again, Jessie. You'd better stop drinking if you can't control it."

"Nooo!" Jessie screamed, beside herself. "Why won't you listen?"

Whimpering, she fell to her knees and wrapped her arms around her mother's legs. "Don't leave me! I beg you. Don't leave me alone with him!"

Liz gave Bill a look. "I'd better stay. You go on home. Call the hospital in the morning and tell them I'm sick."

Bill nodded. "I'm sorry about this, Kevin. I don't hold with men hitting women, but I can see why you felt you had no recourse."

"I appreciate your understanding, Bill."

"Come on, Jessie," Liz said, lifting her weeping daughter to her feet. "Let's get you upstairs."

Jessie obeyed, her breath hitching with sobs. Inside the bedroom, trembling with fear, she clung to her mother.

"Don't leave me! Promise you won't leave me alone with Kevin."

"I won't," Liz said.

"Lock the door," Jessie pleaded. "Please lock the door!"

<hr />

When her mother roused her in the morning, Jessie awakened feeling dazed and confused. Her mind seemed to be in some kind of fog. Her body ached all over.

"It's time to get up, honey. I've filled the bathtub. What you need is a nice soak." Liz raised the blinds to let in some light, as Jessie rose from the bed.

Her mother turned and gasped. "Oh my God! You have a black eye! I had no idea Kevin hit you so hard." Liz helped her remove the soiled nightgown. "Jesus, Mary and Joseph!" her mother exclaimed.

"W-what?" Jessie mumbled, bewildered.

"Look in the mirror."

Jessie stared at scratches and bruises that covered her legs and torso without comprehension.

"I'm sorry. I never suspected Kevin beat you so badly," Liz said, chagrined. "You didn't have a black eye last night, but it takes time for bruises to form. Come on, let's get you a bath."

Jessie shuffled into the bathroom with Liz leading her by the hand, then Liz eased her into tub to soak. She floated blankly in the water's warm embrace until her mother returned to help her dress. Afterward, Liz hustled her and the children out to the car. "I'm taking you home."

Sitting at her mother's kitchen table, drinking coffee, a blurred recollection of events began to coalesce in Jessie's mind. She was relieved to finally be home and safe. Thank heavens her mother had seen the light at last.

Kevin didn't notice Jessie and the children were gone until he entered the house for supper. He'd been harvesting all day.

"Damn it!" He kicked the leg of a kitchen chair. Liz must have taken Jessie and the kids to her house. He wasn't putting up with this shit. He hopped into the car and drove to his in-law's place.

Blackjack and Tar Baby began barking furiously at the sound of a car coming up the driveway. Jessie knew it wasn't her father if the dogs were barking like that. She grabbed the shotgun off the gun rack, and started toward the cabinet where her father stored the ammunition.

"What are you doing?" Liz demanded.

"Kevin's coming! I need the shells."

"No!" Liz said in alarm. "There isn't going to be any shooting in my house. Calm yourself down!"

Jessie stared at her mother. "B-but—"

"Put it back," Liz ordered.

Jessie reluctantly obeyed. She wasn't in the habit of defying her mother, and it was her house and her gun.

Kevin rattled the doorknob. They both jumped.

Finding it locked, he left the porch and tried other doors.

Jessie and Liz scurried around the house, peering through the windows, trying to follow Kevin's movements, hoping he'd leave without making trouble.

Kevin remembered the spare key and sneaked back around front as soon as they lost sight of him. Slipping the key into the lock, he quietly opened the door and ran upstairs before they knew he was in the house. He grabbed a sleeping child under each arm and hurried back down the steps.

Liz and Jessie tried to block his way but he pushed past, knocking them aside.

Tossing the kids into the car, he sped off.

The women stared after the vehicle until it disappeared.

Liz walked back inside and dialed Kevin's phone number.

She let it ring until he picked up. "Bring Laura and Joey back this minute!"

"Tell my wife that if she's concerned about the children, she should come home," Kevin replied and hung up.

Enraged, Liz grabbed the phone book and found the number for the state police. Two troopers arrived in record time. They listened sympathetically to the women's story, but said there was nothing they could do to get the children back.

Kevin was a relative and hadn't broken in—he'd used a key. He was the father of the children and, as such, had the right to take them anywhere, anytime he wished. Since it was clear that neither woman had been injured, they couldn't simply go over to the farm and arrest him.

The troopers looked apologetic. "We're sorry, Mrs. McKenna, but if you want to press charges for the assault and battery, which occurred earlier and in a different location, you'll just have to wait until Monday morning and see a magistrate."

Jessie and Liz watched in disbelief as the troopers departed.

CHAPTER 37

YOU KEEP ME HANGIN' ON

When Bill got home from work, Liz filled him in. He phoned Kevin immediately. "My daughter's sitting here with a black eye! You told me you only slapped her once to snap her out of an hysterical fit."

"I'm sorry, sir. I might have hit her harder than I thought. She was screaming like a banshee, and I just lost it."

"Why did you take Laura and Joey?"

"Jessie's drinking is out of hand, sir. I'd hoped that when the campaign was over and things were back to normal, she'd cut back on the booze. But that just didn't happen. I don't think it's safe to leave Laura and Joey alone with her, and you and your wife both work. My sisters can take care of the children until this situation is straightened out."

"So you plan on going to marriage counseling then?"

"Yes, as soon as we can get started. I want to save my marriage and get Jessie the help she needs."

"Okay. It sounds like you two need a cooling off period, and professional help is definitely in order. Laura and Joey are precious and deserve to have parents who act in their best interest. Let us know as soon as you get an appointment set up."

"I'll get right on it. Thanks for understanding, Bill."

Jessie watched her father hang up the phone with a sense of unease. What she'd heard didn't make much sense.

Her father turned toward her. "Thank God, Kevin's willing to go to counseling—but I think we need to have a frank talk about your drinking, Jessie."

"My drinking? What's that supposed to mean?"

"Kevin said you've been drinking heavily during the whole campaign. You got drunk last night and had a fight with your husband. It's no wonder Kevin lost it when you started screaming, and then ran down the road in your nightgown."

"He's lying. I wasn't screaming and I didn't run down the road because Kevin slapped me. He tried to sell me to a man in Argento's. The guy wouldn't take me when he found out that I was Kevin's wife. Kevin tried to punish me afterward, and I ran because I was terrified."

"That's enough!" Liz exclaimed. "You can't possibly expect us to believe Kevin tried to sell you to a man. He just finished working like a dog to win an election. Why would he jeopardize that to sell you to some guy? The whole idea is preposterous."

"But—"

"You were drunk, honey," Bill interjected. "You probably misunderstood what was going on. Kevin couldn't do something like that anyway, it's illegal."

Jessie groaned. "You don't understand. You think Kevin's normal—he's not. My life's been a nightmare since the day we got married. I tried to talk to Mom, but she wouldn't listen."

"Your father and I have always believed that it's wrong to take sides. Parents too often favor their own child, to the detriment of their child's spouse. In retrospect, we should have persuaded the pair of you to get help sooner, but you must accept your share of the blame for letting things get out of hand. You've no business getting drunk and fighting with your husband like white trash."

Jessie shook her head and buried her face in her hands. *What was the matter with them? Why wouldn't they believe her?*

"See here," Bill said, exasperated. "Laura and Joey are too precious for two self-centered people to tear their world apart. You have a responsibility to your children. Think of them instead of yourself."

"Right," Liz added. "Kevin has agreed to marriage counseling. There's no point in prosecuting him and destroying the dream he's worked so hard for. He'll be better able to provide for you and the children with his new job—but if he's in jail, he won't be earning a living at all."

Jessie began to worry about Blue and Rio. She knew she couldn't trust Kevin to feed them. She asked Sandy Hanlon to help her ride them home to her parents' place Sunday afternoon.

Just to be on the safe side, Sandy's new boyfriend, Josh, drove them to the farm during the afternoon milking. He'd be able to provide some protection if necessary. Fortunately the Grand Prix was gone, and Kevin and the children weren't home.

They saddled the horses and rode off with Dusty following. Jessie was relieved. Although Cletus would feed him, she didn't know what would happen once the bag of dog food in the barn ran out.

More than a week passed before she and Kevin could meet with a professional therapist.

On the way to the first session, Kevin told her it was all her fault that they had marital problems. She wondered why she had even dared hope that he might change. He was just the same as he always was. But maybe, if she was lucky, the counselor could actually talk some sense into him.

The therapist, Sharon Hartshorn, began by interviewing them together.

"What areas of friction in your marriage seem to be the biggest problem, Mr. McKenna?"

"Well, my wife's a good, but misguided, woman. I come from a traditional sort of home where women know how to please a man. Unfortunately, Jessie didn't. Her mother worked outside the home, and it was understandable that her father helped out, but Jessie doesn't work, and I don't want that kind of marriage."

Jessie gave only brief, noncommittal answers to the counselor's questions. She wasn't quite sure how to bring up the real reason they needed professional help. She'd been too vain to be seen in public without covering up the vestiges of her black eye with makeup.

Sharon made some notes and checked her watch. "We have some time left. I think I have everything I need from you for now, Mr. McKenna. Why don't you take a seat in the waiting room while I collect some background information on Jessie's childhood."

"Of course," Kevin said and departed.

Sharon waited for the door to close. "You weren't very forthcoming in front of your husband. I'd like to know why."

"I tried to get my husband into marriage counseling before, but he refused because he believes everything is my fault. The only reason we're here today is because he beat me up, and he wants to avoid prosecution. My parents think I should give him another chance."

"If you care about saving your marriage, professional therapy is the only way to do it. A lot of abusers do come around if they successfully complete counseling. You shouldn't return home unless Kevin does finish counseling. Abuse is all about control, and he must learn that he has no right to harm you, or demean you, or order you around. Do you understand?"

"Yes, I do."

"Explain to your parents how important it is for you not to return to your husband until he finishes therapy. Otherwise, the abuse will only escalate."

Jessie relayed Sharon's recommendation to her parents. They agreed to allow her to stay with them until Kevin finished counseling. However, they made it clear that they preferred not to discuss the problems she had in her marriage because it was the province of the therapist.

*   *   *

With nothing to do but sit home alone all day and think about her problems, Jessie was going stir-crazy. Counseling was obviously going to take time, and she was uncomfortable living on her parents' charity.

She figured she might as well start looking for a job.

Ann offered to drive her to the farm one night after bowling so she could get the Grand Prix.

Jessie went to every business in Mansfield that might conceivably have unskilled entry-level positions, and asked if she could fill out a job application.

She was shocked to discover that her associate's degree overqualified her for the few entry positions available. The retail stores had already done their hiring for the holiday shopping season. All the other the jobs open to women in the classifieds required typing and short-hand, skills which weren't on her resume.

Frustrated by the fruitless job search, she got together with Ann for drinks at Argento's. There, they could talk about things that were best left unsaid during bowling or in front of their parents.

Mia promptly waited on them.

Jessie wasn't quite sure how to take Mia, but she didn't want to be rude and request another waitress. She noticed that Lonnie wasn't manning the bar. When Mia returned with the drinks, she paused to talk.

"By the way, Jessie, I heard something I thought you'd like to know about."

"What?"

"Kevin was in here the other night with Sam Leland and a couple of other guys. Lonnie overheard Sam saying some nasty things about you. Later, Lonnie asked if I knew what you'd done to Sam for him to bad-mouth you like that."

The words sliced through her heart like a knife.

"I can't imagine why Sam would say nasty things about me. I've never done anything to him. But he's Kevin's friend, and he's probably taking Kevin's side since we've separated. I appreciate you telling me, though."

"I told Lonnie that I didn't know anything. I asked him what Sam said, but he wouldn't tell me. I tried hard to find out, too, but Lonnie wouldn't give."

"Well, thanks for trying."

"Just so you know," Mia replied, and went back to work.

Ann's eyes widened. "I wonder why Sam would say bad things about you? Can you think of anything you might have done to offend him?"

"No, not a thing."

"But why?" Ann exclaimed. "Heck, you two were practically ready to have an affair. Can't you think of anything he might have taken the wrong way?"

"No. I'm not a tease. If he wanted me, he could have had me. I wasn't trying to push him into doing something he didn't want to do. I don't see how a man would be offended by that."

"Didn't you think about going to him after Kevin beat you?"

"Yes, but I didn't."

"Why not?"

"For one thing, I looked terrible. I didn't want Sam to see me like that. For another, Kevin agreed to marriage counseling. I had to give him another chance, if only for our children's sake. I owe them that. It would have been wrong to go to Sam, no matter how I feel about him."

Ann lit a cigarette and appeared thoughtful. "Maybe Sam was insulted when you didn't come to him. He might think you were just teasing him before."

"No. I don't think that's the reason."

"Well, if he liked you and you liked him, I wonder why he *didn't* start an affair with you?"

Jessie shook her head, her heart in turmoil. "I don't know. Kevin was suspicious, for one thing, and there wasn't exactly time to plan anything. I just can't believe Sam said something awful about me—so awful that Lonnie wouldn't even repeat it to Mia. I've never done anything to Sam that's false. And he knows Kevin runs around on me."

Ann shrugged. "But all Sam really knows is what Kevin told him, and that wouldn't be the truth. You should go to Sam and talk to him, find out why he said what he did."

"No. I can't go near him," Jessie said. "I've given myself to him already. All he has to do is take me. We aren't going to talk."

"I don't understand you. If you were ready to have an affair with Sam before Kevin beat you, why not now? What's the difference?"

Jessie fingered her drink. "There's something going on, a game the guys are playing against me."

"Are you serious?" Ann exclaimed. "What kind of game?"

"Mike and Johnny made no secret of the fact that they'd like to have an affair with me. But neither of them ever got physical. I thought it was a little strange, and it took me awhile to figure it out."

"So shoot."

"Apparently, according to the rules of the game, all the guys in the inner circle are permitted to have affairs with each others' women, without censure, provided the woman can be tempted into making the first move."

"That's weird."

Jessie nodded. "Anyway, the woman gets used and tossed aside, but all the guys still remain buddies."

"So how does that affect you and Sam?"

"Sam is in the inner circle. Even though he's made it clear he wants me, everything he's done so far is technically within the rules. If Sam were to make the first move, then he'd have to risk something to have me. But if I go to Sam, he can have me and hand Kevin a divorce on a silver platter, along with custody of the children, too."

"I didn't think of that. Do you really believe Sam would betray you?"

"I was hoping he loved me. But after what Mia said, I can't trust Sam, and I know I can't trust myself."

"But do you honestly think Sam would choose Kevin over you?"

Jessie shrugged. "Sam would have to choose between us sooner or later. I think he's made his choice. I just wish he would've tried to find out the truth about me before he did."

CHAPTER 38

DRAW OF THE CARDS

Saturday afternoon, Sandy stopped by to see how Jessie was doing. "If you're still looking for a job, I may have found one for you."

"Where?"

"Well, you know I've been working at Oakridge Farm because Mrs. Smithson was so impressed with my riding, she offered to lend me her best horse and school me for the Olympic equestrian team. Anyway, a groom at Waverly Hall named Emma Turner quit, and they're shorthanded. I told Mrs. Smithson that you were looking for a job and were qualified."

"Great. Who do I see to apply?"

"I'll get Mrs. Smithson to tell Mrs. Waverly you're available, but you'll have to pass muster with the stable manager, Moira O'Day."

***

That evening the phone rang. Jessie picked it up.

"Hi. It's me, Kevin."

"Yes."

"It's been long enough since you were home. Couldn't you see your way clear to come back now?"

"Sharon advised me not to do that until we've progressed further in therapy, and you missed last week's appointment."

"My sisters don't want to watch the kids anymore. They said they've done enough, and they don't understand why you haven't come home yet. If you don't return now, I'll have to hire a full-time sitter."

"Then I'm afraid that's what you'll have to do until we've completed all our sessions. We could go more often, if you like. It would speed things up."

"I can't. I've got too many commitments."

"The campaign is over. What else do you have to do?"

"I'm busy, that's all. The kids miss you."

"I'd be happy to have Laura and Joey here."

"No. I can't trust you to give them back."

"Then all I can do is visit."

"All right, you can visit. But it seems to me you're being a little extreme. I said I was sorry. I agreed to counseling."

"I think it's best to listen to Sharon and follow the program so we can get a fresh start on the right track."

"Have it your way then," Kevin said and hung up.

Jessie arrived at Waverly Hall at six a.m. Monday morning. Moira, a short gray-haired stout woman, was bustling about supervising the feeding of her charges. She scrutinized Jessie carefully. "Are you here to try out for the job?"

"Yes. Mrs. Smithson recommended me to Mrs. Waverly, and said I was to report to you this morning."

"You're late."

"I was told to come at six."

Moira ignored that. "Do you have any experience with horses?"

"I qualified for my 'B' rating in Pony Club."

"All right then." She pointed to a black horse with a white star. "Get Ritual out of his stall, so I can watch you groom him and see if you know your way around a horse."

Ritual eyed Jessie with suspicion but she murmured soothingly, her movements slow and deliberate. Moira watched her every move with a critical eye as she groomed and saddled the animal, but Jessie had been drilled by horsewomen of the old school and didn't find it intimidating.

"You know your business," Moira pronounced. "Take the tack off, put him in the paddock, and start mucking out the stalls."

Jessie gave Ritual a pat as she led him outside. "Well, buddy, it looks like I'm in."

When she returned to the stable, Moira introduced her to the head groom, Steve Mitchell, a shaggy-haired fellow in his mid-twenties. He pointed out the pitchforks, and they dug into cleaning the dirty stalls.

After a bit, Steve looked at her through the iron bars on the upper part of the stall partition. "So you're a McKenna, huh? I heard of a Johnny McKenna. Are you related?"

"Yes, he's my brother-in-law."

"Which one are you married to?"

"Kevin—but we're separated."

"Any particular reason, if you don't mind my asking?"

"I'd rather not talk about it," she said and changed the subject. "How long have you worked here?"

"Since I got back from Vietnam."

"Oh, um, so where did you learn to work with horses?"

"I grew up on a stud farm. My pa was the stable manager."

"Why don't you work there?"

"Pa and I don't get along. This job was open." He shoveled another forkful of manure into the cart and looked through the bars again. "Do you and your husband have any kids?"

"Yes, a girl and a boy."

"What are their names?"

"Laura and Joey."

"So how old are they?"

"Laura's almost two and a half, and Joey's around fifteen months."

"So how come you're shoveling shit instead of staying home with the kids and raking in alimony, if you were hitched to Kevin McKenna?"

"I'd rather not discuss it," she replied coldly, and concentrated on ferreting out manure from the straw.

"Suit yourself," Steve said and began whistling a tune.

Jessie stopped by the farm on her way home from work to visit with Laura and Joey. She parked the Grand Prix and swallowed hard. Although she and her mom had sneaked into the house to get some of her things, she hadn't seen the children since Kevin took them.

Suzy's car was in the driveway and that surprised her because Suzy hadn't graduated from high school yet.

Jessie entered through the mudroom and saw the children playing with toys on the braided rug in front of the wood stove.

The sitter was in the rocking chair and looked up.

"Hi, Suzy. Kevin said I could visit the kids."

"Mommy, Mommy," Laura squealed excitedly and ran to her. Jessie bent down and picked her up for a hug.

Joey scurried over, and Jessie scooped him up with her free arm. After some hugs and wet kisses, the load grew so heavy she had to put them down, but she kept her arms around both of them.

"You bedder now, Mommy?" Laura asked.

"Better? Oh, of course I'm better after all these kisses."

"Daddy sez Mommy's sick. Mommy haf to stay wif granmom."

"Oh, um, yes I still need to stay with grandmom."

"I miss you, Mommy. Peas get bedder soon."

"I'll come home to stay as soon as I can," she said, fighting back tears. "Let's play now. Show me your new toys."

Joey scrambled to beat Laura to the pile of toys and began banging with a small wooden hammer on a play workbench.

"No, Joey," Laura scolded, and hurried over to put a peg in the hole. "Dis way."

After playing with the children for awhile, Jessie was finally free to ask the sitter a few questions.

"I thought you were still in school, Suzy. Are you going to be watching the children from now on?"

"No, Mrs. McKenna. It's just for today and tomorrow. I told Kevin I could take off a few days to help him. My cousin, Krissy Combs, graduated from high school last year, and she's going to take over starting Wednesday."

Jessie immediately took note of Suzy's use of the familiar, instead of calling Kevin "Mr. McKenna." She wondered how long that had been going on. The girl had never done it before in her presence, and her parents had raised her to know better.

Suzy had been baby-sitting the night of the fight, and Jessie wondered what Kevin told her about their split. Not the truth, surely. He'd certainly covered himself well with the story he fed Laura and Joey about mommy being sick.

Jessie turned her attention back to the children. "Let's get your coats and go outside to play."

"No," Suzy said sharply. "Kevin says you can only see them in the house."

"I wanna go ow-side," Laura whined.

"No, sweetie," Suzy said in a soothing tone. "Your daddy said it's too cold to go out today."

"But I *wan* to," Laura pouted.

"No, honey, not if Daddy says you can't," Jessie said, and quickly proffered a toy. "Show me how this works."

The distraction sufficed, and Laura began playing again.

"I think maybe you should go home now, Mrs. McKenna," Suzy said, eyeballing her.

"I was just leaving." Her ruse had failed. Obviously Kevin had warned Suzy not to trust her. However, she would be back—and she wasn't giving up.

Jessie managed to get to the farm and visit the children each day after work. The new sitter, Krissy, seemed a little immature, but claimed she had a year's experience as a full-time babysitter. She watched Jessie like a hawk.

On Friday, Moira handed out the paychecks. Jessie held it in her hand and looked at the total. It wasn't much, but it was hers.

"Hey," Steve said. "Can I bum a ride to the tavern to cash my check? I'll buy you a beer."

"Okay, but I have to pick up my girlfriend, Sandy, at Oakridge. We carpool together."

They drove to the local watering hole. Steve offered to introduce them to the bartender, who was amenable to cashing their paychecks in exchange for buying a few beers.

"Do you need a ride back to your trailer, Steve?" Jessie asked. "I really have to get going."

"What's the hurry?"

"My children are expecting me to visit."

"I have to run too," Sandy said. "I have a date tonight."

"No problem," Steve said. "See you tomorrow."

⸎

The following week, Jessie had the stable routine down pat. She knew all of the horses and where everything went. On Friday, Mrs. Waverly personally came down to the stable to hand out the paychecks. She complimented her on the noticeably cleaner and softer bridles and saddles.

"I'd prefer that Jessie do the tack from now on, Moira."

"Of course."

Steve frowned. "Shit!" he exclaimed, as soon as Mrs. Waverly left. "That isn't fair, Moira, and you know it. Cleaning the tack in a nice warm room, with the radio on and coffee to drink, is a lot easier than doing the horses."

Moira gave him a look. "You've no one to blame but yourself. You should have been doing a better job all along."

Jessie felt bad for Steve. "Do you want a ride to the tavern?"

"Sure, no hard feelings."

When she tried to start the car, nothing happened. "Damn. It's happened before, but I think I can get it going if you'll jiggle the wires under the hood while I turn the key."

Steve climbed out and lifted the hood. He shook the wires while she tried again. The engine remained stubbornly mute.

He wiggled the wires some more as she tried a third time.

It wasn't working.

Finally, Steve just shook his head. "Sorry, but I don't see anything wrong that I can fix for you. You should take it to a garage."

"It's been to the garage three times, and the mechanic said he couldn't find anything wrong."

Steve closed the hood. "Take it somewhere else then. It's probably a bad solenoid."

"That's what my beautician said, but the mechanic wouldn't listen. He just laughed and said he never heard of beauty school teaching girls anything about solenoids."

Steve chuckled. "Well, there's a garage a few miles away that works on the horse van. I'll give them a call, and they'll come and tow it, but I doubt if they'll get to it until Monday."

"Sounds good to me," Jessie replied. "I better call Sandy."

Sandy phoned Josh and asked him to come get them. When he arrived, they went to the tavern and stayed for pizza. Josh and Steve hit it right off. After eating, Steve challenged Josh to a game of pool. The girls remained at the table, chatting.

Sandy lit up an after-dinner smoke. "So how are things going between you and Kevin?"

"I don't know. He hasn't returned to counseling."

"It must be tough doing without sex after being married."

Jessie laughed. "Heck, I had to do without sex even when I was married. But the hardest part is trying not to cave in and run to Sam."

"Do you still think you can't trust him?"

"I'm not going to take a chance on losing my kids."

"You're stuck between a rock and a hard place, Jess. I wish I could help."

The guys returned to the table, wisecracking about their game.

"Hey, I had a little talk with Josh here," Steve said, "and we were wondering if you girls would like to come over to my trailer and play some cards?"

"I don't know," Jessie said.

"Come on," Steve appealed. "It gets lonely living on the edge of the pasture. I used to play a lot of cards in 'Nam, and I don't get much chance to play anymore."

Sandy smiled. "It's cool with me. Come on, Jess."

"All right. I'll call my parents and let them know."

They bought some six-packs at the bar and headed to Steve's trailer. They settled around the kitchen table with fresh beers. Steve got out a deck and shuffled expertly. "Five card stud," he announced and dealt the cards.

After several hands they switched to wild-card draw. Jessie soon began winning more than she lost. She was enjoying herself so much, she lost track of time. Steve kept the beers coming.

Sandy reached for her cigarette pack. "Oh shoot, I'm out."

Josh checked his smokes. "Me too."

"You can have some of mine," Jessie offered.

Sandy grimaced. "I can't stand those damn nonfilters. I don't know why you smoke them."

"Ann wanted me to start smoking with her. Dad said I could, as long as I didn't smoke any candy-ass cigarettes."

Steve held out his pack of menthols. "Have some of mine."

"No, thanks, we don't like mentholated cigarettes," Josh said and checked his watch. "The tavern's still open. We'll pop out to get some cigarettes and be right back."

Jessie glanced toward the kitchen window. "Look, it's snowing! Maybe we should call it quits."

"Nah, we're having too much fun. Besides, I've got four-wheel drive in the Cherokee."

"All right," Jessie said reluctantly.

Sandy and Josh pulled on their down jackets and left.

"How about some five-card stud until they get back?" Steve started dealing without waiting for a reply.

Time dragged on with no sign of the Cherokee returning for over an hour. Jessie glanced uneasily at the clock. "It's half past two. The tavern's been closed for a while now, and it's less than ten minutes away."

Steve walked to the door and opened it. There was already six inches of snow on the ground, and more was cascading down from the sky. "Maybe they got stuck."

"Josh has four-wheel drive," she said flatly.

"They might have gone parking somewhere."

"They left over an hour ago, and they knew we were waiting for them."

"Then I guess they're not coming back." He shut the door and began to gather up the cards. "I don't know about you, but I'm beat. It's time to call it a day and hit the sack."

"B-but I can't stay here!"

"Well, it's a long walk to the barn through the snow, and the hayloft's not too warm on a night like this, but suit yourself."

"All right," she said, defeated by logic. "I'll sleep on the sofa."

"You can sleep in the bed," Steve said. "I'll take the couch."

"No, that's okay, I'd rather sleep on the sofa." She was so tired it didn't matter where she slept, and she didn't want to deprive a hard-working man of his own bed.

Steve went into the bedroom and brought a pillow and blanket out for her.

She pulled off her work boots and went into the bathroom. When she emerged, Steve insisted that she sleep in the bed. She was too tired to argue with him anymore. "Okay, thanks."

Steve headed into the bathroom.

Jessie retrieved her purse and boots, then went into the bedroom. She stripped to her underwear and slid under the blankets with a grateful sigh. She was asleep as soon as her head hit the pillow.

Steve came out of the bathroom stark naked. He went into the living room and grabbed his pillow from the sofa. Then walked into the bedroom and climbed under the covers.

He fondled Jessie's breast and waited for her to wake up.

She stirred and opened her eyes. "What are you doing?"

Steve got on top of her and pinned her down before she realized what was happening.

"Let me go!"

He just grinned.

"Come on, Steve, leave me alone. It's not fair."

"All's fair in love and war, as the saying goes."

Jessie struggled, but she couldn't break away with her arms pinned back and Steve straddling her hips.

"Listen up, sweetheart, I did my trick in Vietnam and you're gonna do yours tonight. Nobody asked if I wanted to go, and I'm not askin' you. We can do this the easy way or the hard way, it doesn't much matter to me. But we're gonna do it, so you might as well enjoy yourself—understood?"

"Yes," she replied hopelessly.

"So how's it gonna be?"

"Easy."

"Good. I like it better that way myself. Now get up and take the rest of your clothes off. I want to watch you while you do it."

She nodded and Steve released her.

Numbly, Jessie climbed out of bed. She couldn't believe this was happening. How far could she run in a blizzard? She probably wouldn't even make it to the door. Steve would be on her in a flash and rape her just like he threatened. There was no point in messing with a man who knew how to kill people.

Unhooking her bra, she felt a flush of embarrassment followed by an odd sense of detachment.

She didn't find Steve particularly attractive or repulsive. Until now, she'd felt completely indifferent toward him. His features were ordinary, and not the sort she even found interesting. She hadn't known him long enough to like him for his personality, and surely wouldn't in the foreseeable future.

At the moment, the thought of him kissing her on the mouth was nauseating, and she hoped he would just screw her and get it over with. She could steel herself to him rutting between her legs, but kissing seemed far too intimate to endure, and almost blasphemous, considering that its very nature was evocative of seduction or mutual desire. This was neither.

She pushed her panties down over her hips and pulled them off.

Steve's gaze traveled over her breasts, then to her belly, and down to the triangle of dark hair between her legs. He sucked in his breath.

"You're a nice looking girl with your clothes on, but I never dreamed you'd look so great with them off."

She said nothing and lingered there in silence, hoping to delay the inevitable.

Steve patted a spot on the mattress next to him. "I'm waiting."

Resigned to her fate, she got into bed and lay down beside him.

Her body was rigid with tension, and she cringed when he touched her breast. But he didn't try to kiss her on the lips, and she was grateful for that. Seeking refuge inside herself, she tried to dissociate. If she remained tense, it would hurt a lot when he entered her.

But Steve took his time, playing with her breasts, teasing her nipples, kissing and caressing her body until she felt a mercurial shiver of desire.

His mouth and his hands aroused the most exquisite sensations she'd ever known. She lost herself in a delirium of pleasure, reveling in her abandon. He brought her to climax twice before he entered her.

Steve had never felt a woman so hot and wet before. She was like a wild thing, primal as the molten fire at the heart of the earth. When he came, it was like launching into space and sailing to the stars.

Drenched in sweat, he lay tangled in an exhausted embrace. It was a long time before he had the strength to move. When he rolled off of her, he realized the bed was a wreck.

"Dammit, woman! Look at the mess you've made of my bed. I never knew a woman could get so slick and hot inside, and have so many orgasms. What are you, anyway? Some kinda witch?"

She laughed wickedly. "Go to hell."

Later in the night he roused her, and drove her to abandon again.

Sometime before dawn, Jessie awakened. She turned over and studied Steve's face as he slept.

She never dreamed such an ordinary looking fellow, whom she felt no attraction to, could have taken her to such heights of erotic bliss.

Steve could have just screwed her and not bothered about whether she enjoyed it, so in a way she had to be grateful for what he did.

Apparently, Kevin hadn't been a very good lover. It was only her own passion that had made having sex with him seem so wonderful at first. He certainly never made love to her like this, and he almost never wanted to do it twice in a row.

She leaned over and kissed Steve softly on the cheek. "Thank you," she whispered.

He woke and pulled her on top of him. "Do me now."

Steve awakened to a blinding light. He blinked in confusion before realizing it was only the brilliance of the sun reflected by the snow. Normally, it was still dark this time of year when he got up for work.

He slapped Jessie playfully on the butt. "Get up, lazybones. We're late for work."

She groaned and snuggled deeper under the covers.

Steve disappeared into the bathroom. When he came back out, she was still in bed. "Hey, Jess, get a move on. I'll make some coffee."

Jessie groaned again, then reluctantly rose from the bed. She froze when she caught a glimpse of the dresser mirror.

A strange woman was reflected in the glass.

How on earth had a stranger gotten into the room?

Her hair was a wild tangled mess, sticky with dried sweat. Purple blotches tattooed her neck and breasts. Her eyes were fey, canny, and feral.

She looked like a witch.

With a chill, Jessie realized the woman staring back at her was herself. She hurried into the bathroom and recoiled when she saw her face in the mirror over the sink. Her eyes were so dark and dangerous she couldn't bear to look at her own reflection while washing up.

Back in the bedroom, she pulled on her clothes and cautiously gave herself a once over in the dresser mirror, careful to avoid meeting her own eyes. The turtleneck hid most of the passion marks on her neck. But Steve wasn't likely to have a blow dryer, so there wasn't much she could do with her hair except tie a bandanna over it.

Jessie put on her boots and started to leave, but hesitated at the door, suddenly mortified. In the rush to get ready for work, she hadn't thought about having to face Steve.

Bracing herself, she opened the bedroom door and proceeded to the kitchen.

Steve was sitting at the table drinking coffee. "Help yourself. The mugs are in the cabinet by the sink."

She poured herself a cup and sat down, keeping her eyes lowered.

"You aren't saying much this morning," he remarked.

"What is there to say?"

"You're a great lay, Jessie."

She looked up. "You aren't so bad yourself."

He smiled. "Take my advice. Do the men of this world a favor—turn pro. The pay is better than what you're getting now. You're sitting on a gold mine."

"I'm not a machine," she snapped.

"Suit yourself. I don't know what kind of problems you and your husband had, but sex obviously wasn't one of them."

"Actually it was."

"Come again?" he said, looking puzzled.

"My husband wouldn't have sex with me often enough to keep me satisfied."

Steve chuckled. "Well, I can see where that might be a problem. He probably had to throw you out of the house to get some sleep. I expect he's got himself a tame woman by now, something he can handle, instead of a wild thing like you."

"It wasn't like that."

He shrugged. "Come on, woman, finish your coffee. We haven't got all day. The boss is going to be pissed as shit."

She drained her mug and put on her down jacket. Steve started to open the door then paused. "Why don't you come over for supper next Saturday? There's someone I'd like you to meet."

"Who?"

"My fiancée. She'll be home from college for winter break."

Jessie's mouth fell open.

"What's the matter?"

"You screwed me all night long, and you're engaged to another girl?"

"So what?"

"It's rotten, that's what! How do you think she'd feel if she ever found out?"

He shrugged. "What she don't know won't hurt her, and you aren't going to tell her. You've got two good reasons to keep your mouth shut—Laura and Joey."

She sucked in her breath. She had no intention of disillusioning Steve's fiancée about her Prince Charming. But if Kevin ever found out, he'd win hands-down in court. "We'd better leave separately and take different routes to the barn."

"Ladies first," Steve said, and held the door open.

The alchemy of newly fallen snow had transformed the dull winter landscape into a sparkling sugar-frosted world. The sky looked so blue Jessie wanted to swim in it. She paused on the step, hating to mar such pristine beauty with a footprint, and wished she could float off into the air.

But she knew she had to go, and buoyantly stepped out into the snow.

She'd found a man, but that didn't get her—or any other woman—respect. What she needed was a man like the man who had asked her to waltz—someone who wanted her, but didn't want to make her a whore.

⚬⚬⚬

When Sandy arrived at Waverly Hall to pick her up after work, Jessie gave Sandy a piece of her mind about abandoning her with Steve.

"I thought you needed to get laid."

"If I was going to break my marriage vows, I'd rather have done it with Sam," Jessie retorted.

"All right, I'm sorry," Sandy said. "So how was it?"

"Let's just say Steve beat Kevin hands down."

CHAPTER 39

POOL OF TEARS

Kevin brought the children over to visit her parents for a few minutes on Christmas Day, before hustling her off to eat Christmas dinner with his family over at Kathleen and Frank's. The minute she walked through the door, the atmosphere seemed charged with static. Her father-in-law didn't bother to acknowledge her. And everyone else was stiffly polite. Frank's parents, Earl and Ima Morgan, acted as if she was wicked Queen Jezebel herself.

Aunt Julia and Uncle Hal weren't there. Julia had the flu, and Hal had stayed home with her. That was disappointing because they would have been kindness itself.

Luckily, Mike arrived with Lynette. Although Mike acted standoffish, having Lynette there gave her someone friendly to talk to. While they only made small talk, Jessie sensed an aura of sympathy.

It was heartbreaking to watch Laura and Joey open presents and play with their cousins. She knew they wanted her to come home, but Kevin hadn't bothered to return to therapy after the first session. Each week he'd come up with some excuse at the last minute for not making the appointment.

Kathleen, Mary Clare, Maria and Ima ensconced themselves in the kitchen after cleaning up from dinner.

Jessie was certain that they were gossiping about her and tried to avoid the kitchen altogether, but Kevin asked her to refill his drink and she needed another herself.

When she entered the kitchen, Mary Clare looked up and smiled. "We're so glad you came today. Christmas is such a special time for children, and it would have been sad if you didn't spend it with them. So how do you like your new carefree life as a career woman?"

Jessie bristled. They clearly believed she'd wronged her husband and children. If only they knew the truth, but Christmas Day, in front of Frank's parents, was hardly the place to air her grievances. "I don't know what you mean, Mary Clare. I'm only working so my parents don't have to support me while things get straightened out through counseling."

"Well, Kevin can hardly wait for you to come home, and *he* said you were dead-set on a career. Naturally, I assumed you enjoyed working more than staying home with the children."

"I see, but that isn't the case. I hope to save our marriage and I'm glad to hear that Kevin does, too," she replied wryly. "Excuse me, but Kevin asked me to bring him a drink."

As she left the room, she heard Frank's mother pipe up.

"Well," Ima huffed, "butter wouldn't melt in her mouth. No wonder she's such a cold mother."

✤

Steve's fiancée spent the bulk of the holidays with her parents, and Jessie found it impossible to stay away from him. Although she didn't want to hurt Amy, Steve might as well have been the Pied Piper as quickly as her resistance crumbled. She knew her sexual addiction to Steve was dangerous. He loved Amy, not her, and there was always the possibility that Kevin might find out what she and Steve were doing on their lunch hour.

✤

Not long after Christmas, a new sitter answered the door at the farmhouse.

"Mommy, Mommy," Laura squealed in delight when Jessie entered the kitchen. Joey ran to greet her as fast as his little legs could carry him. It was amazing how quickly he'd grown since the day Jessie had left home.

She'd only been playing with the children a little while when Kevin suddenly walked into the house. A tremor snaked through her and she stiffened. Usually she tried to be gone before he came in for supper. She was still angry about his refusal to return to counseling.

"Hey, Jess, I need to talk to you for a minute," he said. "Bethanne, do me a favor and take the kids into the rec room."

"Okay," the sitter said, and led the children away.

Jessie faced Kevin squarely. Maybe he'd finally come to his senses and decided to return to counseling.

"Um, I have something to tell you... I-I figured you'd better hear this from me, rather than read about it in the paper first."

"What is it?" she asked, suddenly uneasy.

"Sam is dead."

"What?" Her heart stopped, then plunged into free-fall. *Sam dead? No! This couldn't be real!* But the look in Kevin's eyes told her it was true. "How? What happened?"

"Nobody knows for sure. They found him early this morning. His motorcycle must have skidded off the road. He was pierced through by a metal fence post and bled to death."

Oh God! Not like that. An image of Sam writhing in agony, bleeding out until he lay cold on the ground, flashed into her mind. Nausea twisted through her gut. She swayed on her feet, sickened.

"But why? Was he drunk? Did his brakes fail? Did someone run him off the road?"

"Look, I told you all I know," Kevin snapped. "If you want to know more, read the paper when it comes out."

Jessie staggered out of the house blinded by tears. She drove home reeling in shock and headed straight to the barn.

She fed the horses and the cows in a haze of pain. It hurt too much to cry. She still couldn't believe Sam was dead.

Blackjack and Tar Baby sensed something wrong, but they soon went off to play. Dusty sat faithfully by her side as she sat on the steps of the loft crumpled in grief for over an hour. Finally, she got up and went into the house for a cup of coffee.

Liz looked up from the kitchen table where she was reading the evening paper. "Hi, honey, dinner will be ready in about fifteen minutes."

"I'm not hungry." She poured herself a mug of coffee. "If I'm not back inside in time for supper, don't wait for me. I know Dad will want to eat as soon as he gets home."

Her mother didn't ask her to elaborate, and Jessie was grateful. So many ups and downs had occurred since the day she fled from Kevin, her mother had become used to her withdrawing.

She didn't want to talk to anyone about Sam. She couldn't even mention his death without revealing the depth of her feelings. *How could he suddenly be gone from her life?*

She'd tried to put Sam out of her mind after she'd found out he'd been bad-mouthing her. Why torture herself with his betrayal? But tonight she couldn't hide from her feelings.

She'd been in love with Sam since he first showed up on her doorstep. *Nine months pregnant,* and he said pregnant women were beautiful. Whatever else Sam was or did, he always made her feel like a woman.

It had taken every ounce of willpower she possessed to sit next to Sam in his car in Club Roma's parking lot, listening to that tape, and pretend she was only there for the music. All she wanted to do was make love with him. But he was her husband's friend and she respected that, so she resisted the temptation.

But once Kevin threatened her family, he no longer deserved her faithfulness, and she had no qualms about engaging in an affair with Sam after that. Although she knew it might be risky, she didn't think he'd betray her until Mia's revelation.

Jessie wanted Sam so much she hadn't even tried to imagine it. She wanted him straight, like whiskey, not some fantasy. And she'd waited patiently to see desire for her that he could not mask behind cool gray eyes.

She would never forget that night.

Now she had to ask herself if that night had been worth waiting for. She could have just thrown herself at him, but she wanted him to feel the same way about her as she did for him.

Only Sam knew the extent to which he was willing to risk his friendship with Kevin to have her. They both knew they were playing with fire. No matter how much she loved Sam and how easy it was to regret waiting, if they had become lovers, one way or another it would have led to disaster, and perhaps violence.

She wandered the dark woods, weeping, with the ever vigilant Dusty trailing behind. The pain was so deep, she howled and screamed into the night like a demented creature.

After midnight, she returned to the house.

At five a.m. she called off sick from work.

⁓

Jessie avoided reading the newspapers all week. She didn't know if there would be anything in the daily paper, and she didn't want to find out. When the local came out, she shunned it like a contagion. She couldn't bear the thought of reading about Sam's death in black lines of type, with the words of the coroner coldly and objectively recounting the details. If she didn't see it, it would be easier to pretend it wasn't real.

Life seemed to have lost all flavor now that Sam was dead. Driving home alone from the bowling alley late at night, the spirit world called to her time and again. If she was dead, she could be with Sam. She drove fast, without regard to the consequences, because she didn't care if she lived or died. Often enough, she thought about letting go of the wheel.

But then she would think of Laura and Joey.

If she hadn't given in to the temptation of having an affair with Sam for their sake, while Sam was still alive, how could she abandon them now?

◦◦◦

Kevin wanted Jessie to attend the swearing-in so his public persona would remain untarnished. To persuade her to show up, he promised to resume therapy sessions with Sharon as soon as he officially took his oath of office. He even offered to build a new house on the farm so she wouldn't have to live with his brothers. After the inauguration, however, Kevin continued to stall.

She had no recourse but to file for divorce in an effort to force him back into counseling. She called her attorney, Jeff Dickerson, and told him to draw up the papers. She couldn't go on living in limbo and missing her children, while they were cared for by immature, incompetent babysitters.

Jessie continued her visits to the farm after work. She arrived one day to see the latest sitter, Harlene, irritably checking her watch, waiting for Kevin to arrive. The girl had a dental appointment scheduled for right after work, and Kevin had promised to be home in time for her to get to her appointment.

But Kevin was late. *What luck!*

Jessie feigned sympathy, commiserating over the fact that Kevin was never on time for anything. She offered to watch the kids until Kevin came home, but the sitter demurred.

Under the watchful eye of Harlene, Laura and Joey led Jessie upstairs to see their stuffed animals. Jessie always kept her keys in her pocket when she visited the farmhouse, just in case a chance to grab the children ever presented itself. She casually put her purse down on the bureau and left it there to allay the sitter's suspicions when they returned downstairs.

Laura asked to go potty, and Jessie put her on the potty-chair in the kitchen. After a few more worried glances at her watch, Harlene finally left.

Jessie fervently prayed for Laura to finish peeing, but then Laura grunted and started to have a bowel movement.

Suddenly Kevin rushed in and asked where the sitter was.

"She was late for her dental appointment and had to leave," Jessie replied smoothly, masking her emotions. "So, have you given any thought to returning to marriage counseling?"

"If you hadn't filed for divorce, I might have forgiven you. But it's too late now. I'm going to counter-sue for divorce and full custody. Kathleen's going to testify that you're an unfit mother. I have possession and possession is nine-tenths of the law. You'll never win custody."

The doorbell chimed. Kevin left to see who was at the door.

Hearing Kevin talking to somebody in the front hall, Jessie grabbed Laura and Joey. When she got to the mudroom door with the kids, she saw Kathleen's car parked directly behind the Grand Prix, blocking any escape. One of the boys was disappearing into the dairy with a milk pail. *Damn!* If she tried to sneak out now, Kathleen's other kids would see her.

The next thing she knew, Kevin snuck up behind her and ripped Laura and Joey out of her arms. He dragged them into the kitchen and slammed the inside door, trying to lock her out.

She clung tenaciously to the doorknob so he couldn't get it closed far enough to lock. They wrestled over the handle in a frantic tug-of-war, but Kevin finally won. Jessie pounded on the door, demanding entry.

"Go away or I'll call the cops!" Kevin yelled.

"Go ahead!" she exclaimed, certain the cops would side with her. "My purse is upstairs, and I can't leave without my keys."

Grudgingly, he opened the door. The children led the way upstairs, with Kevin bringing up the rear. Jessie exhibited as much outward calm as she could muster. She planned to follow the kids into the master bedroom, lock the door, and call the police. Surely they'd help her take the children home.

The ruse almost worked, but some instinct must have warned Kevin. He lunged for the door before she could get it locked. They struggled fiercely over the handle. She couldn't get the door latched, and he couldn't get it open enough to get inside.

Kevin reached in and grabbed her arm, pulling her between the door and doorjamb. He slammed the door against her, to break her resistance, and pushed his way inside. Lifting her bodily, he tried to toss her over the banister down to the hall below.

Jessie clutched frantically at the balusters to keep from going over the rail. Kevin hauled her back and pressed her neck against the banister with his forearm, choking her. He was going to kill her. She couldn't breathe and she was ready to pass out.

There was only one thing left to try. Maybe, if he thought she was dead, he'd stop. She instantaneously relaxed every muscle and slumped against the rail. Kevin grasped her and hurled her down the stairs. He ran down, picked her up, and threw her out the front door.

A moment later, he tossed out her purse.

Jessie couldn't move at first. At last, she painfully made it to her knees and crawled to the car. She wasn't sure how badly she was hurt, but being thrown down the staircase wasn't as damaging as being thrown eight feet straight down.

The back cramps got worse through the night, and Liz got so worried she took her to the emergency room. The hospital notified the state police. A trooper arrived and took a statement, but that was all. He refused to arrest Kevin for assault, or go out to the farm to check out the broken balusters that would corroborate her story. All the trooper had to do was ring the front doorbell. If anybody at all opened the door, the damaged balusters would be in plain sight.

Jessie was forced to file a complaint with the magistrate in order to prosecute Kevin. They were so short-handed at Waverly Hall, Mrs. Waverly begged Jessie to come back as soon as she was able. She was on pain killers for several weeks and in a neck-brace during the two months it took to get to trial.

Kevin got off scot-free. He claimed she'd accidentally tripped on the stairs, but suffered no serious harm. The defense lawyer told the judge that the X-rays showed no broken bones, and that Jessie trumped up the charges to help win a big settlement in a divorce. The judge ruled there was no evidence of a crime—just her word against her husband's— seemingly unaware that the X-rays didn't rule out a sprained neck, just a fracture. If Kevin had broken her neck, she'd either be dead or paralyzed.

∽

After the criminal trial fiasco, Jessie became concerned that she hadn't heard a word from Dickerson about a court date being assigned for her divorce suit. She was forced to call him to check on the progress of the case. He insisted she make an appointment so he could explain things in depth. She arrived at his office, mystified.

"Mrs. McKenna, in response to the suit I filed on your behalf, your husband has countersued you for divorce and custody on the grounds that you deserted him."

"Deserted him? I was being abused. How dare he say that?"

"He can say anything he wants. The thing is, you left, and technically that's desertion."

"But you know I was abused."

"Knowing something and proving it in court are two different things. You already learned that in the criminal trial. That's why you should have prosecuted your husband the first time he hit you, instead of trying marriage counseling. A black eye speaks for itself, and a criminal conviction would've gone a long way to help your case. As it stands, your husband has every legal right to charge you with desertion—and you are the one who must prove otherwise."

"If that's the case, why didn't you warn me he might pull something like this?"

"I advised you to prosecute at the time."

"My parents didn't want me to, but if you had given me any idea of how bad things could get, I certainly would have pressed charges."

"It isn't that *bad*," Dickerson said quickly. "Your parents can testify to your bruises, and your mother can testify that Kevin pushed both of you around the night he kidnapped the children. That'll establish that you had good reason to leave, and you took your children with you. It just isn't as weighty and clear-cut as a criminal conviction."

"I have photos of my black eye, and Mike saw him punch me. Can't you have Mike subpoenaed?"

"To begin with, he's a hostile witness, and he'll probably leave the state to avoid the subpoena until the trial is over."

Jessie looked Dickerson squarely in the eye. "I want him subpoenaed anyway. Mike might leave the state to avoid testifying, but I'd rather see him inconvenienced instead of complacently going about his business."

"All right," Dickerson replied sourly. "There's one other problem I think you should know about."

"What's that?"

"It's in Kevin's best interest to delay going to trial for as long as possible. A good lawyer can delay a case like this for at least a year, and Kevin has a very good lawyer."

"How is that possible?" she asked with a sinking feeling.

"You'll find out every trick lawyers use before this is through, but time is money, so let me get to the point. Under the state Equal Rights Amendment, which was recently signed into law, your husband has equal claim to custody of the children, even if he's found at fault for the divorce."

Jessie's eyes widened. "But that would be depriving a child of his mother for no good reason, as well as punishing women for filing for divorce against an adulterous or abusive mate!"

"Exactly. Before, under the *tender-years* doctrine, mothers were given custodial preference because mothers normally stay home with preschool children while fathers work. Courts were loathe to interfere with the strong bond between mother and child, and force a young child to be raised by a babysitter or a second wife—if the mother wasn't unfit and not at fault for the divorce."

"That just stands to reason, so why would the state E.R.A. change it?"

"Unfortunately, under the Equal Rights Amendment, the time the children spent in your care is nullified. Ground-breaking rulings in other states have discounted it as a sexist advantage. Kevin's lawyer will use that argument, and the time the children spend under Kevin's care will count in his favor."

"That isn't fair. They're being raised by babysitters. He's on his third already. You can't count that in his favor."

"I don't, Mrs. McKenna, but some judges are interpreting it that way, and Kevin's lawyer will structure his case on that."

"That's terrible. How many women would file for divorce against an adulterous or abusive husband, if they thought they stood a good chance of losing custody of their children?"

"That's why a criminal conviction would have helped your case, but it's too late to prosecute your husband now."

"Would another witness to abuse help? One of the sitters saw him twist my arm. Her name is Suzy—Susan Hicks."

"Give me her address and I'll put her on the witness list."

"I want her subpoenaed just to be on the safe side."

⚬⚬⚬

Jessie waited anxiously for news of a trial date, until one afternoon she came home from work and her mother told her to call the attorney right away.

"Did we get a court date?"

"He said it was important, but he didn't give any details."

Jessie phoned the lawyer's office. The secretary said Mr. Dickerson still had time to see her that day, if she came over as soon as possible.

———❧———

Dickerson waved Jessie into a chair in front of his desk.

"Do you like your job?" he asked.

She arched an eyebrow, puzzled. "Not really. I was hoping you were going to tell me we have a trial date."

"No, we don't, but I need to talk to you about the case before we proceed any further."

Something sounded fishy. "What is there to discuss? I thought we covered everything last time."

"Actually, we never discussed settling out of court."

"Kevin wants to concede?"

"No, of course not, but he doesn't want to go to trial if it isn't necessary. He's willing to offer you something."

She narrowed her eyes. "I'm insulted that you even believe I'd consider any such thing."

"I'm obliged by law to tell you that he's willing to offer you a deal to settle out of court."

"Since it's legally required, I'll listen," she replied tartly, thoroughly steamed that she'd driven to town in such haste only to hear something she could have easily declined over the phone.

"Basically, he's willing to give you a cash settlement to sign a no-fault divorce agreement granting him custody."

"Tell him I said no. We'll see what a judge has to say when he finds out that Kevin's charge of desertion is a lie."

"It isn't as simple as that."

"What do you mean?"

"As your attorney, I have to advise you to take the best deal you can get. The only leverage you have is custody of the children. Kevin will be willing to pay for that. He'll weigh what he has to pay his lawyer for a long, drawn-out court case versus what he has to pay you. I'll make him an offer he'd be a fool to refuse, and get you enough money to live on and finish college so you don't have to work at a dead-end job like you have now."

"I have no intention of giving up custody of my children for monetary gain."

"I'm trying to do what's best for you."

"I don't think so," she retorted.

"Very well, but you should know Kevin claims he can produce witnesses who will testify to incidents that prove you're an unfit mother."

"Then they'll be committing perjury."

"Perjury is difficult to prove and usually not prosecuted in civil cases, unless it's egregious. Most things are a matter of perception. Slanted testimony can make you appear unfit without being an outright lie. Raising such specters can carry a lot of weight in a judge's mind and are difficult to disprove. Under the state Equal Rights Amendment, Kevin has just as much right to full custody as you do. And remember, possession is nine-tenths of the law—and Kevin has possession. You have a lousy case, and there isn't a chance of salvaging it."

Jessie eyed him coldly. "If you aren't willing to fight, I'll find a lawyer who will."

"Suit yourself," Dickerson said. "But when you find another attorney, you'd better tell him everything up front, because if you try to hide things like you did with me, you'll look like a fool in court."

She stopped in her tracks. *Did Kevin know about Steve? He hadn't filed for adultery.* "What's that supposed to mean?"

"You know what I mean."

"No, I do not. I want an explanation."

"Don't play games," Dickerson said. "Remember what I told you about not having any skeletons in your closet? Why didn't you tell me that you'd been committed to a mental institution?"

Her jaw dropped. "I have no idea what you're talking about. If Kevin has said something like that, it's a lie."

"I have it from an impeccable source."

"If you mean Dr. Herman Gross, he's a good friend of Kevin's. I wouldn't put it past him to tell you something like that so Kevin could use it to bluff. But I've never been committed to a mental institution."

"I was told to expect you to deny it, because you have no memory of being institutionalized."

Jessie stared at him, flabbergasted. "I've led a full and active life. My school records will show I seldom missed a day, and I was an honor student. I was active in 4-H and Pony Club. I have relatives, friends and neighbors who can testify that there's never been any missing time in my life when I could have been institutionalized."

Dickerson shook his head. "Mrs. McKenna, I know your doctor prescribed tranquilizers. And the source who brought this to my attention came from your side. They have no reason to lie."

"Before you believe somebody else, instead of me, make them show you the medical records—there are none. And I told you what sort of hell I lived in. I was prescribed Valium because of stress-induced skin-problems, not because I was crazy—just ask my doctor. I'm not signing anything. I'll take my chances in court." Jessie stood and walked out.

She drove home in a state of turmoil that alternated between anger and anxiety. The state Equal Rights Amendment was having the exact impact on child custody that its advocates had claimed it wouldn't, and its detractors had warned women about. Although Jessie had never aspired to be a mother and homemaker, she'd always respected the sacrifices stay-at-home moms made. And worse still, someone had convinced her attorney that she was mentally unstable and unfit to have custody of Laura and Joey.

Jessie couldn't figure out who in her own circle would've lied to Dickerson, or what they had to gain by falsely claiming she'd been committed. She clung to the hope that a sympathetic judge might see Kevin for what he was, and rule in her favor.

⌘

The scrumptious scent of baked ham and string beans wafted from the kitchen when Jessie entered the house. Her parents had started eating without her, but that was understandable given the lateness of the hour. They looked up in unison and saw her somber expression.

"What's wrong?" Liz asked.

Jessie pulled out a chair and sat. "Kevin's going to try to prove I'm an unfit mother. He claims he can produce witnesses who will testify to that."

"That's ridiculous!" Liz exclaimed. "How dare he?"

"Don't worry, honey," Bill said. "To do that, someone would have to lie, and Kevin would be suborning perjury. It's just a bluff."

"No, Dad. Kevin's relatives can claim the house was a mess, or that I tried to get a job because I didn't like staying home with the kids. They can blow small things out of proportion without lying outright under oath. The whole case will revolve around the fact that I took tranquilizers, I was the one who left, and Kevin can pretend he was only concerned about the welfare of the children when he abducted them. That's why you never should have talked me out of pressing charges the first time he beat me up."

"But how could we have known Kevin wasn't sincere when he apologized?" Bill asked.

"You could have believed me, instead of him."

"You agreed to try marriage counseling. What were we supposed to think?" Liz countered.

"I couldn't keep fighting both of you. I buckled under the pressure."

"All right, what's done is done. I'm sure Dr. Lieberman will testify on your behalf."

"There's something else. Dickerson says a source told him that I was committed to a mental institution. I told him it wasn't true."

Bill's jaw dropped.

Liz exclaimed, "Those underhanded McKennas!"

"You'll have to talk to Dickerson because he doesn't believe me. He said Kevin will give me a good settlement if I sign a no-fault divorce agreement giving him full custody. And Dickerson wants me to take it because he doesn't think a judge will award me custody under the state E. R. A. since possession is nine-tenths of the law."

"Dickerson's right," Liz said. "Kevin has a lot of power in this county. He can delay a trial for a long time, and he'll more than likely win anyway." She looked at Bill. "If Kevin's willing to give Jessie a settlement—"

"I'm not giving in without a fight!" Jessie declared, aghast.

"There's no point in fighting a battle you can't win," Liz said. "Kevin keeps the children on the farm. We haven't seen them since Christmas, and he's refused to let you see them ever since you tried to take them. Children need stability in their lives. You could have them every weekend. With a settlement you can earn a degree that will enable you to make a decent living, and you'll be in school during the week anyhow. Besides, you can't live with us for the rest of your life—this is Rick's home too. We don't have room to raise the kids."

"I'm not giving in! I don't understand why you want me to."

Jessie fled to her room and flung herself on the bed.

Fifteen minutes later, her mother opened the door. The scent of coffee drifted into the room. Jessie was so furious she didn't want to acknowledge Liz's presence. But the smell of coffee made her stomach rumble, and she hadn't had anything to eat since lunch. She sat up to accept the steaming cup, feeling like a traitor to herself.

"I know you don't understand why I said what I did," Liz began, "but you don't know how sick your father really is."

"What do you mean?" Jessie exclaimed, stomach clenching.

"I never told you that your father had more than one heart-attack. Stress is a big factor in whether he has any more."

"You should have told me, Mom."

"I didn't want to upset you. That's why I really resigned from my job in January. I've worked every day since you entered first grade. Now I want to spend as much time with your father as possible. I don't want to lose him over a long, drawn-out custody battle your lawyer says we can't win."

"I won't give up without a fight."

"You aren't the only person this affects. Your father misses Laura and Joey—they're his only grandchildren. If you aren't allowed visitation for a year or so, while a lawsuit you're likely to lose plays out, Joey's so young he'll forget who you are, and Laura might too." Liz paused. "Kevin loves the children as much as you do. I'm sure he'll take good care of them. I know it's hard, but you need to be realistic. None of us knows how much time we have left on earth. Think about what it means to your father."

Liz patted her on the hand and left.

Jessie looked at the mug of sweet creamy coffee and drained it. But it was a bitter brew she had to swallow. Although it was possible Laura might still remember her, there was no question Joey was too young to remember her—if Kevin continued to deny her visitation, and his lawyer delayed the trial for a year.

Now that she thought about it, it had to be her mother who was Dickerson's "impeccable" source. That was the only thing that would explain why he hadn't asked to see any proof. And how could she hope to win custody if her own mother was working against her? She would rather die than do what she had to do, but Kevin was holding all of the cards.

⌒⌒∞⌒

Jessie phoned Dickerson the next day and set up an appointment to sign the no-fault agreement. After penning her signature, she almost vomited.

A few days later, the attorney called and asked her to come into the office with her mother. He declined to elaborate over the phone.

They arrived somewhat bewildered and waited expectantly for Dickerson to explain himself.

He looked at them in silence for a moment before speaking.

"First, I want to say that never in my experience as a lawyer have I ever come across a man as unprincipled as Kevin McKenna. He has refused to accept the terms of the no-fault agreement that his attorney led me to believe he would sign off on. Kevin refuses to provide a lump-sum settlement in the amount he originally agreed to. He will only give Jessie the Grand Prix and ten dollars a week alimony for three years."

"Ten dollars a week? You can't be serious!" Liz exclaimed.

"I can hardly believe it myself, Mrs. Daniels. It's absurd, and Kevin's lawyer knows it. I reminded him that we stood to gain a lot more from a day in court, but he said Kevin was adamant. I don't know what your daughter did to make him so mad, but I've never come across a case like this."

Jessie glared at Dickerson. "I told you what kind of man you were dealing with, but you didn't believe me—neither of you believed me."

"That's enough, Jessie!" Liz snapped, knowing she was more to blame than the attorney. It'd been she who'd gone behind Jessie's back and had a parley with Kevin about a settlement, then encouraged Dickerson to pursue it. "We'll go to court."

Two weeks later, Bill had another heart attack. Dr. Ryder got him stabilized and said he would be allowed back home temporarily, but his only hope was a risky operation. The chances were only fifty-fifty he'd pull through, and even then he might only live six months. Ryder told Bill to get his affairs in order.

Liz asked Jessie to phone Kevin and find out if he would allow the kids to visit Bill, in case he didn't make it through surgery. But Kevin refused to let her father see the children unless Jessie agreed to sign the papers giving him full custody.

Bill and Liz begged Jessie to sign the no-fault agreement. Even Dickerson phoned and told her to sign it. "You can always sue for custody later," he assured her.

Bill lived through the operation, and Liz was ecstatic.

Shortly thereafter, Ann reported that Kevin was openly squiring a nondescript dishwater-blonde named Sheila around town.

Although her father made a remarkable recovery, it was cold comfort to Jessie. Whenever the children came for a visit, they wanted to know why they couldn't live at Granmom and Grandad's like her.

Rick had come home from college after final exams, acting surly and depressed. When his grade report arrived, he was forced to confess to his parents that he'd flunked out and wouldn't be able to return in the fall for his senior year. Jessie managed to feel some sympathy for her brother, but hoped that her parents now realized how foolish they'd been to short-change her education to spend more on Rick's.

Mrs. Waverly's niece arrived to work at the stable during the summer, enabling Jessie to take two months off. Working six days a week didn't give her much time with Laura and Joey, and her father told her not to worry about the money.

The children began showing signs of neglect when Jessie picked them up on their scheduled visitation weekends. They were often filthy and dressed in grubby clothes, with no clean clothes to bring along with them for the weekend. Their nails were dirty and untrimmed, and it was obvious their hair had been left unwashed for days. They both manifested signs of cradle cap.

During visitation one day, Laura innocently informed her grandfather about Kevin's paramour staying overnight at the farmhouse. "Den Sheila sez it's beddy-bye time. Nitey-night now—and no more drinks of wooder. Den Sheila gets in bed wif Daddy."

Bill nearly went through the roof. Liz had to physically restrain him from going to the farm and shooting Kevin on the spot. "Whatever you think about the afterlife, I'm not having you go to hell for premeditated murder. Now calm down. How do you think Laura and Joey will feel growing up knowing their grandfather killed their father?"

"I never thought he'd neglect the children!" Bill exclaimed. "Why else would a man want custody if he didn't love his children? I believed Kevin when he said he didn't consider the separation agreement the end of the marriage—that all he wanted was stability in the kids' lives so they could come here for visitation without him having to worry about Jessie kidnapping them again. He promised that the children would be well cared for."

"I know, but killing Kevin will send you straight to hell. Whatever we did, we did because we thought it was best for Laura and Joey. We didn't know Kevin was lying about *everything*!"

"I betrayed my daughter. And I betrayed my grandchildren because of my own selfish desire to spend time with them before I died. I was just so afraid of never seeing them again."

Bill wept for the shame of what he'd done.

Distraught, Liz phoned Dickerson about Kevin's behavior.

"I'll warn him that a judge might look askance at him having his mistress stay overnight, and that your daughter can file suit to contest custody—if the children are being raised in a morally unfit environment. That'll put a stop to it," he said. "But if your daughter wants to contest custody, she can't file suit until after the anniversary date of the day she left the marital domicile passes in November."

Liz was mollified, and Bill figured there was still hope if the mistress was out of the house.

Jessie wished her father had killed Kevin, but she didn't want her dad to go to hell for it.

⚬⚬⚬

The second week of August, Bill went into the hospital for the last time. The doctor said there was nothing more to be done and Bill was failing fast. Bill told Liz that he wanted to talk to Jessie alone, so Liz and Rick left to grab some supper in the hospital cafeteria.

Jessie wondered why her father wanted to see her by herself. Bill labored for breath.

"I had... no right to ask you... to... sign your children away... just to satisfy my own... selfish... desire to see them," Bill said hoarsely. "They... need you. You're... their... mother. A good... one. Better than... your own mother." He paused, out of breath. "Can you... find it in... your heart... to forgive me?"

Jessie didn't know what to say. The betrayal cut too deep. Kevin never would have gotten away with what he did if her parents had taken her side. But she didn't want her father to go into eternity thinking that she wouldn't forgive him. She saw the growing anxiety on his face as she hesitated to respond. It all hurt too much to say the words "I forgive you" just like that. Yet, she knew it was her Christian duty to forgive.

"There's nothing to forgive Dad." *After all, hadn't she trusted Kevin to take good care of the kids, too?* "I did it because I love you."

"I've been... a fool. I believed... all the lies. I never knew... I had... a daughter... of... such fine caliber. I can... only guess... what it... must've cost... you... But... don't think... I... didn't... appreciate it." Bill struggled for breath. "I... wish... I'd spent more... time... getting to know... you... instead... of... favoring... your brother... But now... I... have... no time... left."

Liz and Rick returned to the room and Jessie left to get something to eat. The gratitude her father expressed didn't ease the profound pain she carried inside. Somehow she had to forgive him for not cherishing her as much as her brother, or trusting in her veracity when she'd needed him.

Bill prayed with Father Martin before he died. At his last, Bill wanted to believe in life after death so he could see Laura and Joey again. Bill confessed his sins to the priest, who absolved him and anointed him. It was a great comfort to Liz to know that her agnostic husband, who had lost his faith in formal religion and Christ's promise of eternal life, had turned back to God. After the sacrament, Bill fell into a comatose state. A few hours later, he drew his final breath.

"Your father was the best husband," Liz sobbed afterward. "How can I live without him? How can I live without him?"

When they got home that night, Jessie tearfully called Kevin to inform him that her father had passed away.

Kevin chuckled with glee. "I'm glad your father's dead! I'm glad that it hurts you!"

She hung up on the maniacal laughter ringing in her ears. Sometimes she didn't even think Kevin was human.

CHAPTER 40

A KING'S RANSOM

After the funeral, Rick enlisted in the Air Force. Jessie was sick of shoveling shit for a living, and working six days a week gave her little time to spend with Laura and Joey on their visitation weekends. She couldn't afford to go back to school, and jobs were scarce in Mansfield. She applied for every opening she could find with no luck.

Frustrated, she broke down and phoned Kevin. She told him that if he didn't get her a normal job somewhere—and fast—she was going to stand on the corner of Main and Market in Mansfield, and get herself arrested for soliciting. She didn't need to tell him how that would look in the local paper.

Kevin got her a job as a teacher's aide at Rendale Elementary School. As a salaried employee, she actually made less than minimum wage—but the hours were much better than the six-day-a-week horse farm job.

Jessie wanted to fight the no-fault agreement in court. But she knew she had to wait until after the one year anniversary date of the day she first separated from Kevin. However, when the right time finally rolled around in November, Dickerson adamantly refused to handle the case. Jessie found a new attorney, Mr. Shank, who was willing to file suit on her behalf.

Laura and Joey were sick over and over throughout the winter. But while they'd been sick before, it now seemed like every other Saturday she was taking them to the pediatrician. Although Jessie paid for the office visits and medications, neither the babysitters nor Kevin stuck to the proper dosing schedule when giving the kids their antibiotics. Far too frequently, Jessie would pick the children up for visitation, and the sitter would hand over a bottle of Amoxicillin still partly full, when it should have been empty days before.

❦

The winter months cycled on through spring and summer, and into another school year, without a court date being assigned.

A new aide appeared on staff that September named Darlene Dorn. Darlene looked like she wasn't long out of high school, and spoke with a Southern accent. She had waist-length light brown hair and wore a long, flowered skirt and peasant blouse like a hippie chick.

At lunch, Jessie noticed her sitting alone at a table in the break room and went over. Darlene looked up from the book she was reading.

"Do you mind if I sit down?" Jessie asked.

"Why no, please do," Darlene said, closing the book.

It was a paperback Bible, not the romance novel Jessie had expected. "So where are you from? I can tell by your accent you weren't born around here."

Darlene smiled. "I was born in Winston-Salem, North Carolina, but Daddy moved our family here a few years back."

"Did he move here for work?"

"Yes and no. Daddy drank a lot and used to beat Momma all the time, but he finally got arrested for drunk-driving. In jail, he met a preacher who witnessed to him, and then Daddy turned his life around. The preacher moved up here to pastor another church. But Daddy missed his fellowship and decided to move our family here, too."

"Oh," Jessie said. "It must have been rough watching your father get drunk and beat your mother. It's a good thing he saw the light and changed."

"Oh yes, praise the Lord. Now we have a home where there's love and peace. But it was too late to save my older sister. She'd already stolen money from Daddy's strongbox and run away. Now she's shacked up with a rich old man, but seduces guys nearer her own age on the side. I don't think she's truly happy, but she thinks she's sophisticated and liberated."

Jessie opened her lunch bag and took out a tuna sandwich.

Darlene pulled a sandwich and an apple from a brown paper bag on the table. "So how long have you been working here?"

"Longer than I expected to be. My husband abused me and ran around on me all the time. Then he tried to pimp me out one night, but the guy walked out when he found out we were married. Afterward, my husband beat me up because he thought I was falling in love with another man."

Darlene's eyes widened. "Who wouldn't fall in love with another man with a husband like that? But who'd believe a fella would try selling his own wife to some other man for sex?"

"My parents didn't believe it either. They didn't want me to file criminal charges because my husband promised to go to counseling, but he stopped going so now I'm here."

"Don't you get alimony?"

"That's a laugh. My divorce case has been floating around in limbo for almost a year now. My husband has lots of powerful friends, and I'm still waiting to get on the court docket."

"It must be tough not being free to get on with your life and find a husband who loves you."

Jessie regarded her with surprise. "Oh, I don't think you understand. I'm a Catholic. I can't get remarried—at least not in the Church. And if I get married in the courthouse, I'd be living in sin, so I wouldn't be welcome at my church again."

Darlene frowned and took a sip of soda. "Well, St. Paul told men to love their wives and give of themselves for them, like Christ sacrificed himself for the Church. The Bible also says that if the unbelieving depart, let them depart. You're under no obligation to a man who broke covenant with you. You can get married in my church, if you ever want to."

"Gee, um, that's good to know." She didn't want to inquire further, in case Darlene went to one of those holy-roller type churches. Jessie crumpled up her sandwich wrapper and napkin, and put them back in the paper bag. "Well, it was nice talking to you."

"It was a real pleasure gittin' to know you, too," Darlene said.

Jessie hadn't actually considered the idea that she could be wholly free of Kevin. She felt alienated from God, knowing in her heart of hearts that she didn't have the willpower to give up sex for the rest of her life, the way Catholic doctrine taught. If she had been capable of living like a nun, she'd have joined a convent long before she met Kevin.

It was more out of politeness than curiosity, however, that she found herself eating lunch with Darlene again.

Jessie told Darlene about the time Kevin kept laughing at her pain during natural childbirth, saying she deserved it because the fall of man was all Eve's fault, but he didn't even believe in God.

"The Bible says Eve was deceived, but Adam sinned willfully," Darlene said.

"I was always taught the fall of man was Eve's fault because Adam just couldn't resist her."

Darlene shook her head. "Even God seemed to think Adam had more willpower at his command than your church seems to give him credit for. That's why God promised Eve a redeemer—one who wouldn't be contaminated by Adam's sin."

"I never heard it explained like that before."

"You should read the Bible. It might surprise you."

"I used to read it sometimes. But if you ask me, the Apocalypse sounds like St. John took some acid and had a bad trip."

Darlene chuckled. "I never heard of a saint tripping."

"I sure hope St. John was hallucinating, otherwise something really bad is going to happen."

"Yes, and probably within our lifetime."

Jessie looked at Darlene, horrified. "What kind of God would let something so dreadful happen?"

Darlene shook her head. "You don't get it. People were created with free will. If they keep on going down the road they're on, they'll bring it on themselves."

"Hopefully not, if the U.N. succeeds in getting nations to beat their swords into ploughshares."

"War is just a symptom of a deeper problem. Man's real problem is rebellion against God. How many people really try to always obey all of the Ten Commandments? Yet, if everyone did, we'd barely need police, much less armies."

"That's true."

"Beating swords into ploughshares is a reference to the prophesied millennial Kingdom of God, which will come about at the second coming of Christ. Yet too many people foolishly think they can create Utopia without God, like the Communists have tried to do and failed. But all such efforts are doomed to failure, because what's really required is spiritual regeneration and self-control. Unregenerate man's worldly utopian visions always end in tyranny because they can only be enforced by force."

"You're right."

"The Bible warns us to beware of such things. It foretells a time to come when certain men, drawing their power from Satan, will try to take over the Earth and form a one-world government. People will fall for it because it'll sound like the best way to solve mankind's most pressing problems. An elite plutocracy will unite behind one individual who, with lying signs and wonders, demands to be worshipped as if he were God. This individual is known as the antichrist or Beast. Instead of truly helping, he tries to enslave everybody—no one will be able to buy or sell without the Mark of the Beast. And those who refuse to worship him will be hunted down and killed. Look it up in the Book of Revelation, chapter thirteen."

"The Book of the Apocalypse is so confusing, I never made it that far," Jessie said ruefully. "I had no idea something like that was in there."

"It can be confusing but going to Bible study helps. There are other related passages in different parts of the Bible that scholars have gleaned to fill out the overall picture. But chapter thirteen will give you a pretty good idea of what'll happen in the end times."

"If it's already been foretold, what hope is there?"

"Well, it's not engraved in stone, like the Ten Commandments, so we can still avoid it."

"What do you mean?"

Darlene smiled. "There's a how-to-escape-Armageddon clause in the Book of Malachi."

"What?" Jessie exclaimed. "Who's Malachi?"

"Oh, he's a lesser-known Old Testament prophet. Not one preachers preach on much."

"So there really is an escape clause?"

"Yes, read the end of the last chapter sometime," Darlene said. "Do you still go to your old church?"

Jessie hesitated. In truth, she hardly ever went to Mass anymore. "No, not much. Getting a divorce is considered morally wrong, and I don't want some priest judging me."

"Then why don't you come to my church?"

"I didn't just run away from my husband. In a moment of weakness I also committed adultery, and I'm not going to give up sex for the rest of my life. I don't know of any church that's keen on scarlet women."

"Hmm," Darlene said. "The woman at the well was divorced more than once, and living with a man she wasn't married to."

⌐∞⌐

Jessie began to have nightmares about the eerie things that had happened while she was married to Kevin. She'd kept those memories buried as a sort of mental defense mechanism, but she'd never truly forgotten. She knew most people would think she was crazy if she spoke about it. But after getting to know Darlene, she felt safe confiding in her.

Darlene didn't seem shocked when she told her about Kevin's declaration that he was a "god" and how he'd demanded to be worshipped.

"Well, I've heard there are psychiatrists who think some mentally ill people have multiple personalities. So it's either that or Kevin could be possessed by a demon. Jesus distinguished between healing people from aliments that were caused by disease, and healing those who suffered from possession."

"My mom says Kevin's a sociopath."

"But he wasn't just unfeeling and mean to you. He demanded that you worship him and that's more than likely demonic."

⌒∽⌒

Darlene knew more about the Bible than anyone Jessie knew, except the clergy. So when Darlene continued to invite her to attend services, she finally decided to accept just to satisfy her curiosity.

The following Sunday evening, Darlene picked her up and drove her to a white clapboard building with a steeple on the outskirts of Mansfield. *The Rock of Ages Chapel of Love* was the name carved on the sign at the entrance. Underneath that was stenciled: *Reverend Elijah Johnson.*

Darlene led the way across the packed parking lot and opened the door. Inside were rows of crowded pews, but no altar—just a stage-like platform and a lectern for the preacher. To the right of the stage was a band with two guitar players, a drummer and a singer.

Jessie sat down with Darlene just as the preacher appeared. He was a florid man with thick white hair and a long beard, dressed in a dark blue suit. He nodded to the band and they struck up an old Southern hymn.

Jessie had to follow along in the hymnal because she didn't know a single word.

When the band was finished, the preacher began a sermon on the parable of the prodigal son: how he'd squandered his birthright, but had finally come to his senses. At the conclusion of the sermon, Reverend Elijah invited everyone who was ready to receive the Lord as their savior to come forward.

Softly, the band began to play.

It was more an act of desperation than understanding that compelled Jessie to move forward, something like her attempt to escape from Kevin across the bridge. As she knelt to pray, her eyes were opened, and she saw herself as she really was.

Sin covered her like grime. Her garments were filthy rags.

Tears of shame welled in her eyes and scalded her cheeks, then the veil parted. She had a piercing glimpse of Christ dying on the cross, writhing in agony, to atone for the sins of the world. Her mind recoiled in horror, and she almost retched.

Only true love could have borne that crown of thorns—a love she didn't deserve.

She moaned and wept. She was so unworthy of such a gallant sacrifice, yet she had only to accept the bloody cup of grace He offered her. Choked with tears, she was barely able to mouth the words asking Him to be her savior.

As soon as the plea passed her lips, she knew she'd entered into the mystery of the ages. A shimmering cloud of grace enveloped her and joyous rapture filled her soul. She felt like a virgin bride on her wedding day.

The King of Kings had paid her ransom to the god of this world. She was alive in Christ and free at last.

She wasn't Kevin's wife anymore—death had parted them. Kevin was one of the living dead. He thought he was a god but he was wrong. He was the puppet of the prince of darkness who owned his soul.

CHAPTER 41

MOCK TRIAL

At long last, her divorce trial was scheduled for mid-December. As the date approached, Jessie held her breath hoping it wouldn't be postponed again. It appeared to be going off this time as scheduled, but after all the shenanigans Kevin pulled postponing the assault trial, she wouldn't know for sure until they got into the courtroom.

The morning of the trial dawned cold and cloudy. Jessie was so sick with nerves she could barely drink a cup of coffee.

Liz insisted she take a Valium pill.

⸎

They got to Mansfield early to meet with Mr. Shank at his office and walk to the courthouse.

Jessie swallowed hard and took her mother's hand as they approached the building. It was an imposing, turn-of-the-century, brick structure anchoring the square in the center of town. She'd already been inside the building for Kevin's swearing-in. However, like most citizens, her mother had never seen the interior. Kevin's criminal trial had been held in a different building.

"Wow, look at the wonderful woodwork," Liz whispered as they entered the stately, domed courtroom.

Jessie's gaze searched the room for key witnesses. Every one of the McKennas was there except Mike—even Kathleen's mother-in-law, Ima Morgan, had shown up. Jessie wondered if Mike had left town to avoid the subpoena. Suzy was nowhere to be seen either. Perhaps she was just late. She could provide an objective and independent witness to the fact that Kevin was physically abusive. Jessie wondered what Kevin's attorney would think when he learned Kevin had twisted her arm to force her outdoors in an evening gown to round up loose cows.

Ann and Sandy came in, opening their mouths in awe as they gazed at the magnificent woodwork and high, domed ceiling. They clustered together until Shank told Jessie it was almost time to start.

"Good luck, honey," Liz said and left to sit with Ann and Sandy.

Kevin entered with his attorney, Mr. Maloney, who'd done his best to malign her during the assault and battery trial. Today, he was dressed in a custom-made Glen-plaid suit. The chestnut color of his hair contrasted sharply with the pallor of his skin. He fixed her with a piercing gaze then turned his attention to Kevin.

The bailiff appeared and announced, "All rise. Circuit Court for Concord County is now in session. The honorable Royce Thornton presiding."

A side door opened and the judge entered. He was a distinguished looking gentleman in his mid-sixties, who walked with the dignified bearing associated with the gravitas of his office. He took his seat, adjusted his flowing robes for comfort, and nodded to the bailiff.

"Everyone, please be seated," the bailiff said, then the clerk of court stepped forward. He read the docket number and suit, "Jessica Marie McKenna versus Kevin DeMarco McKenna," along with the names of the attorneys representing the parties. With the formalities over, the judge looked at Jessie's table.

"Call your first witness, Mr. Shank."

"I'd like to call Mrs. Elizabeth Daniels."

Liz went forward and took the oath, then seated herself in the witness box.

Shank gave her a reassuring smile. Liz straightened up alertly. "Mrs. Daniels, I like to call your attention to November

1974, the Friday after Election Day. Can you please tell the court what happened that day?"

"Yes, my husband and I received an early morning phone call from my daughter saying there was an emergency. When we arrived at the farmhouse, we found her in hysterics. She told us Kevin had beaten her—"

"Objection!" Maloney interrupted. "Hearsay, your honor."

"Sustained," the judge said. "The witness is instructed to testify only to the facts she observed first-hand."

"But—" Liz sputtered.

Shank waved her to silence. "Only tell the court what you saw and did, not what your daughter told you."

In mute distress, Liz looked at Jessie, then gathered herself to try again. "I arrived at the farmhouse to find my daughter battered and bruised. I took her and my grandchildren home with me that very day."

Shank nodded. "You were concerned for their safety?"

"Objection! Leading the witness, your honor," Maloney said.

"Sustained."

Liz's mouth dropped open. She looked at the judge, then over at Jessie.

Shank took a breath. "What kind of mother is your daughter, Mrs. Daniels?"

"Oh, she's a wonderful mother."

Maloney spoke up. "Your honor, this is a biased witness."

The judge gave him a sharp look. "I'm aware of that, and I'll be weighing the testimony accordingly." Thornton turned back to Shank. "Please proceed."

"You may continue, Mrs. Daniels."

Liz flashed Maloney a look of disdain and continued. "As I was saying, my daughter is a good mother. Kevin never appreciated how difficult it was to care for two children, born so close together, and still manage to campaign with him for more than six months."

"So your daughter and her husband were having marriage problems?"

"Oh, yes. As a matter of fact, Kevin asked her for a divorce well before the general election."

"Objection, your honor, hearsay."

"Sustained."

Liz looked flabbergasted. "But my daughter came to me and asked for help. Can't I even talk about that?"

"I must caution you to refrain from outbursts, Mrs. Daniels," the judge said. "Would you care to rephrase, Mr. Shank?"

"No, your honor. I've no further questions.

"Mr. Maloney?"

Maloney stood and fixed his gaze on Liz. "Your daughter never filed charges against her husband for the so-called beating she claimed he gave her, isn't that right, Mrs. Daniels?"

"Well, her father and I—"

Maloney interrupted. "Your honor, please instruct the witness to answer 'yes' or 'no' on cross-examination."

"Answer 'yes' or 'no,' Mrs. Daniels," the judge said. "You're not allowed to elaborate."

Liz pursed her lips and glared at Maloney.

"Your daughter never filed charges, did she?"

"No."

"Exactly. In fact, her husband told you she sustained her injuries when he tried to subdue her because she was in an alcoholic rage. Isn't that so?"

"But—"

"Your honor," Maloney appealed.

The judge sighed. "Confine yourself to 'yes' or 'no,' Mrs. Daniels."

"Yes, but—"

"No further questions, your honor," Maloney said, and returned to his seat.

The judge looked at Shank. "Any redirect?"

"I'd like to save that for rebuttal, your honor."

The judge nodded. "You may step down, Mrs. Daniels. Call your next witness, Mr. Shank."

"I call Mrs. Kevin McKenna to the stand."

Jessie's stomach knotted with tension. She told herself to relax, then rose and walked to the stand with measured steps. She swore the oath and seated herself in the witness box. She folded her hands in her lap and waited for Shank's first question.

He smiled reassuringly. "You left your husband after a severe beating, did you not?"

"Objection, your honor, he's leading the witness."

"Sustained."

Shank sighed. "Please tell the court why you left your husband."

"He ran around on me and beat me up."

"Objection!" Maloney declared. "Mrs. McKenna didn't file suit for adultery."

"Mr. Shank, the witness must confine herself to the facts pertinent to the case in hand," the judge said.

Jessie felt a sense of unreality descend upon her. How could she win if she wasn't allowed to testify about the extent of Kevin's untoward behavior?

"Let's try again, Mrs. McKenna," Shank said. "You left your husband because he beat you. Then what happened."

"My parents wanted us to try marriage counseling, and they talked me out of pressing charges. I was raised Catholic and I always believed divorce was wrong."

"Why did you file suit?"

"My husband kidnapped the children—"

"Objection, your honor," Maloney snapped. "There was no prior court designation of custody. Mr. McKenna had the right to take his children anytime, anywhere he wished."

"Sustained," the judge said. "The witness is instructed to stick to the facts, not make judgmental allegations."

Jessie gave Shank a helpless look.

"Just continue with what happened after that," he said.

"My husband stopped going to marriage counseling, so I filed for divorce."

Shank smiled. "Thank you, Mrs. McKenna. I've no further questions."

Maloney leapt to his feet and approached the stand. He gave Jessie a scornful look. "Isn't it true, Mrs. McKenna, that on the night you claim your husband beat you, you were drinking at Argento's bar from around seven until around closing?"

"Yes, but—"

Maloney interrupted. "Yes or no."

"But—"

The judge leaned toward her. "Confine yourself to 'yes' or 'no,' Mrs. McKenna."

"Yes," she said through gritted teeth.

"Isn't it also true that in late April 1975, you were signatory to a No-Fault divorce agreement offering to give up custody of your children in exchange for the sum of fifteen thousand dollars?"

"Yes, but—"

"You must confine yourself to yes or no."

"Yes."

"Your honor, it's abundantly clear that Mrs. McKenna was only interested in money and not concerned about her children. No further questions, your honor." Maloney turned and sat down.

"Any redirect?" the judge asked Shank.

"Yes, your honor."

"Proceed."

"Mrs. McKenna, would you please explain to the court why you signed that document."

"It wasn't about the money. At the time my father was very ill and my mother didn't feel there was room in our house with my brother living there. Kevin was pressuring me into signing by keeping us from seeing the children. My father wanted to spend time with them before he died," Jessie said, doing her best to protect her mother's reputation by not revealing her betrayal.

Besides, she had no proof that her mother had been the one who'd accused her of being insane to Jeff Dickerson. And it seemed best not to bring up the subject of mental illness, lest Mr. Maloney try to exploit it.

The judge looked at Shank. "Why would you advise any client to sign something under pressure?"

"Your honor, I was not Mrs. McKenna's attorney at that time."

"You mean she did not have legal representation?" Thornton scowled at Maloney. "This is highly irregular."

Maloney hurriedly spoke up. "Your honor, it was Mrs. McKenna's attorney, Jeffery Dickerson, who offered my client the deal. They came to us. There was no pressure involved."

"Do you have any further redirect, Mr. Shank?"

"Not at this time, your honor."

"Call your next witness."

"Your honor, I'd like to call the social worker in charge of the case, Mrs. Clarence, to the stand."

The social worker was sworn in and testified as to her findings. "While I believe Mr. McKenna is providing a good home for the children, the interests of the children would be better served if they were with their mother."

Maloney got up for the cross-examination. "You're prejudiced against fathers, aren't you, Mrs. Clarence?"

The social worker looked him straight in the eye. "No, sir."

"Your honor," Maloney said, "there's a long-standing cultural prejudice against fathers having sole custody that may have colored Mrs. Clarence's findings. The state's Equal Rights statute allows no room for favoritism of the mother. I can cite rulings from several other state courts with such statutes."

"That won't be necessary," the judge said. "The court is well aware of the relevant legislation and rulings that pertain in this case."

"Then I have no more questions of this witness, you honor."

Shank declined the redirect.

"Call your next witness," the judge said.

"I'd prefer to hold my other witnesses in reserve for the rebuttal phase, your honor."

"Very well," the judge said. "Mr. Maloney, you may proceed with your case."

Maloney stood and called Maria to the stand. She praised Kevin to the skies, and claimed to have no knowledge of any abuse or beating precipitating Jessie's flight.

"Kevin told me she was tired of being a mother and wanted a career. I know she answered several classified ads seeking employment. In fact, my daughter Mary Clare and I tried to discourage her. We talked to her about the importance of staying home with young children and waiting until they were old enough to begin school before starting a career."

"You weren't surprised that your daughter-in-law left?"

"No."

"But lots of mothers work full-time and still take care of their children."

"Jessie never seemed to take any pleasure in caring for her children, not like normal women do. So no, it didn't surprise me when she left." Maria looked at Jessie, then at Judge Thornton. "I'm shocked that she would accuse my son of abuse. I certainly never witnessed any, nor did anyone else in the family."

"Objection, your honor," Shank said. "Mrs. McKenna can't testify as to what other family members may or may not have seen."

"Sustained."

Mary Clare took the stand next and corroborated Maria's testimony about Jessie looking for a job. "She just didn't seem to enjoy being a mother. In fact, she even said she wished she could give her children to me to raise."

Jessie winced, remembering the unwary words provoked by the devastation she'd felt when Kevin walked into the house with Karen Blackburn on his arm. One after another, the McKennas entered the witness box and praised Kevin to the skies, then derided Jessie's maternal feelings and homemaking abilities.

"I'd like to call Ima Morgan to the stand," Maloney said, startling Jessie.

Ima was sworn-in and seated herself in the witness chair, looking prim and proper. "You've known the McKennas for a long time, haven't you, Mrs. Morgan?"

"Oh yes, almost twenty years."

"And in all that time, have you ever known Kevin to be anything but upright and honest?"

"No, sir. Why he's one of the finest young men I've ever met."

"So you have no reason to believe he'd abuse his wife."

"Of course not. Why that's utterly ridiculous. Although, it's a wonder he didn't, given the way his wife carried on. I remember when Kevin was busy campaigning, she used to swim naked in the pool at night when her brothers-in-law were home."

Jessie almost choked. She turned to look at Shank, wondering why he hadn't raised an objection. He was staring at her with his mouth open. Jessie kicked him under the table.

"Aren't you going to object?" she hissed.

"Oh, um, objection, your honor," he said, rising. "How would Mrs. Morgan know Mrs. McKenna swam nude in the pool at night?"

Ima straightened her spine and turned to the judge. "My son told me Jessie swam naked in the pool in front of her brothers-in-law, in an effort to seduce them."

Shank jumped back up. "Objection!"

"Sustained," the judge said. "Mrs. Morgan, you may only testify as to what you saw first-hand."

"Oh, but I never actually saw anything first-hand."

"Then please step down, Mrs. Morgan." The judge frowned at Maloney. "Do you have you any other witnesses?"

"I'd like to call Doris Daugherty to the stand.

Jessie turned in surprise and saw Doris coming forward. After she was sworn-in, Maloney asked Doris if she'd ever watched the McKenna children.

"Well, sir, one day Miz Jessie needed to go out to the liquor store an' asked me to mind little Laura and baby Joey."

"Was Mrs. McKenna having a party or some sort of get-together that necessitated a trip to the liquor store?"

"Nosir, not that she said. Mr. Kevin and Mr. Johnny was out, but Mr. Mike came home early and—"

"Objection, your honor," Shank said.

"On what grounds?"

"Relevance, your honor. Kevin McKenna didn't file suit against his wife for alcoholism or adultery."

"Sustained," judge said.

Maloney simply grinned. "No further questions."

Doris stepped down and kept her eyes averted as she passed by the table. Jessie felt sure Doris feared for Bert's job, and she couldn't blame her for testifying on Kevin's behalf.

"Do you wish to call anymore witnesses?"

Maloney glanced at his watch. "Yes, your honor. But, if the court pleases, this would be a good time to break for lunch."

"Mr. Shank?"

"Agreed, your honor."

"Then court will recess an hour and a half for lunch."

⌇

Jessie pulled Shank aside outside the courtroom. "Mike isn't here, and neither is Suzy."

"Well, the sheriff's deputy couldn't find Suzy to serve her. In fact, her parents said she was out of town visiting relatives."

"She goes to community college and classes are still in session. Why would she be out of town visiting relatives?"

Shank shook his head. "I'm only telling you what the sheriff's department told me."

"What about Mike?"

"I told you I didn't want to subpoena him—he's a hostile witness. We're better off without him, unless, of course, you'd prefer he testify about your habit of swimming naked in the pool at night."

"That was taken out of context. I didn't make a *habit* of swimming in the pool naked. It only happened once, late on a stinking hot summer night. The farmhouse isn't air-conditioned and I couldn't sleep. My husband was already asleep, and Mike and Johnny were out. Mike came home early, but Johnny never saw a thing. Besides, what the heck was Ima doing on the stand bringing the subject up at all?"

Shank smiled grimly. "Maloney's good. He doesn't want Mike on the stand, and Johnny wasn't an eyewitness, but he painted a picture in Judge Thornton's mind of you swimming naked as Eve, and few men could forget that."

"Mr. Shank!" she gasped.

"Oh, um, I—I didn't mean that the way it sounded."

Jessie cringed. Of course he did. And right after lunch she was going to have to walk back into Judge Thornton's courtroom wondering if he was still picturing her naked in his mind's eye, not to mention that slimy Mr. Maloney.

～✦～

As soon as court resumed in the afternoon, Maloney called Joseph McKenna to the stand.

Joe got up looking like the prosperous businessman and prominent citizen he considered himself to be. He approached the bench to be sworn in, held up his right hand, swore to tell the truth, and took his place in the witness chair. Maloney went through the formality of establishing that the McKenna family went back more than five generations in Concord County, and asked Joe his opinion of his son's parenting skills.

Joe made Kevin sound like Superdad and Supermom rolled into one.

"What about your daughter-in-law, Mr. McKenna?"

Joe looked over at Jessie and sneered. "She's nothing but a gold-digger who trapped my son into marriage and was no better than a cat for a mother to little Laura and Joey. The house was always a mess. My wife was all the time going over to the farmhouse to help keep it clean. When Jessie brought baby Joey home from the hospital, she handed the baby to me as soon as she stepped into the house and said, "Take this." She was already tired of holding it. All Jessie cares about is the money. She thought she'd divorce my son and get her hands on it, so she wouldn't have to work another day in her life."

"Objection!" Shank exclaimed.

"Sustained."

Maloney tried not to smile. "Is your son well-off financially?"

"The farm belongs to my wife and me. Kevin's paid a salary, just like Mike. Jessie was unhappy with being on a limited budget, and Kevin had to keep her on a tight rein."

"Objection, your honor, hearsay," Shank asserted.

"Sustained."

"I have no further questions." Maloney returned to the defense table and sat down.

Shank rose and approached the witness box for the cross-examination. "Mr. McKenna, you own a large and prosperous farm, isn't that so?"

Joe swelled with pride. "Yes, we have the best milking herd in the county."

Shank nodded. "You and your wife live here in Mansfield, and you're retired from farming, are you not?"

"Yes, I retired in March 1973 and moved into town. Kevin moved his family into the farmhouse so he could stay on top of things better."

"I see. So Kevin was in charge, not Mike?"

"Yeah, on account of he's older. Plus he's the one who worked out all the plans for modernization, x-cettra."

Shank smiled. "So it's fair to say Kevin was the son who worked the hardest to make the family farm prosperous?"

"Well, yes."

"Isn't it odd that if Kevin's the son you put in charge, you haven't increased his salary in several years?"

"Farm profits are put back into the farm. My son assures me his salary is adequate to meet his needs. He's a County Commissioner, as you know," Joe said and beamed at Kevin.

"But if the farm is profitable, Kevin can surely request a higher salary if need be?"

"Well, that's not up to him. It's my farm, and I decide who gets paid what. And that hussy of a wife of his won't get a damn penny, not if I have any say about it!"

"Your honor, please caution the witness."

"Mr. McKenna, refrain from invective," Thornton said.

"No further questions," Shank said.

"Call your next witness, Mr. Maloney."

Kevin took the stand. He offered testimony about the amount of his salary, and said his wife hated motherhood. "She wanted to abort our second child, but I managed to talk her out of it."

Jessie's jaw dropped. It was such an underhanded lie she had to stop herself from jumping to her feet with an objection.

Kevin then told the judge how much he loved being a father. He claimed he tried to save the marriage, but Jessie stopped going to counseling.

Astutely eliciting half-truths and lies, Maloney smoothly concluded his questioning. "The respondent rests, your honor."

"Any rebuttal Mr. Shank?"

Shank rose. "No, your honor."

No rebuttal? Jessie was so stunned she couldn't move. She tried to say something, but nothing came out.

"Very well," Thornton said. "Court will recess while I retire to chambers to consider the testimony presented on behalf of the complainant and the respondent."

The judge stood. "All rise," the bailiff said.

Jessie rose reflexively. She grabbed Shank's sleeve. "What about our rebuttal?"

"We don't need one. The McKennas were obviously prejudiced and spiteful, and their testimony isn't going to outweigh Mrs. Clarence's. Judges almost always give the social worker's testimony the most weight in awarding custody, especially when there are no unbiased witnesses. Don't worry. The judge is smart enough to see the McKennas for what they are."

CHAPTER 42

APRIL FOOL

Day after day, Jessie waited in high anxiety. She prayed the judge would make his decision in time for Christmas. When the holidays passed and the winter months trudged on, Jessie was beside herself wondering what was taking so long.

Laura and Joey had been sick frequently before, but Kevin had become even more neglectful since the trial. Laura had a persistent stomach virus. Joey had tonsillitis over and over. And Kevin was being uncooperative about visitation.

The farmhouse was absolutely filthy. Kevin didn't clean and neither did the babysitters; nor apparently did his lover, Sheila. The bathtub had brown and green rings. The brown rings were dirt, but Jessie wasn't really sure what the green stuff was. Algae, maybe?

~∞~

When April arrived, Ann called her on the phone one day after work.

"Jessie, why didn't you call me right away?"

"Call you about what?"

"The judge's verdict."

Jessie's chest constricted. "What do you mean?"

"Didn't your lawyer phone and tell you?"

"No, I didn't even know there was a verdict!"

"Well, I hate to be the bearer of bad news, but a friend of mine works at the same company as Kevin's girlfriend, Sheila. During lunch, she overheard Sheila bragging to her friends in the cafeteria that Kevin had won full custody."

"Oh no, oh God!" Jessie's heart clenched tight with pain, and her head spun. "I can't believe this! You say Sheila was bragging about it over lunch today? And my son-of-a-bitch lawyer hasn't even told me yet?"

She thanked Ann and rang off. Liz wanted to know what was going on. Jessie gave her a brief summary, then phoned Shank and gave him a piece of her mind. He claimed he wanted to set up an appointment and break it to her gently, which smacked of total bullshit as far as she was concerned. "Kevin's lawyer obviously phoned him. There's no excuse for you not phoning me!"

Liz waited until she hung up. "I'm sorry, honey, I never dreamed it would turn out like this. I wish I'd let you shoot Kevin."

"You should've. It would have been self-defense."

"I don't understand how that judge could have believed the McKennas."

"It would have helped if Shank put on a rebuttal."

"He explained why he didn't, and it made sense at the time," Liz said.

Jessie said nothing. She went to her room, changed into a T-shirt and a pair of jeans, then headed for the barn.

She began cleaning the stalls, weeping in despair, and pondered all that had happened.

If only her parents had listened, it never would have come to this.

The pain piercing her heart was more than she could bear. She'd lost Sam forever and for what? She could have played the whore and gone into court for custody and done just as well. Even the most flagrant adulterers were allowed visitation.

What good had all her efforts at virtue done her?

If only she'd had a crystal ball. She could have had Sam, and the custody outcome would be the same. Sure she would have been the talk of the town, and the scandal would have humiliated her father, but Sam would still be alive. Whether he betrayed her or not—he'd still be alive. The timeline would have changed, and he wouldn't have been on the motorcycle that fateful night.

But the hardest thing of all was being denied custody of Laura and Joey.

Why? Hadn't she prayed hard enough? Hadn't she done her best? Why was God punishing her like this?

She scooped manure and soiled straw into the wheelbarrow on autopilot, packing it high and tight, her tears streaming down her cheeks like a waterfall. Over and over she cried out to God: "Why?"

By the time she finished the fourth stall, despair overwhelmed her. Exhausted from weeping, she sank down on the steps to the loft, and buried her face in her hands, wondering if she had the strength to go on living. Every doubt about the existence of God came flooding in like a crushing weight on her soul. If God had a purpose for her life—and all that had happened—she could not fathom it. "Please, just give me a sign," she wept, "or else I'll go insane."

"BELIEVE."

The word hung in the air, though it seemed to have been spoken only in her head. Yet she did not think it was just her imagination. Peace of mind filled her, enveloping her in a soft soothing warmth, and the feeling of despair departed.

Coming to herself, Jessie got up to empty the wheelbarrow. She stopped in her tracks and stared, stupefied. The urine soaked, manure-laced straw was stacked four feet wide and piled higher than her head. Steve had taught her how to pack a wheelbarrow as full as possible to reduce trips to the manure pile, and teased her about not being as good as he was. But this... this was unbelievable... impossible even.

She studied the towering mound balanced on the narrow base of the wheelbarrow, wondering how she'd even done it. Normally, if she was careful, she could get two stalls worth of manure on one load. She never put any more on because it became too heavy and unwieldy. Obviously, in her distress, she'd forgotten to empty it out before starting in on the last two stalls.

If she hoped to get out of the barn without the wheelbarrow tipping over, she'd have to unload at least half of it. Her gaze traveled to the shallow drainage ditch in front of the barn door, which she dug each winter to keep snowmelt from running inside. She hadn't gotten around to filling it in yet, and the only way over the ditch was an eight-inch wide plank. Ordinarily this was not a problem. However, with the load so tall and wide, she would be unable to see around or over it to align the wheel of the barrow with the plank. And that was assuming she could even lift it.

Evaluating her options, she realized the worst that could happen was that the load would tip over and she'd have to clean it up. She grabbed hold of the handles and gave a mighty heave. The wheel barrow barely came off the ground. Her arms felt like they were going to tear out of the sockets. Her grip broke and the barrow hit the ground with a dull thud. No way was she going to be able to push it across the barn floor and maneuver it over the plank bridging the little ditch.

"Believe."

She was startled to hear the voice again, but grasped the handles for one more try. The load lifted as easily as if the manure and sodden straw were mere wisps of cloud.

Impossible! she thought. Instantly her muscles strained against the real weight. She swiftly corrected her mindset, and the load became light once more. Apparently the Law of Gravity was in partial suspension, but only if she kept faith.

For a nanosecond she wondered how she'd ever get across the plank, but hastily banished any scintilla of doubt. The wheelbarrow sailed over the ditch and across the barnyard to the manure pile as if it was borne on wings.

CHAPTER 43

BLACK FRIDAY

The phone was ringing when Jessie arrived home from work. She hurried to unlock the door and grab the receiver. "Hello?"

"Hi, it's me, Kevin... um, listen, I have some bad news. There's no easy way to say this, so I'll just say it—Ellen's dead."

Jessie's stomach dropped. "What? How?"

"She killed herself."

"Oh, no! Oh my God."

"Look, I can't talk now. I'll fill you in later. Jack called me over right away. He's in pretty bad shape, and somebody has to deal with the police and the coroner. I'm going to stay here and do what I can. I know it's not your weekend to have the kids, but the sitter has to leave at five. Can you pick the kids up and keep them this weekend?"

"Sure, I'll go get them right away. Tell Jack that... that I'm very sorry. Call me tomorrow and let me know how he and the girls are doing."

"Thanks," Kevin said and hung up.

Jessie blinked away tears and put the receiver back in the cradle. She went out to the car and drove over to the farm in a daze. She could hardly believe that Ellen, of all people, had committed suicide.

Why Ellen? She always seemed to have it so together. It wasn't Ellen who'd been the lousy homemaker, the depressed mother, or the runaway wife. No one accused her of being addicted to Valium or being a drunk or unfit mother.

Ellen had moved in social and political circles with poise and charm. And she was universally admired by everyone who knew her. So why?

If only she'd known how to talk to Ellen, maybe she could have done something. But she hadn't kept in touch because Jack and Ellen were more Kevin's friends than hers. She hadn't wanted to behave like the resentful type, downing Kevin to everyone they'd known. Although she had no qualms about correcting the lies Kevin circulated about her when anyone brought them to her notice, she had no intention of proactively seeking out his personal friends and trying to disillusion them.

Only Carol Kramer had ever asked her why she left Kevin, and Carol simply couldn't believe it.

When Jessie pulled into the driveway of the farm, Laura and Joey squealed with delight and came running to the car. "Mommy, can we go to your house?" Laura asked.

"Yes, Daddy said you could."

"Goody, goody," Joey said, hopping up and down. Jessie opened the car door and hugged them both. "I just have to talk to the sitter. Go get whatever you want to bring."

⁓

Jessie managed to keep up a cheerful façade until her mother got home, but inside, her heart ached for Ellen's twin daughters. They were only a little over sixteen and still in high school.

When Liz got home, Jessie briefly told her what happened and asked her to take over amusing the children so she could go off and cry by herself. She didn't want them to know what was going on.

Liz nodded sympathetically. "Go ahead outside, honey, and I'll get the kids to help me start supper."

Jessie fed the horses and cows, then walked out into the pasture and sat on a fallen log. There she broke down in sobs.

Dusty hovered nearby, but Blackjack and Tar Baby soon wandered off.

After her sobs slowed, Jessie considered her friends' marriage and the things that led up to Ellen's suicide. *Were all those other women worth it, Jack? How do you face your children?*

⁜

Kevin showed up a little past noon on Saturday. Jessie was surprised when she realized it was him knocking on the door. She was only expecting a phone call.

His face was haggard, and his eyes were red and swollen. He followed her into the kitchen and sat down heavily in one of the chairs. She quickly poured him a cup of coffee.

"Thanks." He took a sip and bowed his head, cradling the cup with his hands. "Where are the kids?"

"Mom took them shopping."

"Good. I'd rather they didn't hear what happened. But I think you should know."

She nodded. "I'd like to know."

Kevin raised his head, blinking back tears. "Ellen planned everything carefully. The twins had been invited to a sleepover Friday night and were driving there straight from school. So Jack thinks that's why Ellen picked Friday to kill herself, figuring he'd find her body and the note she left when he got home from work."

"I see."

"Anyway, Ellen closed out her bank account and deposited the funds equally into the twins' passbook savings. She left the bankbooks on the table with a note to Jack. Then she stuffed the crack under the garage door with a sheet, climbed into the car, and started the engine." His voice broke. "Jack found her when he got home."

A lump rose in Jessie's throat. "It must have been dreadful."

"Jack called me right away. God, it was terrible. I thought he was losing his mind. Ellen's note said that if it was the last thing she ever did, she hoped to ruin his political career." Kevin choked back a sob. "Jack felt so guilty he wanted to kill himself. I told him killing himself wouldn't make anything right. It wouldn't bring Ellen back—and somebody has to raise the kids."

Kevin buried his face in his arms and wept. When he raised his head, tears were streaming down his cheeks. "I was so scared. I thought I was going to lose Jack. I *had* to keep him from killing himself. It was awful. I held him all night long. I couldn't bear to lose him, too."

"I know." She saw the human being in pain, not the fiend, and put a comforting hand on Kevin's shoulder. She wished that she could touch him and give him life, like the Blue Fairy had touched Pinocchio. But no power on earth could save Kevin until he had a change of heart. Without contrition there was no absolution.

<hr />

After supper on Tuesday, Liz picked up the evening paper to read it with her after-dinner coffee. "The obituary for Ellen Richardson lists the viewing times, but doesn't say how she died. Do you want to read it?"

"No," Jessie said. "I just can't."

Liz nodded. "Well, there's a viewing scheduled for Wednesday night and another on Thursday night. When do you plan on going?"

"I'm not."

"*What?*"

She looked at her mother. "I don't want to go to the funeral home and see Jack suddenly remorseful, while Ellen lies cold in her coffin."

"But you *must* go. Ellen was a friend of yours. What will people say? They'll think worse of you than they do already."

"I can't! How am I going to act normal, knowing Jack has Ellen's blood on his hands? How can I walk up and say I'm sorry for his loss? It's all his fault that Ellen's dead," she sobbed. "And I can't bear to see her lying in a coffin."

Liz put down the paper. "Get yourself together and do it for Ellen. Besides, it'll be a closed casket—carbon monoxide poisoning isn't pretty."

⌒∞⌒

Jessie drove to the funeral home Thursday evening, her anger toward Jack mounting with every mile. He'd broken Ellen's heart, made her life gall and vinegar until she couldn't face another day, not even to see her daughters finish growing up.

Jessie understood exactly how Ellen felt. It was only by the grace of God it wasn't herself lying in death's embrace.

The parking lot was nearly full, and the building was mobbed. Ellen and Jack had many friends and acquaintances.

Jack looked ghastly. The twins clung to one another crying quietly as the people in line moved forward to express their condolences. When it was Jessie's turn, she was so choked with emotion she could hardly speak.

Jack looked at her with tears in his eyes and clutched her extended hand in his.

"I'm so sorry," she managed to say, blinking back tears.

Jack glanced at the coffin and squeezed her hand tightly, then looked back into her eyes. "Thank you so much for coming."

She nodded, unable to speak, and walked over to the casket.

It was closed, just like her mother said it would be. Lovely roses covered the glossy wood. Candles gently flickered on either side of the bier.

Jessie knelt to pray, and her anger drained away. All she felt was pity. The children were innocent, yet they had to suffer for their parents' sins. Everyone was lost. They all thought they could play with sin and get away with it, but everything had gotten out of control. They never were in control. They had all been deluded by a master of deceit.

In a whisper, Jessie echoed the words of Christ on the cross: "Forgive them, Father, for they know not what they do."

She rose and left the building, blinded by tears. She was almost to the car when she heard someone calling her name.

"Jessie—Jessie, wait!"

She turned. Marcella was running toward her with open arms. They embraced, and Jessie began to sob.

"Hush now, I know," Marcella said. "I'm sorry, but I must get back inside."

Jessie nodded, incapable of speech, and wiped at her tears as Marcella headed back. Jessie knew she'd never be able to handle the funeral. Kevin would be there to give Jack support, the same way Jack would have supported him if it had been the other way around. It would be unbearable to watch the men Ellen once loved, put her body in the ground.

CHAPTER 44

THE POINT OF KNOW RETURN

Jessie hoped Ellen's death had affected Kevin enough to change him, but that was not the case. Rumors of his affairs continued. She wondered how he could feel so much sympathy for Jack's children, but not see the damage he was doing to his own.

The babysitters Kevin hired changed more often than the seasons, and were more incompetent than ever. Although Kevin's longtime mistress, Sheila, routinely stayed overnight at the farmhouse on weekends, the house was still a mess.

The children were no better off with Sheila around than with the inept babysitters. They were still filthy and invariably dressed in grubby clothing when Jessie picked them up for visitation. Their skin had a gray tinge from ground-in dirt. Laura's hair sprouted rat's-nest tangles. They both had recurrent cradle cap. And their too-frequent illnesses continued.

During visitation, Jessie made sure the children had a routine that was as normal as she could make it. She bathed them, trimmed their fingernails, combed their hair, and dressed them in clean clothes. She read to them, played games, and served nutritious meals.

Laura and Joey romped with the dogs and often begged for rides on Blue. Jessie decided they were ready for their own pony. As good as Blue was, he was far too large for small children. However, a good child's pony was worth its weight in gold—and gold she did not have.

The prices people were asking for even half-wild, mediocre ponies were already beyond her means. But she began reading the for-sale ads and checking out ponies with Sandy, who was able to recruit a willing pony-clubber to test ride the animals.

Luckily, her mother offered to lend her two hundred dollars to add to the two hundred she'd managed to save. With little more than a hope and a prayer, she persisted in her quest. She'd all but given up when a new ad appeared in the paper.

Accompanied by Sandy and the obliging junior equestrienne, Jessie doggedly set out to view the next prospect.

The farm where the pony was stabled turned out to be a ramshackle place, and her spirits sank. A partially collapsed barn looked dangerous. The house's bare clapboards were weathered gray and some were missing. Honeysuckle and brambles weighed down the rusty barbed-wire fencing around the pasture.

When the lane curved around the corner of the barn, Jessie saw a weather-beaten old fellow waiting by a shed. He wore faded denim overalls, a green cap with a Muncy Chief hybrids logo, and a plaid shirt. A red paisley bandana trailed from his back pocket.

Standing placidly beside him was a plump dapple-gray pony with a creamy-white mane and tail. The pony pricked his ears at the car, but remained quiet at the sound of the tires crunching on the gravel. He looked at everyone inquisitively, but didn't try to pull on the lead rope or shy away.

"Howdy," the farmer said, "I reckon you be Miz McKenna, the lady who called about the pony?"

"Yes, sir," Jessie replied. "This is my friend Sandy Hanlon." Sandy nodded. "And Cathy Maitland here is the girl who's volunteered to put the pony through his paces for us."

"What's his name?" Cathy asked.

"Buttons," the farmer said. "He belonged to my tenants' daughter, but she outgrew him and theys just left him here when they moved away."

"Are you sure they aren't coming back for him?" Jessie asked.

"Well, the pa got some factory job in the city, and they left here owing two months' rent," the farmer said, then pointed to a grove of trees in back of the farmhouse. "I live in the trailer over yonder, and they leased the house. The pa helped me on the farm and hired hisself out for odd jobs and such. But theys been gone more'n a month now, and the pony needs his feet trimmed, and who knows what, that I cain't pay for."

"I see," Jessie said, as Cathy saddled and bridled the pony. His feet did need trimming, but he was well-behaved.

"Anyways, I got the legal right to sell him for the rent that's owed, plus Buttons needs took care of, so I put an ad in the paper."

Cathy put the pony through the drill, and he proved to be amenable. Jessie stepped up beside him and clapped her hands sharply. Buttons flinched, but he didn't spook. She pulled out a scarf and flapped it. He pricked his ears and looked, but didn't shy away.

"What ya doin' that for?" the farmer asked.

"Just to see how safe he'd be around small children," Jessie said. "How much do you want?"

The farmer rubbed his chin with his fingers. "How about four hundert?"

"Sold," Jessie said. Cathy hopped off, and Sandy helped her remove the tack. "We'll be back with the cash and a horse trailer in an hour."

❦

Buttons was kept a secret from Laura and Joey until they arrived the following weekend. They immediately asked to go to the barnyard to see the horses.

"Can we ride Blue, Mommy, can we?" Laura asked.

"Well, there's something else we have to do first," she said, sliding open the barn door. It creaked along the rollers, and light flooded the dim interior of the barn. Blue and Rio poked their heads out of their stalls and nickered, then a small dapple-gray head with a tiny star appeared over the door of the nearest stall.

Laura squealed with delight. "Oh, thank you, Mommy!"

"Yippee! Yippee!" Joey exclaimed, hopping up and down.

"Can we ride him now?" Laura asked.

"Yes, of course."

"Me first," Joey hollered.

"No, me!" Laura shouted.

"Now calm down. You shouldn't yell around ponies," Jessie said, pleased to see Buttons taking it in stride. "You can ride double."

The pony proved to be so well behaved and calm around the children that in only a few weeks Laura and Joey were riding him without a lead line for short stretches. Buttons was so mindful of the children, whenever they handled and groomed him, that there were no tears from inadvertently stepped-on toes. He was not only the answer to her prayers, but a genuine treasure.

The children rode Buttons, played with the dogs, splashed in the stream, and chased lightning bugs. And Jessie told them every fairy tale she knew. Laura's favorites were *Snow White* and *Sleeping Beauty*, where a prince's love awakens the princess from a death-like sleep.

⁓

One stinking-hot Saturday, near the end of August, Jessie was out by the barn supervising the children grooming Buttons, when she heard a car coming up the driveway. Dusty, Blackjack and Tar Baby began barking.

She walked to a spot where she could see whose car it was, but still keep an eye on the children. It was Kevin in the Caprice. The top was down, and someone was in the passenger seat beside him.

What the heck is Kevin doing here? she wondered, approaching the car. The passenger was a handsome blond guy in his early twenties. He was so beautiful he could have been a model for Narcissus.

Jessie halted, embarrassed. She was wearing a T-shirt without a bra and very short cutoffs because she planned on taking the children wading after their ride. There wasn't exactly time to change. She decided to brazen it out.

The passenger side of the car was closest to her and she leaned on the door. The blond guy ignored her. It seemed a little peculiar even though she could see he was rolling a joint. A clear plastic bag of high quality marijuana was on the seat beside him.

Kevin, however, exhibited the typical male response to a braless female, wearing shorts up to her ass, even though he tried not to let it show. "Tell the children Daddy's here to see them."

Jessie raised her eyebrows. "Are you sure you want them to see you with your friend here rolling joints?"

She bent seductively over the passenger door, her breasts prominent enough to give the guy an eyeful, and smiled. "It looks like good stuff, too."

The guy didn't even blink. She couldn't pick up a thing from his vibes, not even the slightest spark. This was interesting.

The corner of his mouth curled into a sly grin. Jessie looked at Kevin, then back at the guy, and smiled a knowing smile.

Kevin scowled. "Come on! I haven't got all day."

Straightening up, she turned and began to sashay off with swaying hips. This was the final test.

She spun on her heel so quickly, Kevin was taken by surprise. He immediately turned his head away, trying to pretend he hadn't been admiring the view. The blond guy didn't have to pretend. He couldn't have cared less.

When the children got to the car, all traces of the marijuana had disappeared. Kevin made a great fuss over them, but didn't ask to see their pony. The young man stared off into space, his cold blue eyes ignoring everyone.

It was a scene Jessie found tasteless at best. Why would Kevin even bother to come here when he was out with a pretty-boy sex-toy for some fun?

She didn't believe for one moment that Kevin missed Laura and Joey that badly. After all, she only got them every other weekend. Did he actually expect her to be jealous of his latest score?

What a contemptible bastard Kevin was, too shallow and self-absorbed to appreciate the true nature of the relationship God intended between men and women. Nor did he realize that he disrespected her sex at his own mortal peril.

Kevin had hurt their children by splitting their family apart. He'd marred so many lives, yet he didn't even care.

When Kevin kissed the children goodbye and shooed them away, loathing filled her. She didn't quite catch the comment he made to his friend as the children dashed back to the pony. The blond guy lit the joint while Kevin started the engine. He and his friend cruised away, careless laughter echoing in their wake.

White-hot anger shook her. She could feel the ancient power stirring in the deep, uncoiling and slithering upward. A curse formed on her tongue in a rage so great she thought she would burst if she did not utter it. Teetering on the brink of the Abyss, she marshaled every ounce of will she possessed. Jessie swallowed hard and painfully, forcing the curse back into the deep unspoken.

Her heart hammered in her chest and her pulse raced, as if she'd stumbled near the edge of a cliff. Thank God she'd managed to keep her balance. It was wrong to use such power for revenge.

Perhaps, someday, Kevin would repent and be saved—if a man who seemed to have sold his soul could be saved. As for herself, she would rather serve in Heaven than serve Hell.

"Vengeance is mine, saith the Lord," she said to herself, for the Lord had paid her ransom with His blood.

Jessie met Ann at the bowling alley Wednesday evening for their weekly summer league game. The opposing team was late. While they waited for them to arrive, she told Ann about Kevin's curious visit accompanied by the blond Narcissus.

Ann laughed. "God only knows how many girlfriends and boyfriends he has, but he still gets off on your body. What a jerk."

"Yeah, I know."

"Did you ever find out why Sam was bad-mouthing you?"

"No, but I can guess. I don't think Kevin could stand the thought of Sam falling in love with me, so he probably told Sam I was having an affair with Jack."

"I bet you're right. That sounds exactly like something Kevin would do. By the way, have you heard the latest?"

"No. What?"

Ann's eyes danced. "You'll never guess—Mike McKenna is engaged to be married."

"You're kidding." But Jessie could see Ann was serious. "To Lynette?"

"No. A girl named Angela. She's a little on the plump side, but not bad looking. And get this—she's a real goody two-shoes who goes to church every Sunday."

"Really?"

"Yeah, and get this—she's a virgin."

Jessie raised an eyebrow. "How do you know she's a virgin?"

Ann smiled knowingly. "I've got my sources. Besides, I could see it in her eyes if she wasn't. So, can you believe it? Mike McKenna and Miss Goody Two-shoes."

"I suppose it makes sense," Jessie said thoughtfully.

"How's that?"

"It's the only way Mike can eat his cake, if she isn't giving out free samples."

Ann burst out laughing. "You just kill me sometimes."

Jessie chuckled. "Who's Lynette going out with now?"

"Nobody. She's turned into a nympho. Mark saw her in a bar one night trying to pick up any guy she could. She came on to him but he turned her down, then she left with some other guy."

"That's sad. What about you and Mark? Have you set a date?"

"We picked Valentine's Day because it's so romantic. This coming February 14th I'll be Mrs. Mark Wilson at last."

"That's wonderful." Ann's dream was finally going to come true. She'd certainly waited long enough for Mark to stand up to his parents. "How are Mark's mother and father taking it?"

Ann shrugged. "They don't like me any better than they did before."

"What about your parents?"

"They're refusing to pay for the wedding because we started living together, but there's nothing they can do to stop us. Mark has his master's and we're both working. By February we'll have enough saved to pay for a nice wedding ourselves."

"I'm so glad you two are finally getting married."

"Thanks." Ann fingered her engagement ring. "Listen, I've been thinking. Remember Brian—the cute guy you went out with for a while in college—I was thinking of having a party and inviting him. It's about time you got on with your life, and maybe he's the right guy for you."

Jessie wasn't sure matchmaking was Ann's strongest suit. Look what had happened the last time she'd tried to fix her up. But Jessie had always liked Brian and Ann was right, it was time to get on with her life.

"Okay. Go ahead and invite Brian, and let's see what happens."

The opposing team failed to show by forfeit time, so the girls bowled for their personal scores and left. Sundown was drawing near. The valleys were already deep in shadow, but the low rays of the sun were still blinding.

Jessie pulled her sunglasses out of the case and put them on to protect her eyes from the glare. She started the engine of the Grand Prix then turned the headlights on to help other drivers who might have trouble seeing because of the sharp changes in contrast. She drove home musing over Mike's engagement to a churchgoing girl. Perhaps there was hope yet for Pan's lost boys.

Jessie – symbolizes Persephone (Proserpina): a type of Eve in myth.

Kevin – symbolizes Hades (Pluto), Lord of the Netherworld. Kevin has ties to the underworld of drugs and prostitution in Concord County.

Pool – According to legend, Hades used magic to entice Persephone away from safety, and she's pulled into the underworld through the pool of Cyane (a minor goddess or spirit of the pool), who cries out against the sacrilege he perpetrates [Ovid, *The Metamorphoses*]. *(Drugs and magic share the same root word.)* Jessie's fall into the pool represents a metaphysical descent into the Netherworld. *(Pools symbolize portals into the otherworld of myth and magic.)* She comes under Kevin's spell when she's drugged and raped: a parallel to the rape of Persephone.

Seed – Hades tricks Persephone into eating the seeds of a pomegranate (a fertility symbol). Zeus insists she become Hades' bride, under the "law of abode," because she has consumed the food of the dead. Jessie is unable to resist Kevin's skillful seduction. She accepts Kevin's seed through intercourse and social mores require that she wed him.

Sam Leland – symbolizes Adonis, the handsome prince whom Persephone loved in rivalry with Aphrodite (Venus), the goddess of sex/eros. Sam pursues sexual pleasure. Like Adonis, he dies an untimely death in the prime of manhood. Adonis was gored by a wild boar and bled to death. Sam is gored by a fence post and bleeds to death.

In mythology, Orpheus unsuccessfully attempted to rescue his wife Eurydice from the realm of the dead after she was killed by a serpent's bite. Early Christian catacomb art depicted

Jesus as Orpheus, indicating they believed He had succeeded in defeating sin and death and Hades, thus enabling the future resurrection of the dead.

In *Madonna of the Pomegranate*, Botticelli depicts the Christ-child holding a pomegranate: the forbidden fruit that brought Persephone under Hades' dominion. Afterward, her cyclical life and death begins. Persephone's ultimate redemption from Hades' dominion was an important aspect of her cultus.

After the fall, Eve eventually dies. And each generation of her offspring lives then dies. The temptation, fall and redemption of Eve is the romance at the heart of the universe.

ABOUT THE AUTHOR

G. M. Trust has been interested in mythology ever since she saw Walt Disney's *Fantasia* as a child and was struck by the sad queen held captive by the god of the underworld. A former student nurse and professional racehorse groom, she became a stay-at-home mother of five. Now widowed, she was happily married for over thirty-seven years to a remarkable man.

Mrs. Trust is an avid reader and lover of books. She was a member of Romance Writers of America for fourteen years and is a member of Pennwriters, Inc. This is her second published novel.

"There are two ways to live your life.
One is as though nothing is a miracle.
The other is as though everything is a miracle."

Albert Einstein